PROBABLE CAUSE

9-21-04

PROBABLE CAUSE

M. L. Donato

Writers Club Press
San Jose New York Lincoln Shanghai

Probable Cause

Writers Club Press
an imprint of iUniverse, Inc.

For information address:
iUniverse, Inc.
5220 S. 16th St., Suite 200
Lincoln, NE 68512
www.iuniverse.com

ISBN: 0-595-21195-X

Printed in the United States of America

To all women
Never fear past mistakes, present struggles, or future dreams.

Contents

Acknowledgements

Many thanks to my "editors" (Tom A., Chris L., Ann M., Donna P., & Steve P.) for their constructive criticism on everything from authenticity to grammar.

Special thanks to Sergeant Ivy Brenzel, a 12–year veteran of the Moscow, Pennsylvania, Police Department, for providing me with insights on women in law enforcement; information on the Pennsylvania Crime Code, legal system, and police investigation and paraphernalia; and support of this gone–on–way–too–long obsession of mine.

Prologue

The Nice Way Or My Way (Five Years Earlier)

"Man, it's snowin' like a bitch!" the young man remarked, holding open the door to the women's dormitory. Midnight neared, and eight inches of a heavy, wet snow had already blanketed the ground, severely limiting travel around campus. A few four–wheel–drive security vehicles maneuvered along the hilly roads, but that was about it. Those that ventured out did it on foot. And even that became a challenge.

His female companion stepped inside, brushing a layer of flakes from her hair and jacket. The snow had started falling about two that afternoon and was expected to continue until daybreak with a total accumulation of twenty inches or more. Weather forecasters across the state were calling it "the storm of the decade."

The young man smiled, a handsome, well–built, nineteen–year–old African–American, his perfect set of white teeth a sharp contrast against his dark skin. "I had a rockin' time tonight. How 'bout yourself?"

The girl, his same age, answered the question with a broad grin of her own, playfully twirling the chain with her room key around her fingers. "Wasn't bad."

"Wasn't bad? You were par–*tee*–in'."

"Get real. I'm not even buzzed."

He raised an eyebrow skeptically. "Guess I'll be headin' over to my dorm, back out in that bad–ass blizzard."

She immediately caught his hint. "Would you like to come up to my room for a while, watch some TV?"

"Sounds cool."

"Now don't get the wrong idea," she warned as they headed up the stairway. "We're only going to watch TV."

"Of course."

She glanced back at him for an instant before opening the door to the third–floor corridor. Refraining from behavior she'd later regret was going to be difficult: A battle against the lingering effects of all the beer she had consumed at the frat party. She'd never admit that doing it with a black guy had always been one of her sexual fantasies. But it was only a fantasy, she told herself, never meant for reality. Besides, she was already involved in a relationship with someone else.

He stood beside her, hands in his jeans pockets, as she unlocked the door to her room. "Ever made it with a home boy?"

Her eyes widened and she grinned, opening the door. She flicked the light switch, illuminating the small, two–bunk room with dim light from the overhead fixture. "Can't say that I have." She removed her jacket and tossed it onto her roommate's bed.

He did the same. "Ya don't know how good we are, 'less you never tried us."

She brushed off his remark. "Uh–huh."

He sat down on the worn carpet, pulling off his high–top sneakers, and leaned back against the side of her bed. "Your roommate's gone for the weekend?"

"Yeah. She went home yesterday to beat the snow." She turned on the portable television on the windowsill and adjusted the channel. "This show okay with you?"

"Don't know. Can't hear it."

"What're you deaf?" She increased the volume and sat down on the floor, an acceptable distance away from him. She bent forward to remove her boots—a little too quickly. Caught in a whirlwind of dizziness, she froze in mid–bend and closed her eyes.

He paid close attention to her actions. Wasn't even buzzed, she had said. He knew better.

As the rush subsided she opened her eyes and slowly looked up, trying to focus on the poster on the wall across from where she sat. "Maybe I drank a little more than I thought."

He moved closer, began rubbing her shoulder.

"I thought we were going to watch TV."

"Tube's on, ain't it?" He now had both hands on her shoulders, kneading her tense skin expertly.

She turned her back toward him, sending him a message to further his advances. It felt good, and she wanted to relax, keep the dizziness away. She closed her eyes and slouched back against his chest.

He pushed her long hair away from her neck, brushing his cheek over hers. "How 'bout it, white girl? Wanna get busy?"

Her eyes flew open as his lips touched the soft skin of her neck. She started to protest his unmistakable actions but the whirling in her head returned, and she wasn't quite sure what was happening. He turned her toward him, covering her mouth with his.

With her guard down he took full advantage, slipping one hand around her back, the other across her lap. His lips moved down her neck.

She closed her eyes again, felt him push her against the side of the bed. She rested her head on the mattress, his mouth returning to hers. This was a fantasy, her fantasy. It wasn't real.

His hand slid over her breast, lingering, then slithered down to her waist. "You hot, girl." He lifted her head from the mattress to ease off her sweater. She opened her eyes, trying to focus on his face. He was pulling her bra off—and grinning.

"Want some dark meat bad, don't you, babe?" He lifted his eyes to meet hers. She exhaled harshly but couldn't speak. His fingers touched her breasts roughly, and she watched, it seemed from a distance, as he lowered his face to them.

Then it happened.

Jolted back to reality by his mouth devouring her flesh—almost animal–like—the girl gasped out his name and grabbed his wrist as he reached for the snap on her jeans. "No, don't!"

He ignored her, breaking the grasp, pulling open the snap. The force of the pull released the zipper, and her jeans fell open.

"C'mon," she protested, trying to squirm away from his hold. "Stop."

He lifted his face, cursing. "Stop? No way. You want this bad."

She stared into his eyes, frightened and confused. "No, I don't want this. You're hurting me. Let's just watch TV, okay?"

"You can't be stoppin' now!"

"Yes, I can! Get off me!"

He snickered. "I don't like bein' rejected."

Her eyes widened with fear, a sobering, real fear. "I said, get off me!" She struggled to work her way out from underneath his body.

"Don't be doin' this!" He viciously grabbed a handful of her hair, forcing her head back against the bed. He straddled her with his powerful, athletic legs, pushing his entire weight down across her hips. "You gonna finish this! Got it?"

A scream started deep down, but his large hand covered her mouth in a split–second, before the cry could alert other dorm residents. He was banking on the TV audio to drown out the sound of his impending onslaught.

"Don't be doin' this! Don't make me hurt you. You won't scream if I move my hand, will you now?"

She tried to shake her head, struggle from his grasp. But he tightened his grip on her hair, held it taut to the mattress until he saw tears form in her fearful eyes. "Will…you…now?" he repeated, pronouncing each word slowly, clearly. He wanted to make sure she fully understood his intentions.

The pain he was inflicting on her, the restraint he *had* on her, were more than sobering. She stared into his cruel, determined eyes and nodded, slightly, conceding to his demand.

"I knew you'd see it my way." Cautiously he lifted his hand from her mouth.

She had to remain calm, composed. The last thing she needed to do was panic. She tried to convince herself this was not happening, but as his hand slid down her throat, the reality of the situation could not be denied. "Please. You have to understand. I'm sorry if I led you on. But I don't want to do this. Please don't do this to me."

"I already told you, you *got* to do this! It's either the nice way or *my* way. The choice is yours." He lowered his face to hers, smothering an unwanted kiss on her lips.

She somehow managed to turn her head from his violating mouth. "Fuck you." She refused to give in, to satisfy him. Despite his threats, despite his position over her and his weight advantage, she began to fight him—fiercely, freeing her hair from his hold. She grabbed onto the back of his shirt, struggled to pull him away, to squirm out from underneath his unlawful confinement. Another scream started inside her, but again his large hand stifled the sound.

Her sudden defiance was totally unexpected—and more than he could handle by physical strength alone. She was a strong girl, and he was now in an all–out war to hold her down.

"Bitch!" His fist hit her stomach with the force of a Mack truck. He laughed as she buckled over, breathless. But his laughter quickly turned to rage, and he seized her hair again. His arm flew around to the back pocket of his jeans, and he pulled out his ultimate re–enforcement.

Panic shot through the girl's body as her horror–filled eyes fixed on the object in his hand. She sucked in air, searched for one last desperate attempt to escape the inevitable.

"Looks like you be the one gettin' fucked. Ain't that right, white girl?" He jerked her head back, placing the steel blade against her exposed throat.

"Okay, okay," she cried. "I'll do whatever you want. Just, please, don't hurt me, please."

She'd lost her battle for freedom.

CHAPTER 1

Entering Highlands County

Renee Maselli stared down at her June day–planner. In thirty minutes she had a meeting with a sales representative from the local radio station concerning an advertisement for the train excursions. She slouched forward, resting her face against her outstretched hand. The proofs for the county's annual brochure were still laying among a stack of letters and requests for information that had gone unanswered for over a month.

Renee Maselli was beginning her third week of employment at the recreation and vacation bureau sitting behind a desk covered with a backlog of tasks that had been left behind by the previous tourism coordinator.

She reached for her empty mug and hurried out of her tiny office for the coffeemaker, needing another shot of caffeine before she left for her meeting with the radio salesman. As she refilled her mug she peered down the narrow hallway, watching the secretary in the reception area turn away from her computer to answer one of the two ringing phone lines.

Quiet. Definitely not.

Renee returned to her desk. Pushing a strand of her thick, dark hair away from her eyes, she glanced out the window. On the sidewalk in front of the bureau office building an aluminum soda–can discarded by an inconsiderate pedestrian rolled across the concrete then dropped over the curb into the gutter.

Clean. Not really.

And then Renee remembered the attempted carjacking last week at the shopping plaza.

Not safe either.

She laughed aloud, visualizing the brand–spanking–new sign that greeted motorists out at the county line: *Entering Highlands County—Safe, Clean, Quiet*. Maybe when the coal and lumber industries flourished in the region. Maybe then Highlands County *was* safe, clean, and quiet. But that era ended over twenty–five years ago, before her birth. Now the tourists came, year–round. Boating, fishing, camping in the summer. Skiing and snowmobiling in the winter. The train excursions had begun seven years ago, combining history with the natural beauty, the result of a joint venture between the recreation and vacation bureau and county government system to bring additional—and much needed—tourism dollars into the rural, mountainous county.

Renee reached for the brochure proofs and quickly scanned through the text while sipping her coffee. She was going to have to spend the better part of the afternoon scrutinizing the draft for errors or changes. This year's brochure was long overdue. It usually went to press in May, but its publication sat dormant since the last tourism coordinator quit at the end of April.

As Renee grabbed a pencil to circle an error that leaped out at her, the secretary from the reception area appeared at the doorway.

"Two things," the young redhead announced, handing Renee a pink message slip. "First, a lady from a church group in Elmira, New York, wants to know if she could reserve an entire coach for the August 15 run."

Renee leaned back in her chair and rolled her eyes. "Tell her the train derailed and ran off a cliff."

The secretary giggled. "Don't let the boss hear that."

"Ah, he needs a life. What's the second thing?"

Before the secretary could respond, a police officer appeared in the doorway.

Renee motioned to the cop. "This is the second thing?"

Grinning, the young female officer leaned against the doorframe with her arms folded across her chest. "What? You're not happy to see me?"

Renee gestured to the secretary. "This is my sister Lisa."

"Nice to meet you." She glanced over at the uniformed carbon copy of Renee. "Is there anything different about you two?"

"Of course," Renee said. "I'm better looking."

Lisa laughed, moving into the tiny office and sitting in the chair before her sister's desk. "But I'm smarter."

"I always thought identical twins did everything alike."

"Not us," Lisa said. "We only *look* alike."

"What's up?" Renee asked her sister.

"The usual. Some old man told me I was too pretty to be a cop and to get a woman's job."

Renee tried unsuccessfully not to laugh. "What'd you tell him?"

"I ignored him."

"How could you work with all those guys?" the secretary asked. She could never handle a police officer's job.

"What guys?" Lisa said. "I have a female partner. We were paired up 'cause none of the good ol' boys wanted us."

The telephone rang at the secretary's desk, and she excused herself to answer it.

"Probably another excursion reservation," Renee sighed. "That's all we've had all morning."

"How about lunch with Alex and me?" Lisa asked. "About one o'clock."

"Don't you usually meet Jim for lunch on Mondays?"

"He has an interview with the school board this afternoon."

"How could I forget that?" The opening for a German teacher at the high school had been the topic of many conversations between Jim and Lisa and her family ever since the old teacher announced his resignation in mid–March. He was moving to Connecticut and this past school year had been his last with the Highlands County School District. "It's looking good, huh?"

Lisa nodded, her face brightening. "Real good. There's one other applicant, but Jim has two years of subbing experience. The other guy doesn't."

"He's got the job," Renee said with confidence.

"They're hiring another math teacher, too. Did I tell you that?"

"No. Why's that? Someone else leave?"

Lisa shook her head. "They need another math teacher to cut down on class sizes. The state education department said the district's math scores are below the state average and smaller classes are required for effective learning."

"Makes sense."

"How 'bout lunch?"

"Sounds great. Now do me a favor?"

"What?"

"Get that train out of my sight."

"What train?"

"The one on your sleeve. I've had it up to my eyebrows with this train stuff."

Lisa shifted in her seat so Renee couldn't see the keystone–shaped patch on her right uniform sleeve. On a green field, encircled with the words *Highlands Regional Police*, a steam locomotive overlay a crossed ax and coal pick. The excursions had become so popular in their short existence depictions of the turn–of–the–century locomotive could be found throughout the county: on building facades, on restaurant placemats, even on the local police cars and uniforms. "How's this?" She pointed to the patch of the American flag on her left sleeve.

"You're going to be late for your meeting at the radio station." The voice came from the doorway, and both sisters looked up surprised.

"Chill out," Renee told the short, stout man. "I'm leaving in a few minutes."

"I need you to stop at the newspaper office after the radio station and talk to the new editor there about a write up on the excursions. He just called me. Here's his name." Her boss handed her another pink message slip. "And you have to get to the printer this afternoon with those proofs."

Renee made a disgusted face. "The newspaper? I'm not prepared for an interview, and I haven't thoroughly checked the brochure for typos. Why does all this have to be done today?"

"Because we're way behind on everything. Tomorrow's the first of July, and this promotional campaign should have been wrapped up in May."

"What's another day? It's already two months past schedule."

"I want everything handled today. Understand?"

Renee stared up at him, stunned by his harshness. During her first two weeks he had seemed pleasant, and Renee figured she was going to enjoy working for him. She was now second–guessing her first impression. "Fine. I'll take care of it all somehow."

"Good." He shifted his attention to Lisa, the other half of the infamous Maselli twins. He recalled these two young ladies, all 5'11" of them, leading the Highlands High School girls' basketball team to the state championship seven years ago. And if that wasn't enough fame, he thought resentfully, their father was chairman of the county board of commissioners, elected this past November—without his vote—for a third four–year term.

"Can I do something for you?" he asked Lisa, a touch of sarcasm in his voice. He refused to address her as Officer Maselli. As far as he was concerned she only wore that badge because her father sat in the head honcho's seat over in the courthouse.

Lisa sensed his irritation and stood up. "Yes, as a matter of fact, you can."

"What's the problem?" He never realized how tall the Maselli girls were; he had to look up to meet her eyes. It angered him even more that her height, coupled with the authoritative look of that navy–blue uniform, made him feel inferior. How could a fifty–year–old man feel inferior to a twenty–four–year–old *kid*?

"There's a Honda parked behind this building, near the train station. Do you know who it belongs to?"

"It's mine. Why?"

"Well…" Lisa tried hard not to smile, "I'm afraid it's parked too close to the tracks. Freight coming down from New York won't be able to pass through."

His face flushed. "We pay the rail authority good money to use those tracks for our excursions. I don't think they'll mind my car back there."

"Not if you don't mind having it plowed over by a two–hundred–ton locomotive."

"I never had this problem before."

Renee slouched down in her seat and turned to look out the window. Her boss was flirting with trouble; Lisa had a short temper.

"I'm asking you to move your car away from the tracks, or you'll get a ticket. You're parked illegally. Understand?"

"I understand all right." He stormed back toward the director's office. "Someone is going to hear about this."

"Just move the car."

His office door slammed shut. Lisa looked down at Renee.

Renee stared up at her twin, fighting off a growing grin. "I don't think I'm going to last a month. You're going to get me fired."

"You loved every minute of it. What's up his ass today?"

"I have no idea." Renee turned away and cupped her hands over her mouth, muffling her sudden, uncontrollable laughter.

Lisa headed out of the office, trying to contain her own smirk. "See you at one."

❧ ❧ ❧

Matthew Ehrich rolled out from underneath a late model Pontiac and stood up, wiping his grease–covered hands on his equally greasy coveralls.

"Needs more work than I thought," he informed the other mechanic bent over the engine of a sporty white Chevrolet Camaro. "I need a break before I put her on the lift."

Matt grabbed a cup of coffee from the office and stepped outside for some air. It was a cloudless summer day, the temperature already nearing seventy–five degrees, and the activity along Main Street was busy as usual. He leaned against the white stucco exterior of his auto–repair garage, sipping his coffee and enjoying the warm, fresh air.

An elderly woman passed by on the sidewalk, and he was politely saying hello when he caught sight of a cop placing a ticket under the wiper of an illegally parked car up the street. He watched nervously as she stepped back onto the sidewalk and headed in his direction. He would do it today. He couldn't hold back any longer.

"Morning, Officer Griffin," he called to her as she approached the building.

She cut across the asphalt lot to talk with him. "Morning, Mr. Ehrich."

"Any bank stickups today?"

"Nope, none today. Hasn't been one in Highlands County since I've been here."

"That's too bad."

"Bite your tongue, Matt. I'm not paid enough to have to deal with a bank robbery. So how's it going?"

"Good, how 'bout yourself?"

"Can't complain, I guess." She glanced inside the garage, noticing that the other mechanic, a handsome, dark–haired guy was staring at her from under the raised hood of a Camaro. Smiling, she waved and called to him, "Hi, Brian."

Abruptly he directed his attention back to the car's engine, never acknowledging her greeting.

Shrugging, she said to Matt, "Not too sociable, huh?"

"Neah, he's shy—"

"Excuse me," she politely interrupted, hurrying over to a middle–aged man who was about to cross the street in front of the shop. Out of the corner of her eye, she had seen him toss an empty cigarette pack onto the sidewalk. "Sir, please pick that up."

The man turned to face her. "What?"

"I saw you throw that cigarette pack down. Pick it up."

He grumbled under his breath, bending over to retrieve his litter.

She returned to Matt as the man again attempted to cross the street.

"Aren't we tough, Officer Griffin?"

"You don't know how much I hate litter bugs. And cut the Officer Griffin act. You know my first name."

He had to do it now. She'd given him a perfect leadoff line. He gulped down the last of his coffee then said it. "Okay, Alex. Since you insist I use your first name, what are you doing Friday night?"

Her blue eyes widened with surprise. "Working, four to midnight. No holiday for me this year."

"How 'bout Saturday night?"

"Midnight to eight. Are you trying to ask me out?" A huge grin spread across her face as she looked up into his pale green eyes.

He smiled back, blushing as her eyes continued to hold his gaze, but didn't answer, couldn't answer. He was tongue–tied.

"I'm off Thursday and Sunday," she said, rescuing him from embarrassment. "Pick a day." She had been hoping for this invitation for quite some time. Perhaps since the first time she had seen him in those soiled coveralls, his blond hair disheveled, his face and hands covered with dirt and grease. But that smile of his, revealing a perfect set of pearly–white teeth, got the best of her. She could only imagine how good he'd look in a pair of chinos and a golf shirt, with his hair neatly combed and his trim body smelling of aftershave instead of antifreeze. Passing by the garage had secretly become her favorite part of the daytime foot–patrol.

"Thursday night?" he suggested.

"You're on. Where're you taking me?"

"The Lumberjack for a few drinks. Is that okay?"

"Sounds great. Do you know where I live?"

Matt paused, blushing again. "Ah, no."

She removed a small notepad and a pen from her shirt pocket and jotted down her address. "It's a one–story clapboard with gray shutters up on Grove Street, a couple blocks before the high–school sports complex."

"I'll pick you up about eight."

"I'll be ready." She handed him the paper, glancing into his green eyes one last time. "I've got to go. I have to meet Lisa by the post office."

He said good–bye but remained outside as she continued down the sidewalk, trying hard to contain his elation. He adored her long honey–brown hair, always pulled back into a ponytail while on duty. He had wanted to ask her out for about a month now but couldn't get up enough courage until today. The guy who was voted "Class Flirt" in high school—that same person who had rushed into an ill–fated marriage three years ago—couldn't muster up enough guts to ask someone out. What a joke, he thought. But dating since his divorce had been difficult, and she was different from the other women. She was a cop.

Cop or no cop every time he looked into her brilliant blue eyes, a surge of sexual excitement would swell within him. As far as he was concerned Alex Griffin was the perfect lady—even if she did carry a semiautomatic pistol at her side.

When she disappeared from his sight Matt returned to the Pontiac.

"I did it," he told Brian Haney, the other mechanic still involved under the hood of the Camaro. "I finally did it."

Brian did not look up from the engine.

"That's nice," he replied, uninterested.

Renee Maselli rapped softly on the doorframe of the tiny, unimpressive office. "Excuse me. Are you Rick Stanton?"

The young man sitting behind the old desk looked up from a pile of papers scattered haphazardly before him. He immediately set his pencil down and stood, whisking his long bangs away from his dark eyes. "Renee Maselli from the recreation and vacation bureau, I presume?"

"Yes." She stepped inside the office, pleasantly surprised. "How'd you know?"

"Lucky guess." He moved around the desk to greet her with a handshake. "Rick Stanton, editor of the *Highlands Journal*."

"Nice to meet you." She extended her hand.

"Likewise." He motioned for her to sit in one of the plastic chairs before his desk. "Would you care for some coffee or tea?"

"No, thank you."

"Then pardon me, please, for a second while I run out to the coffee machine. I've been dying for another cup since about ten–thirty."

Renee sat down, propping her canvas briefcase against the chair legs while he went for his drink. She glanced out the long, narrow window that gave way to the late–morning activity along Centre Street, a thoroughfare intersecting Main Street in the heart of Mountain View's downtown business district. Her eyes then began wandering around the office. She noticed the diploma from Temple

University hanging on the wall to the left of his desk. Master's degree in journalism. On the wall opposite the diploma, Philadelphia sports paraphernalia surrounded a large poster of the city's skyline.

"Sorry to keep you waiting." He returned to his desk with a large mug of black coffee.

"No problem." She smiled warmly. "I see you're from Philly."

"Yep," he said proudly. "And no offense, but I wish like hell I was still living there. This town is too slow–paced for me."

Renee laughed, adjusting her peach–colored skirt. "Give it some time. The town grows on you."

"I'm sure it will," he replied dubiously, his eyes inconspicuously following her hands as they straightened the sheer material then moving downward to inspect her long, shapely legs.

"Shall we begin the interview?" Renee reached inside her briefcase for the notes on the excursions she had quickly composed prior to leaving the bureau office.

"Sure. One second." Rick picked up his pencil and rummaged through the paperwork on his desk for his notepad. "I'd like to start out with some information on your background, and then we'll get into the excursions, if that's okay with you?"

"That's fine." She watched him push aside a pile of what appeared to be invoices and requisitions, producing a yellow legal pad. Disorganized but curiously handsome, she thought, like a California college boy. Neat, dark hair, except for the unkempt bangs hanging before his eyes.

He jotted her name at the top of the page. "Are you related to Robert Maselli, the county commissioner?"

"He's my father."

"Oh. His name has come across my desk every week since I've been here. He seems to be a busy man."

"That he is," Renee said. "But he loves his work. He puts a hundred and ten percent into everything he does for this county."

"From what I've read I believe it. Tell me about your position with the bureau."

"I've only been at the job for two weeks, but I did spend two and a half years with the Mountain Region Vacation Council."

"Tell me about that organization. Where is it located?"

"It's a tourism promotion agency covering the six counties in this region of the state. The office is located in Williamsport over in Lycoming County. It's funded through both private and government dollars. In fact, the Highlands Bureau is a member of the Council."

"How far of a drive was that?"

"Thirty miles, one–way."

"Did you attend college before that?"

"State University of New York in Binghamton. I have a BS in travel and tourism."

"And what exactly is your job title?"

"Tourism Coordinator."

He wrote her personal information alongside her name then looked up, habitually brushing his bangs over the top of his head. "We're sort of in the same boat. I've only been here six weeks, but I've been in the newspaper business since graduating from Temple, almost five years."

"In Philadelphia?"

He nodded. "I worked for the *Journal's* parent company, Penn Publishing. I was transferred here when your old editor was let go. I used to be a reporter, then a community editor covering Delaware County for the *Delaware Valley Tribune*, another subsidiary of Penn Publishing."

"Congratulations on your promotion then." She shifted in the chair, crossing her legs.

Her skirt rode up, and he eyed her right leg, exposed from mid–thigh, as it hung over her left one. He had a fixation with women of Mediterranean descent. Renee Maselli was no exception.

"Thanks, but northeast Pennsylvania was not exactly where I wanted to be promoted to."

"Why not? The perception of this region being off the beaten path is totally false. We've got all the conveniences of the cities here. And we also have acres and acres of beautiful farmland and forests, and most importantly..." She smirked. "Clean air."

"You've sold me. Now tell me about these train rides."

"The excursions are now in their seventh year. The bureau developed the idea of running them to boost tourism in the area. They were initially funded by the bureau, the county commissioners, and through fundraisers and donations from the public. The bureau was looking for a way to combine the rich railroading history of the county with the pristine surroundings." Renee paused, reviewing her notes for a moment, giving him time to write down everything she had said. "The five passenger coaches were purchased from the Trans–Pennsylvania Railroad. They're authentic coaches used by the TP between New York City and Pittsburgh in the 1920s and 30s. The locomotive is a restored Shay purchased from the state of West Virginia."

"What exactly is a Shay?"

"It's a type of steam locomotive that was used to transport lumber and coal through mountainous terrain. It's designed with three vertical pistons connected to a crankshaft on the engineer's side, the right side that is. This design allows the locomotive to negotiate rough track with tight curves."

"I gather the steep terrain in West Virginia is similar to that up here," he interrupted, peeking up at her through those stringy bangs. "Even the industries, huh? Coal mining and lumbering."

She nodded enthusiastically. "Right."

"And I'm safe to assume the name of the excursions, Highlands Scenic and Historic, was derived from the county's bygone industries and rural landscape."

"Yeah, that was hard to figure out, wasn't it? How do you know so much about the excursions?"

He pointed to the computer terminal set up to the left of his desk. "All I did during my first week here was scan through the old files to see what's been happening in the area. What about the scenery along the route?" he asked, hastily resuming the interview. "What's there to see?"

Renee hesitated, straining her thoughts for an effective reply. Her mind was blank. "Trees," she finally muttered through a giggle.

"No?" He dropped back in his swivel chair, laughing. "Trees? Here? I find that hard to believe."

She lifted her hand to her forehead, hiding her eyes from his stare. "I'm sorry," she chuckled, "but that's all I could think of." She let her hand fall into her lap, recomposing herself. "Seriously most of the route *is* through woodlands, but it also passes by some open fields and farmland and some pretty streams and ponds, even a large wetland."

"A wetland? Yeah, I guess that sounds more intriguing than a swamp."

"Hey, don't knock the swamp. The plant and wildlife habitats are quite diverse."

He sat momentarily silent, flipping the page of his notepad, continuing his longhand on the first few lines of the second sheet. "Okay, got it all," he said, emphasizing the last period with a forceful prod. He looked up at her again, his hand systematically clearing the hair from his vision. "Now for the boring stuff. Give me the facts, the numbers. You know, revenues generated from the excursions, number of riders, ticket costs, et cetera."

"The numbers are rather impressive," Renee said, reading off the statistics she had included with her notes: twenty–eight excursions and over ten thousand riders annually, a million dollars in revenues, including tickets, souvenirs, and food.

"I guess these train rides are a *big* deal."

"Yes, they are. And we're certainly grateful for any kind of free publicity that's offered to us."

Rick wrapped up the interview after another ten minutes, mostly with questions on the logistics of operating the excursions.

"May I call you if I have any further questions?" he asked, setting his pencil alongside the legal pad.

She slipped the notes back into her briefcase. "Certainly. I'd give you a business card, but unfortunately I don't have any yet. They're still at the print shop."

"No problem. I've got your name and number written down. I know we'll be seeing each other again. It's inevitable in our line of work. Here's one of my cards." He removed a beige card from a holder alongside the computer and stood, moving around the desk.

She rose from the chair, briefcase in hand, and reached for the card. "Thank you. And thank you again for your interest in the excursions. A feature article in the paper will be greatly appreciated."

He escorted her to the building exit. "I'll have something for you in Wednesday's paper. It'll be somewhere between the first and third pages."

She smiled gratefully. "I'll be looking forward to it. Nice meeting you again."

"Likewise." He watched as she walked up the sidewalk toward Main Street. Those long, dark legs moved with such poise.

Rick returned to his desk and opened the top drawer, removing a computer printout of an article that had appeared in a March edition of the *Highlands Journal* seven years back. His eyes focused on the headline: *Lady Wolves Win State Basketball Championship, Finish Season 30–0.* He had discovered the article while scanning the computer files for other information. The title had piqued his curiosity, so he began reading the text. Two paragraphs from the top he had learned of Renee Maselli's existence. She had scored ten points to help propel the Highlands High School girls' basketball team to a 51–48 victory over North Allegheny.

He leaned back in the chair and interlocked his hands behind his head. In his six weeks of living in this boring little town—he likened Mountain View to Mayberry, the country–bumpkin hamlet of 1960s television—only one other woman had caught his attention the way Renee Maselli had.

Lisa Maselli.

Officer Lisa Maselli.

Alexandra Griffin stood before the dresser mirror in her bedroom, removing her contact lenses. Twenty minutes earlier she had completed a mile jog around the high–school track two blocks up the street. It was essential for her to keep in shape, for both her job and her health. Exercise kept her blood sugar in check.

Alexandra Griffin had been living with type 1 diabetes for nearly half her life. Daily rituals included monitoring her blood sugar, injecting insulin under her skin, and jogging. Upon return from each run she'd poke a finger with a lancet and squeeze a drop of blood onto a chemically treated strip. Insertion of the strip into a portable meter would produce a digital reading of her glucose level. And each time that reading would be low. Six ounces of fruit juice, however, always averted any looming insulin reactions.

Alex slipped on her gold–rimmed eyeglasses and carefully rinsed her contact lenses in the saline solution, storing them away in plastic cylinders. Frowning, she stared at her "four–eyed" reflection in the mirror. Alex hated her glasses. She liked her appearance much more with the unnoticeable lenses.

Four years ago her sight had worsened to the point of having to wear corrective lenses all the time. She rotated between glasses and contacts, and because she could never get used to herself in glasses, she wore the lenses in public, saving the glasses for the confines of her private life.

She changed into a clean pair of shorts and tee shirt and headed back to the kitchen, through the short hallway and living room of the small, one–story house she rented in the Heights section of town. She ran a glass of water from the tap and checked her diabetic survival kit: her supply of insulin vials, syringes, needles, pen cartridges, lancets, oral glucose, and injectable glucagons. Only six syringes and twelve cartridges remained. She used the syringes to administer her slow–release insulin twice daily. The pen cartridges contained quick–acting insulin needed before each meal. She made a mental note to stop at the pharmacy after work the next day and get more of each. Everything else was in abundance. She wouldn't have to worry about any of those supplies for several weeks.

Alex reached into a cabinet under the counter for a box of cat food, filling Oscar's empty dish in the pantry off the kitchen.

A stray Maine coon she had discovered pilfering her trash four months ago, Oscar lay sleeping under the table. It had been love at first site, his thick gray fur, those big green eyes, and that feather–duster tail melting her heart instantly. She took him to a vet for shots and had him neutered, welcoming him into her contented life.

"Rough day, huh, Oscar?" She peeked through the chair legs at her feline housemate then headed outside to her small vegetable garden in the backyard. It had been ten years since she'd planted tomatoes and lettuce and zucchini. She was still living at home with her parents in Wilkes–Barre the last time she even *had* a backyard. The laid-back life she found in Highlands County was long overdue.

She weeded and watered the small patch, picked a few leaves of lettuce and went inside to wash them.

A knock came at the front door. Alex closed the faucet and left the lettuce to drain in the kitchen sink while she went to answer it.

Swinging open the louvered door between the kitchen and living room, she started at the sight of her ex–boyfriend standing on the front porch peering through the screen door. She had ended their calamitous relationship a month and a half ago and hadn't seen him for the past couple weeks, which had suited her just fine. She was free, without condition, of his smothering disposition.

"What do you want, Kyle?" she greeted him coldly, standing before the screen, her hand resting against the back of the door, ready to slam it in his face in a split second.

Kyle Lawry got right to the point of his visit. "I hear you've got a date with Matt Ehrich."

Anger seethed within her. "Your buddy at the garage couldn't wait to tell you, huh? The little wimp has nothing better to do."

"That's why you dumped me," Kyle fired back. "You were lookin' for a better bed partner. Well, you picked a good one. Ehrich's a real charmer. Couldn't keep that glamour queen he married so now he's back on the prowl, I see."

Alex drew in a deep breath. "I want you to leave right now. My personal life is none of your business anymore."

"I can't believe you're doing this to me."

She closed the door in his face, pressing her back against the oak panel. She heard him shout an obscenity as he stomped off the porch.

A red flag waved in her mind, her stomach clenching with a helpless, nauseating fear. Do not negotiate with him, a voice from within warned. You did the right thing by cutting him off, by not allowing him to challenge your decision.

Alex's date with Matt Ehrich would be the first with someone besides Kyle since she had moved to Mountain View nine months ago. She suddenly realized she had just met the real Kyle Lawry.

And he was even more absurdly jealous than she had surmised.

Alex exhaled in frustration. "What have I gotten myself into?"

* * *

The early–evening sun shone brightly in the western sky as Lisa Maselli sat on the front porch of her family's house on Fourteenth Street, feet stretched over the railing, eyes closed. Her feet ached, as they always did after the long and usually boring downtown patrol, and it felt good to sit back and relax.

Lisa didn't mind working the foot patrol every Monday through Wednesday, although she and Alex Griffin had been assigned to the downtown because no other officers had wanted it. Shifts and patrols were established by seniority, and since they had been the last two full–time officers hired, they were expected to work the "shitty" shifts. So every Monday, Tuesday, and Wednesday, Lisa and Alex would walk up and down the streets of the commercial district ticketing parking violators and directing traffic during rush hour.

Lunch was ordinarily the highlight of the day patrol, the time when Lisa and Alex would unwind from the morning's monotonous routine over a sandwich and soft drink. Today's half–hour break with Renee at the Rail Line Restaurant hadn't been a let down.

It began as usual with daily gripes and small–town gossip. But as they waited for the food to arrive, after Alex had returned from the ladies room where she'd administered her insulin discreetly, Renee recounted the details of her meeting with the newspaper's new editor less than an hour before. She had just finished describing the guy when she informed them of his move from Philadelphia.

"What did you say his name was again?" Lisa recalled interrupting her sister in mid–sentence.

"Rick Stanton," Renee had answered. "Why?"

Lisa raised her eyebrows, glancing oddly at her partner across the table. "The DUI we picked up on Mountain Gap Road."

"Whoa, wait a minute," Renee chimed in. "You two know this guy?"

Lisa remembered Alex eyeing her matter–of–factly.

"We stopped him for speeding about five, six weeks ago," Alex said. "What a piece of work."

"I don't believe it." Renee was shaking her head, the bewilderment on her face evident. "He was arrested for driving drunk? But he seemed so nice."

Lisa sat silently, staring at Alex as Renee's eyes bounced back and forth between the two of them.

"He was very polite," Renee insisted.

"He's *probably* an okay guy," Lisa said. "He had a few beers too many, that's all."

"What'd he do? Make a total ass of himself?"

"Among other things."

"What? What'd he do?"

Lisa crossed her arms, resting them on the tabletop. "He was drunk, and he got verbally abusive. And to be totally honest he said some lewd things."

"Are you sure this is the same person?"

"It's the same person," Alex said. "Your description is right on the nail, so is the fact he moved here from Philly. His driver's license still had a Philly address when we arrested him."

"What a jerk," Renee then had whispered. "He actually mouthed off to you guys?"

"Not to Al," Lisa said. "He had a problem with me."

"He must have *known* who I was this morning," Renee realized. "I wonder why he never mentioned any of this to me."

"C'mon, Renee." Lisa had almost laughed at her sister. "Would you broadcast that you were arrested for DUI a few days after moving to a new town? And I'm sure he doesn't want people to know about his rash behavior, especially because of his position with the paper. He *did* apologize to us when we took him home, and I'd like to believe he meant it. But I could be wrong. He could be president of a women haters club for all we know."

Lisa opened her eyes, staring up at the blue sky. *I bet you give good head* Rick Stanton had said to her that Friday night as she attempted to explain his legal rights.

Lisa laughed bitterly. Insults came with the job; she had learned to accept that. In fact, the variety of snide comments made by the public—and by fellow male officers—no longer upset her. In a few years

Lisa would be laughing at them all; she'd have that law degree. She'd spend another year or so with the police department then apply to a law school somewhere in the Northeast. She wouldn't have to put up with the workplace hierarchy anymore—or the abuse that came with her badge. Her ultimate career goals were to establish her own practice here in Highlands County, make a comfortable living, and most importantly, be her own boss. Like her mother, who had run a successful real–estate agency.

Painful memories of her mother's death resurfaced as Lisa glanced around the neighborhood at the modest clapboard houses and small neat lawns.

Ann Marie Maselli had passed away five summers ago, after a long and agonizing battle with cancer. For several months afterward Lisa could not accept her death. The loss of her mother had been the abysm of what Lisa considered to be the worst year of her life.

It had begun with a long–term separation from Jim. He had gone to Europe to study for a semester in France and Germany, to enhance his skills and understanding of their languages and cultures. She had been alone, away at college with her mother's suffering and Jim's absence constantly on her mind. Concentration on basketball and on her criminal justice studies had sunk to the point where she had been in jeopardy of flunking out of college and losing her athletic scholarship. Jim had returned home in late May of that year, but her mother would lose her fight for life three weeks later. The world had been crumbling around her, and she despised herself for using her mother's illness as an excuse for all of her problems.

"How 'bout a game of twenty–one?"

Lisa gasped, startled by the unexpected voice. She looked over only to see her younger brother standing alongside her with a basketball in his hands.

"What are you jumpy about?" Tony Maselli said.

"I didn't hear you open the door."

"So how 'bout a game?"

"Why aren't you working?" She wasn't in the mood to play basketball.

"Night off. I'm working the rest of the week." Monday nights were usually slow at the supermarket, and the manager had taken all but one of the bag boys off the schedule.

"Where're your buddies then?"

"No one's around. They all had plans."

Lisa gave in to him reluctantly. "Okay, I'll play. But you're going to lose."

"We'll see."

They stepped off the porch and walked over to the garage alongside the house. A basketball hoop was attached above the overhead door.

"Go first," Lisa said.

Tony aimed for the basket but missed. Lisa grabbed the rebound and fired the ball through the net.

"What'd I tell you?" She caught the ball before it fell to the ground. "Do yourself a favor, stick with football."

"Don't worry. I had no intention of switching."

Lisa moved to the foul line, a crooked chalk mark across the asphalt, to shoot her bonus point. With little hesitation she raised the ball and pushed it up. Again it was right on target. She had played her last game with the North Penn University Lady Mountaineers over two years ago. Still, her basketball talent hadn't diminished.

She threw the ball to Tony. As he attempted his second shot a Pontiac Grand Prix pulled up to the curb in front of the house.

"Game's over," Lisa announced, heading for the car. "Your new German teacher is here."

"I'm taking Spanish next year," Tony teased, watching Jim Ostler emerge from the car.

"The job's mine," Jim told Lisa. "But it won't be official until the board meeting tomorrow night."

"You knew it was yours. I'm so happy for you."

He smiled mischievously, sliding his arms around her. "Let's go celebrate."

"How and where?"

"I've got a bottle of wine. Let's go to the pond then watch the sun set on the cliff."

She grinned and kissed him suggestively. "It's a deal."

* * *

Lisa and Jim lay on a blanket near the fence at the edge of Seneca Cliff, watching the street lights in the town below sparkle against the growing darkness as the last light of day faded behind the western mountains. A local landmark, the cliff afforded a spectacular view of Mountain View and the surrounding countryside.

"I love this spot," Lisa said. She had been atop the cliff countless times before, but she never seemed to tire of the view.

"I like Becker's Pond more. Let's go back. I can't get enough of you."

"Whatever happened to that quiet boy who asked me out in eleventh grade?" She slid her hand through his blond hair, gently rubbing the nape of his neck with the tips of her fingers. "I thought you were so cute."

"I'm so glad I got the courage to ask you for a date. I thought you'd laugh in my face. But look at us now. We can finally start making wedding plans."

"Wedding plans? We've only been dating *eight* years. Don't you think you're rushing it? Besides, I don't even have an engagement ring."

"Yet."

Lisa lifted up on an elbow. "We have to talk."

"What's wrong?" He looked at her, concerned.

"Nothing. We just need to talk about our future, about me going to law school."

"You still want to go, don't you?"

"Yeah, but I'll have to move away for a while. You won't be able to come with me. You have to keep this job."

His hand lightly touched her cheek. "We'll work it out somehow. Don't worry. Nothing will keep us apart."

"I love you," she whispered.

"I love you, too."

"I wish I didn't have to work on Friday." Lisa sat up on the blanket, gazing down at Pine Creek silently flowing through town. "I want to go with you to the faculty clambake. It was nice they invited you and the other new teacher. Any idea who it is?"

"None whatsoever. I wish you didn't have to work either. I hate going to this alone."

Lisa frowned. "I know, but I have to work two holidays a year. Al and I got stuck with the Fourth and Thanksgiving this year."

"I understand," he said, sitting up alongside her, pouting. "I guess."

She watched him fake that pathetic facial expression and couldn't help laughing. "Ah, poor baby."

He reached over for her hand, guiding it to the snap of his blue jeans. "You owe me for not being able to make it Friday."

"No way. Not here. If we ever got caught we'd lose our jobs. I'd be a disgrace to my father."

Jim sighed, feigning dejection. He began rubbing circles around her knee, teasingly, then slowly inched his left hand upward, inside the leg of her baggy shorts. He glided his finger under the band of her panties. "Ah, c'mon. No one will see us," he insisted, his right hand moving inside the other leg of her shorts. "I'll return the favor. In fact, I'll go first."

Lisa released a short, intense moan, and the smile on her face assured him his verbal and physical enticements would soon overwhelm her.

He maneuvered himself down on all fours, his hands still working their magic inside her shorts. Automatically she arched her body backward, propping herself up on outstretched arms.

"C'mon, Lisa. Don't fight it."

She glanced up at the first stars of the night twinkling in the dusk sky. "No, we can't," she pleaded, her voice less than convincing. "Someone might show up. A lot of people come up here. Let's go in the car."

"You don't want to do that. You want to do it here." Jim went down between her legs, massaging the soft, sensual skin of her thighs with his lips, driving her shorts as far up as the material would allow. "C'mon, lady cop, show me what you're made of."

His tongue slipped under her panties, and she cried out. He knew exactly how to push her buttons. Lisa shivered as he relentlessly teased her with his mouth, provoking her to reciprocate the pleasure.

He paused, looking up, his devilish blue eyes begging for satisfaction. "C'mon, lay down the law. I'm a bad boy."

"Oh, yeah?" she moaned, her heart racing with exhilaration. "*Real* bad?"

"As bad as they get. What are you going to do about it, huh?"

"I don't know. I'll...think about it."

He lifted himself up, pushing her down across the blanket and straddling her. "Let me show you *how* bad I can get." He smothered her lips with a deep, powerful kiss then yanked her shorts and panties down over her knees.

"Jimmy," she gasped, momentarily ashamed. "We're going to get caught. C'mon, cut it out." But as his tongue encircled her navel then traveled lower still, her less–than–threatening protests evolved into a mixture of euphoric sighs and moans. She gave no further thought to being discovered. The pleasure he was giving her was mind consuming, and she could think of nothing else but the caressing, probing of his mouth, leading her to orgasm.

"Oh…oh," she cried, thrusting herself upward as the powerful release surged through her body.

Jim rose to his knees, his eyes pleading for pay back.

"You're so bad. I *have* to do something about it." She pulled herself to her knees, flush from the gratification he delivered so effortlessly, and met him face to face. "You're going to pay good."

The elation on his face was unmistakable. He reached for her shoulders, pulling her face to his. She kissed him savagely as he gripped her, felt her hands trail down his back and around his waist to the snap on his jeans.

"Punish me," he muttered, falling back on his heels. Her eyes filled with lust as her fingers opened his zipper. She recalled for an instant that lewd remark Rick Stanton had made to her while intoxicated.

I bet you give good head.

Smiling, she thought of a response to Stanton's comment: Oh, yes, I do, but *you'll* never find out.

CHAPTER 2

Destiny Unknown

Alex Griffin slid a frozen pizza into the oven and grabbed a bottle of fruit juice from the refrigerator.

"I'm starved," she said, turning toward the kitchen table.

"You're not going to have an insulin reaction?" Lisa asked half–jokingly. She sat at the table dressed in gym shorts and a sweaty white tee shirt with the words *North Penn University Basketball* printed across the front. A bandanna around her head kept her long bangs away from her forehead and the rest of her dark, shoulder–length hair in place.

"Don't you think I know better than that?" Alex said. "I've only been poking my finger and shooting up for thirteen years now."

"After that run we had I thought you'd be drained."

Alex tipped the juice bottle toward Lisa. "Plenty of sugar in this, and I load up on carbs before running so my sugar doesn't drop dangerously low. How 'bout some juice?"

"Sure." Lisa rested her tired body against the back of the chair. "Thanks for asking me to run tonight. I haven't in a long time. It felt good."

"Any time you want to come along, ask. I run every night."

"Hey, have you seen the new reserve they hired to fill in for vacations?"

"No. Why?"

"I saw him today for the first time, while I was finishing up my reports."

"And?"

"He's got braces."

"Braces?" Alex laughed. "I can hear the gibes already."

"Wait till the seniors at the high–rise see him."

Alex filled two glasses with the fruit juice and set them on the table. "Are you meeting Jim tonight after the school–board meeting?"

"Yeah, about nine. I'm thrilled he got this job. This was the break he was waiting for. If the other German teacher hadn't moved, he'd be subbing for a long time, or looking for a position elsewhere."

"You two won't have to leave the area now. What about your law school ambition?"

"Jimmy said not to worry about it. We'll work out something."

"I'm sure you will."

"Since we're on the subject of men, do you think Kyle will bother you anymore about seeing Matt Ehrich?"

"I don't know. And I'm a little concerned about his behavior."

"Forget about that jerk," Lisa said.

"Kyle did say something that took me by surprise."

"What's that?"

"He said something about Matt not being able to keep that glamour queen he married. I never knew Matt was married. I guess that small talk we make when I see him on foot patrol really *is* small talk. I don't think I know anything about his life outside the garage."

"Matt was married for about two years. He's been divorced for about a year now."

Alex wasn't sure how she felt about that revelation. "What happened?"

"It was rumored his wife ran off with the ER doctor at the hospital."

"Wow. That's...terrible."

"Don't dwell on the past. Life dealt him a bad hand. We can all relate to that. Give him a chance. He's a great guy."

Alex grinned. "A charmer I've been told."

He was alone in his bedroom.

He sat on the edge of the bed, staring down at the faded newspaper photograph clipped from an old issue of the *Highlands Journal*. Specifically he was peering at her, third from the left, surrounded by four other women and a man.

"Soon," he whispered to the photo. "You and I. It's gonna happen. Real soon."

CHAPTER 3

Weaving Tangled Webs

Renee Maselli sipped her second cup of coffee while reading over a letter sent to the bureau in late May. It was from the activities coordinator of a school district in a neighboring county. The woman expressed an interest in taking a fifth–grade class on one of the excursions. She stated the experience would serve as both a class outing and a valuable lesson on the state's rich history of railroading, mining, and logging.

"What a great idea!" Renee jotted a reminder in her day planner to make a diligent attempt at contacting this woman. The concept of school trips could open up a whole new avenue for marketing the excursions, she thought, placing the letter in a folder labeled "Immediate Attention."

"Busy?" the office secretary asked, tapping lightly on the doorframe.

Renee looked up from her desk, her eyes narrowing with suspicion. "Why? The boss doesn't want something done right now, does he?"

"No. There's someone here to see you."

Renee set her pencil down and straightened in her chair. "Who is it?"

"Rick Stanton, from the newspaper."

Renee eyed her contemptuously. "Oh? Send him in, please." She blew out her cheeks, quickly rehearsing a denunciation in her mind, as the secretary returned to the reception area to show him down the hallway.

"It's nice to see you again," she said through a phony smile when he appeared at the doorway. She didn't bother to get up from behind her desk. "To what do I owe this visit?"

"Three reasons," he said, holding a folded newspaper under his right arm. He detected the bitterness in her voice and surmised she had spoken to her sister about him. "May I sit down?"

She shrugged, motioning him toward the chair in front of her desk.

He brushed his bangs back and sat where instructed, sliding his hands inside his pants pockets, the paper still tucked out of her sight.

She rested her elbows on the desktop. "What can I do for you?"

"Well, first, I brought you today's edition of the *Journal*."

"That wasn't necessary," she replied coldly. "We get the paper here at the office."

He tossed the paper onto the desk. "I gave the piece on the excursions first-page billing. I wanted to deliver it in person."

"And why's that?"

He exhaled loudly. "You've talked to your sister about me, haven't you?"

Renee scratched her chin. "Hm, my sister? Would that be my twin sister, the cop? The one you tongue lashed a few weeks ago?"

"You know then."

"Oh, yeah."

"That's the second reason I'm here: To apologize. I couldn't tell you on Monday. I wanted our meeting to be professional, civilized."

"I see," Renee replied dubiously. "You knew who I was then, didn't you? It wasn't a lucky guess."

"Actually, yes and no. I didn't know *you*. I knew your sister. But I knew what to expect when I met you, since the two of you are identical."

She certainly couldn't dispute that. "And did you already know Lisa and I were the commissioner's daughters?"

He nodded timidly. "It's kind of hard not to know, with all the press your family's gotten."

Another fact she couldn't argue. Still, she felt uneasy, deceived, and was determined to voice her displeasure with his backdoor tactics. "I'm sorry you were stopped for driving drunk," she said nonchalantly. "But I guess you know now you can't mess around with the local yokels."

Rick sighed. "I apologized to your sister. I was wrong for what I did, the drinking and speeding, and making the crude remarks. But I haven't been convicted yet. We're all entitled to our day in court. I'm still awaiting a hearing date."

For an unknown reason Renee pitied him, though she couldn't express her sympathy. Instead she reached for the newspaper he had set on her desk and unfolded it, directing her gaze away from him.

A small grin brightened his face as her eyes fixed on the paper's headline lauding the train excursions. "I acted like an absolute jerk that night with your sister, and I'm sorry about it. And I'm sorry I kept it from you on Monday. Can we wipe the slate clean and start over?"

She hesitated at first, scanning the article, but then looked up, meeting his dark–brown eyes with her own. "This is fantastic. I'm impressed. It's going to help us a great deal."

He smiled tentatively. "Was that a yes?"

She wanted to tell him no. No, it's not okay to wipe the slate clean and start over. I've already branded you a liar and a drunk and a pervert. And I'm not going to be taken in by your innocent, schoolboy looks. But she didn't tell him no. She didn't answer at all. "What was the third thing you wanted to see me about?" she asked, deliberately avoiding a response.

"I was wondering if you'd like to have lunch with me today? It's the least I can do to show my sincerity."

She pondered the invitation for a long moment, finally deciding to accept for no reason other than curiosity. "Okay, fine. Lunch it is."

The relief on his face was unmistakable, as if he had been exonerated from a first–degree felony. "Twelve–thirty okay with you?"

Renee leaned back in her chair, studying the mysterious person before her. Lunch, she believed, would be anything but dull. "Twelve–thirty's fine."

* * *

Inside a classroom on the second floor of Highlands High School, Jim Ostler sat behind the teacher's desk, flipping through the pages of an introductory German textbook. Satisfied with its contents he closed the book and looked up at a bare bulletin board on the back wall. Several display themes ran through his mind. Months, days, holidays, maps of German–speaking nations, facts, flags. He could hardly wait until September. He'd finally have his own classroom, his own textbooks, his own students. No more subbing and no more working at his father's hardware store. His four years of studying foreign languages ultimately had paid off.

He was searching for the advanced German book when someone appeared at the doorway. Jim glanced in that direction, watching a petite blond woman step into the classroom.

"It's been a long time, Jim Ostler," she said, nearing the desk.

"Yes, it has. So you're the new math teacher. Congratulations. I had no idea you were back in town till I saw you last night at the board meeting."

"Pittsburgh was a drag. This job was my ticket home. I wanted to congratulate you last night on your appointment, but you hurried out."

"I was meeting someone."

Paula Sedlak smiled assuredly. "Lisa Maselli."

"You remembered."

"I thought you'd be married by now. How long have you been dating? Since our senior year, right?"

"Yeah. Eight years."

"Remember all the fun we had with the marching band? Do you still play the trumpet?"

"No." He briefly thought back to the bygone days when they donned those god–awful, green–and–white band uniforms and so proudly marched across the football field or paraded down Main Street on holidays and special events. "How 'bout you? Ever pick up the old alto sax?"

"Not since my college days."

"You headed west after Penn State, to the City of Steel, huh? I always thought Pittsburgh was a great place. What happened?"

"I worked for an Allegheny County school system with six–thousand students. I couldn't handle the metal detectors and the armed guards in the hallways. I had to get out. I was home sick."

Jim smiled warmly. "Welcome home."

"Thank you. I should go. I have to look over some algebra books."

"You, too, huh?" Jim pointed down at the desk cluttered with German books. "That's what I'm doing."

"It's a good idea for us to get our books now. We'll have plenty of time to work on lesson plans."

"I'm looking forward to September."

"Me, too," Paula Sedlak said. "I'll see you and Lisa on Friday then?"

"You'll be seeing me. Lisa has to work."

"On the Fourth of July? What does she do?"

"Law enforcement."

"She's a cop?"

Jim chuckled. "Yes, she's been a cop with the regional police for about two and a half years now. It's experience for law school. I'll see you on Friday. We could reminisce some more."

"I'd like that." Paula Sedlak left the classroom. It felt good to be back home.

"Smoking or nonsmoking?" the perky, young hostess greeted Renee and Rick as they stepped inside the Towne Diner.

"Non…" Renee started to say, but then realized she had no idea of his preference. She glanced back at him.

"Nonsmoking will be fine."

The hostess escorted them to a small table against the back wall.

"I'm sorry," Renee said. "I'm so used to saying non, I didn't think about asking."

"I only smoke when I'm aggravated."

The young woman set menus on the table and walked away.

Rick pulled out a chair, allowing Renee to sit down.

She watched his moves as he joined her across the table. She couldn't believe she had accepted this lunch offer after his Monday–morning trickery. But his apology seemed sincere, and she decided he deserved a second chance to prove his professionalism.

"I've been here a few times before," he said as they opened their menus. "The food's not bad."

"Not bad for what? A hick town?"

His eyes peered at her from across the top of the menu. "Is everyone around here this brutal?"

Renee laughed. "Okay. My fault. I wasn't being fair."

They sat silently for a few moments, reviewing the lunch specials. Renee decided on a turkey sandwich and set the menu at the edge of table while Rick continued to ponder over the food choices. She found herself staring at him, musing over his mystique. He was youthfully handsome, and although those long bangs hanging over his eyes gave him the appearance of a carefree twenty–year–old, she calculated his age closer to twenty–seven or twenty–eight.

Rick finally decided on a bacon cheeseburger. A few moments later a plump waitress appeared at the table, and they ordered.

"I'm glad you gave me this opportunity," he told Renee as the waitress headed for the kitchen. "I didn't want you thinking I'm a terrible person. However, I'm not so sure your sister doesn't think that of me."

"I never thought you were a terrible person. A jerk maybe." Renee fiddled with her flatware. "And, actually, my sister doesn't think that either. She believes your apology was sincere."

"Really?" His dark eyes widened with surprise. Perhaps he misjudged Lisa Maselli. He then wondered about Alexandra Griffin, the one with his mother's steel–blue eyes. "What about her partner? What's she like?"

"Alex?" Renee detected a bit of paranoia in his voice. "She's a great person, really laid back. You sound…are you afraid of what they're going to tell the magistrate at your hearing?" Her own words hit like a ton of bricks. The obvious was there all along, practically slapping her in the face, and it took her this long to figure it out. "I get it now," she said resentfully. "You're using me. You're trying to get on their good side, so they'll drop the charges."

"No, no, that's not it at all." He ran his hand through his bangs, disconcerted, his face burning red. "I don't want people around here looking at me with contempt. I don't want some old lady to see me on Main Street one day and say, 'There goes that drunken newspaper man who had the audacity to mouth off to our police officers. He's from the city, and that's where he belongs, not here in our quaint, little, God–fearing community.' I made a stupid mistake, and I don't want to be labeled a troublemaker. I may not *be* from a small town, but I *know* what goes on in one."

Renee sat speechless, her fork frozen in her hand. She felt her own face flood with color and wanted desperately to crawl under the table. "I…I'm sorry for jumping to conclusions. Perhaps I'm the one who should be paying for lunch."

He laughed, ending their momentary clash. "You can buy the next one."

"The next one?" Renee wondered if there was more to this invitation than met the eye, and she couldn't decide if she felt flattered or frightened by his remark.

"A strictly business lunch. If that's what you'd prefer."

The waitress returned with their drinks, allowing her time to think of a polished response.

"I guess that depends on you," she said, raising the glass of iced tea to her mouth for a refreshing swallow.

"What'd you mean?"

"Come clean, Rick Stanton. I don't want to be second–guessing you. I want to know what you've been reading about my family and me on your computer over there. And why?"

"Huh?" He took a swift sip of his soda, spilling a few drops on the tablecloth.

Renee studied his actions. "I can understand you've learned a lot about my father since the commissioners are in the paper every week. But how did you know about me? I'm certainly not mentioned in the police log or in any articles pertaining to county government. How did you find out that *I* existed?"

"Honestly?"

"Honestly."

Rick leaned back in his seat, playing with the condensation on his glass. "I stumbled onto an article about your basketball state championship."

"You *stumbled* onto an article? I don't think you *stumbled* onto anything. You were *searching* for something with the name Maselli in it. What was it you were looking for?"

The color drained from his face. "Maybe this lunch was a mistake."

"No, I don't think so. Look, Rick, be honest with me. You're new in town, you had a bad experience with my sister, and now here I am having lunch with you. Don't you think it's reasonable for me to be a little suspicious of you?"

"Okay, the truth."

"The truth."

"Okay, here it is. I thought your sister was a knockout, but I have this thing about female cops. I…honestly, they scare me."

"They scare you?" Renee burst into laughter. "I'm sorry, really, go ahead."

"It's a male ego thing."

She pursed her lips, suppressing another bout of laughter. "I suppose."

"Anyhow," he continued, his fingers nervously drifting up and down the glass. "I wanted to learn more about her. I was curious, that's all. I found the basketball article and that's when I found out about you. There was even a picture of the team and your coach. You were all holding up that big gold trophy. It must have been an awesome feeling, huh?"

"Nice try. But I'm not changing the subject yet. If you thought my sister was attractive then why'd you mouth off to her?"

"It's the male ego thing, I told you. I was had by two female cops, and I couldn't handle it."

"Why didn't you give Alex a hard time?"

His stomach clenched with a flash of his mother's punishing blue eyes. "Your sister was doing most of the talking."

"I see. For future reference I happen to respect police officers, male or female, and you can forget about my sister. She's been involved with the same guy since high school and…" She paused, fighting off a condescending smirk. "He doesn't have a problem with her being a cop. Not in the least."

"Thank you for that tidbit of information," he said half–sarcastically.

"Where does that leave me? Why am I sitting here having lunch with you? Is it because I look exactly like Lisa and don't wear a badge or carry a gun?"

"Honestly?" he asked.

"Honestly."

"Yes."

"Is that why you called the bureau and wanted to do a story on the train excursions? Because you wanted to see what the cop's other half was like?"

Embarrassed, he looked down at his flatware. "Yes. And now you *do* think I'm a terrible person. I'm sorry."

"Terrible? Naw. A jerk maybe."

"Really?" he asked, disheartened.

"Honestly?"

He raised his eyes to meet hers. "Honestly."

A comical smile appeared on her face. "No. I'm kidding. Actually I'm a little flattered. Do you know how many people in this town can't tell Lisa and I apart?"

"Probably a lot."

"We used to fool our teachers in school, even some of our dates, until Lisa started going steady. And even *he* had a crush on both of us."

"Why'd he pick Lisa?"

"Because he got to know her, through a study hall they were both assigned to."

"Will I get to know you?"

Renee raised her eyebrows presumptuously. "You might. The bureau and the *Journal* always have worked closely together in the past."

A huge grin spread across his face. "Is that right?"

"Absolutely."

"What do the bureau and *Journal* usually do for the Fourth of July?"

"Right now the bureau has no plans."

"What a coincidence. Neither does the *Journal.* Maybe we should get together, for the betterment of the community."

"Absolutely not," Renee replied, holding a smile as his abruptly vanished.

"I'm sorry. It was only a suggestion."

"I don't work on holidays," she said. "But if you'd like to do something for the betterment of the two of us, I may reconsider."

Rick's smile returned. "Really?"

"Sure. Why not? Have anything in mind?"

"Surprise me."

"Okay, if you insist. Just be prepared."

Kyle Lawry sat at the bar inside Vic's with a beer before him, waiting for his buddy. The Main Street tavern was his usual stop after work each day. He had no reason to rush home from the furniture store. He lived alone in an old house in the Heights section of town.

For the past two days Alex and her date with Matt Ehrich had consumed Kyle's thoughts. He refused to accept her decision to end their relationship. As far as he was concerned it was a temporary interlude. It simply had to be. She belonged to him.

Kyle gulped his beer then ordered another. Nursing his second drink he recalled the first time he had seen Alex. It was last October, and she had been moving into the house four doors down from his place. He introduced himself and offered to help with her unpacking. She had reacted with aloofness, leery of his intentions. She was new in town with a law enforcement background, and he was a very forward stranger.

Gradually he won her trust, first as a friend, and then, for a short–lived time, as a lover. Her appearance had been the main reason for his attraction to her: long, permed hair and captivating blue eyes.

But as the relationship grew, her honest and extroverted personality began tangling him in a web from which he could not escape.

Then she had drifted astray, befriending some state troopers and other guys in town. It hurt him to argue with her, but he didn't like her flirtatious behavior. She was his.

He was helplessly bound to Alexandra Griffin.

Now Matt Ehrich was threatening to destroy that allegiance. If Kyle couldn't have her, no one should, especially not the likes of that Casanova.

Kyle and Matt had graduated high school together. Matt was a known ladies man, and Kyle always had resented Matt's popularity with women. It seemed Matt managed to seduce every woman in town, including that hot number he waltzed down the aisle. Kyle had been delighted when he read Ehrich's divorce decree in the newspaper a year ago.

Alex would be another notch on Ehrich's bedpost, Kyle was sure of that, and he couldn't deal with it. As much as he desperately tried, Kyle could not shake the effects she had on him. He had been her only lover since her move to the county. That he knew without a doubt. He knew *everything* about Alexandra Griffin.

Kyle Lawry drained the last of his second beer as his friend from the garage joined him at the bar.

"What's goin' on?" he asked, ordering a beer for his buddy and yet another for himself.

"Ehrich is laying the work on." Brian Haney pulled his baseball cap off and set it on the bar. "I gotta start lookin' for another job. I can't stand the pretty boy anymore."

Kyle stared at Haney, alarmed. "You can't quit now. Not with him trying to get into Alex's pants. I need details."

"For crying out loud!" Brian grabbed the beer bottle set before him. "Why can't you forget about her? She ain't worth it. No broad's worth the pain or aggravation."

Kyle snickered. "You haven't gotten laid in who knows how long. Maybe if you'd get some balls and ask someone out your attitude would change."

Brian Haney laughed loud and hard. "I'm doin' fine. You're the one who's hung up on women. I'm telling ya, Lawry, get a life."

CHAPTER 4

Chemistry 101

Matt Ehrich pulled out a chair at a corner table inside the Lumberjack nightclub and allowed Alex to be seated. "I thought it'd be nice to bring you here tomorrow night, since a band would be playing."

"This is fine with me," Alex said as Matt sat across from her. "There's no music to shout over."

"What would you like to drink?"

"A diet cola."

"A diet cola? That's it?"

"I stay away from alcohol. I'm a diabetic." Alex produced a medical information tag from inside her blouse. It was attached to the silver chain she wore around her neck. "Here's the proof. I wear this in case of an emergency."

Matt was shocked. He had always visualized diabetics as being either overweight or elderly. "Do you take insulin?"

"Five times daily."

"You actually give yourself five shots a day?"

"I'd be dead if I didn't."

He shuddered, trying to imagine how on earth he would give himself an injection. "Where do you do it? In your arm?"

"In the arm, in the leg, in my stomach. I rotate spots every day. I use a syringe twice a day and this neat device that looks like an ink pen the other three times."

"Do you have to watch your diet, too?"

"Uh–huh. I have to count carbohydrates and exercise. And my eyes are starting to show signs of retinopathy, a condition that affects diabetics. I've been wearing contact lenses for about four years now. My vision is blurry without them."

"Were you born with diabetes?"

Alex shook her head. "No, I was diagnosed at fourteen."

"And you're what now?"

"Twenty–seven. How 'bout you?"

"I'm thirty–one. Alex, I'm sorry about your problems."

"Don't be. It's my life as I'm used to it."

He blushed. "I'm sorry for feeling sorry."

"You're blushing again. You blushed when you asked me out."

"I'm sorry."

"Stop apologizing."

"I'm acting like an idiot, aren't I?"

She met his eyes and grinned. "No way."

Embarrassed, Matt forced a smile. "How 'bout that diet cola now?" He waved over a waitress.

Alex couldn't take her eyes away from him. He looked exactly as she had imagined out of those greasy coveralls: strikingly handsome. She noticed the roughness of his hands as he ordered her soda and a mixed drink for himself. They were the hands of a skilled laborer. Grease was embedded in the crevices of his palms and under his nails. Unattractive, she thought, yet strangely desirable.

"Tell me about yourself," Matt said.

"Like what about myself?"

"Like anything. Where'd you grow up? Why'd you decide to become a cop?"

She smiled; the cop question seemed to be everyone's favorite.

"I'm a full–fledged coal cracker. I grew up in Wilkes–Barre."

Matt listened intently as she spoke. It was the first time he'd seen her out of uniform and with her hair down. He had found her attractive in her police blues, neat, professional, even somewhat sexy. But now, as she wore a slightly revealing blouse with her long hair flowing past her shoulder blades, Matt was convinced she was one of the most beautiful women he'd ever laid eyes on.

"I didn't decide on law enforcement right away. I actually went to college for environmental science with a minor in sociology."

"Where at?"

"Colorado State."

"Get out! Why so far from home?"

"Colorado State has outstanding environmental programs, and I love the mountains and being outdoors. I couldn't pass up four years in the Rockies. Those sociology courses I elected to take included criminology and police science. I've always had an interest in law enforcement, maybe from watching too many cop shows on TV..." She held his blank stare for a few seconds then laughed. "I was joking about the cop shows. Anyhow, after graduation I applied for a job with the National Park Service. I wanted to combine my love for the environment with my hankering to play cops and robbers. I was sent to Arizona for Park Ranger training, including instructions on firearms. I worked for the NPS for four years at two different parks."

"Which ones?"

"Organ Pipe Cactus National Monument in Arizona and Independence Historic Park in Philly."

That blank stare reappeared. "Organ Pipe what?"

"Organ Pipe Cactus. It's in the Sonoran Desert on the border with Mexico."

His lack of geographic knowledge immediately showed. "I'm sorry. I'm still clueless about this Organ Pipe place."

She giggled. "It's a desert wilderness with extraordinary plants including the organ pipe cactus, which is rare to the United States. I basically spent my time there on border patrol. The park is a hot spot for drug smugglers and influxes of illegal aliens from Mexico. I was transferred to Philadelphia after two years."

"Some environment Philly was. Did you like it there?"

"I tolerated it. While I was working at Independence, I decided to take a stab at the municipal police officers training program. After I became certified, I worked two jobs for over a year, at the park during the week and as a part–time officer for a township in Chester County on the weekends."

Matt's brows raised up. "Jeez," he remarked as the waitress returned with their drinks. "In one uniform and out the other. Did you have two guns as well?"

"Two different issues. One was a nine–millimeter semiautomatic, like the one I have now. The other was a thirty–eight service revolver."

Matt sipped his cocktail, shaking his head in astonishment. "Do you feel naked without a gun at your side?"

Alex smirked, swallowing some of her soda. "No, I hate them. I'm carrying fifteen pounds of extra weight when I wear my duty belt."

"How'd you end up here?"

"First I moved back to my hometown. I was getting tired of Philly so I applied for a vacant law–enforcement position with the state fish and boat commission. I got the job, but a year later the governor made some cuts, and I was laid off. I went back to working part–time patrols for another police department until I saw an ad in my local newspaper that Highlands Regional was hiring a full–time officer. So here I am—the newest cop in town."

"You must be overqualified, with all that experience you've had."

"I wish. From what I've been told, off the record, some people cried nepotism when the department hired Lisa, the commissioner's daughter, although she was the most qualified for the job. The police board wanted to show the public they weren't playing favorites by advertising the next full–time opening outside the county."

"Then you've got two strikes against you," he said, smiling.

"What'd you mean?"

"You're a female cop, and an out–of–town cop, working the good ol' boys' network."

"As much as I'd like to argue that, I can't. You're absolutely right, but I've learned to deal with it."

"What's it like working for the police department? You and Lisa are the county's first female cops."

"A lot of guys find it difficult to work with us. Why do you think they assigned me with Lisa? Until I was hired she worked with reserves. The chief hated the fact the police board hired either of us, and the guys with seniority refused to work with us, so we were paired up. Most of the guys, including the chief, are hoping deep down we'll screw up."

"Is it like that everywhere?"

"No, not everywhere. But, hey, it doesn't bother me. I look at it as a challenge. Ever since I developed diabetes my life has been nothing but one challenge after another. I'm capable of doing the job, and I love the work. If the guys here don't like it then that's their problem, not mine."

Matt continued to sip his drink, intrigued by her career and fascinating past. "Who's on the police board?"

"One elected official from each of the municipalities in the county. The regional police force was created to better serve the rural areas and provide round–the–clock protection at an affordable cost to the communities. We have four to six officers on duty each shift. We handle traffic and crowd control, vehicle–code violations, accidents, and minor offenses. The state police handle the hard–core crimes and back us up when we need assistance."

"And the police board basically runs the show?"

"Ted Peterson, the chief, runs the department. However, he has to answer to the board; they do all the hiring and firing." Alex raised her glass. "It's your turn," she announced, wanting to test his integrity. "Tell me about *your*self."

"Compared to your life after high school, mine is rather dull. After I graduated I started working as a mechanic for the man who used to own the garage. He retired about six years ago and offered to sell me the business since he had no family. I somehow managed to get a loan from the bank to buy it. It was the best move I ever made. Business is great."

"That's wonderful, a credit to you. Not everyone can be his own boss."

He was unimpressed with his life. "I'm just an average blue–collar Joe."

"A very attractive one." Alex caught his green eyes and prompted for more information. "I find it hard to believe no one has snatched you up. A single guy in his early thirties, that's a rarity these days."

His eyes glazed over, and he set his glass down. Alex noticed the sadness immediately. She wished she hadn't been so aggressive in seeking out his past.

"I'm sorry," she said with sincerity. "I put my foot in my mouth, didn't I? If I've touched on a sensitive subject, please—"

"It's okay," he assured her. "It's no big secret. I'm…divorced."

"I'm sorry."

"I'm finally beginning to realize I dove into my marriage wearing a blindfold. I learned the hard way that my ex–wife and I had nothing in common. I was twenty–eight and thinking I needed to settle down. Cindy was twenty–four and much too materialistic for my means. She was a medical transcriber at the hospital and wanted way more than I could give her. The physical relationship was there, but that was about it. When we weren't in bed we were at each other's throats. I guess it was fitting she left me for a doctor. He could buy her the world on a silver platter."

The sympathy Alex felt for him was genuine and, gazing into those cheerless eyes, her heart and soul ached with emotion. If they hadn't been in a public place, she imagined herself kissing him, softly, wanting to ease the sorrow.

"Is she still in town?" she asked. "Your ex–wife?"

"No. She followed him to Boston when he completed his residency at Highlands Memorial."

"Matt, I'm sorry."

He sighed. "All we're doing is apologizing to one another. Let's stop the condolences. I don't want you thinking I'm a sad sack."

Alex again found her eyes drawn to his. There was chemistry between them that could not be denied, an attraction so strong it almost frightened her. "You're far from being a sad sack, Matthew Ehrich."

"Would you like a cup of coffee?" Alex said to Matt as they stood on her front porch. It was nearing one in the morning, but she was reluctant to say goodnight. Besides she didn't have to start work until four the next afternoon.

"How could I refuse?"

Inside the living room she turned on a lamp near the couch. Oscar greeted them immediately, slinking into the room from the hallway and hopping into a chair.

"So this is Oscar, found living in a trash can."

"The one and only."

"He's beautiful." Matt glanced around the small, cozy room, decorated in an eclectic manner, a mix of country and contemporary furnishings complementing one another. He noticed a large oil painting of a Southwestern landscape on the wall near the swinging door to the kitchen and commented on it.

"That's a painting of the cliff dwellings found in the Four Corners area of Colorado. They were inhabited by the Anasazi, ancestors of the modern–day Pueblo Indians who mysteriously vanished in the thirteenth century. I bought it at a flea market when I was at Colorado State."

He was impressed by her knowledge, by her intriguing past, and felt out of her league. She had studied in the Rockies, worked in the Arizona desert. He had never ventured far from Highlands County, except for a honeymoon cruise to Bermuda.

"Please, have a seat," Alex offered. "I'll put the pot on."

Matt nestled on the couch, and she started for the kitchen.

"Wait. Come here for a second," he called, motioning her to sit alongside him. "Please, forgive me, but I've been wanting to do this all night long." He pulled her close, covering her mouth with his.

The kiss was long, intense—and perfect, as Alex somehow knew it would be.

"I've been waiting for that all night long," she confessed. Instinctively their lips came together again.

"You're incredible," he breathed, lowering his mouth to her neck.

She closed her eyes, savoring the feel of his sensual lips on her skin as his hands trailed down her arms to her waist, his chest pressing against her breasts. After a few minutes of heavenly pleasure, she reluctantly commanded herself to speak. "I have a rule not to let a man get past first base on the first date. If you keep this up I might break it."

He lifted his head and forced an awkward smile. His face instantly flushed with embarrassment. "I'm sorry."

"We have to stop this apologizing." She raised her hand to his chin, guiding his face back to hers. Her kiss was undeniable, meant to erase any guilt he may have had.

Reluctantly pulling away she drew in a breath to calm the burning, wildly arousing sensation that awakened every inch of her body. "How 'bout that coffee now?"

"That'd be great. You're working tomorrow from four to midnight, right?"

"Yeah."

"How 'bout a picnic lunch at my house? Say about noon? I'd love for you to see my place."

Alex could hardly wait. "Noon it is."

CHAPTER 5

Red, White, And Flashing Blue Lights

Rick Stanton tossed a six–pack of cola into his Nissan. He would have preferred a six–pack of beer, but in light of his pending DUI hearing and the fact he was trying to befriend the sister of one of the cops who had busted him, he wisely chose to bring the soda along instead. He rented a three–room apartment above a flower shop at the edge of town. It would only be a ten–minute drive to Renee Maselli's house.

Horseback riding. That was the surprise. He had agreed reluctantly. He had never ridden a horse in his life, never had the desire to do so. But he was going to do it today, the Fourth of July. He had spent his previous Fourth celebrations at backyard parties in Philadelphia. This year he was saddling up a horse and riding through the boondocks. Had he finally lost his mind?

Rick shook his head and laughed to himself as he pulled onto the highway and drove toward the downtown. He couldn't get the Maselli twins out of his mind. Those long legs. Those deep brown eyes. Their thick, silky hair and Mediterranean complexions. Lisa Maselli had aroused him initially, and now he had a chance at seducing her civilian sibling.

As he slowed the car for a red light on Main Street, he thought back to the night he had been stopped for speeding. He had been in Highlands County only five days. It was a Friday night, and he had been angry. Angry he had no companions or anywhere to go. He had purchased a six–pack at a local watering hole and driven around the Godforsaken countryside. He drained his fifth can and turned onto Mountain Gap Road. He had no idea where the rural roadway led, but it was a straight stretch of pavement so he floored the gas petal. He recalled feeling the buzz from the alcohol and cursing his former boss, that self–important bitch.

That's when he had seen the flashing red and blue lights in his rear–view mirror. He slammed his fist against the steering wheel and pulled to the side of the road. It had been his boss's fault. She had done this to him, made him move to this hick town. He hastily shoved the beer cans under the seat, praying his breath didn't reek of alcohol. He looked in the mirror again, catching sight of the two cops in the police vehicle, a white sport utility vehicle with blue markings. "Just what I need," he had mumbled to himself. "Two broads." The driver was talking into the radio microphone, undoubtedly running his plate number through the system for registration and stolen vehicle information.

He quickly reached around for his wallet while watching the young officers finally emerge from their vehicle and approach his car, expandable batons and pistols arrogantly affixed to those oppressive navy–blue getups. It had been a little past eight, still light enough to make out their features in the mirror, and he recalled being astounded by their appearance. Nothing like the female cops he had seen in the city: They were burly, unattractive women, probably all lesbians. These two had been knockouts, as straight as a Kansas highway. And bitches, he automatically had presumed.

He shifted his eyes to the side–view mirror. The tall cop stayed behind, inspecting his trunk and backseat. The shorter one cautiously approached his door window, her kinky light–brown hair hanging behind her head in a long, thick ponytail.

"Evening," she said to him. "License, registration, and proof of insurance, please."

Without saying a word he removed his identification from the wallet and passed it to her through the open window. His eyes instantly fixed on her face. She was stunning, her brilliant blue eyes beautiful but ice cold. Like his mother's.

He watched her give the documentation to her partner, taking note of the name on the silver tag she wore opposite her badge. Griffin. A WASP. White Anglo–Saxon Protestant. Like him. Like his mother.

"Put your hands on the wheel where I can see them," she had instructed as her partner returned to the police vehicle to run his numbers through the system.

Definitely a bitch. He felt those icy eyes bearing down on him as he sat silently, gripping the top of the steering wheel. He contemplated saying something but quickly decided against it. He didn't want to rouse suspicion. He needed to get out of the detainment with as little damage to his wallet—and ego—as possible.

It seemed like an eternity, but the tall one finally returned with his documents. "Mr. Stanton, your license and registration have Philadelphia addresses. Are you visiting someone in Highlands County?"

He looked up at her face then zoomed in on the nametag. Maselli. Italian. Catholic. Under any other circumstance he'd have made a play for this one. Rick remembered being amazed by her height. An Amazon if he'd ever seen one, close to six feet, his own height. Despite the sudden physical attraction he had to her, she made him feel like a peon, tipping her head down to look through the window opening.

"No, my company just transferred me here," he had replied with a tactical politeness. "I haven't gotten a chance to change my address yet."

"How long have you been living here?"

"Five days."

"Okay, that's fine. But you only have fifteen days to report the change to the Department of Transportation, so make sure you do it as soon as possible."

"I'll take care of it right away."

"Do you know why you were stopped?" she asked.

He didn't appreciate the quiz since he knew a lecture would follow. But he wanted the belittling ordeal over with before they discovered he had been drinking. "I suppose I was going a little fast."

"You were clocked doing sixty. The speed limit is posted at forty–five on this road. And since you *are* from Pennsylvania you should know you're also required to wear a seat belt."

"I *do* know that. I forgot. And I promise I'll pay more attention to the speed–limit signs."

"I'd appreciate that. This road may be straight here, but it gets narrow and windy ahead. It would be in your best interest to slow down and buckle up."

"I understand."

Then the blue–eyed one spoke up: Griffin.

"Mr. Stanton, why are you out driving *this* road? There's not many houses along this route, and no one travels down here unless they live here, especially not someone who has just moved to the county."

He fumbled for an answer as the two of them stood glaring at him, waiting patiently to pounce on him like a cat preying on a mouse.

"Have you been drinking?" Griffin asked.

"No. N…no way. I was bored and decided to go for a ride, that's all."

"You wouldn't lie to us, would you?" Maselli slipped his license and registration into her shirt pocket.

"No," he insisted.

She reached for the door handle any way. "Step out of the car, please."

His threw his head back against the seat. They had him by the balls.

"Look, ladies," he said, trying to salvage what little of his manhood he had left. "That's not necessary. You can rest assured everything's on the up and up."

"We'll be the judge of that," Maselli informed him, opening the door. "Get out of the car, please."

Exhaling harshly he slid out of the Nissan. The seat rose with the shift in weight, releasing one of the empty beer cans underneath. It rolled onto the floor mat, and Blue Eyes spotted it immediately.

"Would you like to explain that?" she said.

He glanced back at the mat, cursing under his breath. He had no means of escape, no choice but to fight back, defend his masculinity.

"Mr. Stanton," Maselli began, "we have probable cause to believe you are driving under the influence of alcohol—"

"Yeah, yeah, yeah." He waved his arms nonchalantly. "Save your sermon for someone else."

He must have pissed her off because the tone of her voice grew sharp, stern. "No, I'm sorry, I can't do that. You are required by the law to perform whatever sobriety tests we feel necessary to prove your coherence. If we cannot determine by these tests that you are *not* under the influence of alcohol, you will be taken to the local hospital for a blood sample. If you refuse to give a blood sample, your driver's license will be suspended automatically for one year."

"You're joking, right?"

"Be quiet, please." She had been extremely angry; he could tell.

"I bet you give good head."

She folded her arms across her chest. "Are you through yet?"

He saw her face flushing and assumed her blood pressure was rising. "No, not really." A cocky grin added to his defiance as his eyes lewdly scanned her body from head to toe. "Do you know what I'd like to do to you right now?"

"Sir, that's enough." Griffin reached for her handcuffs and moved between them.

Maselli's hand came up to stop her partner's intervention. "No, it's okay." Her blazing eyes scorched his. "Why don't you tell me, Mr. Stanton? What is it that you want to do to me?"

He stared at her wide–eyed. She had thrown him off guard, and he didn't know how to react to her provocation. "Oh, no," he muttered, shaking his head. "You're trying to trick me. No way. You're not pinning another charge on me."

Maselli backed off. "Okay then. Are you going to cooperate, or would you rather we arrest you right now for obstruction of justice and disorderly conduct?"

He hadn't answered, his eyes nervously shifting back and forth between the two of them.

"What's it going to be?" Griffin demanded, and his attention quickly turned to her. They were doing it again: quizzing him. That's all his mother had done to him. Quizzed and lectured. Never a kind word, never an 'I love you.' Just grilling and sermons.

"Okay, okay, you win. I've had a few beers." He raised his hands to signal surrender then added, "Fucked again." He had always been coerced by women. By his mother, by his boss—by these two high–and–mighty cops.

"Pardon my French," Griffin had retorted. "But you're *fucking* yourself."

He looked up into the twilight of the late–spring sky and sneered. "Yeah, right."

They showed him no mercy. He had been forced to walk a straight line, one foot in front of the other; stand on one foot and count off forty seconds; recite the alphabet; extend his arm and bring it in quickly, touching his nose with his index finger. All to no avail. They had not been convinced of his sobriety and escorted him to the hospital, had his car towed to the state–police impoundment.

At the hospital he had learned their first names, overhearing a conversation with the lab technician. Later, when they dropped him off at his apartment, he felt compelled to apologize for his foolhardy behavior. He owed that feeling to his mother. She had always made him apologize, sometimes for words and actions he thought harmless.

"Apology accepted," Lisa Maselli had said. But another lecture followed. "I hope you never cross our paths again, and I mean that in a good way. Nobody would have to deal with us if we'd all use a little common sense. And one more thing: If you *should* get pulled over again, by us or any other law enforcement officer, don't get abusive or use gutter language like you did tonight. I realize you were angry, I could understand that, but try to look at it from our perspective. We had no idea who you were, and we have to take threatening remarks seriously."

Before heading up to his apartment he leaned against the vehicle and spoke through the open window on the passenger side. "Alcohol does that to me sometimes, makes me angry and abusive."

"Then don't drink," Alexandra Griffin had said. "Alcohol messes me up, too, not in the same way as you, but I have enough sense to stay away."

Yet another lecture. Women loved to preach. "Goodnight, Officers."

He hadn't seen either Lisa Maselli or Alexandra Griffin after that night. Two weeks later he had received notification by certified mail that his blood alcohol was over the legal limit and he was being charged with Driving Under the Influence. The letter had included the name and phone number of the public defenders' office, in case he needed free legal representation.

He thought perhaps he could beat the rap on a technicality. But when he had met with a public defender, the young man informed him all the required paperwork had been completed promptly and properly and signed by Patrol Officer Alexandra Griffin.

"You don't have a leg to stand on," the lawyer had said. "The only way you're going to beat these charges is if the arresting officer doesn't show up for the hearing, which is highly unlikely."

He still awaited the hearing before the local magistrate. You never know what could happen between now and then, Rick thought haughtily.

He was oddly happy Lisa Maselli hadn't signed the complaint. He didn't want to hate *her*. As he turned onto Fourteenth Street the thought of dating Renee Maselli thrilled him. He saw it as an opportunity to befriend that tall, intimidating woman he had met on Mountain Gap Road, less the badge.

This was the other circumstance.

Alex hopped out of her Chevrolet Tracker and hurried up the three steps of her front porch. It was already past three–thirty, and she had less than a half hour to freshen up, check her blood sugar, slip into her uniform, and get to the borough building to report for second–shift duty.

The afternoon with Matt had her aglow. She had arrived at his house, a two–story Victorian on the North End, about noon. He had a holiday feast waiting in his backyard: barbecued chicken, crabmeat with cocktail sauce, fresh fruit salad, coleslaw, celery and carrot sticks, and plenty of ice–cold diet soda. She had politely excused herself to the bathroom to shoot up before eating. She didn't want to ruin his appetite by using the insulin pen in his presence. It took some time to get used to dating a diabetic. Alex had been through this several times before. Most men had accepted it without a problem; a few could not. Everyone came with baggage. Diabetes was hers.

They enjoyed the meal at a picnic table, under the shade of a large red maple secluded from the neighbors by a tall hedgerow on either side of the yard. Afterward they nestled on a creaky wooden swing suspended from the roof of the back porch and chatted. When she reluctantly said good–bye about three–fifteen to drive home and get ready for work, each had learned they had a number of things in common. They both hated high–school chemistry, the Dallas Cowboys, and heavy–metal music, but fancied the New York Yankees, country music, and outdoor activities, especially hiking and camping.

Since she didn't have to start work until midnight on Saturday, they made a date to meet for lunch at one o'clock and spend the afternoon sailing on Lake Iroquois. A lawyer–friend of Matt's owned a small sailboat and often offered its use to Matt. His friend was out of town for the holiday weekend, so the boat was available. Matt couldn't think of a better way to spend a beautiful summer day.

Alex reached into her purse for her house key. As she swung open the screen door, she caught sight of an envelope hanging from the mailbox. Odd, she thought, since no mail was delivered on a federal holiday. She pulled the envelope from the box. It was blank. No name. No address. Nothing. Curiously she ripped it open and found a note card, the front a lovely picture of red rose petals scattered over piano keys. Inside were the words, "I love you."

"It can't be," she muttered. She hastily shoved the card back into the envelope and peered up the street at Kyle's house. Somehow she sensed he was watching her at that very moment, and a frightening sensation chilled her bones. She quickly turned around and fumbled to unlock the door. She couldn't deal with this now. She had no time to think clearly. Glancing at her watch she rushed into her bedroom. It was three forty–five.

⁂

Renee Maselli greeted Rick Stanton at the front door donned in blue jeans and a red tank top and holding an empty backpack.

"Ready?" she asked, smiling.

He hesitated, preoccupied by her appearance. His eyes wandered down to her breasts, the tank top hugging them perfectly. "Yeah."

Rick tossed the canvas pack onto the backseat of the Nissan, and they hopped into the car, Renee directing him to the stables five miles west of town. When they arrived he stuffed the soda into the pack and strapped it to his back.

"I can't believe I'm doing this," he said, anxiously following her into the stables. "How bad is it going to be?"

"Would you chill out? I've ridden a hundred times. All you have to do is hang onto the reins. They're trail horses. They don't leave the paths."

She picked out two mares, and he paid for two hours of riding. Unsupervised riding. She was an experienced rider, negating the need for a trail guide. The stable hand saddled up the sable mares, and Renee effortlessly mounted hers.

"Coming?" She looked down at Rick. He was standing alongside his horse, contemplating which foot to lift into the stirrup. Renee and the stable hand exchanged smiles.

"Got to be from the city," the hand remarked.

Rick shot the young man a wicked look. "How 'bout showing this uncoordinated *city* guy how to get on this creature?"

The hand explained how to mount the mare and helped him into the saddle.

"Ready?" Renee asked, a broad grin on her face.

Rick grabbed tightly onto the reins. "Lead the way."

They headed across a grassy field to a trail leading into the thick woods. The path wound its way upward, through the trees, to the top of Big Pine Hill. Forty–five minutes after heading out they reached the pinnacle. Renee halted her horse in a grassy clearing, and Rick's mare automatically stopped behind them.

"Check out this view." She swooped her arm outward. "This has got to be the best spot in the county aside from Seneca Cliff."

Rick's eyes scanned the panorama. Endless, gently sloping mountains, dairy and vegetable farms nestled in the valleys between the lush green ridges.

"I don't see anything. Just a lot of mountains and trees."

Renee dismounted the horse. "That's what you're supposed to see. This is God's country."

"You got that right." Rick awkwardly jumped from his mare.

She took the horses' reins and led them to a couple sturdy trees, fastening the ropes to the trunks. As she turned to rejoin him her eyes inconspicuously inspected his attire. Faded blue jeans, snug around his small, firm butt, and a green–on–white football shirt. Holding back an improper grin of approval, she thought how appealing he looked in the rustic outdoors. Even those eccentric bangs, mismatched with the remainder of his trim hair, complemented the laid back garb of rural America. She cracked a subtle grin, thinking there may be potential to turn this professed city guy into a country boy.

She plopped down on the grass. "Sit awhile," she said, patting her hand on the ground. "Enjoy the peace and beauty."

He pulled the pack off his back and joined her on the grass. Smiling, he whisked his bangs away and gazed at her.

"What are you looking at?" she asked.

"Beauty. That's what you said to do."

Her face flushed. She looked away. "I meant the scenery."

"Oh, oh, the scenery. The mountains and trees." He reached inside the backpack for two cans of cola, handing her one. "I'd much rather look at you."

Flustered, Renee plucked the tab a little too swiftly. It snapped off.

"No problem." He took the can and reached into his jeans for a small army knife. "I carry this baby with me all the time," he said, unfolding the blade from inside the handle. "You never know what to expect."

Never know what to expect. Those words bothered her. And at that moment she thought it foolish to invite him to this spot. He was a stranger, and they were miles from habitation.

Thumb against the blade's flat surface he pushed down on the tab. "I'll drink from this one. It may be a little rough." He handed the other can to her and returned the knife to his pocket.

They sat quietly for a few moments, sipping their refreshing drinks. Finally Rick broke the silence. "Tell me about the rest of your family."

"Haven't you read about them already?"

She was teasing, and he laughed. "No, honestly, I haven't."

She disclosed a bit about her younger brother, told him about her mother's suffering and untimely death.

"I'm very sorry," he said with sincerity, seeing tears well in her eyes.

She cleared her throat and quickly turned the conversation to her father.

An accountant by trade Robert Maselli had first dabbled in politics seventeen years ago when he ran a successful campaign for a seat on the Mountain View Borough Council. During his eighth year as a member of council, some of the county's top politicians persuaded him to seek a seat on the Highlands County Board of Commissioners. Vowing to run the county government system fairly and efficiently, he had won the election hands down. Keeping to his original game plan his first bid for reelection four years later had been another landslide success. However, last year's election had been anything but a shoe–in. Renee explained that her father's political foes had tried to discredit his pledge of fairness in the hiring of county employees by questioning the appointment of her sister to the regional police force.

"They conveniently overlooked the fact the police force is not run by the county commissioners," Renee said, a touch of resentment in her voice. "And they also passed over my sister's qualifications. She had the highest civil–service test score of all the applicants. Simply put, the male chauvinist pigs causing all the ruckus were looking for an outlet to vent their displeasure of having a female on the force."

Rick's lips curled upward, and Renee rolled her eyes.

"I know. You think the same way. I'm afraid that's one subject we'll never agree on. But anyhow, it's your turn," she said, draining the last of her soda.

Rick spoke about his life in Philadelphia. An only child of divorced parents his stories centered on his father, an architect, and his friends from high school and college. Although he lived with his mother until starting college, he had never developed closeness to her. She was always too busy with her corporate banking career, and Rick had longed for weekends with his dad. He casually mentioned his passion for computers, especially desktop publishing, and a desire to some day write a novel—a steamy thriller set in southeastern Pennsylvania.

They spent nearly a half hour on the mountaintop, talking about their families and avocations, before heading down to the stables. During the drive back to town Rick asked Renee how it felt to win a state championship.

"Awesome," she answered. "We had such vocal, devoted fans. It was a once–in–a–lifetime experience."

Cued by her response Rick drove downtown to the borough park. He jumped out of the car and opened the trunk, reaching inside for a basketball. "Feel up to a game of one–on–one? First to hit forty wins."

Renee eagerly grabbed the ball from his grasp. "If you're up to it. We weren't state champs by luck."

They headed for the court. "Loser buys dinner," he joked.

"I hope you've got enough money, loser. I'm starved."

And a loser he was; she beat him forty to thirty–six.

"No more challenges." She sank down on the court to catch her breath. It had been a long time since she'd played, and her leg muscles were cramping from the vigorous exercise.

He joined her on the asphalt. "One more." He glided his fingers through her disheveled hair and kissed her. When he ended the embrace she pushed his bangs away from his eyes. His lips instinctively returned to her mouth, kissing her longer, deeper.

Finally, reluctantly, he pulled away, rising to his feet. "How 'bout that dinner I owe you?"

She held an arm out, and he helped her up. "You're on."

Jim Ostler sat on a boulder at the Lake Iroquois overlook, gazing out at the county's largest lake. Three miles long, a half–mile wide, and sparkling with the lights of dozens of small boats, the lake was created by receding glaciers of the Great Ice Age. Several lakes and ponds, including Iroquois, dotted the landscape of Highlands County—a draw for urban tourists. With the establishment of the train excursions, they now came by the thousands.

Jim glanced around at the pockets of people surrounding him at the overlook, awaiting the start of the annual Fourth of July fireworks display. The night was young, and he decided to kill some time. Surveying the huge crowd he figured he must have been one of only a handful of county natives there.

The faculty clambake had lasted from one o'clock to a little past eight–thirty. Jim concluded that Paula Sedlak had not changed much since their high–school graduation. She had been voted "Most Talkative" by her fellow classmates at Highlands High and *still* had the gift of gab. They spent a good portion of the day recalling those carefree days.

"Do you remember the football game up at Northern Tioga?" Paula had asked him, giggling. "Or maybe I should say do you remember the bus ride home?"

Jim had laughed, feeling the heat of embarrassment. "How could I forget? I got two weeks of detention for mooning that old lady."

"We had such good times with the band."

"Yes, we did. But could you believe we actually wore those silly–looking uniforms?"

Paula had burst into laughter. "I used to love those pirate–style hats, especially the white plumes. You have to admit we looked sharp in those green–and–white outfits."

A loud bang echoed across the lake, and Jim glanced upward to see the first fireworks light up the night sky. Gazing at the multicolored explosions he remembered another conversation he had had with Paula Sedlak about old love interests, and he automatically flashed back to the first time he had asked Lisa out on a date.

She was sixteen and a junior. He was a seventeen–year–old senior. It was the end of February, right after the girls' basketball team had suffered a heartbreaking loss that ended the season earlier than most fans expected. He had had a crush on the Maselli twins for quite some time, and when Lisa was assigned to the same study hall with him, his crush quickly grew into an infatuation. Finally, a few days after the basketball season had ended, he pulled Lisa aside after study hall and shyly asked her to a movie. It had taken a lot of courage since he figured a popular athlete like her wouldn't want anything to do with a quiet foreign–language and band enthusiast like him. But she had accepted without hesitation.

Since that day over eight years ago they had remained together. They shared the excitement of the basketball team's state–championship season, attended the same college, mourned the loss of Lisa's mother. Their only long–term separation occurred when Jim had been accepted into a study program in France and Germany. He remembered how he couldn't wait to hold her in his arms and make love to her when he returned from Europe after those five long months.

Jim continued to daydream about Lisa as the fireworks continued to amaze the crowd. He recalled the first time they had made love.

It was New Year's Eve, and he and Lisa were home from college for Christmas break. It was her freshman year at North Penn, his sophomore. His parents had gone to Atlantic City for an overnight celebration, and his older brother was away in the service. He had the house to himself and invited Lisa over for a candle–lit dinner. Halfway through the meal it had started to snow heavily, and he suggested a leisurely walk through town. They spent over an hour strolling the streets in the tranquility of the cold, snowy night, admiring the houses and businesses decorated for the holiday season. Fresh–cut evergreens hung neatly on doors, and each house rivaled the next with sparkling lights. It was nearing midnight when they had returned to the house. He built a fire in the fireplace, and they lay on the carpet before the warmth of the flames, sipping champagne.

Jim's memories grew fonder as he distinctly pictured Lisa setting her stemmed glass on the hearth then taking his away. Her hand trailed down his wool sweater to the zipper of his corduroys.

"I think we should begin the New Year the right way," she had said, the reflection of the flames dancing in her brown eyes.

He knew at that moment their lives would change forever. He remembered his fingers caressing her cheek, slowly drifting across the soft skin of her neck to her thick, silky hair. "Are you sure?" he had asked tenderly. She was still a virgin, and he longed for her first experience with love, his love, to be perfect—unforgettable.

"I couldn't be more sure," she had answered.

A boom in the sky jolted Jim back to the present. An older man sitting alongside him laughed. Jim looked over, embarrassed. "I was daydreaming."

The old man chuckled. "Judging by the smile on your face, you must've been thinking about a girl. Huh, kid?"

"Was it that obvious?"

"She must be something special."

"She is," Jim said, leaving the rest for the old man's imagination. Lisa Maselli was more than special. He lived and breathed for her. She had never been shy about expressing her desire for him, and the openness, trust, they shared energized him beyond comprehension. They had made love a hundred different ways, in a hundred different places, yet each time was as new and exciting as that first night.

God, he loved her. He couldn't imagine a future without her.

CHAPTER 6

Caught Off Guard

Alex steered the police cruiser out of the borough parking lot and onto Main Street. Tonight she and Lisa had town patrol. They wouldn't leave the borough limits unless called to assist the "four–wheelers," department code for the rural unit.

Alex hated the Saturday–night graveyard shift. It conflicted with her meal and insulin schedule. Despite complaints to Ted Peterson about being assigned that tour, nothing had been changed. She had been forced to adjust her daily routine to accommodate the weekend changes, and it hadn't been easy. Alex felt sorry for Lisa having to put up with her irritability during the first few weeks while her body had adapted to the change.

It wasn't bad enough the midnight–to–eight tour had messed up her personal schedule, but it was also the most unpredictable shift. She and Lisa both knew it was a ploy to get them before the police board. But to Ted Peterson's dismay they had been able to handle all the "graveyard" confrontations without any major problems.

"How was your sister's date with Rick Stanton?" Alex asked as they cruised Main Street toward the North End.

Lisa shrugged. "She had a good time. They went horseback riding up at Big Pine Hill, played a game of hoops, and then he took her to dinner at the Lakeside Inn."

Alex raised her eyebrows, impressed, briefly glancing over at Lisa. "Wow, the Lakeside. Maybe he *is* an okay guy."

"He'd better be."

"Renee knows how to handle herself."

"I'm sure she does. But I'm still somewhat leery of him."

"I thought you believed he was being sincere when he apologized."

"I did. I mean, I think so. I don't know, Alex. The guy's a stranger. How do we *really* know what kind of person he is?"

"He's never been convicted of a crime or picked up for any other traffic violations prior to our encounter with him."

"Yeah, I know." Lisa propped her head against her hand. "But I still can't help wondering what it was he wanted to do to me, what he was implying."

"I can only imagine, especially since he cracked the comment about you giving good head."

"Exactly. That's what bothers me." Lisa straightened up, looking over at her partner. She was able to talk openly with Alex, confide in her about personal problems or seek professional advice on dilemmas she encountered on the job. Something she could never do with her previous partners—young, macho reserves straight from the certification program. Alex was an honest person and had far more experience in law enforcement. Alex's tenure with the National Park Service, the Fish and Boat Commission, and the Tredyffrin Township Police Department in suburban Philadelphia cumulatively had yielded a greater variation of critical situations than Lisa would ever face in Highlands County.

"He told Renee he had the hots for me," Lisa continued. "And that's why he arranged an interview with her on the excursions, knowing she would look exactly like me. This may sound totally ridiculous, but I have this uneasy feeling he wants to use Renee to act out his sleazy thoughts."

Alex glanced over at Lisa then quickly shifted her eyes back to the road. "You're right. That's totally ridiculous. The guy was shooting off his mouth because he was busted and half–crocked. I don't think he has malevolence on his mind. I think he's looking for a friend since he's new in town and lonely. *You* piqued his curiosity, but your *sister* is more his type. Face it, some guys can't handle women being cops."

"I suppose you're right. Hear anymore from Kyle, since finding that note in your mailbox?"

Alex huffed. "No. But he's beginning to piss me off."

"You're starting to date again, and it's making him crazy. He'll give up."

"I hope so."

"Tell me about your day sailing with Matt. He sounds like a keeper to me."

Alex swung the cruiser onto a side street, glancing over at Lisa again and smiling. "A keeper for sure. We had a great time. We have so much in common. He's so easy to talk to and a great—"

"A great what?" Lisa urged.

"He's a great kisser. God, those lips…" Alex sighed, recalling the heavenly sensation of his mouth caressing her neck.

"Uh–huh. That's it? No more details?"

Alex laughed. "What? Nothing's sacred to you? I've only seen him three times."

"When are you seeing him again?"

"Monday night. I invited him to go running with me."

"Why running?"

"How else can I get to see his cute butt in shorts?"

An approving grin spread across Lisa's face. "Can I come along, too?"

"No way."

"But you said the other day I could go running with you any time I wanted."

"Oh, shut up." Simultaneously they burst into laughter.

The night dragged on endlessly. By three o'clock they had made only one traffic stop—a woman running a red light on Main Street—and had no calls from the Comm Center.

They bought coffee and snacks at the twenty–four–hour convenience store and stopped back at the station to use the restroom. At three–thirty they were back on the road for another sweep of Mountain View's neighborhoods, heading first for the Heights.

As they passed the high school Alex routinely glanced at the expansive two–story structure. Only this time something wasn't right.

"Check that out." She braked, scanning the entrance to the school. The glass panel adjacent to the doors had been smashed.

"Vandals," Lisa said.

Alex turned into the parking lot and silenced the engine while Lisa radioed the Comm Center, reporting a break–in and requesting backup.

"How long is it going to take for the four–wheelers to get here?" Alex asked Lisa.

"Comm Center, three–five. What's three–two's ten–twenty?"

"Standby," the male voice replied.

They waited as the dispatcher relayed their request to the rural unit.

"Three–five, Comm Center. Three–two's ten–twenty is Lumber Township. ETA fifteen minutes."

Lisa and Alex exchanged worried glances. The backup's response time was too long. Waiting more than five minutes to respond to a situation was against procedure. It was the main reason the regional police worked in partners: To provide a buddy system and limit the risk of danger.

Lisa felt uneasy. They had no way of knowing how many persons were inside the building. "Comm Center, three–five, can we get a ten–thirty–three from the state police if necessary?" She wanted assurance of an immediate backup in case they found themselves in a threatening situation.

"Affirmative, three–five. State police ETA five minutes."

"Ten–four, Comm Center. We're going to check it out. Standby."

They grabbed their portable radios and flashlights and emerged from the car, walking up to the entrance. The eight–foot–high panel had been shattered, shards of glass strewn on both sides of the entranceway.

Abruptly a loud crash from inside invaded the early–morning stillness.

"Definitely vandals," Alex whispered.

Lisa stepped through the panel, being careful of the broken glass. Alex followed. Low–wattage security lights on the ceiling dimly lit the school's interior. They attached the radios to their duty belts and slid the flashlights into their back pockets. They did not want the beams of light alerting the thugs to their discovery. Drawing their pistols they cautiously moved along the edge of the hallway.

Halfway down, it became apparent the racket was coming from a classroom on the left–hand side. Alex moved alongside the doorway with Lisa behind her.

Slowly Alex's free hand slid around the doorframe, searching for the light switch. By chance her fingers touched the metal plate. She looked back at Lisa and nodded. In an instant, fluorescent light filled the classroom.

"What the—"

"Okay, buddy, the fun's over," Alex announced as they appeared in the doorway, pistols aimed in the direction of the startled voice. She quickly scanned the damage: torn window blinds, pages ripped from books scattered across the floor, red paint sprayed across the walls and blackboards.

The teenager flung the paint can frozen in his grasp onto the floor.

"I want your hands up and you on your knees, now," Alex instructed, moving into the room.

As he reluctantly complied, another unexpected noise emanated from farther down the hallway.

"Get out, Billy!" the cornered kid shouted. "We've been had!"

"I'll get him. Call for backup." Lisa headed down the corridor toward the clamor. She turned the corner of another passageway and saw a brawny kid frantically pulling on the side exit–door. "Those doors lock from the outside. You can't get out."

He pounded his fists against the glass, yelling obscenities.

She found a light switch to illuminate the poorly lit area. "Back away from the door. Put your hands up and get down on your knees, slowly."

He ignored her demands.

Lisa repeated her statement, raising her voice.

Defiantly he spun around to face her. Startled she took a quick step backward, immediately recognizing him. She tightened the grip on her pistol. "Turn around, Ryzik! Now!"

"Funny meeting you here, Officer Maselli. Did I scare ya?" Grinning smartly he turned his back to her, raised his arms over his head, and knelt.

She approached him cautiously. "You know the routine. Cross your legs."

He cursed under his breath but did as instructed.

"Can't stay out of trouble, huh, Billy? You're under arrest." She replaced the pistol at her side and brought his left arm down behind his back, handcuffing his wrist.

"What for?" The remark was cocky and rudely patronizing.

"Let's see," she responded with equal condescension. "How 'bout criminal trespass, criminal mischief, burglary, institutional vandalism?"

As she began to recite the Miranda Warning, reaching to lower his right arm against his back, he decided to make a move to get away. She'd never expect it. Swiftly, he struck her shin with the heel of his right sneaker, propelling her backward. The sound of her body slamming into metal echoed through the corridors as she crashed down against a row of lockers, the flashlight thrusting sharply into her lower back.

She moaned in agony and labored to pull herself up on a knee. With lightening speed he tackled her, straddling her hips before she could establish a ground fighting position. He went for her pistol but her right hand instinctively seized his wrist, the loose handcuff clanking off her holster. A large fist came at her face, her left forearm flying up to thwart the blow. She yelled for Alex, struggling to keep a grip on his left wrist and his fingers away from her weapon. She drew her legs up, planted her feet flat against the floor for leverage, and thrust her pelvis toward her left side, knocking him off balance. He tumbled onto the floor, infuriated by her determination to keep him at bay. He maneuvered a hand around to his back pocket, whipping out a switchblade. He rolled toward her, releasing the blade, swiping it at her. Again, her left hand flew up to shield her face, the tip of the knife grazing her forearm.

Lisa gasped through grit teeth, flinching from the fiery tear. The color drained from her face as blood gushed from the cut.

"That ought to teach you a lesson." He reached over her waist for the pistol.

"Freeze!"

His head shot up toward the voice.

"Don't even think about moving!" Alex warned. She stood at the end of the narrow hallway, her hands tightly wrapped around her weapon, one finger resting on the trigger. "Get your hand away from the holster and drop the knife, now!"

His first thought was he could still pull this off somehow. But she was too far away to distract, and her pistol was trained on his chest. He glanced down at Lisa, weighing his options.

Alex's eyes followed his stare. "You cut her again, and I'll kill you the second after."

He sneered. "You don't have the guts to do it."

She had to do this procedurally. She couldn't let her tumultuous emotions take control. "Don't make this any worse for yourself or for me, and don't make me prove you wrong. Move your hand away from the holster and put the knife down."

He pierced her with confident eyes. "Make me."

"You've got three seconds," she warned.

Undaunted he continued to glare at her.

"One…"

No movement.

"Two…"

Still, nothing.

Alex had never been faced with such defiance. Would this be the night? She swallowed hard, slowly moving her trembling thumb over the safety device. She had only done this at the target range. The object before her was now a living, breathing human being, not a piece of cardboard. "Put the knife down. Don't be foolish."

"Can't do it, can ya?"

Alex inhaled deeply, steadying her hands. "Three." The safety released with a click.

"Okay, okay." He tossed the knife onto the floor as if it suddenly got too hot to handle.

She exhaled in relief. "Hands up. Don't move an inch."

He complied, and she cautiously stepped toward him.

"Watch his feet," Lisa muttered. "He knocked me off balance."

Alex pressed her weapon against his back, heeding her partner's warning. She reached for the unfastened cuff that hung from his left wrist and pulled him off Lisa, toward the door. She slipped the free cuff around the metal handle and linked his other wrist.

"Are you okay?" she called to Lisa.

"Yeah, I think so." Lisa winced, sitting up against the lockers. "It's not a deep cut."

"You know this creep?"

"Yeah. Last September I caught him snorting coke and slashing tires on some school buses."

Alex glared at the teenage brute before her. She replaced the pistol at her side and ran her hands over his blue jeans. "What else you got in these pockets?"

"Go 'head, feel me up," he taunted. "I got a hard–on for you."

She ignored him, pulling a wad of twenties and three small plastic bags filled with a white powdery substance from his front pockets.

"Can't kick that cocaine habit, huh?" She shook her head in disgust, slipping the contraband into her shirt pocket and counting the money. Three hundred sixty dollars. "Quite the banker," she said, suppressing a strong urge to slam his face against the glass. "And still wet behind the ears. How pathetic."

"You're gonna be sorry about this, Officer..." He paused to read her nametag. "...Griffin."

Alex grabbed his shirt collar, shoving him against the door. "For your sake, buddy, that better not have been a threat!"

"Suck my cock." He spat in her face.

So much for procedure. She hurled a knee into his groin at full force. His eyes flew open as he struggled for a breath.

"Suck air," she retorted, abruptly releasing his collar. Wiping his saliva from her cheek she watched him keel over, his restrained arms preventing his knees from reaching the floor.

"Mother...fuckin'...bitch," he panted, tears rolling out from under his lids. "Gonna pay f...for this."

"Excuse me?" Alex scoffed, her nerves on edge. She grabbed a handful of his black hair, jerking his head back so she could see his dark watery eyes. "What did you say? I don't think you fully understand the consequences here, buddy. You're not going to get a slap on the wrist this time around. You're going to do some hard time. So I suggest you stop threatening me."

She left him doubled over, whimpering, and went to Lisa. "The big hats should be here any minute." She helped Lisa to her feet, handing her a handkerchief from her back pocket.

Lisa leaned against the lockers, holding the cloth to the gash on her arm. "My back hurts bad."

"You're going to the hospital for an X–ray. And God knows where that knife's been. You need a tetanus booster."

"Where's the other one?"

"I cuffed him to the wall heater. He's not going anywhere." Alex saw that Lisa was trembling. "Are you really okay?"

Lisa shook her head, fighting to keep her composure intact. She couldn't answer. The last thing she needed was for a male state–trooper to see her crying.

Back at the police station inside the Mountain View Borough Building, Alex entered the report information on the vandalism and assault into the computer, while Lisa sat, sipping a cup of coffee. The emergency–room exam had taken nearly two hours, and the first light of day was rising over the eastern mountains.

Lisa hadn't been seriously hurt. She had a bruise on her back but no broken bones. The slash from the knife did not require stitches; the bleeding had stopped before their arrival at the hospital. But it didn't prevent her from getting that painful tetanus booster, and Alex laughed at Lisa's pitiful face when the doctor poked her arm with the needle. "Now you know how it feels," Alex joked, referring to her insulin injections. "How'd you like to do that five times a day?"

As they were leaving the hospital the ER doctor heartedly told Lisa how lucky she had been and then began babbling on about how bad violence and drugs had gotten in Highlands County.

"Why don't you go home and rest your back," Alex suggested to Lisa. "The arraignment's not until nine."

"No, I'm fine," Lisa said, barely above a whisper. She hadn't looked at Alex. Instead she stared at a wall calendar, preoccupied. If she went home her family would be asleep. The stillness would bring back the memories.

Alex glanced up from the monitor. "Okay then. How 'bout coming over to my place after work? I can make us some breakfast before we head over to the magistrate's."

Lisa leaned back against the chair and took another sip of coffee. "Sounds good," she replied, unconvincingly.

Alex finished typing the last few words then printed the report, setting it on the desk. She went to the coffeemaker, pouring herself a cup. "Talk to me."

Lisa placed her plastic–foam cup on the desk. "I can't believe this happened. This kid had it out for me, and I fell right into his trap. Peterson is going to call me on the carpet for this."

Alex walked back to the desk. "You followed procedure."

"Yeah, I followed procedure, but I lost control."

"You were assaulted with a deadly weapon. It could have happened to *any*one."

"It happened to me, and he's been waiting for this moment."

Alex sat silently for a few moments, sipping her coffee. "Don't be so hard on yourself. You told me his whole family is whacked out on drugs, hell–bent on trouble. He's not going through the juvenile system this time. He was on probation from the first possession offense, and he's going to do some hard time."

"I can't believe he caught me off guard. It all happened so fast. I can hear Peterson already."

"Tell Peterson to go fuck himself."

Lisa looked over at Alex and laughed.

"I knew you'd appreciate that."

Lisa closed her eyes, wishing she could forget the whole ordeal, erase every mistake she had made in the past. "I'm sorry I put you in such a terrifying position."

"There's no need to apologize."

"I hate knives. They scare me more than anything else on earth." Lisa shuddered.

"I can certainly understand that."

Lisa nodded, barely, shifting her eyes to the floor. She appreciated her partner's sincerity, but Alex couldn't possibly understand how it felt to be at the mercy of someone else. Lisa had never imagined herself conceding to someone's deviant demands, and in the few times it had crossed her mind previous to that night, she thought she'd be prepared to fight at all costs, mentally and physically. Such was not the case she had unfortunately learned. The knife had dictated it all: submission, humility, utter terror.

Alex stood and moved around the desk. "That was the closest I've ever come to pulling the trigger. But I wouldn't have hesitated if it came to that, not for one second."

Lisa forced a slight smile. "I'm just glad you were there. I owe you my life."

The air was muggy and still. Lisa and Jim lay in the grass near the edge of Becker's Pond as the early–evening sun reflected off the tranquil water.

Lisa's eyes wandered across the small pond to the woods on the far side. What once had been an active dairy farm, owned by the Becker family several decades ago, was now nothing more than overgrown fields frequented by few. She and Jim had discovered the pond while dating back in high school, and ever since, it had become their favorite spot to spend time together, alone.

"I'm not sure I like this cop stuff anymore," Jim said, lightly touching the scar on her forearm. "I don't want you getting hurt again. If anything ever happened to you—"

"Look, I want to forget about it, okay?" Lisa stared up at the sky, agitated. "Peterson's going to call me on the carpet tomorrow, and I don't want to talk about last night anymore."

She rolled away from Jim, imagining how the chief was going to handle her screw–up. He'd have her ass, she was positive of that.

The arraignment had lasted until ten, and William Ryzik, her eighteen–year–old assailant, had been charged with a string of offenses. The magistrate had set bail at eighty thousand dollars. Unable to post the ten percent deposit, the kid had been remanded to the county prison until a preliminary hearing could be scheduled in court. The bailiffs had hauled him off to his jail cell with his seedy family shouting obscenities and derogatory statements at Lisa, Alex, and the female magistrate. His older brother, Dale, even had gone so far as to approach Alex outside the courthouse and issue the veiled threat, "Hey, sweetheart, what goes around, comes around."

Lisa had walked into the house at ten–fifteen. After explaining the ordeal to her family, she headed straight for bed.

Sleep had evaded her. Graphic memories of that February night at North Penn University had come rushing back to haunt her. She had tossed and turned relentlessly, taxing herself to elude a mental replay of the torture, the degradation, she had suffered at the hands of her college rapist. Several times sheer exhaustion had subdued her anguish, but each time she bolted upright in bed, drenched in sweat and gasping for air, seeking an escape from the lifelike feel of that cold, deadly blade pressed against her throat, or from the threatening words of her aggressor's psychological terror, sporadically reinforced with a blow to her abdomen or stiff backhand across the face.

"You all right?" Jim reached over to caress her arm.

She flinched.

"What's wrong?"

She forced the horrifying memories into oblivion. "Nothing. I'm fine."

He slipped his arms around her, holding her tightly. "Are you sure?"

"Yeah. I'm okay."

She lied; he was violating her personal space. But she was determined to ward off those oppressive feelings. *She* was in control of this situation.

He brushed a strand of hair away from her eyes and covered her mouth with his. As the kiss intensified he slid his hands under her shirt and around her back, unhooking her bra.

His lips drifted to her ear. "I'm horny as hell," he whispered heavily, his hands slipping over her breasts.

She labored her hands around his neck as his mouth returned to hers, his tongue probing. Anxiety was building, yet she let him undress her with no opposition, reminding herself Jim was doing this. She was allowing him.

She forced her fingers through his hair, directing his head toward her breasts and away from her guilty eyes. His lips and tongue began massaging one breast, lingering, then slipping over to the other. She sighed, glancing up at the sun then down at the top of his head as his mouth devoured her, physically and mentally. She needed to end this without delay. Her shame was intensifying, invading any minute feelings of pleasure. She was losing the emotional battle.

She awkwardly tugged at his tee shirt. He rose to his knees and yanked it off, tossing it on top of her discarded clothes. He knelt above her, and she immediately reached for the zipper on his jeans. But his hands intercepted her wrists, denying her the satisfaction.

"Not so fast," he said, smothering another kiss on her lips. God, he wanted her, but he would wait a bit longer, heighten his desire.

"C'mon," Lisa pleaded, her heart pounding anxiously.

"What?" His lips covered her mouth again. Finally he released her wrists, deliberately gliding a hand along her inner thigh.

She felt Jim's fingers coaxing her. She gasped, her pelvic muscles tightening. He was tormenting her, playing with her mind. She squeezed her eyes shut and, instantly, Calvin Anderson was above her, his uncompromising, controlling eyes piercing her imprisoned body. "You play with fire, you get burnt." He ground out the words between clenched teeth, running the tip of the knife over the length of her naked, trembling body from her chin down over her heaving chest and abdomen to her crotch. She remembered spinning dizzily, trying to keep alert, calm. "Wanna get fucked with this?" he had taunted, brushing her pubic hair with the edge of the blade. "No, please. Please, don't hurt me," she cried helplessly. His hand came across her face.

"No!" Lisa's eyes flew open, and she sprang upright.

"What?" Jim jerked away from her. "What'd I do?"

She gulped for air, turning away from him. "I'm so sorry." She drew her knees up close to her chest, wrapping her arms tightly around them.

"My God, Lisa, what's wrong? What'd I do?"

"Nothing," she sobbed. "I'm sorry. I was thinking about last night."

Jim slammed his fist against the ground. "I'll kill that Ryzik bastard if I ever see him." Hesitantly he raised a hand to her naked shoulder.

She shook her head, sniffling. "I'm being silly."

"No, you're not." He extended his arms, and she embraced him selfishly.

Lisa held onto him for several moments. She loved Jim so much, despised herself for hiding the truth. She was nothing but a coward—a deceitful coward. She had gotten herself drunk, readily subjected herself to the violent act. Calvin Anderson had targeted her at the frat party to be the recipient of his rage, regardless of her intentions. And she had fallen into his trap. Like she had fallen into Billy

Ryzik's trap. She should have known better. Last night—and five years ago.

Lisa lifted her head to meet Jim's caring blue eyes. This was the man who loved her, and she had willfully betrayed him by inviting a virtual stranger into her dorm room, allowing him to take advantage of her, terrorize her into submission. She had no excuse to deny Jim her body. She'd lost that right the night Anderson had destroyed her self–respect.

"Do you ever wonder what your life would be like if you had asked Renee out instead of me?"

Jim pulled back to examine her facial expression. That had to have been a joke, but the somber look on her face told him it was not. "What kind of question was that?"

"A serious one. Maybe you would have been better off with Renee. She's more levelheaded, more…" Lisa searched for the right word. "Ladylike."

A boyish grin spread across Jim's face as his eyes surveyed her nakedness. "I don't think there can be anymore 'ladylike' than what I'm seeing now."

"That's not what I meant!" she scolded, grabbing her panties and bra.

"I'm sorry, Lise, really," he pleaded, lunging forward to wrestle her for the clothes. "What's bothering you? Tell me, please."

"I hate myself." Lisa wrenched her underwear from his grasp. "That's what's bothering me."

"Why are you saying that?" he asked sadly, reaching for her arm.

"Don't touch me!" She jerked her arm free, and he recoiled, kneeling on the grass, dumbfounded, watching as she hastily redressed herself. "What did you ever see in me?" she shouted angrily, tears welling in her eyes. She jumped up and trampled to the shoreline of the pond. Burying her face in her hands, she sat and cried.

Jim rose to his feet and walked to the water's edge, sitting beside her an acceptable distance away. "Why are you doing this to yourself?"

"I screwed up. Okay?" She lifted her head from her hands and stared out at the serenity of the pond, unable to face him. "I screwed up big time."

Jim frowned at her inability to discuss her shortcomings. He remembered how upset she'd get after playing a lousy game of basketball or scoring poorly on a college exam. And each time she'd refuse to talk about it. She had put herself and her partner in a volatile situation, and she couldn't come to terms with her miscalculation on handling the arrest. She had been emotionally scarred, and he now realized his sexual advances had only added to her distress. She had 'screwed up' as she put it and didn't deserve to be loved. Jim understood Lisa's frame of mind completely. He only wished she would share her pain with him.

"You know, Lise, don't ever think you have to make love to me if you don't want to," he said softly. "I love you so much, please don't ever forget that."

Lisa turned to face him, wiping the tears from her cheeks. "Jimmy, you don't know how much I love *you*. I never meant to hurt you."

He raised a hand to stop another tear that started down her cheek. "Hurt me how?"

She saw the confusion in his eyes and wanted desperately to reveal her secret, beg for his forgiveness. She couldn't. She couldn't bear the thought of hurting him, losing him. She bit back the truth, vowing to herself the events of that snowy February night would remain forever untold.

"For getting angry with you," she said instead. "For pulling away."

"I understand." He slid closer, maneuvering his arms around her. "Can I ask you, though, why you made that comment about your sister being more feminine? Did it have to do with what I said about not liking the cop stuff anymore?"

She nodded, letting out a sheepish laugh. "Sometimes I wonder if I'm being a total idiot by wanting this job."

"Why's that? I think you're perfect for it. You're fair, street smart, athletic, and in no way a pushover. And believe me your being a cop in no way compromises your femininity, at least not to me."

Lisa rested her head on his shoulder. He lifted his hand to play with her hair, and she reached over, lightly caressing the muscles of his bare chest. "I still messed up." She wrapped her arms around him, and he settled back in the grass, gently pulling her down with him.

They lay intertwined in one another's arms, Jim softly stroking her hair. "I'm just glad you're okay."

"Me, too," Lisa sobbed, openly succumbing to her emotional agony.

He kissed her forehead and looked up into the bright evening sky, a lone tear rolling out from the corner of his eye.

He had swelled with pride when she had been appointed to the police force. He admired her courage, her dedication to the job. The only problem: He hated the risks. He wished she'd make a decision on law school soon. He could handle a temporary separation. He could not, however, weather a lifetime without her.

CHAPTER 7

Equal Opportunity Employer

Lisa was already signed in when Alex came through the station door.

"I'm not late, am I?" Alex asked. "Is he here yet?"

"No. He's not here yet. Couldn't you tell? I'm still alive."

Alex initialed the sign–in sheet, greeted the desk clerk, and headed for the coffeemaker. "Want a cup?"

Before Lisa could answer, the main door swung open and Ted Peterson marched into the station.

He whizzed past them. "In my office. Both of you."

Lisa cast a nervous glance at Alex. Reluctantly they walked into his office.

"Shut the door." He dropped a folder onto his desk.

Alex closed the door, and they sat before him. He settled behind his desk and rummaged through a drawer, yanking out a sheet of paper. Angrily he flung the form at Lisa.

"Make damn sure this injury report is completed and given to the clerk before you begin your shift," he growled. "So your insurance claim can be processed without a hassle." He opened the folder and scorched her with his dark eyes. "Officer Maselli, would you care to explain *exactly* how that cokehead managed to get you on the floor?"

Lisa lowered her eyes from his stare. "He knocked me off balance."

"I read that part in the report. I want to know *how* he knocked you off balance."

"How? He kicked me in the shin while I was cuffing him."

"Do you know how close he came to getting his hands on your weapon?"

Lisa lifted her eyes, meeting her superior's condescending glare. "Yeah, I do."

"How'd he manage to get the knife out of his pocket? Weren't you struggling with him?"

"I rolled him onto the floor, and the next thing I knew he was swiping a switchblade at me. My arm got cut because I was trying to shield my face." She held up her left arm so he could see the red scar.

Peterson dismissed her argument. "You lost control of the situation. That's not supposed to happen. You're damn lucky Griffin was there."

"No kidding! Why don't you tell me something I *don't* know?"

"I don't like your attitude, Maselli. Wise up!"

Lisa held her breath, silently counting to five, then exhaled. "Yes, sir. I apologize for my temper."

"You messed up somewhere, and your carelessness could have cost a life, possibly your own," he informed her, no indication of sympathy in his voice.

"I realize that."

"That's not good enough, Maselli. You knew whom you were dealing with. You should've waited for assistance from Griffin or patted him down before handcuffing him. I'm sorry, but I have no choice but to formally reprimand you for your careless handling of the arrest. It will become a permanent part of your record."

"How could you do this?" Alex said. "She was following procedure."

"This does not concern you, Officer Griffin. I suggest you keep your mouth shut. Your fuckup is next."

"My what?"

"You heard me. Now keep quiet."

Stunned she slouched back in the chair and looked away.

"Officer Maselli, you do know after three reprimands you're suspended until a thorough review of your performance is undertaken by the police board?"

"Yes, I'm fully aware of procedures." Did he actually think she was that stupid, not knowing how the system worked?

"And don't think you can whine to your father about this. It won't work."

Lisa tried to ignore that remark, but before she could stop herself, she lashed out at him. "I never expected my father to do anything for me! I don't *need* or *want* his help! I can take my punishment like anyone else."

Peterson glared at her wickedly. "I'm so glad to hear that," he said with venomous sarcasm. "Now go fill out that paperwork. I need to speak with Griffin alone."

She stormed out of his office, slamming the door behind her.

Alex leaned forward on the edge of her seat. "What'd *I* do wrong?"

He removed a few more sheets from the folder. "I'm not sure who messed up more, you or her."

"With all due respect, Chief, I don't think either of us messed up anything."

Peterson laughed cynically. "Tell me one thing, Griffin. You did such a good job in subduing Billy Ryzik, why on earth did you have to go and rough him up?"

"What?" She immediately remembered the young man's threatening statement about paying for her actions against him and his family's contemptuous remarks.

Peterson rubbed the brim of his nose, his eyes casually inspecting her small breasts then rising up to meet her blue eyes. "You heard me. Why'd you do it?"

"I have no idea what you're talking about."

"I'm not in the mood for games," he snarled, scooping up the papers from the file and tossing them into her lap. "The kid told the public defender you pulled his hair, grabbed his shirt collar, pushed him against the door, and kicked him in the balls. He's filing an excessive force charge against you."

Alex skimmed through the complaint forms then placed them back on the desk. "It's my word against his."

"No, you don't understand. The PD had him examined at the hospital. He had bruises on his genitals. Any suggestions on where they came from, if you didn't inflict them?"

Alex felt a sudden heat in her face. She didn't answer.

"Be honest with me, Griffin. Did you rough him up?"

She had to come clean. Lying would only cause more problems down the road. "Yes, I did."

"I appreciate your honesty. I can understand you were faced with an emotional situation, but you had no right to violate Ryzik's civil rights."

Alex stared at her superior officer flabbergasted. "This kid had no reserves whatsoever about cutting Lisa to get at her gun. He wanted to get away at all costs. When I busted him he wasn't the least bit intimidated. In fact he was outraged. He challenged me."

"I know."

"I'm not sure you do. I tried like hell to keep my cool, but I saw Lisa was bleeding, and he was stalling to unnerve me. Even after I had him cuffed and found the coke, he still persisted to taunt me. He spat in my face and told me to suck his cock. That's when I lost my composure. Did he happen to mention that part to his lawyer?"

"Are you through?"

"No. He deserved what he got, and I'm not the least bit sorry about doing it."

Peterson suppressed a grin. "Look, Griffin, I empathize with you. But unfortunately you're going to have to plead your case to the police board. The public defenders' office is filing the papers this morning, and I can guarantee it'll be in this week's paper."

"Is that it? Was this to inform me of the rough road ahead, or are you going to try to do something about it?"

Ted Peterson reclined in his chair, tapping his fingers on the desk. "I guess that depends on what you want to do for me."

"I beg your pardon?"

"I could keep this out of the weekly release so the press doesn't get whiff of it. And I may be able to sway the board in your favor. But..."

The cocksure smile on his face was all she needed to fully understand his intentions. Still, she wanted to be absolutely certain. "What do you want me to do? Work a few double shifts, something like that?"

He ascended from the chair, slithering around to lean against the desk directly in front of her. "I appreciated your honesty, now I'm going to be honest with you. I've had it bad for you since the first day you walked in here—"

"Hold on." Her hand came up, signaling him to stop, and she quickly stood. "I don't think you should go any further. Whatever you're getting at, forget it."

He reached for her shoulder, but she stepped away. "I could solve your problem, and we'd both have some fun. God knows I could use it. I haven't been with a woman in months."

"I'm *not* interested," she said firmly, turning for the door.

He pulled her back. "C'mon, give it a chance."

"Let go of me." Alex tried to break his grasp, but his face was suddenly in hers, his lips forcing a kiss on her mouth. She yanked a handful of his brown hair.

He pulled away abruptly, his dark eyes bearing down on her.

She jerked her arm free. "Don't you ever touch me again."

The wrath of rejection was indisputable as he seized the collar of her uniform, pinning her against the wall. "I could have saved you from the press's humiliation and from the police board. But now you're going to fry."

"Get your hands off me. You're the one who's going to fry. For harassment."

He snickered, that confident grin reappearing. "Like you said before: It's your word against mine. And whom do you think they'd believe? Your so–called harassment complaint would sound like a desperate attempt to get back at the department for disciplinary action against you." He released her collar and walked back to his desk. "Get out of here."

"You bastard." She bolted from the office.

Lisa was sitting in the lounge area of the ladies' restroom, working on her injury report, when Alex stormed past her to the lavatory, shouting obscenities.

"I'm out of here!" She hurled her foot at a stall door.

Lisa jumped up from the couch and hurried into the lavatory. "What the hell did Peterson tell you?"

"You wouldn't believe it if I told you!"

"Oh, no? Try me."

* * *

Renee hung up the telephone for an estimated tenth time since starting work at nine o'clock. "I'm never going to get any work done. How am I supposed to make all the arrangements for these excursions if all I do is talk on the phone?"

Across her desk Rick was smiling.

Renee rose from her chair. "C'mon, let's get out of here before it rings again."

They left the bureau office and strolled to the Towne Diner a block away.

"I hate the phone," Renee said as they entered the popular eatery. "It's a constant interruption."

"I can relate to interruptions. The paper is severely understaffed. I end up doing most of the interviews, as well as all of the editing. I never thought Mayberry would have so much news to print."

She grit her teeth as a hostess showed them to a table. "Stop calling Mountain View Mayberry. That's so *annoying*."

"Before you get involved in the menu..." Rick extended his arm across the table, lightly running his hand across her cheek. "I had a nice time on Friday. I hope you did, too."

She smiled sheepishly, embarrassed by his public affection. "I had a great time."

He returned her smile then lowered his eyes to the menu. They made quick decisions on lunch and ordered. A few moments later the waitress returned with their drinks.

Rick sipped his cola. "I got this week's press release from the regional police before I left the office to meet you," he said tentatively. "For Wednesday's edition."

"Uh–huh. So you know about the incident at the high school."

"Yeah, and honestly I was stunned."

"No town is immune to crime."

"Did you know Lisa's partner is being charged for using excessive force on the kid after he was placed in custody?"

Renee's mouth dropped open. "By whom? What kind of ludicrous accusation is that?"

"By the public defenders' office."

"Wonderful. This is only going to hurt Lisa more."

"I'm under the assumption Lisa and Alex are good friends."

"Very good friends."

Rick habitually played with the moisture on his glass. "I hope you understand I have to print this in Wednesday's paper."

"Now's your chance to get back at them," Renee said with a tinge of resentment. "Go for it."

He took another sip of his soda and slouched back in his chair. "That hurt. It's news, and it's my job to report it. I'm printing strictly facts."

"Do what you have to. I understand."

"Thank you. Can we please change the subject?"

The waitress set garden salads before them and hurried off to another table.

"I'm short one conductor for the train excursions," Renee said. "Do you think you could swallow your city pride and help us country bumpkins out? The bureau pays the minimum hourly wage. It'll be about six hours on Saturdays and Sundays from the Nineteenth to August thirty–first."

"You're kidding, right?"

"No. I'm serious."

"Are you going to be on the train?"

"Yes. I'm a guide. I'll see to it we're on the same coach. How's that?"

"Well…"

She flashed him an enticing smile. "It'll be fun."

"I can think of a few better ways to make some extra cash, but…"

Her persuasive smile grew larger.

He couldn't resist the come–on. She knew how to get what she wanted. "It's a deal. But under one condition."

"What's that?"

"Have dinner with me again, on Friday night."

"That could be arranged."

When Alex had asked Matt to jog with her around the high–school track, he had accepted without hesitation. Now, he was sorry, his aching bones and muscles gruelingly reminding him of his poor physical condition.

"Let's sit for a while," he gasped through gulps of air, trotting in the direction of a bench.

She paced alongside him. "You didn't have to do this. It was only a suggestion."

They sat, Matt throwing his arms over the back of the bench and stretching his legs. "How on earth do you do this every night?"

"It's easy if you're in shape." She looked over at him and grinned. "Obviously you're not."

"Sure, go ahead. Rub it in."

She bowed her head and wiped the sweat from her forehead with the bottom of her tee shirt. Afterward she continued to stare at the ground in a trance.

Matt placed a hand on her back. "Is something bothering you? You've seemed preoccupied since we started jogging."

Alex straightened up and sank back against the bench. "I had a bad day at work."

"Want to talk about it? I'm a good listener."

She shook her head. "I'd rather not. Let's get back to the house. I've got to check my blood sugar and drink some juice."

Matt looked at her puzzled, prompting an explanation.

"Running uses up quite a bit of sugar and to avert an insulin reaction I have to check my blood then replace the sugar I lost."

"What exactly is an insulin reaction?"

"It's a condition that results when there's more insulin than sugar in your system. I could lose consciousness and even die if it's not treated soon after it begins. My body doesn't produce insulin. That's why I have to continuously inject it and balance it with my blood sugar. And just so you know, the main warning signs of a severe insulin reaction are confusion, irritability, and slurred speech. If you didn't know I was a diabetic when I was having a reaction you'd think I was drunk."

Concern showed in his green eyes. "And what am I supposed to do? You're scaring me."

She rested a hand on his knee. "There's nothing to be scared of. If it should ever happen while we're together make me drink a glass of soda, not diet soda, or fruit juice. If I won't take it try to force it. If that doesn't work, I've got packets of glucose gel that could be squeezed between my cheek and gum. I should respond to the soda or gel in about ten, fifteen minutes. If I pass out, you need to inject me with glucagons and call 9–1–1."

"Inject? Me? Gluca…what? Now I'm beyond scared. I'm about ready to hit the panic button."

"Relax. I'll show you what to do. Glucagons cause a rapid, almost immediate, rise in blood sugar. In plain English, they're used to wake up someone who's passed out from a severe reaction."

"This doesn't happen often, does it?"

"No, I don't let it happen. I'm totally aware of myself all the time. But you have to be prepared. I always carry glucose, glucagons, and insulin pens with me, in case I need them."

"Okay, another stupid question from the medical moron here: What on earth is an insulin pen?"

Alex smiled warmly. "It's a device used for administering insulin. Basically, it looks like an ink pen, but it's a needle and vial of insulin hidden in a long plastic cylinder."

"Let's go," he said, anxiously rising from the bench. "So you can check your blood sugar and drink that juice."

They headed across the school grounds. "I'm sorry if I'm frightening you, but you should know."

"I appreciate your telling me. It makes me feel close to you, like you kind of want me to stick around and be a part of your life."

"You're very perceptive. When we get back to my place I'd like to give you a crash course on diabetes and how my survival kit works, if that's okay with you."

He hid his apprehension, because he wanted desperately to stick around and be a part of every aspect of her life. "Yes, I need…want to know."

They crossed Grove Street and walked the two blocks to her house. Along the way they passed by Kyle Lawry's house. He was sitting on the front porch pounding down a beer. Alex tensed but ignored the cold, hard stare he sent her way. There was no alternate route to the track, and Kyle seeing her with Matt only added fuel to the fire. But it was her life, her choice to break off the relationship. Kyle's disturbing behavior would not deter her.

A minute later she and Matt were inside her kitchen.

Alex removed a bottle of fruit juice from the refrigerator. "Would you like some?"

"Please." He sat at the table and unwound. "Did you see the look Kyle Lawry gave us? I wonder what that was all about. He's a friend of Brian's at the shop. Do you know him?"

Alex bit her bottom lip, deciding to be honest with Matt. She set the juice on the counter and leaned her back against the cabinets. "Unfortunately I know him in ways I now regret. I...had a relationship with him for a few months. It turned out to be a total disaster."

"Oh." Matt's surprise showed immediately. He gazed up at her, speechless.

"I know we talked a little about our past relationships on Saturday," Alex explained. "But this one wasn't worth mentioning. It was a nightmare." And might still be, she inwardly admitted.

"You know Brian then?"

"I know *of* Brian. Kyle and he are friends, but I've never met him personally, other than trying to say hello when I see him."

"Brian's real shy, keeps to himself most of the time. I went to high school with both of them, but we never hung out together. Brian's always been somewhat of a loner. His parents are both dead. His father died about twelve years ago. His mother was killed in a car accident a few years back."

"That's too bad." Alex straightened from the cabinets and went to Matt. He pulled her down onto his lap. "Matt, I regret my relationship with Kyle every day. He was so jealous and suffocating. I needed my freedom."

Matt wondered how independent she needed to be. He reached for her chin and softly kissed her. "You'd better check your blood sugar. I'll wait for my drink."

"Don't be silly." She jumped from his lap and poured two glasses of the juice. Grabbing her glucose meter she joined him at the table.

"Brian came to me about two years ago looking for a job," Matt said, sipping his drink. "He was desperate. I needed some help so I gave him a chance. He's a good mechanic, loves working on cars. He has his own school bus. He contracts with the school district to transport the high–school kids to games and events."

"Kyle mentioned that once, about Brian driving a bus."

"I hope I'm not intruding on your freedom by asking if you'd like to go to dinner on Thursday night," Matt said shyly.

Alex was about to poke her fingertip with a lancet but stopped abruptly. "I didn't mean to imply I wanted to be totally free. That's the furthest thing from my mind. I needed to be free of Kyle Lawry's possessiveness."

Matt met her sparkling blue eyes with a bit of concern. "Define possessiveness?"

"He wanted a commitment from me. He'd get jealous if I'd talk to other guys. He even accused me of sleeping around with a couple state troopers who'd asked me out, which was a lie and none of his business anyhow."

"Why didn't you go out with the troopers?"

"I don't date cops. It can get ugly if it doesn't work out."

Matt set his glass on the table. "Well, I'm not a cop, and I'll try not to get too jealous." He winked at her playfully. "But it's going to be hard. You're unbelievably gorgeous."

He made her blush.

"Are we on for dinner Thursday?"

She glanced into his eyes. They were ablaze with excitement. She felt that same exhilaration. "Oh, yeah. Are you ready to begin your lesson on diabetes?"

"You bet."

Lisa found her father sitting on the back porch. This was his usual late–night spot on warm summer nights. It was his time of peace at the end of every long, hectic day as the county's chief elected official.

"I hate to bother you, Dad, but I need to talk to you," she said, resting against the wood railing directly before him.

Robert Maselli looked up at his daughter and saw genuine concern on her face. "Sure, Lise. I'm all ears. You can count on me anytime."

How true, Lisa thought. He always had been there for his children, offering his opinion or sharing his experience, yet always leaving the ultimate decision up to them. She knew how he had felt about her becoming a cop; he had admitted his apprehensions. He had been concerned for her safety, but also leery of the public's reaction to having a female on the force and to their accusations of nepotism. She had *earned* her position with the department with no help from Daddy. It was unfortunate because of his long–standing position in government any success achieved by his children in the county would always be labeled the result of his political influence.

"It has to do with what happened at the school," Lisa said.

Maselli sat upright. At forty–nine he was still a youthful man, dark and distinguished. "About your reprimand?"

"No. It's about Alex."

"Alex?"

"The public defenders' office filed an excessive force charge against her for what she did to Billy Ryzik."

"Are you serious?"

She nodded.

"How's Peterson handling this?"

Lisa turned away, gazing up at the moonlit sky. "He offered to keep it from the newspaper and sway the board in her favor."

"That's great. He's finally showing you two some respect."

"Yeah, Dad, that's really great. And in return all she has to do is sleep with him." She looked back at her father, watching him digest her words in absolute silence.

"That was a ridiculous inference," he finally spoke. "I'm sure she's going to have to do him some favors, put in some overtime or work a little harder. I wouldn't be so upset about that."

"No, you don't understand. It wasn't an inference. It was a literal statement. He told her he has it bad for her. That's why I need to talk to you."

Her father was taken aback. "Are you absolutely sure about this? Did Alex tell you?"

"Yes, after she freaked out in the ladies' room. Dad, I just wanted you to be aware of the situation. She doesn't want to pursue any legal recourse. She can't prove it."

Maselli shook his head, disgusted. "She doesn't have to put up with that behavior. *Nobody* should have to put up with that kind of behavior. I wish you didn't tell me this. I feel like I have to do something about it."

"No! I promised I'd keep it to myself. You can't tell anyone. But I wanted you to know in case he tries to come down hard on her and harass her some more."

"I'm not at all happy about this. I have no authority over the police board, but Ted Peterson's attitude and behavior toward you and Alex should not be tolerated. Promise me something, Lisa, okay?"

"What's that?"

"Keep on him. Be aware of everything he says and does. Maybe next time someone will be around to hear his pitch."

CHAPTER 8

Watchdogs

Alex met Lisa at the corner of Main and Seventh Streets.

"Read what Stanton printed," Lisa said, handing her the *Highlands Journal.* She had stopped at the drug store for a current edition. The stock boy was still stacking the freshly delivered bundle on the news rack when she plucked one from his hand, hastily handed the cashier fifty cents, and hurried outside to find the write–up before her rendezvous with her partner.

Alex unfolded the paper and skimmed over the headings on the front page. Baffled she looked up at Lisa. "Where is it?"

"In the Police Log."

"With all the accidents and boring stuff?" She opened the paper to the third page and scanned through the section titled *Weekly Log: Regional and State Police.*

When she found the piece she read it aloud.

> *Two local teenagers were arrested early Sunday morning after regional police officers discovered them in the process of vandalizing Highlands High School. Officers Alexandra Griffin and Lisa Maselli filed charges against William Ryzik, 18, of Westfall and an unidentified Mountain View minor, age 16.*

They were arraigned before the local magistrate. Charges against the two included burglary, institutional vandalism, criminal trespass, and criminal mischief. Highlands County School District officials estimate the cost for the damages done to the building by the duo will exceed ten thousand dollars.

In addition more serious charges were filed against Ryzik after he allegedly assaulted Officer Maselli while she attempted to make the arrest. Police reports indicate Ryzik apparently overpowered the officer and cut her with a switchblade knife. Officer Griffin, however, was able to subdue Ryzik before he was able to harm anyone further. Officer Maselli was treated and released from the emergency room at Highlands Memorial Hospital.

Ryzik was charged with aggravated assault on a police officer, felony resistance to arrest, reckless endangerment, possession of a concealed weapon, and possession of a controlled substance after cocaine and a large amount of cash were found on him.

Ryzik was on probation from previous drug and criminal mischief charges. He was remanded to the county prison after failing to post his bail.

The Journal has learned the Highlands County Public Defenders' Office has countered the police charges by filing an excessive force charge against Officer Griffin on behalf of William Ryzik. The teenager claims Griffin violated his civil rights by grabbing him by the shirt collar, shoving him against a glass door, pulling his hair, and kicking him in the genitals. Highlands Regional Police Chief, Ted Peterson, has confirmed the charges and reported to the Journal the Highlands Regional force will not tolerate that kind of conduct applied by any of its officers, despite the severity of the charges against

Mr. Ryzik. The regional–police board will hold a closed hearing on the matter on Tuesday, July 15, at 7 PM in the meeting room of the Mountain View Borough Building.

Alex folded the paper and handed it back to Lisa. "Stanton one, Peterson zero. Very low–keyed, and I can't believe he kept it off the first page. He must really like your sister."

"There's no mention whatsoever of my reprimand. I think he's looking for a favor."

"A favor such as…"

"A no–show at his hearing. What else?"

"No way. I'm the arresting officer, and it's an automatic written reprimand for an intentional no–show. I can't afford to screw up with this other problem hanging over my head."

A crafty smile spread across Lisa's face. "Let's take a stroll down to the newspaper office and see what he's up to."

They headed down the sidewalk toward the Centre Street intersection.

"I have a meeting with the union solicitor tomorrow at eleven," Alex said. "He might want to speak with you sometime before Tuesday night."

"Sure. No problem. This whole mess is entirely my fault. I don't know where I went wrong. I did everything procedurally." Her feet came to a halt. "I owe you so much. I wish I could take full responsibility for what happened."

"I don't want to hear that talk," Alex warned, whirling around. "*I* lost my composure. It was nobody's fault but my own. End of discussion."

"But I put you in that situation."

"I said end of discussion." Alex continued down the sidewalk a few paces ahead of Lisa.

"What if they file criminal charges against you?"

"What if they do?" Alex threw her arms out then slammed them down against her hips. "What can I do about it? Peterson sure as hell won't defend me. I guess I'll hope for a compassionate jury, that's all."

"It'll never get that far. I'll expose Peterson myself if I have to."

Alex stopped abruptly, grabbing her partner by the arm. "Watch what you say." She glanced around the sidewalk to see if anyone was in earshot of their conversation. "I don't want to hear you mention what happened with Peterson ever again. As far as I'm concerned it never took place. I'm in a lose–lose situation, so forget about it."

Lisa was already regretting her words. "I'm sorry."

"Forget it." Alex released her arm, and they started on their way again. They turned the corner at Centre Street and, a few moments later, were standing at the reception desk inside the office of the *Highlands Journal.*

"Rick Stanton, please," Alex said to the receptionist.

The blonde woman gave them the once–over, her eyes first inspecting their faces then darting down to gawk at their holsters. It was obvious the sight of guns made her feel uncomfortable. She stood slowly. "Is it official business?"

"You could say that," Lisa replied.

"Right this way." The woman led them to an office at the end of a short, narrow hallway. She motioned them through the doorway and quickly headed back to her post.

Lisa and Alex stood quietly at the door to the editor's office. Rick Stanton was sitting at his desk, back toward them, typing away at his computer terminal, unaware of their presence.

Lisa tapped on the doorframe. "What? No fanfare, no red carpets?"

Rick started, his hands flying off the keyboard then banging back down. He spun his chair toward the voice. Shaken he stared at them.

"We'd like to talk with you for a few minutes, if that's okay?" Alex said, stepping inside the tiny room.

"Y…yeah, sure," he stammered over the words, nervously pointing to the chairs before his desk. "Have a seat."

As they sat, Lisa set her copy of the newspaper on the edge of the desk, noticing the ashen color of his face. "Relax, you haven't done anything wrong. This is a personal visit."

His stare bounced back and forth between Maselli's smile and Griffin's brilliant blue eyes then affixed on Griffin's badge. She sat close enough for him to make out the inscription encircling the Pennsylvania state coat of arms. Patrol Officer, Highlands Regional Police. The number 28 was engraved at the bottom of the silver shield.

"We just read what you printed in the paper about the vandalism at the high school," Alex said. "And we wanted to thank you for keeping it low–keyed."

"Yeah," Lisa added. "It was nice of you after everything you've been through with us."

"What are you thanking me for?" he said coolly, whisking his bangs away from his line of sight. "I printed what was in the press release."

Lisa sensed his discomfort and knew his standoffish reply was a defense mechanism against his psychological feeling of inferiority around them. She wanted like hell to reach across the desk and grab his shirt collar and lay into him about his attitude. She wanted to tell him she wasn't an evil tyrant and she didn't get a thrill out of handing out speeding tickets or making arrests. It was all a part of the job, like writing and editing and interviewing were a part of his job. Believe it or not, Rick Stanton, she shouted inwardly, I'm pretty much like my sister, and out of uniform, buddy, you'd never be able to tell us apart. Guaranteed.

"The last editor would have run away with that story," Alex said. "Screaming headlines. The works."

"I'm not the last editor," he retorted, lifting a pencil from the desk, twirling it end–over–end.

"Why'd you leave out the part about my reprimand?" Lisa asked. "It was in the press release."

"I must have overlooked it," he muttered unconvincingly, then added defensively, "Look, ladies, I appreciate your gratitude, but I was printing a police report in the objective style I usually use. I don't slant my work. Why on earth would I do you two a favor after what you put me through? Thanks to you I'm going to have a police record. Not to mention the astronomical price I'm going to pay, literally and figuratively: fines, license suspension, my insurance premium soaring into space, a substance abuse evaluation. Did I miss anything? Oh, yeah, Highway Safety School. You two have screwed up my life, royally, yet you think I did you a favor. Get real, *Officers*."

Lisa slid forward, resting an elbow on the desktop. "You did it because you're looking for a way out of the charges and because you've got it bad for my sister. And if I weren't sitting here in my blues, you'd have it bad for me, too. Isn't that right, Stanton?"

Rick laughed loudly, leaning back in his chair. Mortified he felt a sudden heat within him and knew his face was scarlet red. He avoided eye contact with Lisa Maselli, looking instead into the steel–blue eyes of Alex Griffin. "Are all you lady cops this conceited?"

Alex shrugged. "Are all you editors this insecure?"

"Insecure?" He laughed again, raising his index finger and thumb under his chin. "I'd be happy to show you how wrong you are on that one. If you can handle me."

"Now there you go again," Lisa admonished. "Mouthing off innuendoes. I don't get it. In case you don't know yet, Stanton, my sister likes you a great deal. She said you were nothing but a gentleman on the Fourth, and believe it or not, I'm the one who went to bat for you when she found out about your little charade last Monday. I told her your apology to us was sincere, and I believed it at the time. So why are we heading down that same ugly path again? There's no alcohol involved this time."

Lisa sat back in her chair, studying his facial expressions. She could see the dread, the insecurity in his deep brown eyes. She sensed he was trying to demonstrate his masculinity, his self–control, by hinting of his sexual prowess. Something's not right, Lisa thought. This guy has a problem, and it's not connected to alcohol like he had previously said.

She got the impression sitting before Rick Stanton that he was frustrated and frightened. Not by them in particular but by any woman with authority. Perhaps paranoia was clouding her judgment, but she surmised one–too–many women had stepped on his toes in the past. That troubled her. She did not want her sister getting hurt.

"Why are you patronizing me again?" Rick demanded. "You're not here on police business, yet you're questioning my statements like I've done something wrong. Why don't you two leave me alone, please. I've got a lot of work to get done."

"We just wanted to thank you for not smearing our names all over the paper," Alex insisted, standing to leave. "I'm sorry you can't accept our gratefulness. We appreciate your professionalism. I wish you'd appreciate ours."

Lisa ascended from the chair and lingered before his desk, staring down at him. "A word of advise, Stanton: You can catch more flies with honey than with vinegar. Remember that, especially since your hearing is coming up. And watch your step with my sister."

Rick swiftly rose from his chair. "You don't scare me, *Officer*. Your sister doesn't need you to baby–sit her."

"Heed the warning. This is the second time you've pissed me off."

They disappeared out the door.

Rick dropped into the chair, burying his face in his hands. A few seconds passed before he lifted his head, releasing his breath in a loud hiss. His eyes wandered to the window, catching sight of them crossing the street in front of the building.

An array of emotions flooded his thoughts as he watched them walk along the sidewalk toward Main Street. Resentment. Disrespect. Arousal. Burning desire. He rested his head on the top of the chair and stared up at the chipped white paint on the ceiling. He loathed what they represented; yet he couldn't help fantasizing about Lisa Maselli. "She must be incredible in bed," he whispered, running his hands through his hair. "I'd have her eating out of my hands."

He snickered. "But then again don't I already?"

He could have easily annihilated both of them in the newspaper, *his* newspaper. And they knew it, coming here to thank him for his soft heartedness. He laughed hard and long. "Yes, officer ladies, you'd better be thanking me 'cause I can destroy you tomorrow, or any day after that. This is only the beginning."

He continued to peer at the ceiling, mentally sorting his perceptions of them. Lisa Maselli had enlivened him from the minute he had laid eyes on her as she approached his car window that fateful night on Mountain Gap Road. And now he was living a fantasy through her sister. Pure and simple.

But he despised Alexandra Griffin. Although she presented herself as a rational, easygoing individual, she had been the one who officially put the screws to him. And he likened those ice–blue eyes to his mother's brutalizing ones. That association had doomed her right from the start. He detested his mother. He had no choice but to hate Alex Griffin. They were too much alike. And equally violent, he speculated. He could easily envision Alex Griffin hurling a knee into that thug's balls. She must have enjoyed it immensely, probably smiled the whole time he was doubled over whimpering. Like his mother. His mother got satisfaction out of her rebukes.

Her scolding had started in elementary school as lectures and tongue–lashings, mostly for mediocre grades, and then escalated to slaps and beatings during high school. She had never been interested in his accomplishments—he had won over a dozen writing contests—only his so–called flaws: his less–than–scholarly science and math grades, that gang of "hoodlums" he palled around with, his consuming interest in sports.

Several times he had wanted to tell his father about his mother's mistreatment, during those short weekend reprieves they'd spent together. But he never did. He had been scared to death of the repercussions. So he had kept quiet, taken the abuse, and never once fought back.

The fear his mother had instilled in him bred insecurity and wariness of women. Dates throughout high school and his early college years had been few and far between. He had spent many a night alone in his bedroom or university dorm bunk with the latest issue of a girly magazine, self–gratifying his sexual hunger. Then, during his first semester of graduate school, he had befriended a fellow journalism major, a Canadian student of Lebanese descent named Caroline. She was a stunning brunette with olive skin and beautiful dark eyes. His first true experience with love. He had been able to open up to her, and she had helped him to learn to trust women. Their two–year relationship had ended, however, with her return to Windsor, Ontario. Despite their strong feelings for each other, neither could relinquish nationality. Canada would always be her home, the United States his. They never lost touch, though. He still confided in her through lengthy letters, phone calls, and e–mail. Caroline was his saving grace, his pillar of sanity.

His former lover had guided him through the ordeal with his previous boss, the one he had fought adamantly with, mainly over writing styles and copy work. She had convinced him to accept this position in Highlands County, not to buckle under his boss's pressure and quit Penn Publishing all together. He had taken her advice, although reluctant of the adjustments he was forced to make to survive in this small, rural community.

"You've got to stop this," he warned himself under his breath, wiping the sweat that had beaded on his forehead. "You're going to blow it if you don't."

Lisa grabbed a can of soda from the refrigerator and stood at the kitchen window, watching her sister weed her small flower patch alongside the back porch. Renee was on her knees with a hand claw, digging out the grass and dandelions that had invaded her geraniums and pansies. Lisa popped open the can and took a long sip. She didn't want to do this, but the qualms she had about Rick Stanton were eating at her. She rationalized it was best to be honest with her sister now, rather than be sorry later on. Lisa organized her thoughts and went out onto the porch.

"Got a minute?" She plopped down on the bottom step.

"Yeah, sure."

"I need to talk to you."

"Okay," Renee said, continuing to dig without looking up.

"Alex and I stopped at the newspaper today to see Rick," Lisa said, taking a hasty swig from the soda can.

Renee sprang upright on her knees. "You did? Why? Not about the ordeal at the school?"

Lisa answered with a quick nod.

"I thought the article was written fairly."

"Perhaps a little too fairly."

"What was that supposed to mean?"

"I thought maybe he was looking for a favor, a way out of the DUI charge. I'm still not sure what he's up to."

"I don't get you, Lisa," Renee said resentfully. "Why do you think he's *up* to something? You're the one who said to give him a chance, and now you're telling me he's up to no good. I don't understand your logic. I like him a lot. He's going to help out with the excursions."

"That's why we have to talk."

Renee set the claw down on the lawn, dropping back on her heels. "About what?"

"I don't want to interfere with your personal life, but there's something about him that bothers me."

"Like what?"

Lisa intended to tell her sister she thought he had a serious problem with women and she should stay clear of him. But she couldn't do it. What if she were wrong? She'd feel like an absolute fool. A mistrusting, paranoid moron. "I don't know, Renee, maybe it's me." Lisa began to second–guess herself.

"What'd he do this time?" Renee stood up, brushing off the dirt and grass from her old faded jeans. She stepped onto the sidewalk and sat alongside her twin.

"He says the wrong things."

"You wouldn't have instigated it? You can be downright rude when you want to be."

Insulted, Lisa opened her mouth to retaliate, but words eluded her. She flashed back to the morning meeting with Rick, their conversation replaying in her mind. It *was* possible she could have prompted the cheap shots. Even Alex had a few digs. Perhaps she was overreacting. She searched for a way around her misgivings while draining the last of her soda. Finally she blurted out a wishy–washy warning to her sister. "I may have been partially at fault today, but I have a bad feeling about him. Please be careful and stay in public places when you're with him."

"Are you off your rocker? How do you expect me to get acquainted with him in public places? If you get my drift."

"I get your drift all right," Lisa replied. And I had the same idea five years ago. If only you knew, sister dear, she thought sadly. "Do what you feel comfortable doing but always listen to your instincts. Trust me on this one, okay?"

"What are you hinting at?" Renee asked, eyeing her sister with concern.

Lisa sighed woefully. "Reality, Renee, reality."

Alex turned down the bed sheets and changed into an old oversized shirt—the one she wore to bed—and a pair of cutoffs. She replaced her contact lenses with her gold–rimmed glasses, made a cup of hot tea, and retired to the living room to watch the eleven o'clock news.

She flicked on the portable set, lifted Oscar off the floor, and plopped down on the couch, throwing her legs over the armrest.

She stared at the TV, cuddling her cat on her lap. It was ten–fifty and the finale of a prime–time rerun was unfolding on the screen before her.

Her mind drifted off as she waited for the news to air. She thought about Kyle's bizarre behavior. She'd found another note in her mailbox tonight upon her return from jogging. It had read:

> *Will Ehrich protect you from the Ryziks? They're bad news and I fear for you. I love you so much I wouldn't want anything to happen to you.*

Obviously Kyle had seen the piece on the school vandalism in the newspaper, and the implications in his message escalated her alarm. She didn't know if she should fear the Ryziks—or Kyle. The last thing she wanted to do was petition the court for a restraining order against him.

With the legal system on her mind, her thoughts shifted to Ted Peterson and the meeting scheduled with the police–union's solicitor the next morning. She gazed up at the ceiling for an instant then lowered her eyes to Oscar, lying contentedly in the safekeeping of her arms.

"I must've been a bad person in a previous life," she whispered. Oscar lazily peeped at her then resumed his catnap. Alex smirked. "Thanks for the support, buddy."

A knock came at the door. Startled, Alex shot upright, the cat flying from her arms and scrambling down the hall. She glanced at the clock above the television. Eleven–o–two. The news was on, and she hadn't even realized it. Who on earth was calling at this late hour?

Thanks to Kyle's menacing note she hurried into her bedroom for her baton. Returning to the door with the weapon expanded to its maximum twenty–six–inch length and gripped tightly in her hand, she called out, "Who is it?"

The voice was muted but recognizable. "It's Matt."

"For goodness' sake," she breathed relief, opening the door.

From the opposite side of the screen he first noticed her eyeglasses then the baton clutched in her hand. "Is this a new way of greeting guests?"

"You don't want to know." She welcomed him into the living room, tossing the baton onto an armchair.

"I already know. I just read the paper. No, actually I just *started* reading the paper. I only made it to the third page."

"That's what was bothering me Monday night."

"My God, Alex, what happened?"

"Have a seat. I'll tell you about the whole thing. Want a beer?"

He accepted her drink offer and waited on the couch while she went into the kitchen.

"I see you're wearing your glasses," he said as the louvered door swung open and she reappeared with a bottle of beer.

"I forgot I had them on," she gasped, lowering her eyes from his gaze, embarrassed. "I took my lenses out about fifteen minutes ago. I look goofy in these glasses. I'm sorry…"

"For what?" He smiled, amused by her self–consciousness, as she joined him on the couch. "You look gorgeous with glasses *and* with contact lenses."

He was becoming a pro at making her blush.

Matt slurped down some beer then set it on the end table. "Is Lisa okay? The paper said he cut her with a switchblade."

"She's fine. It was only a superficial cut." Alex reiterated the details of last Saturday's graveyard tour. "I have a meeting tomorrow morning with the union solicitor. I have no idea what'll become of it. Or of the hearing for that matter."

"This is unbelievable. This kid resisted arrest, slashed a cop, had cocaine in his possession, and now he's charging *you* with excessive force. Where exactly did the system go wrong? What the hell is the matter with this country?"

Alex let out a short laugh. "I shouldn't have done it, Matt. He deserved it, and I'm not sorry about doing it, but I shouldn't have. It was out of character."

"I wish I could do something for you," he said softly, clutching her hands.

"I need some moral support." She smiled appreciably, gazing into his pale eyes then down at the rough, dry hands that were embracing hers. The thought of those course hands caressing her body's smooth skin wildly aroused her. At that moment she wanted him more than she had ever imagined.

The passion in her eyes was undeniable as her hands wrapped around his neck, her lips covering his. It was a deep, intense kiss—an invitation. Matt's arms maneuvered around her back in response, pulling her closer.

She lifted her lips for the few seconds she needed to connect with his eyes and mutter, "Stay the night, please." Her mouth fell back on his.

Matt's hands hastily ascended over the curves of her back, his fingers surging through her hair. "I'm not dreaming this, am I?"

"You're not dreaming, believe me."

His green eyes fired with excitement. He started to remove her glasses, but she stopped him. "I don't want it all to be a big blur. I want to see you."

He entangled his hands in her wild hair, his lips lingering over hers, teasing, until she kissed him fully. "Alex, I've been dying for this moment." He undid each button on her shirt, holding her gaze the entire time, and eased it over her shoulders, revealing her breasts.

They stripped their clothing off and momentarily surveyed each other.

"God, you're beautiful," he whispered.

Her eyes sparked immodestly.

There, on the couch, they began exploring each other for the first time. He cupped her breasts with his hands and buried his head between her legs, lingering there while she sighed and gasped and cried out. She coaxed him to switch places and took his erection into her mouth, hungry for the taste of him, the feel of him. He moaned euphorically.

She crawled on top of him, her hands raking the hair on his chest. "Matt, I hate to do this," she said awkwardly, rushing the words, "but I...you...need protection. I don't use birth control because of my condition. I have condoms in my bedroom."

Her ability to communicate that to him, uninhibited, only heightened his longing for her. He didn't mind in the least. "I have one in my wallet." He reached down on the floor for his jeans and fulfilled her request, gazing into her eyes with lustful anticipation. "I'm all yours."

She anxiously straddled his hips, guiding him into her. Riding him, she lifted up with her arms, pushed down on him hard. She threw her head back then leaned forward to kiss him wildly, manipulating him until an intense surge of pleasure rocked her body from head to toe. She collapsed on his chest, sweating.

"You're not done." He rolled her onto the floor and lifted her up onto her knees. The bottom of her feet pressed into the base of the couch as he arched her body back against the front of the armrest. He knelt before her, his hands sliding through her hair then tracing the curve of her back with the tips of his fingers. She cried out as her body responded to his sensual touch. His mouth traveled down her neck then farther, devouring her breasts, lingering. His hands descended to her buttocks, groping them, and he abruptly hoisted her off her knees, pulling her lower body to his. She wrapped her legs around his hips as he eased himself inside her. She cried out loudly, driving her pelvis into his, needing, demanding, his full penetration.

He immediately brought her to a second climax. With his strong hands gripping her buttocks and her back pressing against the armrest, he moved slowly, forcefully, disciplining himself to prolong the incredible pleasure she was giving him. But finally he could hold back no longer, crushing her against him as the release enveloped him explosively.

He fell forward, and they both fell onto the carpet, his breath heavy in her ear as he lay on top of her. He buried his face in her disheveled hair, his lips searching for the soft skin of her neck. "Al, that was awesome. I didn't hurt you, did I?"

She sighed, exhausted, satisfied. "No way."

Kyle crouched between the shrubs alongside her house, peering into the living room. It was a muggy night and the window was raised completely, the curtains swaying gently from a warm breeze. He'd seen and heard everything—their unreserved lovemaking.

Anger and betrayal surged through his veins. His notes had meant nothing to her.

Stone–faced, Kyle watched them lay naked in each other arms, laughing and kissing. She'd left him no choice but to come down hard on her.

She had breached their allegiance.

CHAPTER 9

Cause For Alarm

Alex awoke and fumbled for her glasses on the nightstand. Slipping them on she looked at the digital clock. Seven o'clock. She lazily surveyed her bedroom as the bright morning sun filtered through the window. Smiling she glanced at Matt. He slept with his back to her.

Alex climbed out of bed and padded into the living room to retrieve their clothes. She threw hers into the hamper and laid Matt's along the foot of the bed. Quietly she dug out a pair of khaki shorts and a white tank top from her drawers and slipped into the bathroom to shower.

Standing before the sink she scolded her reflection in the mirror. "You were a bad girl, Alexandra Griffin, sleeping with this guy in less than a week's time."

Her alter ego laughed. "But wasn't it worth it?"

Alex showered and dressed, her mind continually returning to last night. Never before had she felt so alive, so fulfilled. They had made love on the couch, on the floor, on her bed. They had not fallen asleep until well past two in the morning.

She glowed, combing her wet hair and pulling it back into a ponytail. She grabbed a bottle of rubbing alcohol and a cotton ball from atop the vanity and headed for the kitchen.

To her surprise Matt was sitting in the living room fully dressed. Perched on the armrest of the couch, Oscar stood guard, dutifully inspecting the stranger who'd invaded his domain.

Matt greeted her with a devilish smile. "Good morning."

"Morning. I thought you were still asleep."

"I just woke up."

She went to him, kissing him deeply. That same reckless abandon she'd felt the night before instantly rekindled. Reluctantly she pulled away, holding open the swinging door. "Breakfast?"

Matt lifted out of the chair, and Oscar dashed from the couch, beating him into the kitchen.

Laughing, Alex set the alcohol and cotton on the table and turned toward the counter. "What can I say? He's the jealous type."

Matt moved up behind her. He glided his arms around her waist and slid open the zipper on her shorts. "I'd much rather have you than breakfast."

She sighed pleasurably, trying to remain detached as he kissed her neck, his hand wandering inside her panties, touching her lightly, making her ache again. "Have you forgotten the rules of the game already?"

He pulled away at once, and she turned to see the grimace on his face. Smiling she fastened her shorts and reached across the counter top for a tiny bottle of clear liquid and a syringe. "Nothing goes down in the morning before two injections and a healthy breakfast."

"I...forgot."

"Take it easy," she said, sitting at the table. "I didn't expect you to remember everything."

He sat alongside her and watched as she rolled the tiny bottle between her hands. "Is that the slow–release insulin?"

"Yep. This I take first thing in the morning and then again twelve hours later."

"Is this going to gross me out more than finger–poking?"

"Don't look."

"No. I need to see how it's done."

Alex soaked the cotton ball in the alcohol and opened the tiny bottle of insulin, filling the syringe with the designated amount of pre–measured units.

"Where are you going to stick it?" he asked.

"In my thigh."

Matt paid close attention. She rubbed a small spot on her left thigh with the cotton and pinched her skin. Without hesitation she inserted the needle into her skin, drew back the plunger slightly, and slowly injected the insulin.

He cringed, looking away.

She held the cotton over the injection site as she withdrew the needle. "That's it."

"When do you use the pen with the other type of insulin?"

"About fifteen to thirty minutes before each meal, which in this case will be about ten minutes from now. That's the quick–acting insulin, the one that controls the rise in glucose from eating." She broke off the needle and disposed of everything in the garbage. "I'll make us coffee now. How 'bout some scrambled eggs and toast? What time do you have to be at work?"

"No rush. I'll call Brian and tell him I'm going to be late."

She began shuffling around the kitchen.

"Is this condition hereditary?" he asked.

"In my case, yes. My dad's a diabetic and my grandmother was, too. But I'm the only one of three siblings it affected. My older sister and brother don't have it."

"How do your parents feel about their baby girl being a cop?"

She scooped coffee grounds into the automatic–drip machine. "They're not too thrilled."

"What about your siblings?"

"My brother's not happy about it, but my sister's proud of me."

"Are they married?"

"Yep, both of them." She flicked on the coffeemaker. "My sister, Sharon, is married to a college professor. She lives down in Morgantown, West Virginia. Tommy's the oldest, he's a computer programmer in Tampa."

"Do they have children?"

"No. Neither of them does yet."

Matt got up from the table to retrieve a carton of eggs from the refrigerator and help prepare breakfast. "How do you feel about children?" he asked nonchalantly.

"I love kids."

"Me, too. Children were out of the question with my ex–wife, which I guess was for the best, since we split up. But I think I'd make a pretty good dad some day."

"I think you would, too." She deliberately avoided the response she surmised he was searching for. This was not a conversation she had anticipated, not this early in the game. She had no idea where this relationship was headed. Perhaps it was a novelty. A few good rolls in the hay and nothing more.

Somehow she sensed that wouldn't be the case.

She had never felt the need to explain herself to a man until now. Alex looked up from the counter and turned to face him. "This may be far too early for me to say, but I don't want to lead you down a road you may not want to travel."

"What are you trying to tell me?"

She gazed into his bewildered eyes. "If you're looking for someone to…make a commitment, you need to know I never plan on having children. I don't mean to sound like your ex. I, uh…I could conceivably, but it'd be a huge risk with my condition. And I don't want to pass this on to a child."

He stared at her speechless. Suddenly his arms enveloped her, and he kissed her. "I'm sorry for giving you that impression about children. I should've never brought it up. I was making small talk, that's all." His fingers lightly touched her chin. "I love your honesty. And, please, don't think you have to compete with Cindy. There's no comparison."

She lowered her eyes from his stare. "I'm sorry. I overreacted. I just wanted you to know. I don't know why."

But Alex did have a good theory. And she wasn't sure if these unfamiliar feelings invigorated her—or frightened her.

"We're still on for dinner tonight, right?" Matt asked, lifting her chin. "I haven't scared you, have I?"

Entranced she held his eyes for several seconds before replying. "What time?"

"Seven okay?"

"I'll be ready."

"Officer Griffin, do you understand the complaint that has been filed against you?"

"Yes, sir, I do."

The police–union solicitor, a distinguished man in his early fifties, sat at the large conference table flipping through the pages of her personnel file.

He nodded, reading for the fourth time the official complaint filed by the public defenders' office. "I've reviewed your personnel file from the Highlands Regional Police Department, as well as those from your previous employers, and I need to ask you some questions. You have the constitutional right to decline to answer any and all of them if you so choose."

"I understand," Alex said from across the table, her folded hands resting on the oak surface while her feet quietly tapped the carpet underneath.

He wasted no time, reaching over for a notepad in his briefcase and removing a pen from inside his suit jacket. "Officer Griffin—"

"Please, call me Alex. I don't even like being call Officer in uniform, let alone in street clothes."

"Fine. I'm not much for formality either. Alex, have you ever been faced with a situation similar to the one that occurred with Mr. Ryzik? Where a fellow officer's life was in immediate danger."

"No. That was my initial experience."

"Have you been involved in arrests before that involved some type of physical confrontation or the drawing of your weapon?"

"Yes, I have," she answered candidly. "Several times, as a matter of fact, while I was working for the NPS in Arizona. But in those cases the suspects either immediately complied or were subdued by a group of officers. No one's life was threatened."

"Have any occurred here in Highlands County?"

"One I can specifically remember, a domestic."

"Tell me, frankly, what you came upon in the school hallway and the thoughts that were going through your head. Take all the time you need. I'm in no hurry."

Alex drew in a deep breath and released it slowly. The solicitor wrote as she spoke. "I was in the process of placing the first kid in custody, the one apprehended in the classroom, when I heard a loud crash and scuffle down the hallway. I knew something was wrong because Lisa was yelling for my help. I radioed for the state police and cuffed the kid to the wall heater and ran to assist her. I had my pistol drawn and in firing position when I came around the corner. The first thing I saw was Ryzik on top of Lisa. He had a knife in his hand and was reaching for her weapon."

"And did you immediately order the suspect to relinquish the knife?" he asked.

"Yes. He refused. It was at that point I noticed Lisa was bleeding." Alex ran a hand over her hair, collecting her thoughts and visualizing the scene in her mind. "I realize you're supposed to depersonalize yourself in this job, but I couldn't at that instant. Lisa and I are good friends, and I was scared to death. I thought she was hurt seriously or he would kill her at any second."

"Is it correct Mr. Ryzik challenged you to make him give up the knife?"

"Yes, it is."

"When exactly then did he throw it onto the floor?"

"Only after I released the safety on my weapon."

The attorney slouched back in the leather chair, raising the hand with the pen to his chin. "Would you have shot Mr. Ryzik if he refused to comply with your final verbal warning?"

Alex's eyes widened in horror. "I...I...yes. I felt I would have had no choice. My perception was Lisa's life was in danger and I couldn't waste anymore time."

He resumed taking notes. "Okay, so Mr. Ryzik finally got scared and gave up the knife, right?"

Alex nodded.

"And did he comply with your orders as you placed him in custody?"

"Yes."

"And then Officer Maselli told you she was okay and informed you of his previous drug ambitions so you proceeded to search the suspect, finding two hundred grams of cocaine and a large wad of twenties in his pocket?"

"Correct."

"Why'd you brutalize him then?"

"Because my nerves had been pushed to the limit and because he persisted to verbally abuse me. I lost it. I just...lost it. He threatened me. He told me to suck his...cock. He spat in my face." Her eyes locked on the attorney. "He cut my partner with a knife. Where does he get off saying I brutalized *him*? He willfully resisted arrest, and he *assaulted* a police officer."

"I'd like to verify a few personal facts, if that's okay?" the attorney said, fiddling with his pen. "And then I'd like to explain my feelings about this complaint against you."

"Okay, fine."

"You're twenty–seven, correct?"

She eyed the man quizzically. "Yes."

"Your file also indicates you're five–four and weigh one hundred twenty pounds. Is this information correct?"

"Yes."

He set the pen alongside the notepad, folded his hands over the paper, and began to speak. "Alex, your personnel file is flawless. In fact it includes a letter of commendation from the Highlands County School District, lauding the presentation you did at West Highlands Elementary School during Safety Week this past spring. My personal feeling on this matter is this kid is nothing but a cokehead and a troublemaker. He's got a rap sheet from here to the county line. But this time he went too far. He knows it, and he wants to get back at you to maintain his bad–boy image. You probably should *not* have roughed him up, but under the circumstances, anybody could have snapped and done the same things. You're a young woman of average build. You're not a big burly man, or woman, who'd have no problem making a career out of roughing up perps."

Alex exhaled in relief. "Thank you."

"Let me explain what's going to happen on Tuesday night," the attorney continued. "It will be a formal hearing with a stenographer. Those filing the complaint will go through their spiel, and then you'll have the opportunity to rebut their claim. You're allowed witnesses to collaborate your story. Do you feel Officer Maselli can back you up on this?"

"Absolutely."

"Fine. I'll set up a meeting with her prior to Tuesday night. The board will undoubtedly have questions for everyone. Answer them honestly. Like you did here with me. They may make a decision that night or they may request a continuance to decide at a latter date. Best case: dismissal of the complaint all together. Worst case: termination of your employment and filing of criminal charges. I can't see either happening. I'm thinking more on the lines of either a public apology to the kid or a formal reprimand in your file. Can you live with one of those?"

"I can live with the reprimand. I was wrong. But I'm not sure I could bring myself to apologize. I'm not the least bit sorry for what I did. Mr. Ryzik should be apologizing for what he did to us, especially Lisa."

"Would you be willing to risk your job to maintain your pride?"

"I don't know."

"You've got five days to decide," he said, packing up his files in the briefcase.

"What about the chief? Does he have any influence in the board's decision?"

"Certainly. More than likely the board will seek his thoughts on the matter. Why do you ask?"

Alex leaned back in the chair, staring helplessly at her counsel.

"No reason," she told him.

I'm screwed, she told herself.

"No problem," Ted Peterson spoke into the telephone, rummaging through the paperwork on his desk for the monthly patrol schedule. "How many do you need a night? Two...Okay...From?...Four to midnight...Okay...No, no, that's fine. I'll be in touch."

He hung up the phone and wrote out a memo "Highlands Heritage Days, July 25 through 27. Two officers a night, four to midnight." He picked up the patrol schedule and skimmed over the shifts to see which officers he could work into the festival. He hated these community events. They always taxed the department, already shorthanded. He cursed under his breath, dreading the start of the high–school football season. The overtime checks would be burning up the presses and eating into the department's tight budget.

"Part–timers," he mumbled to himself, reviewing the list of reserve officers he could assign to the festival. He was able to work the part–timers into Saturday and Sunday nights but not Friday. Smirking he penciled in the names Griffin and Maselli.

He got up from behind his desk, yawned, and stretched his arms. He walked over to the wall and studied the large, color photograph hanging near the door: the eighteen men—and those two broads—of the Highlands Regional Police Force. He had to admit his officers looked sharp in the photo taken recently on the steps of the borough building.

His eyes fixed on Alex Griffin, front row, last on the right. Man, what a looker. "This is why women shouldn't be cops," he muttered. "You're distracting. You make us think and do irrational things." Like come on to you in the heat of the moment and have you reject me. I hate that, he thought.

Ted Peterson returned to his desk, reclining back in his seat, contemplating his retribution. It wouldn't be an unfavorable statement at Tuesday's hearing, he decided. That would look bad on his part. The kid was a druggie. He assaulted an officer. Griffin's actions, although technically inappropriate, were undoubtedly understandable. He had to defend her. Besides he didn't want to arouse any inkling of suspicion of his feelings for her—or against her.

But soon. Real soon.

I'm going to get you, Alex Griffin.

Guaranteed.

Paula Sedlak plopped down on the porch stoop, opening the notice she just had received in the mail from the Highlands County School District. She read it to herself.

The Highlands County School District has been notified of an all–day seminar regarding innovative instructional techniques to be held on Thursday, July 24, from 9 A.M. to 5 P.M. at Anthracite University in Scranton. Please refer to the enclosed brochure.

The district feels this seminar will be a valuable asset to all teachers recently hired. I strongly urge you attend. Reservations can be made by simply contacting the district administrative offices. I look forward to hearing from you. If you have any questions concerning this seminar, please feel free to contact the superintendent.

Paula beamed, slipping the letter back into the envelope. Perfect timing, she thought. It was a legitimate excuse to spend an entire day with Jim Ostler. It only seemed logical they drive to Scranton together. Why should they both have to travel the fifty miles alone?

Paula found Jim Ostler charming and attractive, in high school and presently. Blond hair, brilliant blue eyes, and a sexy smile—all a part of a tall, lean body Paula had admired since their days with the HHS marching band.

She wondered if acting on her resurgent feelings would be a waste of time. After eight years any attempt at weakening his steadfast commitment to Lisa Maselli would be nothing short of impossible.

Nothing ventured, nothing gained, she convinced herself.

Paula sauntered into the house and flipped through the yellow pages for the number of Ostler Hardware, jotting it down on a small piece of paper. She ran up the stairs to her father's den and removed his brand new world atlas from the bookshelf. She sat before his computer and shrewdly authored a letter to an exchange student she had supposedly met while attending Penn State. A letter that would be e–mailed and require a translation into German. Another perfect excuse. A backup plan.

When she finished the letter, she printed it out and picked up the atlas, flipping through the pages until she found the map of Germany. Her fictitious friend needed a factual place to live. A quiet village. She studied the map and decided on a place near the Czech border called Zwickau. She never thought to check the population index.

With paper in hand, Paula left the computer desk and headed to the telephone.

* * *

At the bar inside Vic's, Kyle Lawry and Brian Haney pounded down their daily round of suds.

"Hey, man," Brian said. "You're not so talkative today. What's up?"

Kyle slammed his bottle down, splashing some of the beer on the bar. He glanced around the establishment to see if anyone was listening. An old man sat at the far end talking to the bartender. Convinced he would not be overheard he leaned close to his buddy's ear and growled, "She slept with him."

"What are you talking about?"

"Alex slept with Ehrich," Kyle repeated. "I saw them."

Brian coughed up a mouthful of liquid. His hand flew across the bar for a napkin, and he quickly wiped his chin. "You what? You *saw* them?"

"I was sitting on my porch last night about eleven, and I saw Pretty Boy pull into her driveway."

"And what'd you do? Tiptoe through the bushes and peep in the window?"

Kyle's eyes blazed with that same seething anger and betrayal he'd felt the night before.

"Are you crazy? That's insane. It's...*illegal.* You need help."

"What'd Pretty Boy say today, huh? Anything?"

"Get real. You actually think he'd tell me he slept with your ex?" Brian reached up, grabbing his buddy's shirt below the neck. "Listen to me, Lawry. You've got to stop this. Let her go before your sorry ass ends up in jail."

Kyle couldn't let go.

He needed to turn up the heat on Alex, make her realize, once and for all, she belonged to him.

Furiously Alex yanked the paper from her mailbox. She was returning from a brisk walk around the school track. She had decided against running. It would have been risky since she hadn't loaded up on the normal amount of carbohydrates needed to keep her glucose level from dropping drastically. She was preserving her appetite for dinner with Matt.

She cursed under her breath, unfolding the note. Her hands trembled as she read the brief message.

I know what you did last night.

Stunned she could not peel her eyes away from it.

"Oh, my God," Alex muttered, her hand covering her mouth in horror. How? How does he know? Has he been watching me? For a split–second her reaction was to march the four doors up to his house and deliver the no–nonsense ultimatum: Leave me alone or face legal recourse.

It was the obvious thing to do. But she recalled from a training seminar on stalkers it was the worst approach. Any kind of contact would be a victory for him. She needed to remain abstinent. Police statistics showed jealous boyfriends usually gave up if their ex–girlfriends continued to avoid engaging them.

She folded up the paper and went inside to monitor her glucose and inject the second slow–release insulin dose of the day, shower, and dress for her date with Matt. It was already past six o'clock, and Matt would be picking her up at seven.

As she showered she deliberated her counterattack on Kyle. She needed to tell someone about her predicament and begin keeping a journal of his actions. With Lisa and Matt as her only confidants, Lisa was the obvious choice. She was an ally within the system—and her best friend.

She'd have to wait until tomorrow to see Lisa. As her thoughts went back to the morning meeting with the union solicitor and Monday's confrontation with Ted Peterson, Alex finally succumbed to the fear of the looming conflicts. Slumped against the shower wall she cried for over ten minutes with the water cascading down her body before drying off and padding into the bedroom to recompose herself and dress. She selected an ivory sundress and a pair of tan sandals. She completed the outfit with a thin gold chain—replacing her medical information tag—a matching gold bracelet, and a pair of hoop earrings. She blew her hair dry and contemplated French–braiding her locks. But, glancing at the clock on the nightstand, she saw she was pressed for time. She quickly combed it out and let it fall untamed.

Matt knocked at the front door exactly at seven, and she invited him inside.

"You look beautiful," he said, his eyes pleasantly inspecting her ensemble.

She smiled, surveying his neat appearance in a plum shirt and pair of tan chinos. "And you look handsome."

"Are you ready? Shall we go?"

She grabbed her purse from the end table, and they drove to the Mountain View Inn, an upscale restaurant on the south end of town. An attractive hostess escorted them to a cozy, candle–lit table away from mainstream traffic.

"I need to do the quick–insulin thing," Alex told Matt before allowing herself to be seated. "I normally do it in the restroom. I don't want to gross out people in public. I'll be right back."

When they were settled at the table together, Matt ordered a glass of white wine and Alex a diet cola, and they made small talk while reviewing the menu. Alex decided on veal Parmesan. Matt ordered filet mignon. Sipping their drinks and snacking on bread and cracker appetizers, Matt tentatively asked her about the meeting with the police solicitor.

"He sounded optimistic," Alex said, nausea churning as she thought about the possible repercussions. "But nothing's certain until the board hears both sides."

She recapped the questions the attorney had asked and her responses. Matt listened intently, intrigued by the procedures of law enforcement. It was a new and exciting avenue of life, and he was enthralled by her intelligence and police skills. Conversations with Cindy had amounted to nothing more than mindless talks about work or the latest fashion trends. She often criticized his business and his lack of a social life. She was a bimbo. The woman who now sat across from him was a sensual, perceptive, and extremely independent individual who expressed her feelings honestly and tactfully. Matt was engrossed by her mere presence.

"Can I ask you something?" Matt said. "How does it feel to hold a gun on someone? Where do you get the guts to do it?"

"When someone or something is in danger, you don't think about guts, you just focus on the situation," Alex answered, the serious tone of her voice unmistakable. "It doesn't happen often, but it comes with the job. It scares me to death, and I pray I never have to pull the trigger."

"Then why do you do it?"

Alex smirked, slightly irritated with his inquiries. "Matt, why are you a mechanic?"

He understood her insinuation and immediately apologized. "I'm acting like an idiot again."

She reached across the table for his hand. "You are not an idiot, Matthew Ehrich. I'm sorry for the sarcasm, but sometimes people go overboard with this cop thing. A lot of people, male *and female*, have a problem with women being cops. They think it's unfeminine. Some guys are actually *afraid* of us."

Matt looked into her brilliant blue eyes and smiled. "Alex, I have to be honest. I was one of those guys for a long time. I was never afraid of you, but I'd see you on the street and talk to you, and all the while I was dying to ask you out, but I couldn't. I was intimidated. By your uniform, by your gun, by the authority you possess. I'm glad I overcame that fear. You're so fun to be with, so fascinating."

She met his eyes, but knew she was blushing. "You're the best thing that's happened to me since I've moved here."

A series of chats continued through dinner. They talked about their families, past relationships, and high–school days, a little politics and a lot about hobbies and interests. When they left the restaurant about ten o'clock Matt had learned even more about Alex. She had played field hockey in high school, lost her virginity at seventeen, and dreamed of visiting all fifty states. Thus far she had set foot in thirty. Alex in turn discovered Matt had been voted "Class Flirt" by his Highlands High classmates, admired former–President Ronald Reagan, and had a crush on a well–known gospel–turned–pop singer.

The night was young. With the early–July humidity hanging heavily in the air, Matt suggested a drive to Lake Iroquois and a leisurely walk along the overlook. Alex readily agreed.

"I love this area," he said as they walked in the moonlight along the path above the lake.

Alex relished the serenity of the water, rhythmically lapping against the large rocks lining the shore. "It's beautiful."

They approached a wooden bench. "Would you like to sit awhile?" Matt asked.

"Sure."

They settled on the seat, Matt's arm slipping behind her back.

Alex nestled closer. "I had a great time tonight."

"Nothing short of first class for you." He caressed her cheek, hesitantly brushed his lips over hers. She responded by kissing him fully.

"There's something between us, Alexandra Griffin. And you know what?"

"What?"

"I like it. I like it immensely. I'm hooked on you, lady. You're unbelievably beautiful, and I love your outspokenness. You're riveting, provocative, and you stimulate me beyond belief."

Alex smiled broadly, boldly, holding his green eyes. "Wanna know what I think of you?"

He buried his face in her hair. "In no uncertain terms."

Alex felt herself trembling as his lips whisked over the soft skin of her neck, arousing her. "I think you're handsome, intelligent, and ungodly sexy. You're a perfect gentleman and an incredible lover." His lips came across her throat. She sighed excitedly, tilting her head back. "And you're addicting." She ran her fingers through his hair, messing it, and lifted his head to meet his eyes. "Let's go back to your place." She slid her hand along his inner thigh.

He smiled mischievously. "Have you ever made love under the stars?"

Alex raised her eyebrows in surprise. She grinned, fully understanding his proposition. "I'd like to exercise my fifth–amendment privilege."

Matt laughed, his hand drifting under her dress. "I'm afraid you've incriminated yourself, Officer Griffin. C'mon."

He led her to the end of the overlook path and down a wooded trail to a secluded section of the shoreline. With a near–full moon above in the summer sky, Matt rested against a large boulder deposited at the lake's edge millions of years ago. Alex slid her arms around his waist, pressed her body against his.

"What exactly did you have in mind?" she asked, baffled, observing nothing but rocks around them.

A devilish smile spread across his moonlit face. He straightened up and maneuvered around so she was propped against the rock. "Perfect positioning." He lifted her off her feet, setting her buttocks on the rock. He stood before her, face to face, as she sat on the smooth, flat surface. He kissed her deeply.

"You're so radical," Alex muttered, offering no opposition as he slowly undid the buttons on the front of her dress, starting at the top and ending well below her breasts. He slid the wide straps of the dress off her shoulders and in the same movement unfastened her bra.

Alex did nothing but hold his gaze while her body responded to his every touch. He bent downward, his tongue finding her breasts. She moaned softly, dropping her head back, her hair caught in a gentle breeze.

His hands trailed down her back, slowly, and she welcomed his advances by allowing him to drive up her skirt and free her panties. He quickly unzipped his pants and prepared himself with a condom from his wallet.

"Ever done it like this before? On a rock?" he muttered heavily, returning to her. He touched her lightly between the legs, making her gasp with anticipation.

She shook her head, her eyes pleading for him. "No," she whispered.

He pressed close to her, entering her. She wrapped her legs around his hips and could see his face twisted with passion, his eyes half–closed, as they moved with the rhythm of the water slapping against the shore.

Together they vanished for a time into a world of pure ecstasy.

* * *

Alone in his room he sat on the bed, resting against the headboard. He drew his knees upward and opened a spiral–bound tablet. He began diagramming his plan, writing out every detail, every intent, every possible obstacle. He lifted the faded newspaper photo from alongside him and placed it on top of the paper. Staring down at her, he smiled demonically.

"It's time," he said, glancing over at the twenty–two–caliber revolver lying on the dresser. "Pay back time."

CHAPTER 10

An Even Score

Alex gave Lisa a lift to the borough building. They signed in at the police station, picking up their assignment sheet and talking for a few minutes with the other two officers on second shift.

"Rural patrol," Alex said. "Thank goodness. I'm not in the mood to deal with the townies."

"Let's hope it's a quiet night," Lisa said.

They headed out to the four–wheel–drive marked with the numbers 3–7. It was Lisa's turn to drive so Alex settled in on the passenger side. They fastened their seat belts, informed the Comm Center they were beginning the shift, and started out for the rural townships north of Mountain View.

"Did the union solicitor get in touch with you?" Alex asked.

"This morning," Lisa said. "I met with him earlier this afternoon."

"And?"

"I told him my version of what happened. He seemed pleased. Al, there's no way charges are going to be filed against you. The kid is a first–class perp."

"Yeah, and so is Peterson. The board is going to ask for his opinion. I'm screwed. He's not going to side with me."

"If he goes against you he'll look like a jerk. How would he justify that? Tell everyone you refused to sleep with him?"

Alex pondered Lisa's theory while they drove north along the highway. Perhaps she was right. Peterson would not be able to justify his negative judgment without a legitimate reason. Alex shrugged, thinking one of her conflicts may have been averted. But he'll get me some other way, she cautioned herself inwardly.

"What's the latest with Renee and Stanton?" Alex asked, turning the conversation away from work.

Lisa glanced over for a second then returned her eyes to the road. "They're going out to dinner tonight. I told her Wednesday night how I felt and to be cautious. What else could I say?"

"What'd she say?"

"Not too much. And I don't know how she took it. Sometimes I think Renee resents my relationship with Jimmy. She's never said anything to that effect but every now and then she'll remind me how lucky I am to have someone in my life. I hope I didn't alienate her."

A few miles north of the borough limits, Lisa pulled off the highway and backed into an area hidden by a stand of evergreen trees. They would be using two wire–transmission poles across the road as reference points to compute the speed of passing vehicles.

"Jimmy got a notice from the school district about a seminar in Scranton," she said, shifting the SUV into park. She slouched back against the seat, looking over at Alex. "Something about teaching techniques. It's being held in two weeks."

"For all the teachers?"

"Just the new teachers. Jimmy and the math teacher, Paula Sedlak. She called him to make arrangements to drive there together. And while she's on the phone with him, she asks if he could translate a letter for her into German to e–mail to a friend she met at college who lives in Germany."

Alex activated the speed–measurement device mounted to the dash and caught the grimace on Lisa's face. "Something tells me you're not happy about any of this."

"C'mon, Al. If this friend went to Penn State, he or she would have been able to read, write, and speak English. Or Paula could use the Internet. There's got to be a website offering free language translations for international e–mails. It doesn't seem logical. She had a crush on Jimmy before we started dating. It's been a long time, and I'm probably being silly, but I never liked the girl. I guess I'm overly suspicious of everyone."

"That you are." From the corner of her eye, Alex operated the speed–timing switches as the occasional car whizzed by on the highway. "Maybe Paula wants to impress her friend by sending the letter in his or her native tongue. A translation from the Internet wouldn't provide the personal touch that Jim could in the e–mail. I wouldn't get all bent out of shape yet."

Lisa sighed then added jokingly, "You're so rational you make me sick."

"Not all the time." Alex turned to face her partner. "I need your help big time."

Lisa met Alex's humorless expression with a bewildered look. She straightened in her seat. "Sure. What's wrong?"

"It's Kyle." Alex reached into her shirt pocket for the note cards and handed them to Lisa. "He left these in my mailbox. One Wednesday night and the other last night while I was out jogging."

Lisa took the cards and unfolded them. Alex watched as she digested the messages, her eyes narrowing in confusion. Lisa dropped the notes into her lap and looked over at Alex. "I understand the first one about the Ryziks. But do you want to elaborate on the second one?"

"Matt came over late Wednesday night after reading about the school vandalism in the paper."

"Yeah?"

"I..." Alex momentarily hesitated but then quickly decided she had nothing to be ashamed of. Lisa was a trustworthy friend. "I asked him to stay the night."

"How did Kyle find out?"

"He must have seen Matt's pickup in my driveway. I'm convinced he's been watching me like a hawk."

A motorcycle sped past them. Lisa glanced down at the speed measurement. Digital numbers flashed a reading of seventy miles per hour. "Forget the bike. We didn't see it. Are you saying Kyle spied on you and Matt?"

"I haven't got a clue, but it sure seems that way. Lise, I think he's got stalking tendencies. I've got to start documenting his actions. And I need you to back me up if it comes down to filing charges against him."

The radio cracked to life, and Lisa signaled Alex to stop talking. "Highlands three–seven, Comm Center."

Lisa picked up the microphone. "Comm Center, three–seven. Go ahead."

"Respond to a ten–fifty, two–vehicle accident, at the intersection of Ridge Road and Highway 181 in Westfall Township," the female dispatcher directed. "Injuries reported. Ambulance and rescue en route."

"Ten–four, Comm Center." Lisa replaced the microphone and reached down for the lights and siren. "We *will* continue this discussion later," she said, swinging onto the highway. "I hate accidents."

Renee sat at the restaurant table, fussing with the pasta on the plate before her. She slowly twirled the linguine around her fork, lifting her eyes every few seconds to watch Rick feast on the meal before him.

The evening had begun with him bestowing a long–stem rose upon her as he greeted her at the front door. He had been nothing but a gentleman from the onset of their date, showering her with flattery, holding open doors. And Renee did nothing but second–guess his every word, his every action. Thanks to Lisa and her vague warning about his alleged insidious conduct.

The gist of their evening had consisted of small talk, with neither mentioning Wednesday's meeting between him and Lisa and Alex. He blabbed mostly about the paper and upcoming articles, and she chatted a little about the bureau and the plans for the start of the rail excursions.

"I know I agreed to serve as a conductor," Rick had said as they munched on fresh garden salads prior to the main course. "But are you going to explain to me, or show me, what I'm supposed to be doing?"

"Of course," Renee had answered, laughing. "I won't throw you to the lions without any training. How 'bout Wednesday night? I'll give you a tour of the train and the lowdown on the conductor's job."

"Fine. Do you have any plans for Sunday?"

"No. Why?"

"It's supposed to be a hot one. Are there any good swimming holes around here?"

Renee immediately thought of the gorge along the Indian Cave Creek. Pristine, private. But Lisa's cautioning words flashed before her: *Stay in public places when you're with him.*

"The pool at the state park," she had answered instead.

"Great. Would you like to go swimming then on Sunday?"

"Yeah, sure."

"And afterward I'd like to cook you dinner at my apartment. If that's okay with you."

"You? Cook?"

"You'll be surprised by my culinary talents."

"Is that so? I didn't think male chauvinists did that sort of thing."

He had laughed at her remark, heartily. "Was that a yes or no?"

It was then she had thrown caution to the wind. "That was a yes." She wanted to afford him an opportunity to prove her sister's suspicions wrong. Renee had always hated Lisa's wary attitude of people. She often speculated why her sister had become so distrustful of everyone. She assumed it arose from the intuitive nature of her profession or dealing with a society mistrustful of the police.

Renee glanced up at Rick once again, wondering if *Doctor Jekyll and Mister Hyde* was seated across from her. Or if her sister simply had a tainted opinion of him.

She couldn't keep quiet any longer. "I have to ask," she said, setting her fork on the edge of the plate. "Were you going to tell me about Lisa's visit on Wednesday, or were you hoping I wouldn't bring it up?"

Rick looked up from his plate abruptly. He swallowed his mouthful of food and set down the utensils. "Is there anything your sister *doesn't* tell you?"

Renee smirked nonchalantly. "No. Not really."

"I didn't want to put a damper on our time together. I'm sorry, but I didn't think it concerned us. It involved the paper and the police. Your sister and her partner thought I was looking for a way around the DUI charge. I don't like it when people think there's an ulterior motive for everything."

Renee shook her head, astounded by the animosity between them. "I'm not sure who's more pigheaded, you or Lisa."

"I suppose we're both equally stubborn. We're set in our ways, and we have certain opinions about one another that can't be swayed."

"Okay, fine," Renee conceded. She did not want to dwell on the issue, not at this particular moment, and ruin the remainder of their date. "I can accept that for now. But this pissing contest between the two of you has to end. Don't you think so?"

Rick stared at her for a long, thoughtful moment. Her last question was more of an implied statement: You will stop this nonsense, or you'll get nowhere with me. He only hoped he *could* stop it.

After dinner they continued the evening at the Lumberjack. A local rock–band was performing, and it didn't take long for them to loosen up with a few drinks and join the large crowd already on the dance floor. But about ten–fifteen or so Rick excused himself and hurried to the men's room. He returned a few moments later, his face as white as flour.

"I feel lousy," he reluctantly told Renee. "Would you mind if we cut our date short?"

"No, not at all. You look terrible."

Outside, in the clear night air, he felt a tad refreshed as they walked to his car. "I'm sorry about this. I feel terrible."

"No, don't. I understand. I'll see you Sunday."

"We're definitely on for Sunday?" he asked sheepishly.

"You bet."

Ten minutes later he turned the Nissan into her driveway.

"I hope you feel better in the morning," Renee said, leaning over to kiss his cheek. "I had a great time tonight. I'm looking forward to Sunday."

"Me, too."

He waited until she safely entered the house.

Renee watched from inside the screen door as he backed out of the driveway and drove out of sight.

Alex shuttled her partner home after work, pulling into the Maselli's driveway a little past midnight. Lisa slid out of the Tracker. "Thanks for the lift. Sorry we couldn't finish our discussion on Kyle. Who would've thought we'd be so busy."

"Don't worry about it," Alex said, resting her hands on top of the steering wheel. "You saw the notes. We can talk more tomorrow night."

Lisa leaned against the door, peering inside. "You can count on me. I owe you my life, for goodness' sake."

"Cut the melodrama already. Going anywhere with Jimmy now?"

"Neah, I'm beat. We're going to hang out on the porch. It's such a nice night."

"See you tomorrow night," Alex said as Lisa closed the door and headed for the house. She backed out of the Maselli's driveway, shifted into first, and started down Fourteenth Street to Main Street. It had been one of the worst four–to–midnight shifts she had ever worked. Nonstop from the get–go: two major auto–accidents, a disorderly conduct call, a vandalism report, and another time–consuming DUI. They had not taken their dinner break until nine o'clock. The deviation in her meal schedule and the night's continuous activity had her utterly exhausted.

As Alex turned onto Main Street and drove through the commercial district, she tried to sort out her predicament with Kyle. But she was too tired to concentrate. Foremost on her mind was the thought of sleep.

At the end of Main Street she made another right and began the ascent up Grove Street. Two minutes later she silenced the Tracker's engine in her driveway and entered the peace and comfort of her home. She switched on the lamp closest to the door and routinely removed her duty belt, tossing it onto the couch for the time being. She needed to unwind before lugging her police equipment to the bedroom closet.

"Oscar," she called for her cat, walking across the living room, surprised he hadn't greeted her at the door as he normally did each time she'd return home. "Wha–cha doin', buddy?"

As she strained to listen for the cat's response to her voice, she heard a strange noise, and a sudden feeling came over her, a sense of something amiss. She froze and held her breath. It was at that moment her eyes fixed on the dark figure leaping from the hallway.

Your gun! Get your gun! But as she spun around to retrieve the pistol, it all happened in the tick of a second: a leather glove seizing her throat, her body being driven backward and slammed against the living–room wall, the painting of the cliff dwellings crashing to the floor, the barrel of a small, gray revolver shoved into her mouth. She hadn't had time to scream or struggle or react in any way. Her heart beat so fast she could feel the pulse pounding against her constricted airway. She stared up in utter horror at the dark eyes bearing down on her through the only openings of a black ski mask.

"Try anything, *Officer*, and you're dead," the muffled voice ground out the words.

Alex tried to speak, but he shoved the gun deeper into her mouth, making her gag on the cold metal.

"The trigger on this piece is real sensitive. You'll be history if you even so much as think about trying to disarm me. Understand?"

Helplessly, she nodded.

With the clamp on her neck and the revolver in her mouth, the intruder slid her along the wall of the unlit hallway toward the bathroom. In one swift move he threw her inside. He flicked on the light as she crashed into the tile wall.

The bone–chilling scream that worked its way out from inside her pierced the air like a knight's lance. "No! How could you?" She staggered forward into the vanity, fighting off nausea. Oscar, her beloved pet, hung lifelessly by his neck from a cord tied to the shower curtain rod, his mouth agape in silent protest. "Who are you? What do you want from me?"

"Let's just say we're evening the score," the intruder growled, reaching out for her uniform collar. He dragged her into the bedroom, dimly illuminated by the bathroom light and a street lamp outside the window. He released her and stood in the doorway, leveling the gun at her chest, blocking her only means of escape.

Alex took a step backward, away from him. She was trapped. Her pistol and baton, her primary means of defense, lay affixed to her belt on the couch in the living room, and she couldn't attempt to physically fight him unless he put the weapon down. She had no doubt he meant business; his index finger was positioned threateningly on the trigger.

Stay calm, she told herself, you need to buy time for an opening to initiate a counter defense. Her eyes frantically scanned his ominous figure. He was close to six feet, not burly by any standard. With the exception of his eyes, dark clothing completely concealed his identity. He wanted to even the score. What score? She felt dizzy, nauseated. Her hands quickly covered her mouth and she dry heaved.

A muted laugh emanated from under the mask. "Scared shitless, huh?" He slowly began closing in on her. "You should be."

She stepped backward, around the foot of the bed, visually searching for a potential weapon she could grab if he somehow became distracted. A brush and her hairdryer lay on top of the dresser. If she expressed compliance maybe he'd let his guard down. "Don't hurt me, please. Okay? I…I'll do whatever you want. Put the gun down, okay?"

Undaunted he backed her into the corner farthest from the door, away from the furniture—putting the brush and dryer well out of her reach. Imprisoning her between the walls and his body, he seized her chin, forcing her head upward. "What'd ya think I'm stupid? I ain't puttin' it down. You ain't usin' any of your fancy police tactics on me. Now, look at me, *Officer*."

"Please," she pleaded, desperately, lifting her eyes to comply with his demand. "I'm not trying to trick you, really. I'll do what you want."

He did not respond to her statement, and Alex sensed the rage within him. She could have easily reached up and yanked the ski mask from his face. But she dared not to. He was concealing himself for a reason: She could identify him. That she was sure of, although she was unable to distinguish his muffled voice. Whatever his intentions, murder was not one of them. He would not have gone through the trouble of covering his features. If she foiled his plans, she would die.

He laughed wickedly, meeting her eyes and relishing the fear he saw there. "It's pay back time, baby."

"F...for what?" she asked, trembling, his words racing through her mind. It couldn't be Ted Peterson? The wrath of her rejection of him couldn't possibly lead to this? He couldn't be this demented. The voice was questionable, but the eyes... She stared into the intruder's dark eyes, her ability to reason running amok. She remembered how the chief had seized her collar and pinned her against his office wall. "Please, I have no idea...I'm sorry. Just put the gun down, and we could talk—"

"Shut up!" He squeezed her throat, holding the barrel of the gun under her chin. "I'll do all the talking. *This*'ll do all the talking." He thrust the end of the barrel into her skin. Then, as abruptly as he had seized her, he released her, backhanding her hard across the face. She bounced off the wall, her lip split.

Her knees buckled, but he pulled her upright, holding her by the throat against the wall. As she gasped for precious air, severe pain coupled her terror. Her head throbbed and her lips and cheek stung, blood trickling from the corner of her mouth. She tried to focus on her assailant's mask but saw only a distorted image. She doubted her contact lenses had been knocked out of her eyes by the blow to her face. No, the heart–pounding terror was causing her blood sugar to skyrocket and impairing her vision; the fight–or–flight response did not function well in diabetics. Breathe deeply, calm down. You can't allow yourself to pass out. You need to be conscious, to be your own witness.

The gun was again pushed into her jaw. "Wipe your face."

She lifted a trembling hand to clean the blood from her chin then rubbed it off her fingers on her uniform pants. There was no way he was going to relinquish the weapon. He came prepared to fight—and win. He was in total control.

His gloved hand slithered down her neck and over her badge. He traced the edges with his index finger, encircling the silver shield. "Does this piece of tin make you feel powerful?"

She did not reply. She stared at the intimidating black mask, seeing the pleasure, the excitement in his eyes as her vision drifted in and out of focus.

"Answer me!"

She shook her head. "N…no. I'm sorry if I—"

"Liar! You think you're hot shit wearing this piece of metal. Ain't that right?"

She started to shake her head again, but he indicated with a sharp thrust of the gun's barrel it was the wrong answer. Alex bit back her pride and told him what he wanted to hear. "Y…yeah. Okay? C'mon, please, you've made your point."

"You ain't talkin' your way out of this, Officer Griffin. You're mine." He raised his arm above her head and leaned forward, pressing his hand against the wall assuredly. He ran the revolver across her bruised cheek, menacingly, then down the side of her neck and under her collar. The feel of the cold metal inside her shirt made her shiver. He pressed the gun into the soft skin above her clavicle. "Unbutton your shirt."

Alex closed her eyes momentarily and a stream of suppressed tears gushed out from under her lids. He was going to rape her. Stay calm, she commanded herself, looking away from him. At some point he's going to have to set that damn gun down, right? To get your clothes off, to get his clothes off. That's when you'll have a chance to fight back. That's what they told her at training. But she was supposed to be teaching self–defense to other women, not trying to use it to prevent *herself* from becoming a statistic.

"I *said* unbutton your shirt. You're challenging me," he said matter–of–factly. "I don't like that."

"Okay…" Pray that he sets the weapon down. Remember his words, his sordid acts. Detach yourself from the nightmare that's about to take place. She raised her hand to the top button of her uniform and fumbled to undo each of the small, navy–blue knobs, stopping at the waistband of her pants. She would not willfully aid this degradation by freeing her shirttails from inside her pants.

He tore her shirt open and slowly encircled her bra with the barrel of the gun. She turned her head away, and he laughed, running his free hand down her neck and under the bra, touching her roughly. She refused to look at him. She knew he was smiling, enjoying his vengeance underneath that black mask.

Suddenly, without warning, he seized the chain with her medical tag, compelling her to face him. He twisted it repeatedly until it was tight around her throat, nearly strangling her. "No more. You won't be so high and mighty after I get through with you."

Alex gasped spastically, searching for air.

"Beg me to let go," he taunted, twisting the chain tighter, thrusting his fist into her jaw. "Let me hear you grovel. It turns me on."

Alex fought desperately to keep alert. Soon she would be completely vulnerable. Her legs were weakening and she was losing the battle to keep her blood sugar under control. "Let go," she croaked. "Please, stop hurting me. I already told you I'll do what you want. Please, I can't breathe."

Another wicked laugh. He released the chain and drove a knee into her crotch. Alex's eyes flew wide open. She doubled over on the verge of blacking out. But he reached around and grasped the top of her ponytail, again forcing her erect. He held her against the wall, allowing her to regain her cognizance. He was drawing it out to watch her suffer. He wanted her aware the entire time.

She tried to calm herself by inhaling deeply. But the reality of the situation was overwhelming, uncontrollable. Her mind shot back to the high–school corridor, where she had kneed William Ryzik in the groin. Her assailant was reenacting on her what she had done to the kid. It has to be his brother!

"Unzip me. Take it out, feel it."

He was making *her* do the deeds; he was not going to relinquish the gun for any reason. Her hand meekly fumbled for the snap on his jeans. She felt strangely disembodied as she pulled it open and slid down the zipper. He was not wearing underwear, and she could not bring herself to touch him. He grabbed her wrist, forcing her to extract his penis from his pants. "Stroke me." He held her hand against him until her fingers reluctantly wrapped around his erection and fondled him robot–like.

"Tell me how much you like it," he moaned, prodding her breast with the gun, pushing his penis against her pants.

Alex cringed with disgust. With every ounce of strength remaining she jerked her hand free and beat his chest. "Just do it." Her voice trailed off into heavy sobbing, giving up on any chance of saving herself. "Just...do...it."

He let out a loud, evil laugh and forced her down onto her knees. She's unable to resist, he observed, watching her cry convulsively. She's physically and mentally drained. The rush from the success of his mastery, his control, inundated him, and he thought he could actually kill her, level the gun at her chest and squeeze the trigger. But he restrained himself. It was not in the plan. He wanted her to live in fear for the rest of her life.

His hand twisted her ponytail, and he pulled her face to his penis, pressing it against her mouth. "Suck me, bitch. Make me come."

She gagged, smelling his putrid body odor.

He tightened the grip on her hair, shoved the gun under her left ear. "Do it, or I'll kill you."

Her lips parted unwillingly, and he thrust himself into her mouth. She cried and gagged repeatedly, but the painful, taut grasp he had on her hair forced her to satisfy his demand. He threw his head back in blissful triumph. "Swal—"

Before he could finish grinding out the word, she wrenched her hair free in a defiant rage and turned away, spitting his semen onto the carpet, some spraying onto her pants. Evidence, you bastard! I swear you'll pay for this!

He struck the side of her head with the butt of the gun, and she collapsed onto the floor, semiconscious. He dropped to his knees, straddling her, and grabbed her neck with his free hand. He wanted her awake. "I'm not through with you yet!"

She struggled to keep her eyes open, hearing a faint wailing in her mind. He was hovering above her. She felt him rip open her pants. Was he using both hands to strip off her uniform? Did he drop the gun? The wailing sound grew louder, and Alex suddenly recognized it was a police–car siren blaring in the street somewhere, not a mental illusion.

He heard it, too, jumping to his feet. He frantically tried to zip up his jeans, cursing.

Alex somehow found a salvaged inner strength. "Someone heard and called the police!" she screamed in raw fury. *"I'm gonna kill you!"*

The siren grew louder, nearer. In seconds he was gone.

Time stood still as Alex lay on the floor, reeling from the shock, listening as the siren faded from earshot. No one was coming to help her, she realized. But the siren had saved her, frightening her assailant into flight.

"Ohmygod. Ohmygod." Alex rolled onto her side and curled up into a fetal position, her body wracking with tremors and intense sobs. "Ohmygod. Ohmygod. Ohmygod…"

CHAPTER 11

The Big Hat Strikes Back

Highlands Regional Police Department
Mountain View, PA
Initial Crime Report
Incident Number: 07–12–01A

Offense: Aggravated Sexual Assault

Victim: Alexandra Griffin W/F

DOB: 3 November

Location: 438 Grove Street, Mountain View Borough

Date: Saturday 12 July

Time: 00:30 hrs

Means: threat of deadly force

Weapons: twenty–two–caliber revolver

Details: Reporting officer and partner, Ptlm. David Romanovich, arrived at 438 Grove Street in the borough of Mountain View at

02:00 hrs, 12 July, in response to a reported break–in and sexual assault. Victim and off–duty Ptlw. Lisa Maselli were at premise upon arrival. Victim described her assailant as follows: white male, 5'10" to 6'0" of unknown age and average build and wearing dark clothing, leather gloves, and a black ski mask. Perpetrator apparently broke into premise, killed her male feline pet, and waited until she arrived home from work at 00:30 hrs. Assailant, armed with a .22–caliber revolver, surprised victim in living room and forced her into bedroom. Assailant proceeded to physically assault and force victim to partially undress herself, fondle and perform oral sex on him by threatening bodily injury or death. It is the victim's and this officer's belief the assailant would have proceeded to commit the act of rape on the victim if he had not been frightened into fleeing the scene by the sound of a siren of a passing emergency vehicle. Case was turned over to PSP Detective, Gregory Van Dien, who ordered Ptlm. Romanovich to stay at premise and await arrival of PSP Crime Scene Unit. Upon request of victim and approval by Det. Van Dien and HRPC Ted Peterson, off–duty Ptlw. Maselli accompanied R/O and victim to Highlands Memorial Hospital for medical–legal exam. Detective Van Dien was to meet victim, R/O, and Ptlw. Maselli at hospital with rape kit and obtain official statement from victim.

Chris Wingate, Ptlm.

Highlands Regional Police Department
Mountain View, PA
Supplemental Crime Report
Incident Number: 07–12–01A

R/O accompanied victim, Alexandra Griffin, and on–duty Ptlm. Wingate to the emergency room of Highlands Memorial Hospital for medical–legal exam where investigating PSP Det. Gregory Van Dien awaited. R/O acknowledges victim is a police officer employed by the HRPD, and further acknowledges victim is R/O's assigned partner. Being the only female officer available approval of R/O's presence during the medical–legal exam was obtained from Det. Van Dien and HRPC Ted Peterson. Det. Van Dien presented rape kit to ER Doctor Kevin Holleran and R/O observed as Dr. Holleran used kit on victim and turned same over to R/O. Evidence sealed in the kit #07–12–01A is as follows:

Envelope 1: Not used. Pubic hair combing not performed. Victim remained fully clothed from the waist down and no vaginal penetration occurred.

Envelope 2: Blood scraped from right pant leg.

Envelope 3: Semen scraped from left pant leg.

Envelope 4: Fingernail clippings.

Envelope 5: Twelve hairs cut from scalp.

Envelope 6: Not used. No pubic hairs cut.

Envelope 7: Filter containing saliva sample.

Envelope 8: Not used. Vaginal region not swabbed.

Envelope 9: Oral swab.

Envelope 10: 10cc of drawn blood.

R/O also collected the following items of evidence from victim:

07–12–01A–E1: shirtsleeve, navy–blue police–uniform shirt

07–12–01A–E2: beige bra

07–12–01A–E3: navy–blue police–uniform pants, zipper broken

07–12–01A–E4: beige bikini panties

07–12–01A–E5: one pair navy–blue socks

07–12–01A–E6: one pair black leather tie shoes

07–12–01A–E7: one pair gold topaz birthstone earrings

07–12–01A–E8: one silver "diabetic" medical information tag and chain

07–12–01A–E9: one black–band Timex wristwatch

07–12–01A–E10: one gold Colorado State University ring, ruby stone

07–12–01A–E11: one HRPD Patrol Officer badge, #28

07–12–01A–E12: one silver nametag engraved with name "Griffin"

07–12–01A–E13: one gold–clasp barrette

07–12–01A–E14: taped loose hairs found on right hand

07–12–01A–E15: taped loose hairs found on neck

07–12–01A–E16: Polaroid snapshot of face, bruise on left cheek, small cut on left corner of mouth

07–12–01A–E17: Polaroid snapshot of throat area, discoloration evident

07–12–01A–E18: Polaroid snapshot profile of left temple, bruise evident

07–12–01A–E19: Polaroid snapshot of vaginal region, bruise evident

R/O turned kit and evidence collected over to Det. Van Dien and remained with victim for further examination and treatment. No additional reports will follow from the HRPD; case has been relinquished to the PSP–Highlands Investigation Division.

Lisa Maselli, Ptlw.
12 July

Lisa signed the supplemental–report form, tossed it on top of the initial report, and buried her face in her hands. She had held herself together the entire night for Alex's sake. Now at eight–thirty A.M. she could no longer suppress her pain and anger. Alone in the police station she began to cry. "Oh, Al. I can't believe this happened. No one deserves this. No one, especially not you."

Lisa set her head down on the desktop, exhaustion from a lack of sleep finally overrunning the adrenaline high she had been on throughout the night.

The nightmare had begun with a phone call from Alex about one o'clock. She had been sitting on the front porch with Jimmy and Renee, her sister talking about her dinner–date with Rick Stanton. Alex had asked her rather calmly to come over immediately, alone. Something had happened, and she needed her. In light of the night's short–lived conversation on Kyle, Lisa had assumed automatically Alex and Kyle had somehow seen one another, had gotten into a fight, and Alex had needed to vent her frustration. Never in a million years had she expected to see the horror before her when she stepped inside Alex's home.

Alex had been sitting on the couch, staring at nothing, her pistol gripped tightly in her right hand and resting on her lap. The oil painting that normally hung on the wall near the kitchen door lay on the floor, the canvas torn, its wood frame cracked. Alex had buttoned her shirt and refastened her pants before Lisa had gotten there, but the bruises and cut on her face affirmed something terrible had happened.

"Alex?" Lisa had asked hesitantly. "Did s…something happen with Kyle?"

Alex let out a short, bitter laugh, her eyes transfixed across the living room. "I was attacked, raped I guess. Funny, huh?"

Lisa remembered trying to speak and not being able to form words. She had stood motionless before her partner, her best friend, paralyzed by her own horrifying memories. She felt sick, her heart pounding through her chest as terror shot through her body.

And Alex had rambled on, in a mindless state of shock and grief. "He busted the lock on the back door. He…killed Oscar. He put a gun to my head, and I thought if I expressed compliance he'd put it down. But he didn't, and I had to do everything he wanted, like a puppet. Except swallow," she muttered bitterly. "I spit it out. Guess I showed him…" Her voice cracked. "Yeah, I showed him…that's when he bashed the butt of the gun off my head. Funny, huh?" Then suddenly, as if the gut–wrenching reality of the ordeal had finally registered, Alex began shouting hysterically, "Ohmygod. Tell me this didn't happen. Please. Tell me. This didn't happen to me. Tell me, please."

Lisa had snapped out of her trance and dropped onto the couch, holding her partner, her best friend, tightly in her arms, listening to her heartbreaking sobs. "I'm so sorry," Lisa had mumbled, choking back her own tears. "I'll get you through this, don't worry." A million things had raced through her mind as a ball of rage formed in her stomach. Two or three times she had tried to twist the pistol out of Alex's hand, but Alex had been gripping it with such perseverance she gave up. After ten minutes or so had passed, Lisa freed herself from Alex's despairing embrace to call the Comm Center. Chris Wingate and Dave Romanovich, the graveyard–shift officers who had relieved them at midnight, responded to the call.

Dave had stayed at the house to wait for the state–police crime–scene unit, who would comb the premise for evidence. Chris had accompanied Lisa and Alex to the hospital emergency room. There they had met Greg Van Dien, a state–police detective. Lisa and Alex were both relieved Greg had gotten the assignment. In the past he had never been cocky, always soft and compassionate.

Greg was married and in his mid–thirties, a ten–year veteran of the state–police force and one of two detectives assigned to the Highlands County Barracks. These were the guys who handled the hard–core crimes—every type of felony imaginable. However, being the only two female police officers—regional or state—in the county, Lisa and Alex were often called by the big hats to witness a rape victim's statement and medical–legal examination for the police procedure known as chain of evidence. Both knew the procedure thoroughly, which had eased Alex's anxiety but had sickened Lisa's stomach. She had to perform her duties as a police officer, rather than be a supportive friend. She didn't want to witness her partner's endurance of the medical–legal, where her body would be prodded and searched and photographed for evidence, and every stitch of clothing and jewelry confiscated and turned over to the crime lab for analysis. She didn't want to *see* any of it. She didn't want to *hear* any of it.

It had taken Alex over a half hour to painstakingly reiterate the details of the assault to Greg, and she had been adamant about her feelings on the intruder's identity. His remarks about evening the score, the resemblance of the act to the incident at the high school, and his implicit threat at the arraignment all had led her to believe Billy Ryzik's brother, Dale, had been behind that ghastly mask.

It had been especially hard for her to discuss the oral copulation. Lisa had sat in a chair, out of Alex's line of sight, listening with that same ball of rage in the pit of her stomach she had felt earlier at the house. Calvin Anderson had not forced her to perform oral sex on him. And, as Lisa had sat, listening to the debasing Alex had suffered through, she guiltily thanked the Lord for sparing her.

The medical–legal exam had lasted over an hour, and Lisa turned over the rape kit and nineteen pieces of evidence to Greg. Before leaving the hospital he pulled her aside and asked that Alex not be allowed to return home until morning, after the crime scene unit had completed its search and removed the evidence.

"I feel bad about this," Greg had said. "Does she have somewhere to go?"

"Don't worry about it," Lisa had replied. "She can stay at my house."

After the male officers had left, Kevin Holleran, the young ER doctor, treated Alex's cuts and bruises with antiseptic. He checked her blood sugar and gave her a shot of penicillin. Alex had questioned him about her chances of contracting AIDS.

"Are you involved with anyone at the present time?"

She nodded.

"If your attacker is HIV–positive there is a chance you could become infected because your cut lip came in contact with his semen. You'll have to wait six months to be tested. Until then I strongly advise your partner use a condom during intercourse. You can't transmit the virus through kissing or oral sex unless his blood is exposed to your body fluids."

Alex just shook her head, running her fingers through her hair, and cried.

Kevin then informed her he had the ER nurse place a call to her physician concerning her diabetes and she would not be discharged until her sugar count was returned from the lab and assessed by her physician. He had sensed her obvious irritation and discomfort so before stepping out to await the lab results he offered her the use of a shower. She declined at first, but when Lisa explained she couldn't return home until morning, she reluctantly accepted. An ER nurse escorted her to the shower facility and furnished her with an array of toiletries, including a toothbrush, toothpaste, and mouthwash.

Lisa had used the time while Alex showered to call Renee. It was four–thirty A.M., but her family needed to know of her whereabouts.

Lisa recalled the shock and horror and sadness in her sister's voice as she explained what had happened. They both had hung up in tears.

When Lisa returned to the ER with coffee, Alex was sitting on the examining table dressed in a pair of blue jeans and a Tampa Bay Buccaneers tee shirt, her wet hair pulled back into a ponytail. Alex's shirt had been a gift from her older brother, a Tampa resident and diehard Bucs fan. She wondered sadly how Alex would break the news to her family. At that moment Lisa had hated herself more than ever, for not having the guts to tell her family about her own harrowing experience.

She handed her partner the steaming coffee, and Alex savored the warmth against her trembling hands.

"I made my gums bleed," Alex said, sipping the coffee, needing to vent her frustration. "I scrubbed so hard...but I couldn't get the taste out of my mouth." She choked back tears. "I can't deal with this."

"You will...in time," Lisa said for a lack of a better response. She, herself, remembered hurrying to the shower after Anderson had left her naked on her dorm–room floor. She had showered repeatedly. But she had not felt clean until Jim returned from Europe and made love to her. She had needed the assurance he still desired her.

Lisa sympathized with Alex, but more so she respected her. She understood Alex had wanted desperately to cleanse her mouth of the violation from the minute her attacker had fled but her instincts as a police officer had told her she would be destroying valuable evidence. It had been her only hope of fighting back, of avenging this repulsive act. Thus she had stomached the dirty taste of him on her teeth and tongue for four agonizing hours so the doctor could swab the "evidence" from inside her mouth. Lisa had washed the evidence from her body immediately afterward. She had chosen not to fight back. You were a coward, she had berated herself as she sat with her partner in the ER. That son of a bitch shattered your life, and you let him get away with it, scot–free.

"I'm dying to get these contacts out. My eyes are so sore," Alex said.

"I'll get you whatever you need for your lenses." Lisa anxiously gulped down her coffee. "You can stay at my house for as long as you want."

Kevin had returned to the room with two syringes in his hand, and Lisa recalled the disgusted, helpless look on Alex's face.

"C'mon," Alex said angrily. "You've already stuck a needle in each arm. What now? I want to get out of here."

The doctor became overtly disturbed. He set the syringes down on the counter and exhaled harshly. "Look, Alex, I got the lab results and talked with your doctor. Your glucose is out of control. You're nearing hyperglycemia. He ordered insulin and a sedative. I'm sorry, but you have to stay here. You have no choice."

His last remark must have shot through her wired mind like a bullet from her assailant's gun. She threw her coffee at his chest. He hollered and jerked backward as the hot liquid instantly soaked through his lab coat and shirt. Alex flew off the table, and Lisa jumped from the chair to restrain her. But before Lisa could pull her away, she violently grabbed the doctor's coat by the lapels. "Don't you dare tell me I have no choice!" she screamed, every last ounce of her suppressed anger exploding into a ballistic rage. "I can take care of myself. I don't need your insulin or your sedative. You got that!"

"It's okay. Take it easy," Lisa had said, wrestling her away from the doctor.

Alex sank to her knees and collapsed against the examining table. "This didn't happen to me..." she whispered, her body convulsing with sobs. "Tell me, please. It's all a nightmare, right?" She pressed her head against the side of the table and wept uncontrollably.

Kevin reached for the insulin and two sterilizing pads and ordered Lisa to hold her still. But Alex didn't resist, her anguish and soaring blood sugar weakening her to a state of sobbing oblivion. He injected the insulin into her left arm and quickly reached up for the sedative, repeating the process in her right arm. Together they lifted her up and laid her on the table, Kevin carefully removing her contact lenses from her overworked eyes and storing them away in sterile cylinders. They let her alone to cry herself into an induced sleep.

"She'll be out in a minute," he had said. "She's got to stay here until morning. It's vital she remain sedated for a few hours. I'm talking a possible life and death situation here."

"Let me ask you something, Kevin," Lisa said to him, after she was positive Alex had fallen asleep. "How many rape victims have you treated in your career?"

"Probably about the same as the number of medical–legals you've witnessed. Why do you ask?"

"You really have no clue?" Lisa's voice had been condescending. "You told Alex she had no choice about the injections. Just over four hours ago she had no choice whatsoever. Get it, Doc? I suggest you be a bit more compassionate and selective in what you say to the next victim who comes through here. And believe me there'll be another."

Kevin had stared at her for a long, hard moment. "I didn't realize…what I said. I was only thinking about her condition, the diabetes that is. It's been such a long night. Wow, I guess I deserved to wear the hot coffee. I feel terrible about this now. You guys are constantly in here with DUIs. How am I going to face her again?"

"I think Alex is going to feel badly about what she did, too, once the shock wears off."

Lisa remained with Alex for over an hour and a half, until almost six–thirty, intermittently dosing off herself. On her way out she informed the ER staff she was going to the police station to complete the report on the medical–legal exam and left the phone number there for someone to call her if need be. Kevin had advised her to return at nine A.M., explaining he would leave instructions with the day shift doctor to discharge Alex only if her blood–sugar count dropped below two hundred. If it had not she was to be admitted for a twenty–four observation.

Lisa lifted her head from the station desk and stared at the crime–report printouts, sniffling and nauseated.

"Hey, are you okay?"

Startled she shot upright and spun around in her seat. She exhaled in relief, seeing Greg Van Dien standing a few feet away. She quickly wiped away her tears. "You scared me to death. Yeah, I'm okay, considering."

Greg pulled up a chair and swung it around, sitting with his legs straddled around the back. "How's she doing? Is she at your place?"

"She's still in the ER. Her blood sugar was extremely high. She had to be sedated for a couple hours. I'm going to check on her in a half hour or so."

He shook his head in disgust. "This one's killing me. Alex is such a great person. So easygoing, and one real good cop."

Lisa choked back tears. "Yeah. Any luck at the house?"

"Some. CSU finished up about an hour ago so she's free to go back if she wants. We removed the cat. We picked up some hairs from the carpet, probably from the cat, or Alex's. We got the semen specimen from the bedroom and a partial sneaker print from the linoleum in the kitchen. We also lifted forty–one sets of fingerprints; however, I'm betting they're all Alex's since he was wearing gloves. The lock on the back door was forced open with a crowbar, and—"

"The lock," Lisa suddenly remembered. "I'd better call her landlord to have it replaced right away. I'm sorry, what were you saying?"

"We found a crumpled cash register receipt from Westfall Lawn and Garden Center under one of the kitchen chairs. Actually, Ted Peterson found it. It must have fallen out of the creep's pocket."

Lisa's eyes widened into saucers. "Peterson? What was *he* doing at her place?"

"He went right over after Chris called him. He said he wanted to help in any way possible."

Chris Wingate had called Ted Peterson to obtain permission for her to witness the medical–legal exam at the hospital. He and Dave

Romanovich had envisioned a conflict of interest, since Lisa was Alex's partner and friend, and some public defender jumping at the chance to use that conflict as grounds for dismissal of the evidence.

"Oh, really?" After his behavior on Monday, Lisa figured Peterson couldn't give a rat's ass about Alex. "What good was finding this register receipt?"

"Dale Ryzik works for Westfall Lawn and Garden. Alex's address was scribbled on the back."

"She was right then."

Greg rested his arms on the top of the backrest. "It sure looks that way. And we have probable cause to bring him in for questioning. I've filed an affidavit with Judge Conroy for warrants to search his house and car. They should be ready in two hours. But if this doesn't pan out I'm going to need you to furnish me with a list of every incident and arrest the two of you had since she's worked here, about nine months worth. I want you to highlight every incident where the person or persons displayed any kind of hostility toward Alex."

"No problem," she said.

Hostility. She had one immediate thought: Rick Stanton. Recalling the traffic stop on Mountain Gap Road and the confrontation in his office, Lisa had mistrusted Rick Stanton since he'd lied about his abusive attitude. But he had a problem with *her*, not Alex. She'd feared he'd hurt her sister because of his resentment, not her partner. He'd cut his date short with Renee last night at ten–fifteen. Plenty of time to prepare himself and drive up to the Heights by midnight. C'mon, she admonished herself, it couldn't be. Your sister is not dating a rapist. No way. You're being ridiculous. You've got not one ounce of proof and no probable cause for any legal recourse. Only a silly gut instinct, which amounts to nothing.

"The siren that scared the creep away," Greg commented, rising from the chair. "It was Dave and Chris responding to a burglary alarm at the Gems and Gold jewelry store downtown. A false alarm. False but fortunate for Alex. I guess someone answered her prayers."

"If it were only a half hour earlier."

"Yeah," Greg sadly acknowledged. "I'm going home for a quick breakfast and shower, then I'm going to talk to some of the neighbors, see if they heard or saw anyone suspicious. After that I'm picking up the warrants and heading straight for Westfall. I'll keep you posted."

She smiled appreciatively. "Thanks."

He went on his way, and Lisa made three quick calls before heading back to the emergency room. She phoned her sister, Jimmy, and Alex's landlord. None of the conversations had been easy; it took a lot to remain composed.

At the hospital Lisa spoke with the day–shift doctor first.

"Her blood sugar's down to one–seventy–five," he informed her. "I gave her her scheduled insulin injections this morning, and she ate a descent breakfast. She's free to go, but her condition is still touchy. Someone should keep an eye on her for a while, make sure she eats. She also needs to see her own medical doctor as soon as possible. Her insulin may have to be adjusted."

"She'll be in good hands." Lisa hesitated before entering the ER. She inhaled deeply, held it momentarily, then exhaled loudly. Slowly she opened the large metal door.

Alex was sitting in a chair, slouched back with her eyes closed.

"Hi," Lisa faintly announced.

Alex's eyes instantly opened, and she straightened in the seat. "Hi. Where've you been? Are you okay?"

"Am *I* okay? How 'bout yourself?"

"Can I go home now?"

"Whenever you're ready. Are you sure you want to go back?"

Alex stood, gathering up her purse. "I have to go back. I have to get on with my life. Could you do me one favor, though?"

"Anything."

"I need to get a new medical information tag at the pharmacy."

Lisa smiled warmly. "No problem."

Warily, Alex's eyes roamed around the living room. She stood inside the front doorway examining her home, appalled by the aftermath of the CSU's hunt for evidence. Black powder used for the fingerprint dustings covered every surface and nothing had been returned to its rightful position.

"You think they could have put just one thing back in its place," Alex said, tossing her purse onto the couch, anger in her voice.

She drew in a breath, mentally readying herself for the inspection. Exhaling she slowly started across the living room, her eyes zeroing in on the spot where her body had been slammed into the wall, her mind replaying the scene in slow motion. The mask, the gun, his merciless eyes flashed before her, and she immediately squeezed her eyes shut, forcing the visions into oblivion.

"I'm not going to run from this," she said with an agonizing determination, commanding her legs to move down the hallway. "Bear with me, please."

Lisa remained a watchful distance behind. She did not want to suffocate her. Alex needed to move at her own pace, make her own decisions.

The bathroom was first. Alex stood at the doorway, staring inside. Like the furniture in the living room, the faucet and vanity were covered with black powder. Her eyes skimmed past the shower stall, but she would not allow herself to visualize the image of her dead pet hanging by its neck. He's gone, she told herself, and you can't bring him back. Just remember the pleasant moments.

She continued down the hall to the bedroom.

"I need you for this one," she said, glancing back at Lisa.

With Lisa at her side, Alex hesitantly stepped into her room. She stood alongside the bed, her eyes fixed on the corner farthest from the door. She refused to look away as the scene came rushing back. She kept her feet firmly planted on the carpet and met it head–on.

She needed to accept it, to get on with the healing process and return to a normal life.

After staring at the spot, transfixed for a long, hard moment, Alex finally turned away and sat on the edge of the bed. "I have to face this," she tearfully acknowledged. "But how?"

Lisa sat down alongside her. "One day at a time."

"What do I do first?" She ran a trembling hand over the top of her hair, the back hanging in a ponytail, frizzy and uncombed. A million things ran through her mind: her family, Matt, work. The thought of confronting them, anyone, anything, everything, terrified her.

"I need a new lock on the door," Alex said, her thoughts reeling out of control. "I need a new badge. I have to clean up this place. I have to go to work—"

"Hold on," Lisa cut her off. "You need to rest. Don't worry about the mess in here. I took care of the lock. You'll get another badge, and *no* one is expecting you to work tonight."

"Why not? This is not going to change my life. And although I appreciate it, I don't need you to take care of me."

"You need to get yourself in order, emotionally and physically. You should only be concerned about your blood sugar right now." Lisa's tone became stern. "Whether you like it or not, the…this…has affected your health, and that should be your first priority."

Alex fought off the tears. She closed her eyes, hearing the word Lisa could not say. She nodded, helplessly accepting the reality of the situation. "You're right. I need to sort this out. I'm sorry for snapping at you."

"I understand. I don't know about you, but I could go for some coffee. I'll make some, if you'd like."

Alex nodded. "Let me get my contacts out and I need to take another shower…brush my teeth again."

Lisa understood that feeling of uncleanliness all too well. "Take as long as you want."

Alex got up from the bed to rummage through her drawers for clean clothes, and Lisa started for the kitchen.

"Lisa, wait," Alex called out, following her into the hallway. Lisa spun around.

"I need to ask you something. Could it have been Peterson? Pay back for rejecting him."

Lisa stared at her partner, taken aback. Could it have been? The eyes fit. A motive was clearly there. Lisa's thoughts immediately went back to the night before. Chris Wingate had called him at home about two–thirty to obtain permission for her to witness the medical–legal exam. Peterson had approved her presence in the ER without any reservations then hurried over to Alex's to see if he could help. Was he trying to have the evidence thrown out? Was he tampering with it? Did Peterson set up Dale Ryzik? Was he using the school incident as a cover for his own revenge? And then Lisa still had ill–at–ease feelings about Kyle Lawry and Rick Stanton. They too knew about the Ryziks and the arrest at the high school through the police press release and weekly newspaper log.

"Is that what you're thinking now?" Lisa asked, concerned. "Are you having doubts about Dale Ryzik?"

"No...not really. All I'm saying is more than one person had it out for me."

"What about Kyle?"

Alex slowly shook her head. "It was dark and his voice was muffled, but...it wasn't him. I think I would have...known if it was him." She became confused, overwhelmed. "He's got a small mole... It wasn't there..."

Lisa bit her lip. She didn't want to tell Alex about what had been found on her kitchen floor, or *who* had found it, until Greg was able to investigate further. But she could see Alex agonizing over the uncertainty of her assailant's identity. She deserved to know.

"Al, they found a register receipt with your address written on it. It was from the garden center where Dale Ryzik works. Greg is bringing him in for questioning and getting warrants to search his premise."

Alex's eyes flew open in shock. She quickly squeezed them shut, staving off another round of tears. The association of a real face with the ominous figure only made the haunting memories more repulsive. And as she pictured Dale Ryzik's seedy appearance at his brother's arraignment, a strong wave of nausea suddenly hit her.

"Oh God," she gasped, convulsively. "Oh God. Oh God. He touched me. He made me…"

She ran into the bathroom and dropped before the toilet, vomiting.

Detective Gregory Van Dien walked across the grounds of the Highlands High School athletic complex. Football stadium and track, baseball field, tennis and basketball courts, the complex sprawled across ten acres behind the school building and bordered the west side of Grove Street two blocks south of Alex's place.

The detective was heading for the parking lot adjacent to the football stadium in search of something, anything, that would shed additional light on the identity of Alex's attacker. The elderly woman who lived catty–cornered from the complex swore she saw a young man donned in dark clothing walking briskly across the lawn to the stadium lot about one A.M. The woman had been the only resident within a two–block radius who had seen—or was willing to admit seeing—someone peculiar at the time the police sirens had been blaring through the neighborhood.

For obvious reasons Greg had been ambiguous in his explanation to the neighbors about what had actually occurred about that time. He had simply stated a break–in had been reported in one of the houses along the street and the perpetrator fled the scene wearing blue jeans and a dark sweatshirt.

Reaching the edge of the stadium lot, Greg stood on the concrete curbing and scanned the expanse of asphalt. He looked up at the light standards and noticed none were located near the end of the lot adjacent to the backside of the bleachers. Probably the darkest part of the lot, he surmised, and the best place to park a getaway vehicle. He headed in that direction.

A garbage receptacle on the lawn near the edge of the pavement was overflowing with trash, and several discarded cans and bottles lay strewn across the grass. Nothing out of the ordinary. Typical refuse from the summertime athletes using the facilities. It had been worth a shot, he reasoned, turning back toward the street.

Out of the corner of his eye he caught sight of a small rectangular object lying on the pavement of the last parking stall. He immediately swung around to investigate. Squatting he observed a beat–up *Night Crew* cassette–tape case. He reached around for a handkerchief in his back pocket. This was not trash; it was someone's possession that had been dropped or had fallen out of a car. He lifted the case at the corners with the handkerchief and brought it up to his eyes to examine it more closely. The tape rattled inside the case, which further led him to believe it was left behind unintentionally.

Greg took the tape back to the unmarked state–police car parked along Grove Street and carefully placed it in a paper bag. He would send it along with the other evidence to the crime lab for analysis.

He jumped in the car and drove to Judge Conroy's office to pick up the search warrants and then back to the state–police barracks. From there he and four uniformed troopers headed out in two police cruisers to Dale Ryzik's place in Westfall Township.

Twenty minutes later they were bouncing down the narrow dirt road leading to the dilapidated trailer deep in the woods. Loners the Ryziks were. Loners and troublemakers. The most despicable of Highlands County's poor white trash, well known to local law officers. They had a rap sheet as long as a Texas mile.

Flanked by the brawny troopers, Detective Gregory Van Dien marched up the rickety steps of the trailer and pounded on the front door.

A thin, haggard man in his late twenties, his dark hair uncombed and his face unshaved, opened the door. "What the hell do you want?"

"Your ass, Ryzik." Greg yanked him outside by his filthy shirt and effortlessly tossed him down the steps onto the dirt.

"What's your problem?" Dale Ryzik sputtered.

"*My* problem?" Greg flew down the steps and pulled Ryzik to his feet. "*You've* got the problem. With women. Don't you, scumbag?"

"You ain't makin' no sense, Van Dien. Get the hell off my land!"

Greg motioned to two of the troopers. "Cuff him."

"No way!" Ryzik shouted, struggling to break free. "I ain't done nothing."

The troopers easily subdued him, handcuffing his wrists behind his back.

Greg removed the warrants from his pocket and held them before Ryzik's eyes. "This one's for your dumpy firetrap, and this one's for that piece of shit you call a car. *You're* going for a ride to the barracks, Daley boy. I got some questions for you."

"I ain't got no answers."

Greg seized his shirt. "You'd *better* have some answers, buddy. You're in deep shit."

"What the hell are you talkin' 'bout, man?" Ryzik pleaded, his voice mixed with anger and confusion. "You ain't makin' no sense."

"We need to discuss your problem with women."

"I ain't gone near her since I got outta prison. I swear."

"I'm not talking about your ex, Daley." Greg tightened the grip on Ryzik's shirt, pulling him closer to assert authority. "And you've outdone yourself this time, preying on one of *us*. Do you know how *much* that pisses me off?"

"Man, I got no idea what's goin' on. You gotta believe me!"

Greg pulled Ryzik's face inches before his, getting a whiff of the foul body odor. "What goes around, comes around, eh, buddy?"

"Huh?" But then he remembered the threat he had made to that female cop at Billy's arraignment. What the hell were the pigs trying to pin on him? "Hey, c'mon now. I didn't mean nothin' by it. I wasn't gonna do nothin' to her. I swear."

"Do nothing to who, Dale? Who are you talking about?"

"I don't know what you're getting at, man. You know who. That cop that did my brother in."

That's it, Daley boy, Greg inwardly encouraged, keep talking. Incriminate yourself. "No, what cop? You tell me."

"You know."

"No, I don't. You said her. I know two women cops. Which one are you talking about?"

"I already told you, the one who busted Billy. Griffin, man, that's her name. But I didn't mean nothin' by it. I swear."

"You've got a lot of explaining to do, Dale." Greg released his shirt and motioned the two troopers who had cuffed him. "Take him down to the barracks. I'll be down as soon as I get a look around here."

"You ain't gonna find nothin'," Ryzik shouted as he was being ushered into one of the police cruisers.

Greg called one of the troopers back.

"Notify the DA and public defenders' office that he's under suspicion and make arrangements with the hospital. We need a blood sample and to have him examined for signs of evidence. I'm looking for loose hairs that could be Alex's, and make sure they check his dick closely for fibers from her pants or saliva from her mouth. I don't think this dirt bag's showered in a week."

The trooper nodded in compliance and returned to the cruiser. Greg watched as they drove off down the dirt lane toward the highway.

He looked back at the two remaining troopers. "Turn that dump inside out. I'm going to search the car."

The troopers went inside the trailer, and Greg headed over to Dale Ryzik's beat–up Chevrolet, slipping the warrants back into his pocket.

He reached into another pocket and removed a sealed plastic bag containing a sterile pair of latex gloves. He snapped on the gloves and opened the car door on the driver's side, peering inside. Garbage was strewn everywhere: empty beer cans, fast food bags, crumpled cigarette packs, papers, clothing. He shook his head in disgust, his eyes immediately taking note of the cassette player under the dash. He pushed the front seat forward and began rummaging through the mess for tangible evidence. A DNA match between Ryzik's blood and the semen stains found on Alex's pants and carpeting, as well as the specimen swabbed from inside her mouth, would be enough for a conviction. But Greg wanted more. He wanted assurance the dirt bag wouldn't get away with this.

He began tossing aside piles of trash, tenaciously rooting through every inch of the car's interior, including the glove box. But he found nothing connected to the assault. Lastly he stuck his hand under the driver's seat, his fingers touching a hard, cold surface. He extracted the object.

Staring down at the small gray revolver, he ridiculed the dumb ass. "Bingo."

He transferred the gun to the cruiser, dropping it into an evidence bag. He made a mental note that the barrel needed to be analyzed for verification it was the same weapon that had been shoved into Alex's mouth.

Greg returned to the Chevy and continued probing under the front seat. He shook his head in disbelief, pulling out a black ski mask and a pair of black leather gloves. "That's it, Daley, hide everything under the seat, don't try to dump them off somewhere. Either you think *we're* that stupid, or *you're* the dumbest bastard alive."

Greg placed the mask and leather gloves in bags together with the revolver and went inside the trailer to inform the troopers the search was over. One of them had discovered a large plastic bag filled with cocaine duct–taped to the underside of the toilet–tank lid.

He had uncovered all the evidence he needed for a solid case against Ryzik—and a bonus drug collar. It would be a sure–fire conviction. And with his prior track record of violence against women and drug abuse, Dale Ryzik would be spending a much longer bout in prison this time around.

And your brother will be spending some time in the slammer as well, Daley boy, Greg inwardly mocked, for effecting your demise. You've both gone too far this time. When you prey on cops, you get burned. Burned big time.

Kyle Lawry paid the bartender at Vic's for a bottle of beer and got change for the pool table. He walked into the back room and set the drink on the edge of the felt surface. Dropping four quarters into the slot he began racking the balls. What a life, he thought. Saturday night and playing pool in a dive bar. Alone.

His mind drifted to thoughts of Alex and Ehrich.

"Up for a little competition?"

Kyle turned toward the voice. "Hey, Bri, missed you last night. Don't tell me you had a date?"

Brian Haney grunted, taking a swig of the beer he had purchased. "Yeah, right. I was working on my bus. I'm gettin' her all set for the Heritage Days weekend. I'm hauling the nerds from the band up to the fairgrounds."

"I'm not sure whose night sucked more. Yours or mine?"

"What'd *you* do? Spy on my boss gettin' it on with your ex again?"

Kyle did not respond to Brian's jab.

"What'd ya do?" Haney repeated.

"Same as I'm doin' now. Played some pool, drank myself into oblivion. Went home 'round ten–thirty, puked up my guts, and fell asleep on the couch."

Brian shook his head. "So you're through with her?"

Again, no reply from Kyle.

"You're through with her, right? I'm telling you, it's for the best. Let her go."

Kyle nodded slowly, cracking a slight grin, his thoughts elsewhere. "Yeah, I'm through with her," he said then mumbled under his breath. "For now."

Brian set his beer down and removed two cue sticks from the wall rack. He handed one to Kyle. "What's your pleasure?"

"Eight ball. Break the rack."

Brian bent over and drove the cue ball into the rack, sending the fifteen balls across the table. The six and eleven balls dropped into the two far pockets.

"Had a little excitement in the neighborhood last night so I heard," Kyle said, gulping down his beer.

Brian was hunched over, sighting the twelve–ball. "What kind of excitement?"

"A break–in of some sort. Some state–police detective was at my door this morning asking if I saw anyone suspicious in the neighborhood about one or so last night."

"Did you?"

Kyle spewed air through his lips. "Hell, no. I already told you I fell asleep before eleven."

Brian snorted. "First time something big happens on your street, and you sleep through it."

CHAPTER 12

Tainted Lust

Jim Ostler was assembling a salami and cheese sandwich when Lisa walked through the back door. Turning away from the kitchen counter he set the slices of meat down and immediately opened his arms to her.

"This has been one of the worst weekends of my life," Lisa muttered, her eyes brim with tears. She tossed her car keys onto the table and succumbed to his embrace, burying her face against his shoulder. The tears poured out.

"I'm beside myself over all this," Jim said tenderly, stroking her hair. "How's she doing?"

"She threw me out." Lisa lifted her head and let out a short, bitter laugh through her sobs. "She told me to go home and salvage what I had left of my weekend. She's doing...okay, now that she knows he's been arraigned and couldn't post bail. But he refused to be tested for AIDS, and that's bothering her, big time."

"Has he admitted anything?"

She shook her head, sniffling. "No way. He's saying he was set up." She looked past Jim's shoulders into the living room. "Are your parents at home?"

"No, they're gone to a flea market for the afternoon. It's okay, Lise, say whatever you're feeling. Talk to me. Get it out. I can only imagine how hard this has been for you."

"It isn't fair. You want to know how I'm feeling?" She pulled away abruptly. "I'm furious! Furious those no–good bastards did this! Alex saved my sorry ass. And what'd she get for it, huh? Where did it all go wrong? I don't…understand. I *hate* them! I *hate* this town! I *hate* what this place has become. No one's safe *anywhere* anymore."

Jim reached out and pulled her to him, steadying her against his body with his strong arms. "I know, baby, I know."

"And to add insult to injury," Lisa cried, lightly pounding her fist on Jim's shoulder, suppressing her need to punch something at full force, "she's got to face Billy Ryzik Tuesday night at the hearing and fess up to *her* behavior. But the worst part is going to be telling her family." Lisa paused, soundlessly acknowledging her inability to do that. "And telling Matt."

"Hey, if he's any kind of decent guy and really does have feelings for her, then he'd better damn well be understanding and supportive."

Lisa searched for the honesty of his last statement in his blue eyes. That was something *she* had sought to hear from him. "Would you feel the same way if it were me who was—"

"Lise, don't even say it. I don't know what I'd do. I can't even bear to think about someone hurting you in that way. I'd…I'd kill them."

She squeezed her eyes shut and a stream of tears ran down her cheeks. "Hold me, please. Don't let go."

His arms secured her against him. She rested her head on his shoulder and wept. I'm so sorry, Jimmy, she silently apologized. That's why I kept it to myself. I couldn't bear the thought of you suffering as a result of my stupidity. I couldn't bear the thought of my mother or father or sister or brother having to deal with such an atrocity.

"I'm here for you. I'll always be here for you," Jim whispered, his hand sliding under her chin. He gently lifted her face, sweeping his lips across her tear–streaked cheek and over her mouth, kissing her openly.

Lisa closed her eyes, yielding to his warm caress. She dropped her head back as his lips slowly trailed down her neck. "You feel so good," she sighed, guiltily desiring an escape, a release, from all the horror of the weekend. "Please don't stop. I need you so bad."

He reached down for her hand and quietly led her upstairs to his bedroom.

❧ ❧ ❧

"What a gorgeous day," Rick commented.

On the blanket next to him, Renee casually surveyed the crowd at the huge public pool at Swiftwater State Park.

Rick propped himself up on an elbow. "I like this place."

Renee nodded, her mind elsewhere.

"Is something wrong?" he asked. "Wasn't this what you wanted to do?"

She nodded again then realized what he had said. She looked over at him, embarrassed. "I'm sorry, Rick. This *is* what I wanted to do. I was thinking about something else. How are you feeling, anyway?"

"Fine. I was feeling much better yesterday morning. What'd you do after I dropped you off Friday night?"

"Sat on the porch with Lisa and Jim, that's all." Renee recalled the phone call Lisa had received from Alex while they had been lounging out in the muggy night air, and her mind began wandering back to the tragic events that had subsequently unfolded.

"I'm beginning to take this personally," Rick said, perplexed by her lack of interest. "Is it something I said or did? Are you sure you want to be here?"

She mulled over whether or not she should tell him what was engrossing her thoughts. "You're going to learn about it tomorrow when you get the police reports. So I might as well tell you. Lisa's partner, Alex, was attacked Friday night."

"Huh?" Rick immediately sat up. "B...by who?"

"Evidence points toward the Ryzik kid's older brother."

"You're kidding?"

"No, I'm *not* kidding. Do you think I'd *joke* about something like this?"

"No, of course not. What happened?"

Renee regurgitated what little details Lisa had disclosed to her over the course of the last thirty–eight hours, explaining that her sister had spent the entire weekend with Alex, and she had yet to see her for any concrete information. "I don't want to know the specifics. This is the most despicable thing that's happened in this town since...as long as I can remember. And I'm sick over it. Alex is one of the nicest persons I've ever met, and it's..." Renee's voice trailed off as she choked back from crying. "I'm sorry. Let's stop talking about it. Okay?"

Rick sat, speechless, lost in his own thoughts of Alex Griffin. She deserved what she got. He turned to Renee. "C'mon, let's go swimming, have some fun. It'll get your mind off everything."

She looked at him blankly but then smiled. "You're right. I shouldn't be putting a damper on our day." She removed the terry-cloth cover–up she wore over her swimsuit and rose to her feet.

Rick stood up slowly, his eyes appraising her figure, clad only in a white bikini. The contrast with her olive skin was enlivening, and he immediately fantasized about what was hidden beneath.

"Forgive me, but I have to say it," he mumbled, unable to peel his stare away from her. "You're doing something to me right now."

Renee boldly inspected his bare chest, not muscular by any standards, but nonetheless appealing. She allowed her eyes to drift lower, approving of his blue swim trunks and long legs. "You might be doing something to *me* right now. Ready for that swim?"

His smile was exuberant. "You bet."

They swam for over an hour and lay out on the blanket afterward for another hour, basking in the sun while conversing. They talked seriously about some national controversial issues and chatted lightly on trivial stuff: TV shows, sports, family, college stories. Renee took note he hadn't mentioned his mother. She asked him why.

"Like I told you before, she never had any time for me. No big deal."

But Renee sensed it *was* a big deal, bothersome enough that he chose not to discuss it. She felt oddly sorry he had divorced parents. *Her* upbringing could have been used as a textbook example. Her mother and father were both loving and supportive, all the while doing their best to mold her and her siblings into independent, wholesome adults.

"Whenever you're ready to leave," Renee said, pulling on her cover–up. "I'm famished. What exactly are you cooking for me?"

"Oh, no, no, no," he teased, slipping his shirt over his head. "A good chef never discloses his mastery until it's served. But you did say you liked fish, right?"

She laughed. "Yes."

It was close to four–thirty when they left the park. He dropped her off at her house to shower and change while he ran to the supermarket for some last–minute groceries.

An hour later Renee stood in the kitchen of his three–room apartment above Village Flower Shop, watching in awe as he assembled a seafood feast. She took it upon herself to set the table while he shuffled between the counter and refrigerator.

"This is a nice place," she commented, searching for his flatware.

He pointed to a drawer near the sink. "The rent was reasonable. I guess I was expecting city prices when I first came here. I'll give you country people that much: Your cost of living is much lower."

A few moments later Rick had Orange Roughy and stuffed potatoes baking in the oven. He went to the refrigerator and removed a head of lettuce, a few scallions, a tomato, cucumber, and stock of celery, and set them all on the cutting board alongside the sink. But before he began chopping up the vegetables for a tossed salad, he took out two stemmed glasses from the cabinet and went back to the refrigerator for a chilled bottle of Chardonnay.

He tilted the wine in her direction. "Can I interest you in some?"

"I'd love some."

He uncorked the bottle and filled each glass, handing one to her. "A toast. To us. And to many more toasts, I hope, in the future."

Renee raised her eyebrows curiously. "To us." She lightly clanked her glass against his. They sipped the wine together, Renee leaning back against the cabinets. Rick moved before her, setting his glass on the counter behind her.

"You're so incredibly beautiful," he whispered, abruptly sliding his hand around her neck, kissing her. He pulled away just as suddenly. "I didn't mean to be so brazen. I'm sorry."

She discarded her glass on the counter then raised her hand to his hair, pushing his eccentric bangs away from his eyes. "Why are you apologizing? Was I complaining?" Her hands slipped around his neck as his lips immediately returned to hers, his arms hastily wrapping around her back. In the heat and hurry of the moment, his left hand caught the edge of the glass on the counter directly behind her. It tipped forward, the wine spilling and instantly seeping across the back of her shirt.

She gasped and pitched forward, the cold, wet sensation sending a shiver up her spine. Looking back at the wine as it dripped down the cabinets and onto the linoleum, she laughed.

"Oh, man! I'm so sorry," he said. "I can't believe I did that. Your shirt…"

"Relax." She ignored the wetness on her back, pulling his face back to hers. "I'm not the least bit concerned about my shirt."

Their lips met for a third time, and the lust between them could not be stopped. Renee figured she was going to regret what she was about to do. She hardly knew this guy. Her sister despised him. But her hunger for the touch and feel of a man had gone unsatisfied for too long a time.

"Rick," she breathed, barely lifting her mouth from his, "are you feeling the same way I'm feeling?"

"Are you serious?" he muttered, his heart racing with exhilaration.

She met his eyes with a sinful gaze. "Oh, yeah."

They barely made it across the living room to the bedroom, entangled in a frenzied passion.

Afterward, lying naked with him on his bed, Renee reeled from the reality of what just had occurred. What she had initiated and allowed to happen.

She had made love to a stranger. And it had been the most reckless, almost painfully fulfilling, experience of her life. His mouth and hands had left no part of her body untouched, and he had fueled her lewd response with the most immodest, indecent utterances she had ever heard. He had devoured her, infiltrated her, brought her to the most intense pinnacle imaginable.

And she had done the same to him, seeing his face awry with pleasure, feeling his body shudder as he climaxed deep inside her, thrusting her buttocks off the bed and holding her pelvis against him for what seemed to be an eternity.

Rick propped himself up on an elbow, his free hand moving slowly across her abdomen, encircling her navel. She closed her eyes, ashamed of her promiscuity, but as his mouth returned to her breasts, his bangs erotically brushing over her skin ever so lightly, she encouraged him to manipulate her again by running her fingers through his hair, pressing his face against her flesh.

"What about dinner?" she breathed, feeling his hand on her inner thigh.

"Do you really care?"

He climbed over her, and she wrapped her legs around his hips, allowing him to enter her again, yielding her body and mind. The second crest was more stimulating, more dynamic, more explosive than the first.

After he dressed himself and went to the kitchen to salvage their dinner, Renee stood alone in his bedroom, staring at her nude reflection in the dresser mirror. As she surveyed her body she scolded herself for acting so sleazy, yet applauded herself for being so desirable. Either way she felt invigorated. She threw caution to the wind and loved every minute of it. Lisa would not have approved of any of this. But who cares? Lisa is never going to know about it.

"Hey, Rick," she hollered into the kitchen. "Got a shirt I could borrow? Since mine is soaked with wine."

"You bet," he yelled back. "Top dresser drawer on the left–hand side."

She slipped her panties, shorts, and bra back on and opened up the dresser drawer for a shirt. As she began rummaging through the clothes, she suddenly realized she had opened the right–hand drawer. "Don't know your left from your right, huh, Renee?" She started to push the drawer shut, but her eyes caught a glimpse of a dark object hidden beneath the pile of clothes. Curiously she lifted up the clothes for a closer look. She immediately wished she hadn't. Her mouth dropped open in horror, and her hand reflexively flew up to stifle any involuntary sound. There, concealed under a stack of shorts and sweat pants, lay a small, gray revolver.

"Holy…" she whispered, quickly covering it up and closing the drawer. "I didn't see that. No way."

She opened the left–hand drawer, removing a yellow shirt. As she pulled it on and combed her hair, Renee frantically searched for an explanation to her discovery, her sister's disturbing warning mentally resounding.

No way, Lisa, you're dead wrong. He's from the city, she reasoned. He probably needed a gun. After all, handguns *are* legal if properly registered. It must be registered, she convinced herself. Why wouldn't it be? Renee thought about Alex's masked assailant who had brandished a small revolver. No. No way, she admonished herself for even letting the notion cross her mind. The state police have found the weapon used in the assault. The state police have arrested the man who committed the act. So stop worrying about it. It's nothing. Purely a coincidence.

She squelched all of her sinister thoughts and defiantly joined him in the kitchen.

CHAPTER 13

Facing Reality

Alex winced under the man's hand tightly clamped over her mouth. She stared up at the intruder, filled with terror. His features were hidden behind a black ski mask, his hot breath sending shivers down her spine as he menacingly whispered in her ear, "It's pay back time."

Her mind raced wildly as she strove for a measure of control. Horror enveloped her as he straddled her waist, securing her arms against the bed. She whimpered like a child pleading not to be punished as he revealed a gun, shoving the barrel into her mouth, and squeezed the trigger. Blood gushed from her wound, while she struggled to survive. Her body lurched forward, laughter echoing in her brain. He fired the gun again…and again and again.

"No!"

Alex shot upright in bed, her deafening scream synchronized with the blaring buzz of her alarm clock. "Ohmygod," she gasped, disoriented, her sweat–soaked body trembling. Slowly reality returned to ease her whirling emotions. It was morning; a stream of bright sunshine warmed the room.

Her hand frantically searched to silence the alarm. She found the shut–off button and swung her legs over the side of the bed. Sitting there, idly, she absorbed a sense of safety in the silence of her bedroom.

She cursed herself for allowing the nightmare to materialize. "You're not going to wreak havoc on my life. No way." She stood from the bed and reached for her eyeglasses. Gathering clean underclothes from her dresser she dragged herself into the bathroom to begin another routine Monday. Today would be anything but routine.

An hour later Alex walked through the door of the police station, donned in her uniform and ready to begin the eight–to–four foot patrol.

Lisa was standing by the computer terminal, reading over the weekend reports. She set the papers on the desk. "Good morning."

Alex cleared her throat. "Morning," she replied, a touch of anxiety evident in her voice.

"How'd you do last night?"

Alex nodded slowly. "Okay."

"Are you sure you're ready to do this?"

"No. But I have to. I need to get my life back in order."

"I have some good news for you," Lisa said. She glanced over her shoulder, making sure the desk clerk was still in the men's room. "I called Kevin Holleran last night to see what could be done about getting an AIDS test on Ryzik."

"What'd you mean? You know he refused to be tested."

"Yeah, that's right, officially. This is strictly between you, Kevin, the lab tech—he's a good friend of Kevin's, and me. One of Ryzik's blood samples went to the crime lab; the other stayed at the hospital. I should be hearing from Kevin later this week."

Alex felt as if the world had been lifted off her shoulders. She breathed a sigh of relief. "Thank you so much. How'd you get Kevin to agree to it?"

"Let's just say he owed it to you."

"He owed it to me?"

"The coffee thing. He feels terrible about what he said to you."

Alex had forgotten about her ballistic behavior at the hospital. "*He* feels terrible? *I'm* the one who owes him an apology. He was only trying to do his job."

"Believe me, he understands. Listen, Peterson's got your new badge and name tag." Lisa motioned toward his closed office door. "He wants to see you before we head out."

Alex drew in a deep breath to mollify her absurd fear of him. So you rejected him, and he became angry over it. But he's not the man who terrorized you, she rationalized. That man is in the county jail, awaiting the crime–lab results and a preliminary hearing. You have nothing to be afraid of.

"Might as well get it over with." She paused, her eyes wandering nervously around the room. Finally she looked up at her partner. "This may sound silly, but… How does my face look? I'm talking about the bruises. Be honest with me."

"Why are you asking me that?"

"Because…" She warded off another tearful battle of her teetering emotions. "Because I hate looking like…this. It's one thing to know about it, but to see the proof…"

Lisa shook her head, that familiar ball of anger sickening her stomach. "Well…"

"I said be honest with me."

"You can't hide them. They'll heal in a few days. You have to give this time."

"Do I?" Alex shot back. "I swear I will not let this affect me!"

Fired by her determination to deny the painful truth, she hurried toward Peterson's office and knocked loudly on the door. Before she heard a response she opened the door and marched inside, leaving Lisa stunned by her outburst.

"You wanted to see me," Alex said. She inhaled deeply to settle her temper.

Ted Peterson stared up at her from behind his desk. He was taken aback by her abrupt entry, his mind completely blank.

He ascended from his seat, his eyes fixing on her bruises. "I…uh…have a new badge and tag for you." He moved around the desk, opening his arms to her. "Alex, I'm so sorry."

She immediately recoiled. "Don't touch me! Don't even come near me! Just give me my badge, okay?"

"I'm sorry…sit, please. We need to talk."

"About what?"

"About you…me…my behavior…what happened."

"Look, I don't want to talk about *any* of those things." She held out the palm of her hand. "My badge, please."

"I need to talk to you. Sit down."

"Don't tell me what to do!"

He expelled a huff of air, awkwardly running his hand over his face. "Is this what you want to do? Play hardball?"

"Excuse me?"

"Do you want to play hardball?"

Anger was building deep inside her. But she refused to lose control in his presence. "No," she replied instead, barely above a whisper.

"Then sit down, Officer Griffin. Whether you like it or not, I'm still your boss."

She glared into his dark eyes, a frightening chill spiraling down her spine.

"Please, sit."

She plopped down in the chair before his desk, and he returned to his seat.

"First," he said, fiddling with the paperwork at his fingertips. "I want to apologize about my behavior last Monday. I was totally out of line."

Alex stared at him coldly, unmoved by his atonement. "Fuck you."

His eyes widened with shock. He shook his head. "Okay. You win. And I deserved that." He reached inside his top drawer and removed a silver badge and nametag. He tossed them both across to the front edge of the desk. "There's your new badge, Officer Griffin. Get to work."

"Why did you go rushing over to my house when you were called Saturday morning?" she demanded.

"I…I wanted to help, to make it up to you for what I did."

"Save it!" She scooped up the shield and tag and was on her feet in a split–second, turning toward the door.

"Have you forgotten about the hearing tomorrow night?" he called to her.

She stopped dead in her tracks, spinning around to face him. "Why are you asking me such a stupid question?"

He sprang to his feet. "Because you can't go through with it. Let me make some phone calls, see if I could get it postponed, or better yet, get that asshole public defender to drop the complaint."

"Hold it a minute. Why *can't* I go through with this? I want this hearing over with and the facts out in the open."

"Because if you admit you roughed up the kid, it may cast some doubt about your demeanor."

Alex stared at her boss, appalled. "Are you saying that I *deserved* it?"

"N…no, Al. Talk to the DA about this. Has he met with you yet?"

She shook her head slightly. "He's waiting till the lab results are returned before he requests a preliminary hearing."

"How long till the results are back?"

"They promised Greg they'd have it all back by Friday. Look, I appreciate your concern, but I'm trying not to let this…affect me, especially not professionally. I have a job to do, and if it means owning up to a mistake then so be it. And whether or not I'm held responsible for my actions at the school, Billy Ryzik still has a preliminary hearing next Monday for the vandalism and assault on Lisa, and I'm going to have to testify then, anyhow. So what difference does it make? If you'll excuse me, I have to get to work."

She walked out of his office.

❧ ❧ ❧

Matt Ehrich called Brian Haney into the garage office, his voice fired with anger.

Brian cursed under his breath and sauntered into the office. "What's the problem?"

"What's the problem?" Matt grabbed a piece of paper from his cluttered desk and shoved it into Haney's chest. "This is the problem! It's the receipt from Mr. Parson's transmission job! Do you see that guarantee written on the bottom? Ninety days or ten thousand miles. Guess what? Mr. Parson called from Williamsport. His transmission blew *again*! He just picked up the car Saturday, Haney. What the hell did you do to it? Huh? I have to pay to have his car towed back here and rebuild the transmission again. That's time and money wasted!"

"Hey, c'mon, Matt," Brian sputtered. "I swear everything was okay when I took the car for a test drive."

Matt exhaled, contemplating a response to Haney's pathetic song and dance. "Maybe if you'd lay off the booze, you'd be able to concentrate more, instead of being hung over every goddamned morning. I don't want to see any of *these* cars back in here for a long time, buddy." He pointed to the three vehicles currently under repair. "Now go do what I pay you to do."

Brian whirled around and stormed out of the office, running headlong into Alex, nearly knocking her to the floor.

Startled she gasped, her hands grabbing onto his forearms to keep from falling. "You scared me to death. I'm sorry for barging in unannounced."

He pulled away from her, reeling backward into a wall shelf, sending an array of automobile parts crashing to the concrete floor. He scurried to retrieve them in stone silence, tossing them back onto the shelf haphazardly, all the while avoiding eye contact with her. He threw the last box onto the ledge and fled to the men's room.

"Wow, he's a little edgy today," Alex remarked.

"He's a born loser." Matt crumpled up the transmission receipt and flung it across the office. "And I just lost a ton of money on a job he botched up." He drew in a breath, simmering down, and turned his attention to her. A smile started to form but instantly disappeared at the sight of her injured face. "Al, what happened?"

She immediately lowered her eyes from his stare, self–conscious and mortified. Reluctantly she mumbled, "I had a rough one Friday night."

"What happened? Who did this to you?"

"Lisa and I were called to a bar fight up in Westfall. We got caught in the crossfire." She was disheartened by her ability to lie so easily. But this was not the time or place to tell him the truth. "I was wondering if you could come over tonight?"

He raised his eyebrows suggestively. "What time? I wanted badly to see you this weekend but with your work schedule and mine, it was impossible."

Alex staved off the nausea churning in her stomach. She'd been thankful his thriving business kept him away over the weekend; the mere thought of intimacy frightened her to death. She wanted to scream, viciously retaliate against someone for everything that had been taken from her. Confidence. Peace of mind. Sexual freedom.

She had to leave before she exploded into a violent rage.

"Anytime after seven is fine," she said hastily. "I've got to go. I have to meet Lisa."

She was gone before he could utter good–bye.

"You're my lawyer?"

Dale Ryzik murmured a profanity under his breath, glaring at the fortysomething woman who seated herself across from him in the interrogation room of the Highlands County Jail.

"Yes." She was not pleased by the tone of his voice. "I'm an assistant public defender for the county. I've been assigned to your case."

Ryzik slumped forward in his chair, shaking his head in sheer disbelief. "I'm accused of beatin' an' rapin' a *bitch* cop, and now I got a *bitch* lawyer to defend me. What the hell are you people tryin' to pull on me?"

"Mr. Ryzik, let's cut to the chase. First, don't you *ever* call me a bitch again. And second, you'd *better* start convincing me it wasn't you who assaulted Alexandra Griffin."

Ryzik did not respond to her statements.

"Did you hear me, mister?"

"Every fuckin' word."

"Lose the profanities," she warned, opening her briefcase and removing his file containing copies of the probable cause affidavit, police report, and emergency–room examination. "Do you understand the charges that have been filed against you, and why?"

He slammed his fist down onto the table. "The cops set me up, that's why. I'm tellin' ya, I swear on a bible, man, I was home Friday night. I wasn't nowhere near that cop's place. I *didn't* do it to her. I swear."

"Mr. Ryzik, don't play games with me. You threatened Alexandra Griffin at your brother's arraignment, you severely beat your ex–girlfriend three years ago, a receipt from your place of employment was found at the crime scene, and three pieces of crucial evidence, including the weapon, were found in your car. You expect me to believe you were set up? C'mon, now. Get real."

"What about the blood and hair samples?" Ryzik desperately pleaded. "I'm tellin' ya. They ain't gonna match..." He peered into the lawyer's dispassionate eyes. "You don't believe me. You're in on it, man. The pigs, all you hotshot lawyers. You're out to get my whole family. You hate us. Don't ya?" Infuriated he sprang to his feet, propelling his plastic chair backward. It toppled over, crashing to the floor.

A correctional officer on guard outside the room immediately responded to the racket. But the attorney waved him back into the corridor. "I'm fine," she told the officer, looking up at Ryzik, her glare hardening by the second. "Sit down, now, you prick! I have a lot to discuss with you. Whether you want to hear it or not."

Dumbfounded he stood speechless.

She rose from her chair, waving an extended index finger in his face. "I can play your game, buddy, if you want. Now you can either sit down or go to hell. I don't give a shit either way. The choice is yours."

Dale Ryzik yanked the chair upright and angrily deposited himself into the seat. "I got *nothin'* to discuss with you."

The woman huffed, inflamed by his smug attitude. She settled in her seat and folded her arms on the table before her. "Tell me. Did it make you feel like a hero? Putting that cop in her place after what she did to your baby brother."

"I didn't do nothin' to her! I don't know what you're talkin' 'bout."

"Then would you be so inclined to answer a few questions?"

"What?"

"Do you have a cassette player in your car?"

"Yeah. So?"

"What do you think of the rock group, *Night Crew*?"

"What are ya gettin' at, lady?"

"Answer my question, please," she said sternly.

"I hate 'em."

"So you don't own any *Night Crew* tapes?"

"Not a one. What the hell does that got to do with me sittin' here? Huh, Ms. Public Defender?"

She ignored him as she began skimming through the reports she had scrutinized earlier. Her attention focused on the physical evidence obtained from the victim: the semen specimens and strands of loose hair. A positive DNA match with his blood sample would place him at the scene of the crime without any reasonable doubt. A trial would be nothing short of a waste of taxpayers' money. A negative DNA match would send the prosecution's case into a tailspin. With conflicting scientific results the theory of a setup could not be ignored. And with all the enemies a police officer procures over the course of a career, the notion would not seem that farfetched.

"Mr. Ryzik," she began a rehearsed sermon, "the results from the state–police crime lab will be returned on Friday. Until then there's not much I can do for you. I suggest you use the time wisely. You have been formally charged with eleven different offenses, excluding the cocaine charges. If the prosecution agrees you may want to consider plea bargaining."

Dale Ryzik leaned across the table, piercing her with his dark, angry eyes. "No…fuckin'…way," he spat, pronouncing each word slowly, firmly. "I ain't gonna plea bargain ov'r somethin' I didn't do."

Alex completed her nightly jog around the school track. The run had soothed her, freed her mind of troubling thoughts. It was a temporary escape from reality.

On her return home she passed by Kyle's house. He was not at home. In two days Kyle would be picking up the latest edition of the *Highlands Journal* and piecing together what had occurred in her bedroom three nights earlier. She wondered how low–keyed and objective Rick Stanton would be this time around.

Lisa had advised she take it one day at time. And right now she had to prepare herself for Matt. She forced her trepidations over Kyle from her mind.

Once inside, Alex checked her blood sugar and drank some juice, half–expecting Oscar to scamper out from under a chair or around a corner. The stillness was heart wrenching.

At seven–fifteen she injected her slow–release insulin then began pacing from room to room, anxious for Matt's arrival. The uncertainty of his reaction to what she had to tell him had been driving her crazy for the past three days. But she needed the time to reorganize her life, to deal with the ugly reality alone.

She hadn't broken the news to anyone in her family yet but decided on calling only her sister in West Virginia. Her brother would be on the next plane out of Tampa to personally see that Ryzik got the proper punishment, and she didn't want to upset her parents, especially not her father, with his diabetes. Dale Ryzik had wreaked havoc on *her* physical vulnerability. She would not allow him to do the same to her father.

At seven–thirty the knock came at the door. Alex hesitated, collecting her thoughts. The dreaded moment had arrived. Her feelings for Matt were genuine, and she didn't want to lose him. She was excitedly discovering he was the man she had always dreamed of, and her passion for him was like none she had ever known before. She prayed he felt the same way about her; the road ahead would be nothing like the carefree, romantic path they had been steaming down prior to Friday.

Drawing in a deep breath Alex greeted Matt at the door. "Hi, c'mon in."

"Hi." His smile stretched from ear to ear as he opened the screen door and entered the living room. "I missed you." He rolled his hands over her shoulders, his lips nearing hers.

"Matt, no." She turned her head to the side, and he quickly pulled away, stunned and disheartened.

"What's wrong? What'd I do?"

She forced a meek smile. "Nothing. You haven't done anything wrong. We need to talk, that's all. It's serious."

His heart sank; she was going to dump him. "It's about us. Isn't it?"

She nodded. "But it's not what you're thinking. Have a seat. This is going to hit you like a ton of bricks."

Troubled he settled on the couch, and she sat alongside him a foot or so away. She cleared her throat, swallowing dryly, and glanced into his apprehensive eyes. Her own eyes brimmed with tears as she looked away. "I didn't get these bruises from breaking up a bar fight," she said, struggling to control her voice. She slouched forward, momentarily burying her face in her hands. When she finally lifted her head she stared at the television set across the room and slowly muttered, "I was ambushed b…by Dale Ryzik Friday night when I got home. He was wearing a ski mask. I d…didn't know it was him, but they found… He…he…sexually assaulted me."

Silence filled the room as Matt absorbed her words.

"What?" he whispered, his face twisted with disbelief. "You were, I…I…don't…" He sat idly, lost for words, a burning heat numbing his body.

"It was pay back for what I did to his brother at the school," Alex said bitterly, her eyes still trained on the television. "He broke in here while I was working and waited for me. He…had a gun. He killed Oscar…"

Overwhelmed Matt's mind raced thoughtlessly. "But you're a cop. I don't understand how he could do this?"

"You think this sort of thing can't happen to cops?" she lashed out, angrily turning to face him. "I thought you knew me. Do you think I'm invincible? Is this what everyone's going to think, huh? That because I'm a cop I could have prevented it. He had a gun, and I couldn't get to *mine*." She jumped up from the couch and hurried into the kitchen. Leaning against the sink with her back to the swinging door, she began sobbing.

Matt followed her but kept his distance. "Al, please. I'm sorry. I didn't mean it that way. I didn't know what I was saying. I don't know *what* to say. I can't believe you're telling me this. I have no idea what happened. Please, don't shut me out. Let me hold you. I want to hold you."

He gently touched her shoulder. She would not turn around.

"Al, please. This can't be happening to us. Don't shut me out like this. Please, let me hold you."

She wiped the tears from her eyes and slowly turned to him, longing for the sense of security the warmth and strength of his body provided as he crushed her to him. He cradled her head against his shoulder, and she wrapped her arms around his waist, holding onto him selfishly.

"I'm sorry I snapped at you. You have no idea what I went through this weekend."

"You're absolutely right," he said tenderly, brushing his chin against her hair. "I have *no* idea what you went through, but I don't want it to affect our relationship. If you want to tell me what happened I swear I'll never bring it up again."

She cleared her throat and acknowledged his request with a slight nod. Taking his hand she led him back into the living room. Together they sat on the couch, and Alex stammered over the details of the assault and the aftermath.

"They found the gun and the mask and the gloves in his car." With the terrifying events still vivid in her mind, she could no longer keep her composure intact.

Matt immediately pulled her into his arms, cradling her sobbing, trembling body. "I'm so sorry, Alex. I wish I could do...something."

"Just don't lose faith in me," she muttered. "I'm going to need a little time."

He squeezed her against him. "Nothing's going to take you from me. Do you understand that? Nothing. You're the best thing that's happened to me." He lifted her chin, gazing into her blue eyes overflowing with pain and tears.

"How could anyone do this to you?" he agonized in a silent rage, watery–eyed, as he slowly raised a hand to caress her discolored cheek. He softly kissed her bruise. "I won't let you go through this alone. Whatever it takes I'll be there for you."

CHAPTER 14

Secret Revelation

"You know what, ladies and gentlemen?" the police–union solicitor said to the nine men and two women of the Highlands Regional Police Board seated at the long, narrow table inside the council chambers of the Mountain View Borough Building. "Mr. Adebratt and his client, William Ryzik, are absolutely correct. No one should be subjected to excessive force or brutalized while being placed under arrest. No one, that is, who recognizes the authority of the police officer placing him or her under arrest."

The solicitor paced before the table. A court reporter punched the keys of her stenotype as he spoke. "But Mr. Adebratt didn't tell you *why* Mr. Ryzik and Officer Griffin ended up in the predicament you heard him describe. Without the cold, hard facts, ladies and gentlemen, I too would believe Officer Griffin overstepped her bounds and abused her authority. But Mr. Adebratt didn't mention Mr. Ryzik was initially placed under arrest by Officer Maselli." He turned and gestured toward Lisa, who sat clad in her uniform behind the small table where he and Alex were stationed. "And Mr. Ryzik overtly resisted. In fact, he not only resisted, he knocked Officer Maselli to the floor, physically assaulted her, and accosted her with a switchblade knife, cutting her arm. Blatantly he defied the orders and actions of a duly sworn police officer. Ladies and gentlemen, the only thing on William Ryzik's mind was to get away, at any cost, because he had two hundred grams of coke in his pocket. He assaulted Officer Maselli for the sole purpose of getting his hands on her weapon—his ticket to freedom. In doing so he escalated the vandalism charges into charges of resisting arrest and aggravated assault on a police officer. And what Officer Griffin saw when she went to assist her partner was William Ryzik on top of Officer Maselli, a knife in one hand and his other hand reaching for her holster. She was bleeding from the cut he had inflicted seconds before."

The solicitor stopped midway along the table, his eyes scanning and making contact with each member of the board. "Now, ladies and gentlemen, I want you to put yourselves in the shoes of these two officers and listen carefully to what occurred in the early morning hours of Sunday, July 6, in the first–floor corridor of Highlands High School."

First Lisa, then Alex, was called to the table to describe the events. As Alex sat before the board explaining her actions, she forced herself to make eye contact with Billy Ryzik, deliberately holding his stone–faced gaze until he looked away in annoyance.

"Thank you, Officer Griffin," the chairman of the police board acknowledged upon the conclusion of her testimony. "Mr. Adebratt, do you have any comments or questions for either Officers Maselli or Griffin?"

Adebratt, Ryzik's court–appointed attorney, stood up. "Yes, I do. But first I'd like to remind the board the guilt or innocence of my client is not the issue of this hearing and everything these two police officers described may or may *not* be true…"

The police solicitor was immediately on his feet. "May I please interject?"

"Go ahead," the chairman directed.

"Mr. Adebratt, are you calling these officers liars?"

"No—"

"Perhaps you didn't see the scar on Officer Maselli's arm. Would that be proof enough your client, in fact, cut her the way she described?"

"That's not the issue of this hearing."

"The hell it isn't! It all plays into Officer Griffin's frame of mind that night. It's the *reason* she acted the way she did."

"Okay, gentlemen, enough," the chairman interjected. "Mr. Adebratt, you had some questions for the officers?"

"I have a few questions for Officer Griffin, if I may?"

"Go ahead."

"Officer Griffin, it *is* correct then, as I gathered from your testimony, that my client did *not* physically resist you when you placed him under arrest."

Alex nodded once. "Yes, that's correct."

"And how long have you been working in law enforcement? Two, three years?"

"Six years."

"Six years," Adebratt repeated, raising his eyebrows, feigning admiration. "And in those six years no other person you've encountered had used foul language or made lewd remarks to you?"

"No, that's incorrect."

"So you're saying you're used to hearing that kind of language on the job?"

"Yes."

"What made *my* client's remarks, quote–unquote, get to you?"

Adebratt was toying with her emotions. But she would not allow him to bait her. Her eyes again fixed on William Ryzik as she spoke. "He didn't just *taunt* me with his filthy mouth. Like I said before he threatened me. He said I was going to pay for it." She paused momentarily, to draw in a deep breath. An eerie stillness gripped the council chambers as she continued to stare down Ryzik, garbed in his prison clothing and flanked by correctional officers only a few yards to her right. She assumed everyone in the room knew his brother had made good on that threat, the bruises on her face undeniable proof. Uninhibited she resumed her response. "He was intentionally provoking me, trying to stall for time. Foremost on my mind was the condition of my partner. I didn't know how severe her wound was, and I needed to subdue him so I could help her. And when I found the coke on him, his attitude got worse."

"Uh–huh," he mumbled, unimpressed, returning to his seat. "I have no further questions."

"Thank you, Mr. Adebratt. Officer Griffin, you may return to your seat," the chairman said, turning to the police solicitor. "Would you like to wrap this up?"

"By all means." He rose from his chair to address the board one last time. "Ladies and gentlemen, you've heard the testimony. The decision is yours. But might I remind you Officer Griffin is a six–year veteran of law enforcement with a flawless record. Look at her. She's five–feet–four and weighs a hundred and twenty pounds. Does she look like someone who makes a career out of roughing up people without just cause? Clearly, ladies and gentlemen, William Ryzik effected his questionable treatment. And, in conclusion, the constitution of the Commonwealth of Pennsylvania empowers police officers to use whatever reasonable nondeadly force they believe necessary to make an arrest and to protect themselves and the public from bodily harm while making the arrest."

"Chief Peterson," the chairman spoke. "You've read the reports. The board would like your consideration on this matter."

Ted Peterson stood from his position at the far right corner of the board's table. "Ladies and gentlemen of the board," he began. "Something went terribly wrong that night at the high school, and I feel Officer Maselli is fortunate to be alive. Officers are expected to be fully aware of the situation they're facing and perhaps this was not the case that evening. However, Officer Griffin should be commended for the manner in which she subdued Mr. Ryzik. She kept her cool for the most part and successfully talked him into relinquishing the weapon without a need for deadly force. I feel an officer must have control over his or her emotions at all times, but in light of the circumstances surrounding this case, I feel Officer Griffin was not acting with any malicious intent."

"Thank you," the chairman replied then addressed the remainder of the board. "Any further questions?"

There were none.

"Fine. We're going to excuse ourselves for a half hour then return with a decision. There's coffee in the lobby if anyone would like some."

"Told you Peterson would stick up for you," Lisa said to Alex, leaning forward to talk into her ear.

"Lucky me," Alex retorted with sarcasm. "He only did it to cover his guilty ass."

At nine–thirty P.M., forty minutes after the break, the board members returned and quietly seated themselves at the table.

"If I can have everyone's attention, please," the chairman beseeched. "It's been a long night, and we're anxious to get this problem resolved. After careful deliberation based on the testimony we heard this evening, we have decided unanimously to instruct Highlands Regional Police Chief, Ted Peterson, to verbally reprimand Officer Griffin for her actions against William Ryzik the morning of July 6 at Highlands High School."

The police solicitor turned and winked at Alex. Smiling with relief she mouthed him a thank you.

Flabbergasted, Adebratt was on his feet. "That's it? A verbal reprimand? That's a bunch of bull."

"I'm sorry, but that's the board's decision," the chairman replied.

"What a crock! I insist the board make Officer Griffin publicly apologize to my client for her actions."

The chairman had about all he could take of Adebratt. The response to this humiliating, unfeeling request belonged to Alex Griffin. "Mr. Adebratt, the board is not going to make Officer Griffin do anything. But I'll be kind enough to ask her." He looked over at Alex. "How 'bout it, Officer Griffin? Would you care to apologize to Mr. Ryzik for your actions?"

Alex turned to confront the younger Ryzik, but she directed her reply to his attorney. "Is your client willing to apologize to Officer Maselli for what he did to her?"

"That's not the issue."

"You're wrong. That's the entire issue. Sir, as far as I'm concerned, your client can go to hell."

After the hearing Lisa bought Alex a coffee and drove to the top of Seneca Cliff. Still clad in uniforms minus their duty belts and weapons, they sat on a large boulder near the fence at the edge, sipping their drinks in silence. The town below basked in the moonlight of the clear summer night and at first glance it was difficult to determine where the stars ended and the twinkling streetlights began.

"This is an awesome spot," Alex said. "You could do some serious soul searching up here."

"Among other things."

Alex looked over at her partner, catching the sinful smirk on Lisa's face. "Yeah? Ever done it on a rock?"

Lisa nearly inhaled a mouthful of coffee. "Here?"

"Anywhere?"

"No. Why, did you?"

"Yeah."

Lisa could not contain her laughter. "Really? How?"

"Let your imagine run wild."

Their merriment faded into a contented silence. They sat with their feet propped up on the rock, listening to the sounds of nocturnal insects.

Alex finally ended the stillness. "Thank you for everything you've done for me these last few days. You don't know how much I needed your support."

"Al, I wish it was all a bad dream."

"Me, too." She peered inside her paper cup, lost in deep thought, swirling the last of the coffee around the bottom. "I hated having to tell my sister. We almost got into an argument over the phone. She wants me to quit my job and move down near her."

"Is that what you want to do?"

Alex looked over at Lisa and slowly shook her head. "No. I want to stay here. I don't want to run from it, and I don't want to lose Matt. He's so right for me. I've never felt this way with any other guy. This is the one. I know it is. I just hope this...doesn't destroy our relationship." Her eyes burned with pressing tears. "No way..." She cleared her throat, warding off another emotional outburst. "I'm not going to cry. I promised myself I would stop doing this."

"There's nothing wrong with crying. Let it out if you have to."

"I hate this! I hate losing control of my emotions."

"It's only a suggestion, but you might want to consider talking to someone at the Women's Resource Center."

"Deja vu." Alex wiped away the few tears that had managed to evade her determination to remain composed. "That sounded like one of our standard how–to–console–the–victim lines. Thanks, Officer Maselli, but no thanks. I'll deal with this by myself."

"You don't have to. You're not alone. Believe me when I say this, I know what you're going through."

Bitterness marred Alex's laughter. "I'm sorry, Lisa, but *how* could you possibly know what I'm going through, huh? Has someone ever...forced you?"

Lisa crushed her empty coffee cup between her hands and met her partner's resentful eyes straight on. "Yes."

Alex's eyes narrowed with bewilderment. Her mouth fell open, but words eluded her.

"You heard right. I said yes. It happened to me…in college." After a five–year suppression it was all coming out—every terrifying, degrading moment. Lisa needed to rid herself of the secret, and Alex needed to know. "By a black football player who I foolishly invited up to my room after a frat party. I had been drinking, and it was the stupidest thing anyone could have ever done—right up there at the top of the list of 'don'ts' every female student is warned about at freshman orientation. And I paid for it, big time. He terrorized me with a knife, and he raped me repeatedly for over an hour. He violated my entire body, and he played with my mind…" Lisa paused to draw in a breath. "And…I never told a soul about it. But I'm telling *you* because I don't want you to make the same mistake I did. You're not alone, Alex, and you need to get your anger and frustration out. Don't bottle it up like I did for all these years."

Stunned, Alex stared at her partner, faltering to form a comprehensible sentence. "I had…no idea… Ohmygod… Did you…know him? What about Jimmy?"

Lisa nervously played with the crushed cup. She was amazed by her ability to recount the events of that horrifying night with little hesitation. In fact she felt strangely relieved to have openly acknowledged it. "Jimmy was in Europe that semester. Did I know the guy? Yes and no. He was someone I saw a lot in the gym during basketball practice. I thought he was a nice guy, good looking, and we happened to run into one another at the party. I had a few beers too many and got way too friendly with him. He offered to walk me home. It was in February and it was snowing like crazy that night. My roommate was gone home for the weekend, so like a real fool I invited him up to my room. I let myself believe I didn't have any intention of sleeping with him, but deep down, I did. For the thrill of it. To realize a fantasy of mine. I was tanked, and I let him kiss me. I let him partially undress me. But then he got rough, and I didn't want to do it anymore. You know the rest. I had to make myself believe, for my sanity, that I didn't lead him on, that he had every intention of hurting me from the get–go."

"Lisa...oh, Lisa," Alex muttered sadly, numbed. "Why didn't you report it?"

"I didn't want my family to have to suffer through a legal battle, not with my mom dying of cancer at the time. And I didn't want Jimmy to find out. C'mon, I was going to betray him. How do you think he'd react to that? And the bottom line: It would have been his word against mine. He slapped me around some, but I had no recognizable bruises. He would have said I was a willing participant, and face it, he was a football player with an athletic scholarship. Football rakes in much more money than women's basketball. Who would they have believed? I was in a no–win situation."

Alex angrily crumpled her cup and flung it over the edge of the cliff. "Fuck them all."

"That's the first time I've ever seen you litter."

"Lisa, I can't believe what you're telling me. I would've never known. How'd you deal with it?"

"I'm *still* dealing with it. You'll always have to deal with it. I have nightmares every now and again. And every once in a while something'll happen that'll make the memories come back—vividly. Like every time I have to witness a medical–legal, the fiasco at the school."

"The knife," Alex muttered. "You told me afterward you hated knives more than anything else. I had no idea."

"*No* one has any idea. I trust everything I'm telling you will stay between us."

Alex gave her word. "Can I ask you a serious question?"

"Sure."

"How did you feel about being with Jimmy after—?"

"Honestly? I needed to control that initial sexual encounter after, and I needed to be in the driver's seat, mentally, when it came to sex for a long time afterward. I had to remind myself every time Jimmy touched me, it was because he loved me and I was consenting to it. I still have to remind myself of that on occasion. But not so much anymore. I have to admit sex with Jimmy is…incredible."

"Quite proud of that, aren't you?" Alex kidded, laughing heartily.

Their laughter intensified to a pinnacle of tears and, suddenly, they were both crying, joy intermingling with sorrow.

"I owe you my life, Al. My screw up at the school caused all this. You didn't deserve any of this. None of it."

"Would you shut up about that already? I'm getting sick of hearing it."

CHAPTER 15

Dirty Deeds

Lisa walked through the front entrance of Ostler Hardware. Jim was behind the sales counter.

"Hi," he said. "Have you seen the *Journal* yet?"

"Yeah. We both saw it."

"And?"

"And I hate to admit it, but Rick Stanton is a professional, tactful writer."

Jim agreed. "Strictly facts, no indication whatsoever of who it was. I was shocked at how many different offenses this creep was charged with."

"The DA will only concentrate on the more serious ones."

"How much prison time are we talking about?" Jim asked curiously.

"Twenty years max," Lisa replied.

"He should be hanged."

"Let's change the subject, okay? It's not my favorite topic right now."

"What's going on with Renee and this Stanton guy?" he then asked.

Lisa shrugged. "I have no idea. She's been very elusive the last few days. She *is* meeting him tonight to go over his responsibilities for the train excursions."

Jim slouched over the counter, his fingers fiddling with the ring of keys attached to her duty belt. "What's happening in town this morning? It's been slow in here."

"Nothing much," she said as the phone rang.

Jim stepped away to answer it. "Ostler's."

Lisa leaned against a shelf, listening as he spoke. She was expecting a hardware–related conversation, but, as the discussion went on, it became apparent it had nothing to do with business, at least not the hardware business.

"Sure," Jim said. "I'll be here tomorrow. About what time?...One–thirty is fine."

"Who was that?" Lisa asked as soon as he hung up.

"Paula Sedlak."

"Now what?"

"She wanted to know if I could translate that e–mail letter into German for her tomorrow afternoon?"

Lisa snickered. "Oh, yeah? I'm glad it's my day off."

"Are you jealous?"

"No."

"Yes, you are. I can tell by the tone of your voice."

"I'm a little suspicious of her intentions, that's all. She had a thing for you in high school."

He laughed. "High school was a long time ago. You're being silly."

Lisa shot him a look of annoyance, which only fueled his laughter. He walked around the counter and down the main aisle to the front door, turning the sign in the window from "Open" to "Closed."

"What are you doing? Your father will kill you."

"Relax." He grabbed a piece of paper and wrote out the words 'Be Right Back.' Taping it alongside the 'Closed' sign, he locked the deadbolt.

"C'mon." He walked into the stockroom, out of sight.

"Whatever you're planning, forget it," she warned, following him. "I'm on duty."

Jim smiled. He removed the portable police–radio from her back pocket and set it on a shelf. "I have this thing about cops." He slid his arms around her waist, backing her against the wall. "I have this fantasy about a tall female cop going down on me while in uniform."

"You're crazy..." Lisa blurted out, giggling, as his lips covered hers, her arms slipping around his neck.

His hand inched upward, undoing the top button of her uniform.

"Whoa." She pulled her face from his. "No, really. I can't."

"Why not?" he breathed, lowering his lips, brushing them ever so lightly across her neck, teasingly.

Lisa closed her eyes. "Jimmy, c'mon. I'm working. We can't do this."

"Why not?" he persisted, weakening her opposition with his mouth, his words.

"I have to meet Alex in a half hour."

His fingers undid the next button. "Yeah, so? That's plenty of time."

"C'mon, cut it out," she groaned, but as he unfastened the remaining buttons, she only continued to verbally protest his advances, less than seriously. "Stop it. I can get into a lot of trouble."

He ignored her objections. "*Fräulein Polizistin, Sie sind in Schwierigkeiten schon.*"

Lisa rolled her eyes. She could only imagine what he had rattled off in German. "*Je suis désolé, le monsieur,*" she retorted in French, playing his game. "*Je ne parle pas l'allemand.*"

Smiling and laughing he maneuvered his hand around her back, unhooking her bra. Not only was he fluent in German but in French as well. "*Mademoiselle officier de police, vous avez déjà des ennuis.*"

She did not fully understand his remark, but the words she'd managed to comprehend were enough to produce a wicked grin. "*Je ai*?"

"*Oui.*"

"Okay then," she giggled. "Just don't tell on me."

"I never kiss and tell, *officier*." He freed her breasts, and twisted himself downward. Slowly, seductively, his tongue encircled each breast, lingering, persisting. She ran her hands through his hair, completely surrendering her resistance.

"I shouldn't be letting you do this," she breathed, resting her head against the wall.

"Not many cops are as unscrupulous as you, or as sexy." His lips and tongue were now caressing her neck, slowly moving upward, over her ear, her cheek, finally meeting her waiting lips. He nudged his body against hers. "How was that for kissing and not telling?"

Her hands trailed down his back, working their way around to his crotch as the police radio ungratefully cracked to life. "Highlands three–one," the male dispatcher called over the airwaves. "Acknowledge."

Panic washed over her as she lunged for the radio, fumbling to operate the portable device.

"Comm Center, three–one."

"Report of a ten–eighty–eight, public nuisance, at the convenience store on Sixth Street. What's your ten–twenty and ten–twenty–six?"

"Three hundred block of Main. ETA five minutes."

"Ten–four, three–one. Respond. Three–two's ten–seventeen."

"Ten–four, Comm Center." She set the radio back down and turned to Jim. "C'mon, hook my bra. I knew this was going to happen."

Jim hastily helped her repair her uniform. She grabbed her radio and planted a quick kiss on his lips. "I owe you one. See ya later."

"Be careful, please," he shouted as she hurried for the door. When she was gone he huffed in frustration. "Damn, I need a cold shower."

❦ ❦ ❦

The doorbell rang.

Dishtowel in hand, Lisa stuck her head around the corner into the foyer. Rick Stanton stood before the screen door, dressed in shorts and a golf shirt. He was several minutes early, and Renee was still upstairs, drying her hair. A shrewd smirk spread across her face.

Let's see how observant you are, she declared inwardly. You think you're so smart, but I bet I could fool you. Lisa tossed the towel on the kitchen counter, inspected her attire—baggy gray shorts and a plain green tee shirt—and walked into the foyer.

"Hi," she said, unlatching the door.

"Hi." He entered the house, smiling, his eyes anxiously canvassing the downstairs. "Anyone else at home?"

Lisa stifled her urge to laugh. "My sister's upstairs. Why?"

"What about your father or brother?"

She eyed him quizzically. "They're out. Why?"

"So it's safe to do this." Swiftly his hand slid around her neck, and his lips smothered a long, fiery kiss on hers.

Lisa had no time to stop him. Thrown off guard, she kissed him back.

Finally he pulled away. "Are you ready to give me that train tour now?"

She stared into his dark eyes at a loss for words. It was the first time since her junior year in high school someone other than Jim had kissed her that way. And it was so…erotic. She immediately dismissed the thought and grinned. I got you now, Stanton.

She burst into laughter. "No, not really. But Renee will be down in a few minutes."

The color drained from his face, his mouth agape. It was then he noticed the fading scar on her arm. His emotions raced wildly.

"Was it all you imagined?" she razzed.

He distanced himself from her, his nostrils flaring murderously. "Wipe that wily smile off your face."

"C'mon now, Ricky, you have to admit it was a classic. I got you good."

He cursed under his breath, chiding himself for falling for her trickery. He curled his upper lip and sneered. "You tongued me good. You're dying for it, aren't you? You want me bad."

"Yeah, right. In your dreams."

"I don't know about that. If that was acting I'd love to experience the real thing."

"I bet you would." Here we go again, she thought. She couldn't help egging on his crudeness. There was something about him that fanned her fire, and she couldn't let it go. I can take whatever you dish out, buddy, and I'm waiting for you to overstep your bounds. Then you'll learn the hard way you're playing in the wrong league.

"Don't flatter yourself."

"If I recall correctly it was *you* who had lustful thoughts of *me*. I distinctly remember some tactless, disrespectful statements emanating from your mouth that fateful night. Didn't anybody ever tell you you're not supposed to mouth off to the law?"

He let out a contemptuous laugh. "You love being a bitch, don't you?"

She pursed her lips, pretending to ponder his insulting inquisition. Grinning smartly she neared him, her face inches from his. "Immensely."

She left him in the foyer as she ascended the stairs to call her sister.

His heart pounded through his shirt, his lips scorched from the blazing kiss. He whisked his bangs back, calming himself.

A few minutes later Lisa returned from upstairs.

"Renee will be down shortly," she informed him then added with civility, "Seriously, Rick, I'm sorry for fooling you and for taunting you. But despite your beliefs Renee and I are a lot alike. I wanted to prove it to you. No hard feelings?" She extended her hand.

Rick stared at her, perplexed, uneasy. "You blow my mind."

"Why's that?" She studied his face, instantly detecting his nervousness. "Look, we got off on the wrong foot. I'm sorry about the DUI, but I was only doing my job. You have to understand that. Don't be so nervous around me. I hate that. I'm not any different from my sister, and really, I'm not a bitch. I'm willing to forget about our rocky start and try again. How 'bout it?" She again gestured for a handshake. "Hi, I'm Lisa Maselli. And you're?"

His eyes narrowed with distrust. "What are you trying to pull?"

"Nothing."

Renee had warned him he best get along with her sister. He supposed now was as good a time to start as any. Hesitantly he accepted her hand, shaking his head in astonishment. "Okay, we'll start over. I'm Rick Stanton."

"Nice to meet you, Rick. What do you do for a living?"

"I'm the editor of the *Highlands Journal.* What about you?"

"I'm a police officer."

"Don't take this personally," he said, "but I don't like women cops."

"That's too bad. A lot of people think female cops are easier to deal with than males. We don't like physical confrontation. We're much better at solving problems by communication than by force. Ever been stopped by a female officer before, Rick?"

He smiled; she was playing this game to show her humanity. He'd play along, give her the impression he was being sincere. "Yeah, by two actually. I was…speeding…and drinking."

"And how'd they treat you? Were they polite and professional?"

He glanced away, his smile growing. "I guess they were as polite as could be expected. But I let my male ego get in the way of my better judgment."

She motioned him into the living room. He settled on the couch, and Lisa plopped down in a chair. "You know, Rick, I shouldn't tell you this, because it makes me look bad, but I was going to let you go.

Since you were new to the area and a not–so–bad–looking guy, I was going to give you a break. My partner, however, caught on to you."

Lisa watched his reaction to her statement blaming Alex for their ill–fated encounter. He nervously brushed his bangs away from his eyes, his feet rhythmically tapping the carpet. Lisa was heeding the very warning she had given him exactly one week ago about catching more flies with honey than with vinegar. I want you to like me, Rick Stanton. I want to learn more about you. I want to delve into your past and dig up something that'll prove your evil intentions.

"How's your partner doing?" Rick finally spoke.

"She's got a strong head on her shoulders. And while I'm thinking about it, the piece you printed in today's paper was written as tactfully as it could have been. I think your professionalism as an editor and writer is nothing short of admirable."

"Like I told you last week it's my style. I don't let personal feelings cloud my objectivity."

"And what are your personal feelings?

He shot her an alarming look. "About what?"

"I don't know. About Alex, about me."

Rick tossed his bangs to the side and began tapping his fingertips together, anxiously. Where was Renee?

"C'mon, be honest," Lisa persisted. "We had an unfortunate run–in, but that doesn't mean we have to be enemies. I've already told you what *I* was thinking that night."

"Yeah, you have." His eyes connected with hers. "Okay, here goes. I'm a male chauvinist pig. I don't like women with authority, and I felt like a peon, an idiot—"

His confession was interrupted by Renee's appearance from upstairs.

"Hi. Sorry I took so long. Ready to go?"

"Yes." He quickly stood from the couch and brushed past Lisa. "Nice talking to you."

A huge smile brightened Renee's face. "It's about time."

Lisa stood from the chair, her eyes trained on Rick. "Yeah. We had an interesting conversation."

⁂

Rick drove his Nissan along the dirt alley that paralleled the railroad spur line behind the bureau building. The five passenger coaches of the Highlands Scenic and Historic Railroad sat on the spur near the train station when not in use.

"You can park anywhere," Renee said.

He silenced the engine midway down the line of coaches, and they slid out of the car.

"We'll be working on the John Schmidt." Renee strutted in the direction of the train's fourth coach. "I'll show you that one."

Rick strolled behind her, surveying in awe the five colossal rail cars identically painted in an eye–catching green, brown, and black scheme. He assumed the green and brown represented the lumber industry, with the black depicting the bygone coal–mining operations.

"Pretty impressive, huh?" She stopped in front of the black metal steps at the far end of the fourth coach. "You'll be standing here, punching tickets and helping people climb aboard."

"That's it?"

"That's basically it. During the excursion keep your eyes on the passengers, make sure no one gets unruly and help them cross from coach–to–coach if they want to walk around."

"Sounds easy enough. I think I can handle that."

She giggled. "Wait till you see your outfit."

"Outfit?" His eyebrows came together in a quandary. "What kind of outfit?"

"Your conductor's uniform. The black–and–brass of the HS&HR, an authentic remake of 1920s railroad attire."

"You've got to be kidding."

"It's not that bad. C'mon, I'll show you the inside."

He watched as she grabbed onto the side rails and pulled herself up onto the first step, turning the latch and opening the brown metal door. A mischievous grin lit up his face as she climbed the remaining two steps to the vestibule, her red shorts riding up her long, dark legs.

I've got it bad for her.

I've got it bad for her sister. He could no longer deny it. He hated her attitude. He hated her authority. But he wanted her in the worst way.

His thoughts returned to the foyer where he had kissed her. Where she had kissed *him*. It was no prank. She wanted him as much as he wanted her.

I'm going to get you, he vowed and boarded the coach behind Renee.

"I'm truly impressed," he commented, examining the vintage interior through the vestibule windows. "These cars are awesome."

Renee pulled out a set of keys from her pocket and unlocked the door to the passenger compartment. She swung the door inward, and they walked inside. "This is it. The John Schmidt, named for the first mayor of Mountain View."

"Is that a fact?" He leisurely started down the aisle, nonchalantly glancing around. "Who were the other four coaches named for?" he asked, plopping down in a seat.

"Let's see." She moved down the aisle, leaning against the back of the seat across from him. "In order as they're lined on the tracks, the first coach is named for Joseph Haul, the man who headed the construction of the railroad."

He listened as she spoke, gazing up at her, never once removing his stare from her deep brown eyes.

Renee started to giggle. He couldn't care less about the coaches' names. She could see it in his devilish eyes. She continued nonetheless.

"The next one is named for Sheldon Runther, president of the county's first coal company. Then there's the Phillip Ikel, founder of the Highlands Lumber Company. Then there's this coach, and the last one—"

Rick reached over for her hand, guiding her onto his lap.

She smiled as he slipped his arms around her waist.

"The last one is named after—"

"I don't care if it was named after Richard Nixon." His hand ascended to the nape of her neck, pulling her face to his. He kissed her.

"I'm beginning to take a liking to this town," he said, his lips fondling the smooth skin under her ear. "Especially the recreation and vacation bureau. You know how to welcome newcomers."

"That's one thing about us rural people." Her fingers began playing with his hair, pushing aside his bangs. "We're real hospitable."

"That you are." His mouth returned to hers, kissing her fully.

When they ended the embrace, Renee looked into his dark eyes, speculating over what was hidden behind them. The thought of the revolver concealed under his clothing troubled her. She needed to know more about him. She needed him to acknowledge ownership of the gun. But she could not confront him with what she had discovered since she had no business opening the wrong drawer. Perhaps a discussion about the police would prompt a mention of his gun.

"Have you and Lisa called a truce?"

"I think so. Your sister was cordial to me and honest. I think we can treat one another civilly."

"Good. Lisa's a terrific person, like me. But she's more aggressive than me, and I hate having that gun in the house."

"I'm sure she's careful about it. You never know when, or if, you might need it someday. I have a gun. It's a twenty–two–caliber revolver. My father gave it to me when I moved out on my own. It's been in his family for years."

Renee faked astonishment, breathed a sigh of relief. "Where do you keep it?"

"In my dresser. Where I can get at it quickly if need be."

He detected a bit of apprehension, fright, in her eyes. He playfully twirled her hair through his fingers. "Relax. It's registered. If you don't believe me you can have your sister check it out."

"Why would I not believe you?" she said, rather insulted. "That's another thing about us country people. Unlike you flatlanders we're not so mistrustful of others."

Everyone, that was, except her sister.

"Hey, man, what's up?" Kyle looked up at Brian Haney, involved under the hood of his school bus. Brian was standing on a stepladder, bent over the engine.

"Got a problem with my oil–sending unit," Brian grumbled, tossing a worn oil filter onto his gravel driveway. "I got Heritage Days in less than two weeks, and state–police inspections start next month. Last thing I need is this baby to fail inspection. I need that extra cash from the district."

"Yeah, for that drinkin' and smokin' habit of yours."

Brian mumbled an expletive then said, "Make yourself useful. Hand me a wrench."

Kyle searched through the pile of tools strewn across the driveway for a wrench.

"What's been happenin'?" Brian made small talk but kept his attention focused on repairing the oil unit. "See that thing in the paper about Dale Ryzik? Think it was your ex he put it to?"

Kyle handed the wrench up to his buddy. "I glanced at the article but didn't put much thought to it."

Brian continued fiddling with the bus. "I say it was her. Didn't you tell me something about a state–police detective askin' questions on Saturday morning?"

"Yeah."

"Much too coincidental. Same time and all." Brian snorted. "And the way I look at it: If it was her, if she couldn't even defend herself without that big, bad gun, then maybe she deserved it."

Kyle simply shook his head, deliberately keeping quiet.

"You know," Brian went on. "If they hadn't have found that stuff in Ryzik's car, I'd be a little scared if I were you."

"Huh?" The color drained from Lawry's face.

"With the way you'd been actin' lately, spying on her and gettin' all bent outta shape 'cause she's sleeping with the pretty boy, it sort of seems like you had a motive to knock her around some."

In an instant Kyle had Brian on the ground, yanking him off the stepladder in one swift jerk. "What the hell kind of friend are you? Why don't you pick up the phone and call the goddamned cops and sing away. How could you be accusing me of such things?"

Brian wrestled himself away and jumped to his feet. "Hey, c'mon now, Kyle, I was bustin' your ass. I wasn't serious, man."

"You got a problem," Kyle said with disgust, waving an index finger in his buddy's face.

Brian shrugged and resumed work on the bus. With his face obscured from Lawry's line of sight, he muttered inaudibly, "And you got an even bigger problem, ol' buddy."

CHAPTER 16

The Last Laugh

"Be right there," Jim called out from the stockroom, hearing the door open. He deposited a box into the garbage and walked out to the retail floor.

"Paula, hi."

"Hi. Are you busy?"

"No. I'm ready to translate. I brought my German dictionary with me this morning."

"I appreciate this." Paula Sedlak discarded her umbrella near the sales counter and reached inside her nylon carry–bag. She handed him the letter and a notebook.

He walked around the cash register and extracted the dictionary from a shelf underneath. "What lousy weather, huh? It's supposed to rain all day."

She leaned over the counter. "Yeah."

His eyes traveled downward; the low–cut blouse she wore left little to the imagination. He picked up a pencil and unfolded the letter, skimming the context.

"Easy enough," he said, and without delay, began to write.

Paula watched as he translated the English words into German with little difficulty, occasionally flipping through the dictionary. "I'm impressed. I hated high–school French."

He paused, glancing up to observe her overzealous grin. "I hated geometry and trig."

"But we both liked music."

"I guess we did. But that was a long time ago."

"It's sort of funny. We couldn't wait to get out of that school, and now we're going back to it."

"Yeah, but this time they're paying us."

They both laughed at his remark.

"Are you looking forward to that seminar next Thursday?" Paula asked.

"The seminar, yes. The long ride to and from, no."

"It won't be so bad," she hinted. "We could reminisce some more."

"I think we covered everything at the clambake."

"I'm sure we'll dig up something else. Did you study overseas?"

He nodded. "In France and Germany for a semester. It was a wonderful experience. It helped my language skills tremendously."

"My friend told me quite a few stories about her homeland. It sounds like a great place to visit."

"It's beautiful. The people are fantastic. In what part of Germany does your friend live?"

"Some small village near the Czech Republic. I think it's called Zwickau."

"Zwickau? In Saxony?" Jim's eyes narrowed with doubt.

Paula felt her face flush with embarrassment. "What's Saxony?" she asked sheepishly.

"It's a German state. Zwickau is not a small village. It's an industrial city with over 100,000 people. It was a part of East Germany before reunification."

Paula tried to camouflage her blunder by giggling dimwittedly. "I'm such a geographic illiterate. I must have mistaken Zwickau for a village that sounds similar."

"Must have." Jim returned his attention to the letter and, continuing the translation, began to wonder if Lisa's suspicions of Paula were valid. Perhaps this whole exchange–student story was nothing but a farce—an excuse to befriend him. Whatever Paula's intentions were, Jim decided, he would deal with them on his own. He did not want to create an animosity between Lisa and Paula. He would be seeing Paula daily at the school come September, and he didn't want Lisa to be uncomfortable with his new job.

No sooner than his thoughts of Lisa had materialized, the door opened and she walked into the store, propping her wet umbrella against the outer edge of the doorframe.

"I hate this weather," she grumbled. "Thank goodness it's my day off. I wouldn't want to be out walking the streets in this monsoon."

Paula swung around and greeted Lisa with a huge, almost phony, smile. "Gosh, I haven't seen you in years. How've you been?"

"I've been well," Lisa replied cordially. "Welcome back to the area."

"Thanks. It's good to be back."

"By the way," Lisa commented nonchalantly. "Is that your car parked right out front?"

"Yeah, why?"

"You're parked alongside the fire hydrant. I wouldn't want to see you get a ticket. The fine is pretty hefty."

Jim shot Lisa a censurable look. "Officer Maselli, I thought today was your day off?"

"It is." Lisa joined him behind the counter. "I thought I'd give her fair warning."

"No, no, thank you," Paula insisted. "I didn't see the hydrant. Let me go move the car."

"No need to." Jim prodded the last period onto the paper. "I'm finished with the letter. Totally *auf Deutsch gescrieben*, written in German. I bet your friend will be surprised to see this in her native language."

"Yeah." Paula packed up her notebook and reached for her umbrella. "I hope she doesn't e–mail me back in German."

"If she does, print it out and bring it on by. Unless, of course, you're afraid there may be something personal in it."

"Not at all." Paula's eyes skimmed past Lisa's to meet his directly. "I'll be in touch before next Thursday. Thanks again. It was nice seeing you, Lisa."

She disappeared into the rainy afternoon.

"What an airhead," Lisa remarked. "How could anybody *not* see that fire hydrant?"

"And you couldn't wait to tell her about it, could you?"

"Hey, I was being nice."

Jim glared at her dubiously. "Yeah, right."

Lisa mocked his sarcasm. "Sorry I missed her arrival, but I was on the phone with Alex. She got the results from the AIDS test on Ryzik."

His scornful look immediately vanished. "And?"

"Negative. He's clean."

Jim sighed heavily. "What a relief."

"You're not kidding." Lisa looked away abruptly, remembering how she had wrongfully rummaged through the North Penn University athletic files one Saturday evening in search of Calvin Anderson's medical records. She needed to know his HIV status, and she had been willing to risk expulsion to ascertain that information. It was a matter of life or death. If Anderson had been HIV–positive her life would have been over. She had nothing to lose by sneaking into the athletic director's office.

"How'd Paula's little German lesson go?" Lisa ridiculed, snapping back to the present.

"Fine. It was no big deal." He didn't mention the mistake about the *city* of Zwickau. But he did make a mental note to check through his atlas at home to verify if any *village* names were spelled similarly to Zwickau. His instincts told him there were none. And by the look Paula had flashed him before leaving, he was convinced she had an interest in him—an interest that went way beyond his language ability.

It was only a ten–minute drive to Matt's house, but it seemed like an eternity to Alex. She sat in bumper–to–bumper traffic along Main Street. The route provided the only means of travel from the Heights section of the borough to the North End, and traffic snarls were common occurrences in downtown Mountain View during the summer months—a nightmare for local folks.

Alex listened to a soft–rock song on the FM station of her Tracker while the wipers rhythmically swept the rain from the windshield.

It had been a long day. She spent the entire morning at the doctor's office, three–quarters of it in the waiting room. After the exam and blood sugar test, her doctor had rambled on about how the trauma from the assault had substantially altered her blood sugar and the necessity to increase her daily insulin intake. That was the last thing Alex had wanted to hear. After all these years she had finally managed to gain control of her disease. Now, with the modification of insulin, a stricter diet would be imperative. She left the doctor's angry and helplessly frustrated. Dale Ryzik was continuing to control her.

It was shortly past noon when Kevin Holleran had phoned with the results of Ryzik's AIDS test. She was moping around the house, feeling depressed, listening to the steady pelting of the rain against the windows.

The call could not have come at a better time. It was a glimmer of hope her life could somehow return to normalcy. Mildly rejuvenated, Alex had spent the remainder of the gloomy day shopping at the plaza south of town. She bought a pair of shoes, silver hoop–earrings, a country music CD, and the latest issue of a women's magazine.

She had returned to Mountain View about five, stopping for a burger and fries at the fast–food franchise. If she had to start a restrictive diet, it would be tomorrow. Today she was throwing caution to the wind.

Alex had then gone for her run—in the pouring rain. She donned her dirtiest pair of sneakers and a water–repellent jogging suit and sloshed a mile around the high–school track.

"Rot in hell, Dale Ryzik," she had rebelliously shouted to the sky, letting the cold rain flood her face and soak her hair. "I'm going to have the last laugh."

Invigorated by her foolish behavior Alex had decided to visit Matt. She returned home and quickly checked her blood sugar, showered, and changed into blue jeans and a three–button tee.

Alex shifted the Tracker into first as she started through the last Main Street light, then into second, finally making it through the congestion. Three minutes later she parked in Matt's driveway and headed up the porch steps.

When he opened the door Alex greeted him with the most exuberant smile he had seen on her face since they had made love at Lake Iroquois. As he welcomed her in and closed the door behind them, her arms wrapped around his neck. She backed him against the door.

Pleasantly surprised by her aggressiveness, yet apprehensive about touching her, Matt just smiled. "To what do I owe this wonderful reception?"

"One word. Negative." And before he could respond in any way to her thrilling news, her lips found his for a long, open kiss.

"I'm so happy for you…" Matt finally managed to mutter. "For us."

They settled on the couch. Matt held her in his arms as she summarized the visit to her doctor, explaining how the stress from the attack had affected her condition and the need for an insulin adjustment. He could see the anger in her eyes, hear it in her voice.

"But I'll be damned if I let him keep on taking from me," she spit out the words with a bitter determination. "He took away my peace of mind, and now he's trying to take my well–being. I won't let him take any more."

Matt played with her hair, comforting her, allowing her to vent her rage and control the conversation. He understood she was suffering through the period of acute reaction to the attack. He also learned from the book on violent crime he checked out of the library Tuesday morning the healing process took months, sometimes years, and the psychological scars would remain with her forever.

He was willing to accept the ramifications of this tragedy. This was the woman with whom he wanted to spend the rest of life, and he was not about to give up on her. This was not going to be a mistake, like Cindy had been.

From the inception of their first date his feelings had been forthright. Alex possessed all the qualities he desired in a woman: independence yet some vulnerability, outgoingness, honesty, adventure, sexual confidence. And, on top of it all, she was the sexiest, most irresistible woman he'd ever laid eyes on—with or without glasses, in or out of a police uniform. Her warm smile, those stunning blue eyes and that long, wild hair drove him absolutely crazy. He was aching to touch her, feel her, make love to her. But he wouldn't assert any pressure. That decision belonged solely to her.

"Would you like to go hiking Sunday afternoon?" he asked, resting his chin on the top of her head and taking her hand, intertwining their fingers. "And afterward there's this great little Italian restaurant just over the New York border. It's only about a forty–five minute drive."

Alex tipped her head to the side to see his face in full view. "Sounds like fun. I'd love to."

Matt gazed into her eyes, wanting desperately to kiss her again.

Alex immediately sensed his fear. She raised her hand, slipping it around his neck. "Please, don't be afraid. It's okay."

Slowly his lips were drawn to hers, and as she responded to his touch, he deepened the tender, unhurried kiss.

"Al, you're incredible," he whispered. "I…love you. I want to be with you for the rest of my life."

Tears stung her eyes. "Matt, I…I feel the same way about you. I just can't make any promises, about being…intimate. I need a little time."

"Hey, hey." His index finger crossed her lips. "It doesn't matter to me. I'll wait as long as it takes. The most important thing to me right now is being with you, being *there* for you."

She buried her face against the soft cotton of his shirt. "I need you so much."

He gently stroked her hair, his stomach knotting with rage. How *dare* you do this to her, Ryzik! How *dare* you take from *me*!

CHAPTER 17

Tailspin

Detective Gregory Van Dien sat at his desk inside the state–police barracks staring down in shock at the crime–lab results. The twenty–page report had arrived a half hour ago from the laboratory in Harrisburg.

"This is it, Daley Boy," he had scoffed. But as he began carefully reading through the evidence analysis, sheer disbelief and an acute numbness quickly paralyzed his thoughts, his ability to concentrate.

Fifty–five pieces of evidence and forty–three sets of fingerprints taken from Ryzik and the scene of the crime had been examined. Most contained nothing of relevance that could be used in the case. The majority of the fingerprints lifted from the scene belonged to Alex, matched against her prints on file with the Automated Fingerprint Identification System where all police officers' prints were stored. One set found on the register receipt belonged to Ted Peterson, also matched against the AFIS file. None were Ryzik's. That was expected, Van Dien rationalized. Several hairs found in the carpeting matched Alex's and her cat's. Some hairs were unmatched. Some were blond, a few dark brown. None matched Ryzik's DNA makeup. Okay, no big deal, Van Dien thought. They weren't relying heavily on the hair, either.

The bomb had exploded when he read, and reread three times, the reports on the key pieces of evidence, those needed for the sure–fire conviction.

His mind *had* to be playing tricks on him. He read them again for a fifth time.

07–12–01A–E3: navy–blue police–uniform pants. *Dried blood-stain on upper right leg matches victim's from sample (Env10). Dried semen stains on upper and lower left leg DO NOT match suspect's DNA composition from blood sample (E20). Semen specimen on pants match those found on carpeting (E53) and on oral swab from victim's mouth (Env9).*

07–12–01A–E14: taped loose hairs found on victim's right hand. *These hairs DO NOT match victim's hair (Env5); DO NOT match suspect's hair (E21). Hair color is dark brown. Origin is from the pubic region.*

07–12–01A–E22: twenty–two–caliber revolver. *Six slugs found in tumbler. No identifiable prints found. Dried saliva found on barrel matches victim's DNA from blood sample (Env10).*

07–12–01A–E23: black knit ski mask. *Several loose hairs found on inner side of mask match hairs found on victim's right hand (E14); DO NOT match suspect's hair (E21). Hair color is dark brown. Origin is from the cranial region.*

07–12–01A–E25: audiocassette tape (Night Crew–Full Moon). *One identifiable set of prints found on tape case match one set of prints found on cash register receipt (E55); DO NOT match suspect's prints (P43).*

07–12–01A–E55: cash register receipt (Westfall Lawn & Garden Center). *Two identifiable sets of prints found on receipt. One set match prints found on audiocassette tape (E25); DO NOT match suspect's prints (P43). Second set, identified through AFIS (File #45732), match those of Theodore Peterson, age 45, Chief of Police, Highlands Regional Police Department, Mountain View, Pennsylvania.*

Greg slammed his fist on the desk. Defeated he buried his head in his hands. It was back to square one. How was he supposed to break this news to Alex? Any sense of security, peace of mind, she had felt from Dale Ryzik's arrest would be viciously shattered.

Her attacker was out there—somewhere, free as a bird, riveted by his ingenious plot and mocking the police this very moment. Greg was sure of it.

"I've got to find this piece of trash," he hissed hell–bent, snatching up the phone.

"I got here as soon as I could." Lisa stepped into Greg's office, her words tinged with concern. "What's up?"

"Sit down." Greg Van Dien motioned to the chair before his desk. "I've got bad news."

She sat on the edge of the chair. "What?"

He leaned back in his seat, directing his gaze away from her. "The DA had no choice but to drop all but the drug charges against Dale Ryzik. We have no solid ground to stand on." He turned to face her. "It wasn't him, Lisa. Nothing matched. The semen, the prints, the hairs, nothing."

"Shit," she whispered, numb.

"There's no doubt in my mind at this point that he was set up. The gun found in his car *was* the weapon. Alex's saliva was positively ID'd on the barrel. The prints on the receipt aren't his, but they match a set of prints found on the cassette tape. Whoever did this parked his car in the school lot and somehow, unknowingly, lost the tape. It was someone who knew what happened at the school with Alex and Billy Ryzik. Someone with dark brown hair who knew what the Ryziks were like. And someone who had it out for her big time. Someone who conspired the whole hideous act and plotted to set up Dale Ryzik. I need your help, Lisa. I need it bad. Who else had a motive to do this?"

Lisa was beside herself. She shook her head helplessly, visualizing Alex's reaction to this inconceivable discovery. Her stomach clenched and fluttered.

Two names immediately came to mind: Kyle Lawry, Ted Peterson. But one reason prevented her from acknowledging her suspicions: She would not betray her partner's trust.

Anxiously she replied, "Don't you think you should be asking Alex that?"

"No! Don't tell me this!" Alex sank onto the couch in her living room, shaking her head wildly.

Lisa dropped alongside her. "Greg's going to do everything he can to find this guy."

"Al, I swear I will," Greg said, his heart breaking. He knelt before her, embracing her hands. "We're going to find this creep. But we need your help."

"I gave you my help," she sobbed helplessly. "It had to be Ryzik. It had to be."

"He was set up. Scientific evidence doesn't lie, not that much evidence. Help me, please. Think really hard. Who would want to do this to you?"

"How the hell do I know?" she screamed in exasperation, refusing to believe what her instincts were now telling her: Her boss had done this to her—his revenge for her rejection. But what if she were wrong? An accusation as serious as this would destroy both of their lives. She'd never be able to live or work in Highlands County. And she was not leaving Matt behind.

She was powerless again. This bastard was going to control her for the rest of her life. Drained of all hope she succumbed to Lisa's arms. "What difference does it make? What can I do now?"

"Keep on fighting," Lisa pleaded, her stomach nauseated from the raw fury surging through her veins. "Don't give up. Don't be the coward I was. This guy will get his in the end."

Lisa glanced over at Greg, studying the bewildered look in his exhausted, heartbroken eyes. Suddenly she realized what she had said: *Don't be the coward I was.* She abruptly lowered her eyes from his stare.

"She's right, Al," Greg said, the greater part of his attention still focused on Lisa as he tried to interpret her words. "We're going to find him. I'm begging you, think real hard. Talk to me. Tell me about any problems you've had with anybody in the past couple weeks, months. I need something to go on. The sooner we get this creep off the streets, the better it'll be for all of us."

Alex gave in to his heartfelt plea. Sniffling she pulled away from Lisa and straightened up, composing herself. "You make a lot of enemies in this profession. Like you didn't know that."

"We're going to go through all your reports and arrests since you've been with the regional police. If there are any incidents in particular where you remember someone giving you a hard time, please, let me know. Also, any acquaintances that might have something against you. Perhaps something you unknowingly did or said to them. I have to leave all options open. And I need to ask you some personal questions. If that's okay?"

She nodded meekly. He produced a small notebook and pen from his pocket and sat in the armchair across the room.

"Do you want me to leave?" Lisa asked.

"I have nothing to hide."

Greg slouched forward, setting the pad on his knee. "I need to know if you've been sexually active with anyone since you've moved here?"

"Yes," Alex answered.

"How active? How many guys?"

"Only two. I dated one guy for about six months. The other I started dating two weeks ago."

"I need to know who they are. This information is kept confidential."

"Kyle Lawry was the first one. He lives up the street."

"What does Mr. Lawry do for a living?"

"He's a delivery–truck driver for Zeller's Furniture Store."

"Has he ever been in trouble with the law before?"

"Not that I know of, other than a few speeding tickets."

Greg wrote as she spoke. "Was it a mutual breakup?"

"No. I broke it off. He was getting too possessive. I needed space. I was having some problems with Kyle prior to that…night. He was leaving notes in my mailbox…"

Alex immediately caught Greg's stunned expression. "What kind of notes?"

"Harassing ones. He found out I was dating someone else, and he was jealous."

"Do you still have these notes?"

"Yes, but…" She began shaking her head. "It wasn't him. He…he has a small mole near his…this guy didn't have a mole. I'm positive it wasn't him."

"Be honest with me, Alex."

"I am being honest."

"I gather he fits the description. Dark hair and eyes."

"Yes."

"I'd like to see those notes."

Alex retrieved the three cards from her bedroom and handed them to Greg. He quickly skimmed over them.

"I don't like the sound of this one," he said, quoting the longhand, "*Will Ehrich protect you from the Ryziks? They're bad news and I fear for you. I wouldn't want anything to happen to you.* Al, this sounds like an implicit threat."

"It could have been. But...I swear, it wasn't him."

"What's he mean by this line, '*I know what you did last night*'?"

Alex became overtly annoyed. "I guess he'd been watching me. He somehow knew I had someone...stay overnight."

"What night was this?" Greg persisted.

"Wednesday. I found the note on Thursday afternoon."

"The day before the assault. Who's your new beau? I'm assuming he was your overnight guest."

Alex shot him an intense look of anger. She did not want Matt involved in the investigation. "His name is Matt Ehrich. Leave him out of this, please."

Greg sensed her irritation and chose to end the interview for the time being. He'd have to dig up more on this Lawry character on his own. He slipped the notebook back into his pocket and stood to leave. "I'd like to keep these note cards, if you don't mind."

"Go right ahead."

"Think really hard about any other confrontations," Greg insisted. "Any inkling of a suspicion or bad vibe about someone, please, tell me about it. I'll be in touch."

Bad vibe. Those words played on Lisa's mind. She had nothing but bad vibes about Rick Stanton ever since he developed an interest in her sister. An interest that arose solely from his misfortune on Mountain Gap Road. Lisa couldn't help conceptualizing that this stranger in town was skillfully, diabolically, carrying out a vendetta against her—and her partner—while using his interest in Renee as a diversion. His belligerent attitude, his lewd remarks all showed signs of insecurity, of resentment toward women with power. *She* had been the target of his brash words that fateful night, but it was *Alex* who had questioned his presence on the isolated road. It was *Alex* who had discovered the beer cans under the car seat. And it was *Alex* who had signed the complaint. Was *Alex* his first target? Would *she* be next? Or was her deep–rooted distrust of strangers completely clouding her judgment? If anything, Lisa rationalized, Alex should be apprising Greg of her confrontation with Ted Peterson. Her rejection of him was clearly a motive. And who better to devise a setup than the chief of police himself.

Alex saw Greg to the door and waited until he backed out of the driveway to turn to Lisa.

"It *wasn't* Kyle," she stated adamantly. "I know what Greg's thinking. But it wasn't him."

"You're one–hundred percent sure of that?"

"Yes! I've *been* with him." She suddenly lost her tact and blurted out, "For crying out loud, Lisa, I've given him a couple blow jobs. And this guy didn't have a mole down there! Okay?"

Lisa stared at her partner, not knowing how to acknowledge her rather blunt revelation. "I really admire your candor," she simply said.

Alex burst into laughter, welcoming the comic release. It was all she could do from losing her sanity.

Lisa got up from the couch. "Why didn't you tell Greg about Ted Peterson? You were having suspicions of him the next day. You told me so. Why are you holding back?"

Alex didn't answer. She hurried into the kitchen.

Lisa followed on her heels. "Answer me, Al. Why are you holding back?"

Alex turned to face her partner, her face pale with confusion, fear. "Because I'm scared to death."

❧ ❧ ❧

Brian Haney answered the telephone at Ehrich's garage.

"Matt, please," Alex said.

"Hold on." He dropped the earpiece and went to fetch the pretty boy. "For you," Brian mumbled, ambling back to the engine of a black minivan.

Matt set his wrench down on the edge of the engine he was working on and wiped the grease from his hands. "I'll take it in the office."

He stepped into the office, out of Brian's sight and earshot, and picked up the phone. "Hello. May I help you?"

"Can you turn the clock back a week or so?"

"Alex? What's up?"

"The crime–lab results came back this morning. Everything came up negative. It wasn't Dale Ryzik, Matt—"

"What? Are you serious?" His arm flew out to shut the door. He turned his back to the work bays.

"I'm dead serious. He's only being charged with possession of cocaine. Matt, I'm terrified. He's out there somewhere...I don't know who it was."

He anxiously ran his hands through his hair. "D...don't worry. I'll come over if you want. I'll stay with you, or you could stay with me. They'll find him...don't worry. Do you need me now?"

"No. I'm leaving for work in fifteen minutes. I'll be okay till midnight. But could you stay with me tonight?"

"Say no more. I'll be there at twelve–o–one. Al, are you going to be okay? Did you eat? Did you check your blood sugar?"

He couldn't see her appreciative smile, but he did hear her faint laugh. "I'm fine. It's not me I'm worried about, it's you."

"Me? Why?"

"Matt, I don't know about being exposed to AIDS now."

"Stop, please. I don't care about that. I want you to be okay, that's all. And I want this animal behind bars. Don't they have anything to go on?"

"Dark brown hair and a *Night Crew* tape." Alex went on to recount the details of Greg's visit and the new course of the investigation.

On the other phone in the garage, Brian Haney dared not to breathe as he listened in on the conservation.

* * *

"This is going to be a good one," Lisa remarked as a young woman cradling a baby in her arms emerged from her run–down house and hurried toward the police car. "I graduated with her and her boyfriend. I'm not even sure if the kid is his. She's slept with every guy in town."

Alex reached for her portable radio. They stepped out of the cruiser and approached the distressed woman.

"What seems to be the problem?" Lisa asked.

"Get him out of my house!"

"Who?"

"Marty. Who else? He's drunk, and he's lost it. I want him out!"

"Has he threatened or hit you?" Alex questioned.

"Both. He slapped me and said he was gonna kill me."

Her stomach knotted with anxiety, but it was imperative she remain focused. "Are there any guns inside?"

The young woman shook her head. "No."

"Where is he?"

"In the living room."

Lisa and Alex exchanged concerned glances.

"Call for backup," Lisa said. She listened intently as Alex spoke with the Comm Center over the portable radio.

"Mike and Sam are on a call, another domestic in Westfall. The big hats got called to an accident in Lumber Township."

"We've got no backup."

"We're on our own," Alex said, accustomed to the usual lack of help. She slid the radio in her back pocket and detached her baton, hell–bent on exerting her authority. "I'll go in." She started for the front door.

Lisa pulled her back by the shoulder. "I'll handle him."

Alex glared at her partner, infuriated.

"Stay here with her and keep trying for a backup," Lisa said, freeing her own baton from her duty belt. "I know this guy. A little height may help."

"Fine." Alex was unable to start an argument in front of the young woman since officers were forbidden to contest one another in a crisis situation. And Lisa had seniority.

"Are you sure you can handle him?" the woman asked skeptically as Lisa headed for the door.

"I'm never sure of anything." Lisa stepped inside and walked slowly through the hallway, guided by the audio of the television set.

"You'd better get the hell outta here," a hostile male voice warned from inside the living room.

With a whip–like motion, she expanded the closed baton to full length, gripping it tightly in her right hand. She cautiously appeared in the room. "Take it easy."

He sprang from the couch, and Lisa quickly stepped back, anticipating a physical attack.

"Get out!"

"C'mon now, Marty. Don't get all excited. I just want to talk."

"There's nothin' to talk about! You got no right bein' here!"

She took a short step toward him. "C'mon, sit down, calm down."

"I said, get out! You got no right bein' here. Who's she think she is, callin' the cops on me?"

Lisa took another step in his direction. "Sit down."

"No!"

"Sit down," she repeated.

"No!"

He was not going to cooperate, and Lisa had no backup. "Sit down, Marty."

"Fuck you!"

She mentally assessed the situation. The word war could go on for an eternity. She needed to act. Raising the baton across her chest she grasped each end. "This is my final warning. Sit down."

And again, "Fuck you!"

That was it. Lisa drove the baton into his upper body. He lost his balance and tumbled onto the couch, the result of her strength stunning him—but only for a second. He leaped to his feet, raising his fist to strike her.

She quickly recoiled, clutching the baton defensively. "You don't want to do that."

His arm stopped in mid–flight, his eyes blazing.

"Rethink it, Marty. You don't know how serious the penalty is for striking a cop. Don't make this problem any worse than it already is. Now sit down."

Reluctantly, angrily, he complied with her request. "You're a—"

"That's enough. Why don't you tell me what your problem is?"

"Right now, *you're* my problem."

"Look, I don't want to be here. Your girlfriend wants you out of the house. Why don't you leave on your own? Save us all a whole lot of aggravation."

"I don't *wanna* leave."

Her frustration escalated with his uncooperativeness. "Your girlfriend said you slapped her and threatened her, and you've been asked to leave. Go home. Sleep the booze off."

He was on his feet once again. "I ain't leavin'!"

"Then I'm afraid I'm going to have to arrest you for assault, terroristic threats, and trespassing. Turn around, put your hands behind your back, and get down on your knees." She reached around her waist for her handcuffs.

"Make me!"

"Don't do this, Marty."

"C'mon, make me!"

"You're resisting arrest. You're only making it worse for yourself."

"I'm outta here!" He pushed her into the wall and bolted past her. He dashed down the hallway and onto the front porch. Spotting Alex in the yard, he flew over the railing, darting through the neighbor's yard toward the street.

Alex freed her baton from her belt and began sprinting after him. She whipped the rod open and flung it at his legs. As he fell facedown onto the sidewalk, she reached for her handcuffs. He attempted to get up, but she pressed her foot against the back of his neck. "Move your hands above your head and lay them flat on the sidewalk!"

Lisa came up alongside her and knelt down to cuff his wrists.

"Great job," she said to Alex, pulling the guy to his feet.

"Guess you couldn't do it all by yourself after all, huh?"

"I'm sorry about that. But I had my reasons."

"Yeah? I'm dying to hear what they were."

Renee and Rick strolled along a path at the borough park. The evening air hung heavy with humidity, hazing over the half moon.

"I'm thinking about doing a piece in the paper on your state–championship team," Rick nonchalantly informed her.

Renee's eyebrows came together in bewilderment. "Whatever for? It's old news. Seven years long and gone. Nobody cares anymore."

"Local sports stories are few and far between in the summertime. I thought it'd be something different. I want to focus on the current lives of the starting five, what you're doing now."

"Believe me, none of us have gone on to bigger and better things. Four of us are still living here. The fifth moved to Philly as a matter of fact."

"Now there's a smart girl." He motioned toward a bench. "Let's sit awhile."

They nestled on the wooden seat, Rick maneuvering an arm around her waist. "Seriously would you oblige me with an interview?"

"You already know what I'm doing now. But this may be the perfect way to get on Lisa's good side. She loves to talk about basketball, and since she played in college, she'll definitely have more to tell you." Renee's face lit up. "I'm sure she'd go for it. I don't know about the other three starters."

"Not a problem," he said. "I'm sure I can work my magic on them."

Who cares about the other three? Rick chuckled to himself. All I want is to work on your sister.

But right now I want you.

Boldly he buried his face under her hair, caressing the nape of her neck with his soft, teasing lips. "How 'bout another tour of the train?"

"In the dark?"

His hand was working its way up her thigh to the edge of her shorts. "I'm still not sure what to do."

She rose to her feet and brushed his bangs away from his dark eyes. "I'm sure you'll know *exactly* what to do."

Lisa and Alex signed out at the police station, Lisa turning the cruiser keys over to Chris Wingate.

"Good night? Bad night?" Dave Romanovich questioned as they officially switched shifts.

"Bad night," Lisa said. "We had a domestic about nine–thirty, just got through with the arraignment."

Chris gazed at Alex, taking note her facial bruises were almost healed. It was exactly one week ago he and Dave had been called to her home. He felt compelled to express his support, especially now that he had learned the assailant was still at large.

"How're you doing?" he asked.

She managed a halfhearted smile. "Okay. Thanks."

"If there's anything you need," Dave offered, unconsciously moving forward to kiss her on the cheek. He stopped abruptly, uncertain of her reaction.

Alex forced another small, appreciative smile, her face flushing with humiliation. "It's okay. I'm not afraid of being touched."

"Al, I'm sorry," Dave murmured. "I wasn't sure. I hate doing this to you." He opened his arms to her, and she embraced him for a long, tearful moment.

Later, standing outside in the parking lot with Lisa, Alex slammed her fist down against the hood of the Tracker.

"When is the awkwardness going to stop?" she lashed out, angry at the way people now saw her, treated her. She was no longer Alex Griffin. She was now Alex Griffin, rape victim. "It's never going to stop, is it?" Her blue eyes lifted up to burn contempt on her partner. "And *you're* not helping matters, either. Why'd you stop me from confronting that guy? What were you afraid of, Officer Maselli?"

"You've got it all wrong—"

"Do I?" Alex squeezed the top of her baton with knuckle–whitening perseverance. "You were afraid I couldn't handle it, that I'd let my emotions get in the way of my better judgment? That's what you thought. Wasn't it?"

"No."

"Oh, no! Then what? Huh? What?" Alex's hands flew up, wrenching Lisa's uniform below the collar.

Lisa grabbed onto Alex's wrists, struggling to free herself.

"Listen to me, partner–friend!" Alex yanked at Lisa's shirt with such force it ripped at the first fastened button.

Stunned, Lisa yielded her resistance. She stood on the asphalt, speechless, frozen in Alex's grasp.

"I can handle whatever's thrown at me!" Alex spit out the words in a ballistic rage. "I've been doing it all my life. Don't you ever second–guess me again! Got that, Officer Maselli?"

Lisa opened her mouth to speak, but Alex silenced her with another persuasive jerk. "When I got this job I thought this place was perfect for me. So laid back..." Her voice trailed off. She swallowed the lump in her throat and relinquished the hold on her partner, overcome with a grave sense of worthlessness. Defeated she turned away. "Boy, was I wrong."

Lisa casually inspected her torn shirt. "May I talk now?"

Alex shrugged, but she refused to turn around. She stood with her back to Lisa, her arms folded across her chest, tearfully staring at the side of her vehicle.

"For your information, Officer Griffin," Lisa spoke calmly, "it wasn't *you* I was second–guessing tonight. It was me. After my screw–up at the school I wanted to prove to myself I could handle the situation. You jumped to the wrong conclusion."

"Yeah, right. Then why'd you comment on your height? Huh? You were afraid I wasn't big enough to handle him."

"No, that's not true. I thought my height would intimidate him a little, maybe he'd be cooperative. I was wrong."

Alex snickered. "Guess you were."

A tense silence lingered for several moments before Lisa spoke again. "Al, I've *never* doubted you. Why would I doubt you now? In fact I look up to you. Have you forgotten I've been in your shoes? I know how you're feeling right now."

Alex squeezed her eyes shut, letting an overflow of tears run down her cheeks. "How could you look up to me?" she mumbled, sniffling and wiping her eyes. She laughed. "You're taller than me."

Lisa joined in the laughter. "Well, look down to you."

"I'm sorry about your shirt," Alex said, turning to inspect the damage. "I'll pay for a new one. I'm sorry for the outburst and the accusations."

"I understand."

"I don't know what to do, Lisa. I'm gonna lose it."

"You've got to tell Greg about Peterson."

Alex shook her head, her watery eyes brim with fear. "But what if I'm wrong?"

Lisa frowned. "What if you're right?"

CHAPTER 18

Destination Canada

It was half past one in the morning when Lisa walked into the living room. She found her entire family still awake and watching the conclusion of a movie on cable TV.

"What's this?" She set the nylon gym bag that contained her uniform and equipment on the floor. "Family night at the Maselli's? And no one invited me." She plopped down in a chair and threw her legs over the armrest.

"It was a good movie," her younger brother, Tony, said. "We didn't want to miss the ending."

"Where'd you and Jimmy go after work?" Renee sat up from the couch.

"Out for a bite to eat and a few beers. I thought you had a date."

"I did."

"He's an interesting young man," her father commented, rising from the recliner, yawning. "But he's got to do something about those bangs." He started for the stairs to retire for the night. "I'm bushed. Good night."

Lisa quickly straightened in the chair. "Hold on a minute, Dad. I've got some bad news."

Her father turned back. "What?"

"The results came back today from the crime lab. Dale Ryzik didn't do it. The DNA didn't match."

"What?" her father gasped.

"*Nothing* was linked?" Renee's eyes widened with disbelief. "What about the gun?"

"The gun, believe it or not, *was* the weapon used. Alex's saliva was identified on the barrel. Somebody set up Dale Ryzik."

Commissioner Robert Maselli stared down at his daughter, speechless, his thoughts immediately returning to the conversation he had with her on the back porch less than two weeks ago. "We need to talk about this."

Lisa acknowledged her father's request with a single nod.

"In the morning," he said then vanished up the staircase mumbling inaudibly.

Tony scooped up an empty bag of potato chips and stood up from the floor. "What was that all about?"

"Nothing," Lisa said. "He's just upset about the whole thing."

"Sounded more like the two of you know something Renee and I don't. But…" Tony shrugged. "Whatever you say." He walked into the kitchen, deposited his trash in the garbage basket, and headed up to bed.

"Tony's right, Lisa," Renee said coldly. "What's going on?"

Lisa sighed, slumping down in the chair. "I can't tell you."

"Why not?"

"Because I can't. It's official police information. All I can say is there may be another suspect."

"Why is Dad involved?"

"Renee, I'm sorry. I can't tell you yet. Trust me on this, okay?"

Renee huffed in annoyance. "Okay, fine." She rose to her feet. "I guess I'll go to bed, too. Got a long day tomorrow on the train. G'night."

"No, wait awhile. Tell me about your night with Rick. How was it?"

"Why the sudden interest?"

"Because I'm trying to like this guy. I want you to be able to confide in me."

"Why do I think there's more to it than you're letting on?"

"No. I'm making a serious effort to wipe the slate clean."

"I'm glad to hear that 'cause Rick's trying to do the same."

"We had an interesting conversation the other night. I'm sure he's got some great qualities I'd like to hear about."

A skeptical grin spread across Renee's face. She leaned back on the armrest of her father's recliner and folded her arms across her chest. "I bet you would."

Lisa eyed her twin precariously. "You want to elaborate on that a little?"

"He's looking to do an article on our title season and what the starters are doing now."

"You're kidding?" Lisa shifted in the chair, slouching forward to rest her elbows on her knees. "Why the interest in high–school girls' basketball?"

"I asked him the same question. He said local sports' stories were hard to come by in the summer with school out of session."

"Oh? Yeah, I guess that's true."

"Would you be agreeable to an interview with him sometime in the next few days?"

Lisa didn't give it a second thought. "Sure. It'll give us another chance to get more acquainted."

"Great. I'll tell him. When would be a good time?"

"Monday after work." Lisa glanced over at the television screen then back up at her sister. "You didn't tell me how your *date* was. And you conveniently slid over your 'I bet you would' comment."

Renee fumbled for a reply, and Lisa began shaking her head, watching her sister's face flush with guilt. "You slept with him, didn't you?"

Renee became angry, defensive. "What if I did? It's none of your business."

"Not too long ago, sister dear, we used to tell each other everything." Lisa got up from the chair. "Sorry I asked." She reached down for her gym bag and headed for the stairs.

Renee was on Lisa's heels. "No, you're not." She reached out for her arm and spun her around. "Yeah, Lisa, I slept with him. Is it killing you?"

"What was that supposed to mean?"

"You know damn well what it means. *You'd* never act so reckless, would you? Not my self–righteous cop sister, who's been sleeping with the same guy for eight years. Here's to your sainthood." Renee gestured with her middle finger. "We did it tonight on the train. How's that for wild? And I slept with him last Sunday at his apartment. In fact I initiated it, Saint Lisa. Is that burning your holy ears?"

Lisa pursed her lips. This was not her sister standing before her, spitting insults in her face. This was Rick Stanton's pawn. Now more than ever Lisa was convinced ice water flowed through Stanton's veins and he was using her sister for more than lustful gratification. There's more to the town scoop than meets the eye; Lisa held firm to that belief.

And she needed to dig up the dirt, uncover exactly what it was that fueled his fire—before someone got hurt. Or—if that ill–at–ease feeling she had about him was proven true—before someone *else* got hurt.

Saddened by her sister's naiveté Lisa said, "It's your life, Renee. Live it any way you want." Quietly she turned and mounted the stairs to her bedroom.

At ten o'clock the next morning Lisa and her father sat at the kitchen table, sipping coffee. Renee had already left for the bureau office to finalize the logistics before the train's noon departure, and Tony was still asleep in his room upstairs.

"Dad, Alex is caught between a rock and a hard place."

Robert Maselli stared off, his eyes transfixed on the handle of the refrigerator door. He began shaking his head. "All that went through my mind last night was what you told me about Ted Peterson two Mondays ago, what he laid on Alex. I can't believe he'd retaliate like...that."

"She hasn't told Greg about Peterson yet, but she's going to today. There's still her ex–boyfriend, although she's convinced it wasn't him. And we have to go over nine months of reports with a fine–toothed comb. Peterson clearly had a motive, and the interrogation won't be pretty."

"Is she prepared for the fallout?"

Lisa lifted the mug to her mouth and swallowed a mouthful of coffee. "How would you feel if she did nothing? If she just let this...sicko get away with it? Peterson knew what happened at the school. And he undoubtedly knows how to set someone up. Unfortunately most people in the county know how the Ryziks are and could have done the same thing. The incident at the school *was* printed in the paper—"

"So it could have been anyone. I feel for Alex to have to go through this. I only hope Peterson is understanding and cooperative. And I pray it wasn't...him."

"Dad, no one knows I told you about Peterson, not even Alex. Let's keep it that way for now."

He reluctantly agreed. "But if there's anything I can do for Alex, I won't sit on the sidelines and watch. I'll do whatever it takes to put this guy behind bars. Mark my words on it."

Lisa gripped the coffee mug with both hands, praying Renee would adopt the same attitude if the state police interrogated Rick Stanton. Greg Van Dien would be reviewing the report on the traffic stop on Mountain Gap Road, which included an official statement on Stanton's belligerent behavior.

It would not be overlooked.

* * *

A thick plume of black steam spewed skyward from the smokestack of the Shay locomotive as it climbed the grade leaving Mountain View, its five coaches crammed with energized passengers in tow.

"May I have your attention, please?" From the front of the coach Renee addressed the entourage of rail buffs on the John Schmidt through a microphone wired to two speakers above each end of the aisle. "My name is Renee, and I'll be your guide for the afternoon. I'd like to welcome everyone to Highlands County and aboard the Highlands Scenic and Historic Railroad. For all you history buffs Highlands County was created in 1858 from a portion of Lycoming County and has approximately twenty thousand residents. We're now rumbling out of the borough of Mountain View, the county seat, population: five thousand. We will be traveling in a southeasterly direction along the course of Pine Creek to the village of Elk Grove near the county line. Highlands County was settled in the mid–1800s by immigrant coal–miners and loggers and grew as a result of these flourishing industries, which provided fuel and building materials for the development of American cities through the early 1900s…"

Rick eyed her from the opposite end of the aisle, listening as she narrated a brief chronicle of the railroad's role in the mining and logging industries and the origins of the Shay locomotive and Trans–Pennsylvania coaches. Leaning against the metal door to the vestibule as the train clanked and rocked along the rails, he cracked a small, haughty smirk. She wore a pair of black slacks, a green button–down tee, and a brown vest with the logo of the railroad embroidered in gold above her left breast. That outfit, he decided, looked sillier than the black–and–brass conductor's suit he had unenthusiastically sported for these absurd jaunts back to the past.

Renee caught his stare. She struggled to restrain from grinning as she concluded her welcoming oration. "Please feel free to ask me any questions. At Elk Grove we'll be treated to a picnic lunch alongside Pine Creek courtesy of the Elk Township Volunteer Fire Company Ladies Auxiliary. You'll then have about an hour to wander around the village before we head back to Mountain View. I hope everyone has a great time. Thank you and enjoy the ride."

She replaced the microphone and teetered down the aisle, stopping several times to chat with passengers or satisfy inquiries. She innocently smiled at the obese woman and antsy child who now sat in the seat where she and Rick had made love the night before.

"Having fun?" Rick teased when she finally joined him at the back of the coach.

"Not as much fun as last night," she said in a low, proud voice, her hand inconspicuously slipping over his buttocks. "Did anyone happen to mention how hot you look in this getup?"

He grinned mischievously, aching from the instant arousal she effected, and moved close to whisper in her ear, "Later."

"Is that a promise?"

"No, ma'am. That's a fact."

Ninety minutes later the locomotive whistle blew as the train approached the Elk Grove Station, locking wheels screeching over the rails like nails on a chalkboard.

"Please don't stand up until we come to a complete stop," Renee instructed the riders from her post at the microphone. "Enjoy your lunch and visit to Elk Grove. We'll be reboarding at three o'clock. Please be prompt."

Renee was the last person to disembark the coach, and Rick held out a hand from his conductor's post at the base of the steps.

"Looks like you got the knack of it," she said as they followed the crowd to the creekside pavilions for lunch. "Playing conductor isn't so bad, is it?"

"I'd like it a lot better if I didn't have to wear this silly outfit. It's not me."

"Yes, it is. You're a small–town boy now."

"Oh, no. I haven't been sold on this country thing yet."

"Have you been sold on me?"

Smiling he reached down for her hand. "That I have."

Joining the four other guides and conductors, they leisurely ate their picnic lunches—hamburgers, hot dogs, a variety of cold salads, and lemonade—along the bank of the creek. Afterward, when the others dispersed to wander through the village, Rick and Renee remained near the train, relaxing on the grass under the shade of an old oak tree.

"What'd you think of the scenery along the way?" she asked. "Pretty impressive, huh?"

He pursed his lips, pretending to seriously ponder her question. "Yes, yes, quite impressive. I particularly liked the wetland."

"Cut it out."

"Cut what out?" He propped himself up on an elbow and brushed his bangs over his hair.

"The sarcasm."

"Okay, okay. Actually I wasn't paying much attention to what was outside the train. Most of my attention was focused on this extremely attractive guide on the John Schmidt, who, if I recall correctly, was the first mayor of Mayberry…I mean Mountain View."

She smirked. "You're real funny."

* * *

It was close to five o'clock when the day's excursion wound down at the Mountain View Station behind Main Street. As the last of the riders departed, Renee rounded up the guides, conductors, and locomotive engineers to review the next day's itinerary and thank them for helping oversee a successful, crisis–free run.

"Your place for a quick shower, my place for a quick shower, then out for a quick dinner?" Rick suggested when the meeting concluded.

"Sounds like a plan," Renee replied. They headed down the alley to his car as the engineers uncoupled the locomotive from the coaches to run it back to the railyard.

Rick sat in the living room while Renee ran upstairs to shower and change. No one else was at home at the Maselli's, and he passed the time by flipping through the stations on the television. He found a baseball game between the Mets and Pirates, but it was the bottom of the ninth with two outs and the contest ended a few minutes later on a fly ball to center field. He flicked the TV off and let his eyes casually wander around the room. A family portrait hung on the wall above him, and he twisted around to study it. He took note Mrs. Maselli appeared healthy and guessed the photograph was at least six or seven years old. He was amazed at how closely the twins resembled their mother. And, although he tried, he could not determine which of the twins was Renee and which was Lisa.

Renee and I are a lot alike, Lisa had said to him Wednesday night, right after she had tricked him.

"I'll be the judge of that," he whispered, laughing to himself, recalling the words Officer Lisa Maselli had uttered when he insisted he hadn't been drinking that fateful night.

"Where do you feel like eating?"

Rick unlocked the door to his apartment, and they stepped inside.

"Somewhere with fast service. I'm starved." Renee walked into the living room and deposited herself on the couch. She kicked off the beige loafers that complemented the pair of sage–green jeans and beige shirt she now wore and stretched her long legs across the cushions.

"How 'bout the Towne Diner?" he suggested, throwing the conductor's jacket over the back of a kitchen chair.

"That'd be fine."

He went into his bedroom. "I thought for sure your boss would be there today barking out orders," Rick kept talking as he rummaged through his closet for a pair of jeans and a descent shirt.

"He'd never be able to handle the pressure or the crowd. And he doesn't know the first thing about trains, other than they run on rails."

"Do you get along with him?" Rick emerged from the bedroom with an armful of clothes.

"I tolerate him," Renee said as he disappeared into the bathroom to shower.

Boredom got the best of her while she waited. She noticed several certificates and trophies showcased on a shelf above the desk across the living room. She rose to her feet, walking over to examine the awards. Writing and journalism awards from high school and college. She pressed her lips together, admiring his accomplishments. The biggest trophy was engraved with the wording *Philadelphia Public Schools All–City English Award, Richard A. Stanton, Roxborough High School.*

"You're quite the writer, Richard A. Stanton," she muttered under her breath. "Among other things." She examined his laptop computer then picked up the July issue of a writers' magazine lying alongside it. A tattered envelope and a handwritten letter lay beneath.

It's none of your business. Leave it be, a voice inside her warned, but the peculiar postage stamp affixed to the upper right–hand corner of the envelope piqued her curiosity. She examined it closer.

The stamp was Canadian, canceled out with a postmark dated over a month ago, and the return address read Windsor, Ontario. The water was still running in the shower so, out of a pure and innocent interest in the international address, she picked up the letter and began perusing the longhand.

My dearest Rick,

I've been concerned about you ever since you called last night. I'm writing this letter because my computer is being repaired, and I can't e–mail you. You can't be having these terrible thoughts again. You've come a long way. Don't regress now. I'm sorry I can't be there to help you through this problem, but listen to me. They were only doing their job. You were wrong by drinking and driving and feeling sorry for yourself. Your mother's beatings are the reason for your hostile feelings toward these two cops, and you know it. But they are not the same as her; no one is the same as your mother. You have to make that separation again, even if the one with the blue eyes reminds you of her. Okay? Please don't do anything rash. You can't keep letting your mother's cruelty do this to you. You have to keep moving forward, stop reliving your horrible past. It was so nice talking to you again. You can always count on me for moral support. As soon as my computer's fixed, I'll send you an e–mail. You're a good person, Rick. Remember that.

Love, Caroline

Renee's hands trembled as she quickly replaced the letter underneath the magazine. Her mind raced wildly. Who was this Caroline person from Canada? What terrible thoughts? His mother's beatings? Blue eyes? Don't do anything rash! Stop reliving your horrible past!

"Oh, no," she whispered, her pulse pounding in her throat. "You couldn't have done those horrible things to Alex. It can't be…true."

Her eyes darted around the room. She had to get away from him, to sort over in her mind what she had discovered before jumping to the wrong conclusion.

She heard the bathroom door open and dashed back to the couch.

"By the way," Rick said, appearing in the living room refreshed and neatly dressed, his wet hair slicked back. "Did you mention anything to your sister about the article on the basketball team?"

She stared up at him with frightened eyes.

Lisa! What did he *really* want with Lisa? Could her sister have been right about those wary feelings?

"Y…yeah. She said sh…she's free Monday after work."

"Great. Tell her to stop by my office." He glanced down at her. She was as pale as her shirt. "You look like you've seen a ghost. Are you okay?"

She shook her head, unable to peel her stare from his dark eyes. Eyes like Alex had described. "I don't know what's come over me," she lied in desperation. "I don't feel so good. Could you please take me home?"

CHAPTER 19

The Guessing Game

Alex stared into the closet, contemplating what to wear for her trek in the woods with Matt.

"None of this garbage," she mumbled, turning toward the dresser. She pulled out a pair of navy shorts and a pale–pink tee.

She dressed, slipped on a pair of sneakers, and French–braided her hair. She wanted it neat and away from her neck. Judging by the late–afternoon sunshine that streamed through her bedroom window, the temperature outside must have been hovering in the high eighties.

As she tucked the braid under and pinned it in place at the nape of her neck, a knock came at the front door. Giving herself a final inspection before the mirror, she smiled, pleased with the results, and went to answer the door.

Matt drove his pickup north through the sparsely populated areas of the county.

Alex relaxed in the passenger seat, admiring the rustic scenery. Throughout the rolling hills and in between stands of virgin forestland, they passed a countless number of dairy farms. The townships north of town were farthest from the interstate and thus escaped the brunt of the summer tourist migration from the metro areas.

"It's so beautiful up here," she remarked, her eyes catching a glimpse of a small stream coursing alongside the roadway.

"I love it up here," Matt said. "No tourists."

Alex continued to gaze out the window as they drove on. Matt kept quiet. She was lost in the beauty and tranquility of the rural landscape against the cloudless blue sky. He didn't want to spoil her engrossment with small talk.

They rode in silence along the main road for another fifteen minutes before Matt turned onto a dirt road. The rutted lane sliced through an endless expanse of dense woodlands.

"If my memory serves me right," Alex said, visualizing a county road map in her mind, "this is state–forest land. I've heard the hiking is great here."

"You've heard right." He glanced over at her for a split--second then returned his eyes to the road.

They passed three hunting cabins along the two–mile journey into the wilderness before Matt steered the pickup into a clearing between the trees and silenced the engine.

"Ready?" He unfastened his seat belt and looked over at her, smiling.

"You bet." Alex hopped out of the truck.

Matt grabbed a backpack from the bed, secured it behind him, and led her to a path marked by the forestry department.

"How far are we going?" Alex asked.

"About three miles."

"Round trip or one–way?"

"Round trip."

"Three miles *total*?" she teased. "I thought we were going *hiking*."

He laughed as they started down the path. "Remember the jog around the track?"

"Yeah."

He looked over at her, smirking. “Don’t push it.”

They meandered their way along the forest floor, climbed over rock formations, strode along and across fallen trees, all the while chatting about trivial subjects. Neither mentioned a word about the search for her assailant.

It was the furthest thing from Matt’s mind.

It silently consumed Alex’s thoughts.

Yesterday at the state–police barracks she had reluctantly disclosed her boss’s attempt at sexual coercion to Greg Van Dien. Tomorrow she would suffer the consequences when the detective confronted the chief with her allegation. The staggering look of disbelief that had hung on Greg’s face while she had described Ted Peterson’s bid at sex for favors remained etched in her mind.

“Al, his prints were identified through AFIS on the register receipt. Did he go to your house afterward to throw us off?”

“I don’t know *why* he was there. But what about the cassette tape? The prints on the tape matched the other set on the receipt. It doesn’t make sense.”

“No, it doesn’t. But he’d certainly know how to botch things up for us. Why didn’t you tell me about him immediately?”

“Put yourself in my position. I’m not even sure I should be telling you *now*. I can’t prove it by a long shot. And what’s going to happen to me if it turns out to be coincidental, huh? How you do think *he’s* going to treat me then? I’m breaking the blue code of silence.”

Greg had shrugged, unmoved. “Let me ask you something,” he had then said, resting his folded hands on the conference table, a touch of annoyance in his voice. “Do you *want* this scum bag behind bars?”

Her mouth dropped. Enraged by his smug attitude she had jumped down his throat. “No, not at all! I thought I’d let him roam freely, maybe give him another chance at getting it right! Or better yet, he could kill me! Then you’d have a big, bad, murder case on your hands!”

"Would you stop that nonsense? I'm *trying* to help you!"

"Look, Greg, I'm sorry." She had drawn in a deep breath, composing herself. "I *don't* know who it was. Okay? And I *don't* want anyone else falsely accused, especially not my boss."

"Alex, I understand, but I have to cover all the bases."

So did she.

Some time today she had to tell Matt. Tell him about everything, everyone: Peterson, Kyle, the three other men she had highlighted unwillingly after reviewing the police reports.

One possible retaliator was a thirty–year–old she and Lisa had arrested five months ago on an indecent assault charge that was subsequently dropped. He had blatantly resisted arrest and had a few choice words for them. Another was an eighteen–year–old who had been charged with underage drinking three months ago. He had insinuated retribution by uttering the words while intoxicated, "If I ever get my hands on you, babe, you'll be screaming." The third person was Rick Stanton, the twenty–eight–year–old newspaper editor who had been arrested for DUI. His lewd innuendoes, however, had been cast at Lisa rather than at her.

She had not felt strongly enough about the malice of any of those individuals, especially not Stanton, to consider them threatening, but Greg had insisted any inkling of a suspicion or motive be brought forthright.

"I'm really doubtful about this Stanton guy," she had said. "He's dating Lisa's sister—"

"He's dating Lisa's *twin* sister? Didn't you tell me the brunt of his vulgarity was aimed at Lisa? I don't get that at all."

"I don't either. But it's none of my business."

"It might be *my* business," he had said, his voice tinged with sarcasm.

Alex hated playing this guessing game. She was being forced to make assumptions. Assumptions that could backfire and create more enemies for herself. Greg's inquiries were becoming increasingly painful and outright intrusive. She was both frightened and appalled by her uncontrollable mood swings, and she wasn't sure how much longer she'd be able to endure the emotional roller coaster ride that had been set in motion within her.

She had longed for this time alone with Matt.

They emerged from the woods into a grassy clearing, the path ending at the bank of a shallow stream.

"Okay." Alex glanced over at Matt. "Where do we go from here?"

He pointed upstream, across the water to an abandoned sawmill.

She assessed the surroundings, looking toward the mill then down at the water. She turned to Matt, her eyes brimming with excitement. "Awesome. How do we get over there?"

He smiled, the expression on her face telling him she already knew the answer.

"See those rocks over there?" He directed her gaze a few yards upstream, to five large rocks that formed natural stepping–stones across the waterway. "You don't mind, do you?"

"Me? Mind?" She eagerly headed for the rocks. "You're talking to an ex–fish–commission officer here. I hope *you* make it across dry."

"I'd better go first. If I fall the ex–fish–commish can catch me," Matt teased.

They started across the rocks, Matt an arm's length ahead of her.

"Be careful," Alex sputtered. "These rocks are a little sl…ippery."

Matt glanced over his shoulder just in time to see her lose her balance.

"What'd you say about staying dry?" He burst into laughter, reaching around for her as her feet slipped into the water. He grabbed onto her arms, but the extra weight drew him into the water as well.

"Told ya you wouldn't stay dry," she giggled, her eyes locking on his.

Instinctively their lips came together.

Alex's hands found his face as his strong arms pressed her against him. After a long moment he released her. Their eyes met, and he smiled.

Alex wanted to say something. She couldn't. She was mesmerized by the sun's reflection in his soft green eyes. Her lips parted yet her mind was blank.

Matt broke the silence. "This water is freezing."

Alex hadn't noticed at all.

They made their way to the other side of the stream. Beyond the nonfunctional waterwheel, under the shade of a small stand of trees, Matt freed the backpack and dug out an old sheet, spreading it over the grass.

They removed their soaked sneakers and socks and unwound. Exhausted and sweating from the heat and long walk, Alex laid back on the sheet, bending her knees upward.

"I'm thirsty," she said, gazing up into the cloudless sky.

"Juice?"

"Yes, please."

His hand slipped into the backpack, and he handed her a twelve–ounce plastic bottle of fruit juice.

She sat upright and twisted off the cap, raising it to her mouth for a sip.

Matt opened his bottle and took a long draw of his own juice. "When was the last time you had a beer or some other sort of alcoholic drink?"

"Ten years ago, on the seventh of June."

He stared at her in astonishment. "I was figuring on a general number of years, not the exact date."

"There's a reason I remember. I was graduating high school in a couple days, and a bunch of my friends and myself went out partying. I learned a hard lesson on how alcohol adversely affects a diabetic. By the time my friends got me to the hospital, I was unconscious and needed intravenous glucose. Needless to say my parents were extremely upset over it. One, because I was underage and drinking, and two, because I was diabetic and drinking. My mother lectured me on my irresponsibility, but my dad got to me. Instead of getting mad at me he blamed himself. His baby girl, the only one of his three kids, had gotten his disease. But I never blamed or resented him and, after that night, I vowed never to touch another alcoholic beverage again."

Matt shook his head in awe. "You're something else."

"What'd you mean?"

"I love your honesty and perseverance."

Alex set her juice on the grass. "I'm glad you said that because I've got a lot to tell you about what went on before I was...attacked. It's all playing into the investigation. Bear with me, please?"

She completely opened up to him. And for a long, awkward moment afterward, Matt was unable to speak, an array of raging emotions silently boiling within him.

"What would happen if I beat the shit out of your boss?" he finally spoke, the seriousness of his voice sending a frightening chill down Alex's spine.

"Matt, don't even think about it. This is not why I told you."

"Okay then. How 'bout Lawry? He...he...he...*watched* us! What kind of sick person is he? Al, I'm...I'm—"

"You're sorry you got involved with me, aren't you? I guess I can't blame you. I suppose I had it coming to me."

"What are you talking about? Had *what* coming to you?"

"Everything. I've got an attitude, haven't you figured it out? Everyone wanted a piece of me—"

"Oh! Oh! Wait! Stop it now!" He tossed his drink aside. "Don't you dare blame yourself. *None* of this is your fault. I don't want to hear you say those things about yourself."

His words bounced right off her. It was happening again. Another round of uncontrollable anger. "Hey, no big deal." She unbuttoned her shorts. "You wanna get it on?"

He stared at her, his mouth agape. She was trembling; he could see it as she reached for the zipper on his shorts.

"No, Al. Don't do this." He intercepted her hand and tried to take her into his arms.

She lashed out. Swearing, she vehemently fought the imprisonment.

He quickly released her. "I'm sorry. I'm sorry."

A blank stare met the dumbfounded expression on his face.

"Alex?"

She managed to shake her head, perspiration beading on her forehead.

"Are you okay?"

The color drained from her face as the world around her began whirling. In an instant she was soaked in sweat.

"W...what's wrong?" he nervously asked.

Spinning. Everything was spinning. Everything was a blur.

Suddenly she collapsed against his body, weak and incoherent. Was she having an insulin reaction? Had the warning signs gone undetected—masked by emotional trauma?

He began rummaging through the pockets of her shorts in search of a counteraction, pressing his memory to recall the instructions she had given him a couple weeks ago. He found the packet of glucose gel. "What do I do with this?" He was miles from a telephone to call for help. "Think, dammit."

Then Matt remembered the fruit juice. She only had taken a sip. He reached for her bottle.

"Please let this work. C'mon, Alex, drink this."

She rejected it.

"C'mon." He held her still and forced the liquid down her throat. He was fearful she'd choke. But she didn't. She swallowed. He held onto her for what seemed to be an eternity, rocking her in his arms, reciting aloud every prayer he had learned from his Methodist upbringing.

It paid off.

Alex steadily regained her cognizance. Moaning she sat up. Her head was pounding. She felt nauseated from acute hunger. "I had a reaction, didn't I?"

"Yeah, I guess so. What caused it? Are you going to be okay?"

"I think so. I don't know what triggered it… The long walk in the heat… The increase in insulin… It had to mess me up. Man…" She wiped the sweat from her brow. "This never happens. I should've seen it coming. I've got to eat soon."

"Are you going to be able to make it back to the truck?"

She nodded. "I just need to get some strength back. The gel should hold me over until I get something to eat."

"Are you sure? You gave me a scare there." He lightly brushed his fingers across her cheek.

"Thank you so much. You must follow instructions well."

He sighed. "Don't make a habit of it."

The twitter of the birds and insects, the rushing water of the clear mountain stream fell on deaf ears. The beauty and peace of the woods only added insult to injury as Alex sank back on her heels and quietly cursed the world.

"I feel like such a fool. I…I have no control over these outbursts. My anger gets so intense the stupidest things will set me off. It comes out of nowhere. I hate it."

He tipped his head to the side and smiled warmly. "It's all a part of the healing process. Don't sell yourself short, Alexandra Griffin. I understand completely."

"Huh?"

"Your outbursts and anger. It's not uncommon after…"

She stared at him, awestruck. "How do you know all this stuff?"

His eyes found the ground. "Please don't be mad. I checked a book out of the library."

"A book on…?"

Mortified he hesitated.

"Matt?"

"A book on…violent crimes. I needed to know. I want to help you through this."

"Oh."

Silence again. Chirping birds and insects. Coursing water.

Without saying a word, she lifted up on her knees and gently grasped his face with both hands, bringing his lips to hers. She kissed him openly. It was an uninhibited expression of gratitude for his sincerity and devotion.

"Alex, I love you so much, it hurts," he said when she finally pulled away.

"Matt, can I ask a favor of you?"

"Sure. Anything. What do you need?"

She pressed her lips together. Choking back tears, she whispered somberly, "The book."

Renee longed for the day to end.

She stripped off her tour–guide outfit and plodded into the bathroom. She showered for over a half hour then slipped into a pair of black shorts and a SUNY–Binghamton shirt and ambled downstairs to fix herself a ham and cheese sandwich.

No one was at home and the stillness only deepened her melancholic mood. She reached into the refrigerator for a bottle of beer and went out to the back porch to eat her "supper" and drown herself in the alcohol.

She had given Rick the cold–shoulder from the onset of the excursion, using a lame "I'm not feeling well" excuse. She sensed he didn't believe her. She didn't care. She had simply tolerated him, answered his questions or comments curtly. She had not smiled or laughed, and she made every attempt to avoid him.

Renee curled up on the porch swing, staring at her sandwich. Her appetite waned, the text of the letter she had found on his desk the night before continuing to haunt her. She tossed the sandwich onto a plant stand and opted for the beer. She twisted the cap off and drained half the bottle in one long gulp.

Don't do anything rash. Terrible thoughts. Mother's beatings. Don't do anything rash. Hostile feelings toward these two cops. Blue eyes. Mother's beatings. Stop reliving your past. Mother's cruelty. Don't do anything rash.

Caroline from Windsor, Ontario, Canada, had written him not to do anything rash. To stop reliving his horrible past. And to make the distinction between the two cops and his mother, even if the one with the blue eyes reminded him of her.

The one with the blue eyes. The one who had endured the "pay back." For what? A DUI charge? Previous beatings inflicted by his blue–eyed mother?

Renee's assumptions spun out of control.

Who the hell was Caroline?

Who the hell was Richard A. Stanton? City boy? Writer? Editor?

Rapist?

She shuddered at the sobering possibility a demonic individual capable of carrying out the unimaginable had manipulated her.

She had slept fitfully the night before, tossing and turning, sorting over what she had secretly discovered in his apartment. A gun. An incriminating letter.

He told her the gun was registered, and the weapon used in the attack had been recovered. The letter confirmed his hatred of women with power. But he had openly admitted he disliked women cops. The mere existence of the gun and letter proved nothing.

So what was eating at her conscience?

The fact her sister had warned her of his odd behavior. The fact a police officer and close friend—*the one with the blue eyes*—had been sexually assaulted.

Renee guzzled the rest of the beer and went inside for another. Plopping back down on the swing, she opened the second bottle, angrily flinging the cap onto the lawn. She swallowed another mouthful of the cold ale and pushed her hair back, holding it atop her head. She stared unseeingly at the early–evening sky, recalling Rick had supposedly fallen ill and driven her home an hour before Alex had been attacked.

The floodgates opened as pieces of the puzzle seemingly came together. She agonized over her options. A horrifying crime had been committed on a friend, and justice needed to be served. It was her obligation to come forward with what she had found.

How? By telling Lisa? By admitting to her self–righteous sister she had been wrong? It would be yet another defeat in the shrouded war against her sibling. Lisa achieved better grades. Lisa led the basketball team in points, rebounds, assists, every statistic imaginable. Mountain Region Athlete of Year according to the *Williamsport Post–Gazette.* Lisa got the collegiate scholarship. Lisa made history. First female police officer in Highlands County. Lisa got all the glory, all the attention.

Lisa got Jim. She envied her sister's monogamous relationship the most. Why couldn't she have been the one assigned to that study hall? Jim Ostler was the cream of the crop. Sincere, devoted, compassionate, intelligent, and from what Lisa had so immodestly described many a night in the privacy of their bedroom, a phenomenal lover. All of Renee's relationships had been short–lived, meaningless.

The thought of Rick Stanton possessing the capability to inflict such a terrifying and degrading vengeance sent shivers down her spine. She had made love to this man. She had trusted him. Had he warped her mind?

She had no answers. She needed answers.

She needed more before pointing the finger, before she could open up to her sister and admit her misgivings.

She would have to confront Rick with the letter and demand those answers. If it were a horrible coincidence, she'd have nothing to worry about.

If it wasn't…

That was a chance she had to take. For Alex's sake.

Renee polished off her second bottle of beer and buried her face in her hands, nauseated. "Please, God, don't let this be true."

Rick threw that god–awful conductor's jacket onto the kitchen table and immediately started on the six–pack he had purchased at the bar down the road.

He flicked on the light in the living room and slouched back in the armchair, feet on the floor, legs spread nonchalantly. He peered up at the ceiling and exhaled in exasperation.

His aspirations were going awry. Renee had shunned him. He had no idea why, but he was not banking on her illness excuse. He was going to have to pour on the charm and have a long talk with her to solve the mystery. He could not fathom a reason she'd shy away from him. He behaved like a perfect gentleman, and it certainly wasn't the sex. Neither held anything back. He couldn't help wondering if her sister had somehow prompted the snobbery he had been subjected to today.

His deep–seated resentment of women consumed his mind as he pounded down the first two cans of beer. By the third can he was out for blood. Soon he'd have her. He had not intended to do this back in early June, when he began plotting to befriend Renee Maselli—the other circumstance. Now, he was being driven. Driven by the taste of her the night she had "tricked" him.

A villainous laugh bounced off the walls of the small living room. "I can play dirty, Officer Maselli. I'm going to get you."

After his fourth can he swaggered over to the desk and removed a folder full of old newspaper articles and photographs. He had dug them out of the archives back in June, soon after he had been charged with Driving Under the Influence. That's when he had learned the tall cop had a twin sister.

At the stereo he searched through a stack of cassette tapes for his favorite. He cursed; it wasn't there. It was probably in the car, either on the console or shoved in the slot on the side of the door. He wasn't running down to the car. He selected an alternative and popped it into the tape deck. Rock music broke the silence.

Rick returned to the chair and stretched out, resting his head on the top of the cushion. He held the photos up to the light and flipped through them slowly, studying each one. Highlands High School girls' basketball team, the year of the state championship. Lisa Maselli with the chief of police, Police Swearing–In Ceremony, two years ago. Alex Griffin with the police chief and some other male cop, Police Swearing–In Ceremony, last October. Alex Griffin with four teachers and the principal, West Highlands Elementary School, Safety Week, this spring.

Alex Griffin. He hadn't thought about her in a couple days. His stomach clenched as he visualized those ice–blue eyes.

He set the pictures aside and began scrutinizing the articles. *Maselli Twins: Lady Wolves' Dynamic Duo. Lisa Maselli Scores Big for NPU. Commissioner's Daughter First Female Cop in County. Maselli Lands Recreation and Vacation Bureau Position. Wilkes–Barre Native Second Woman on Force.* He was especially amused by that piece, the one on Alex Griffin's appointment to the police force. *She was previously employed by the National Park Service, the Pennsylvania State Fish and Boat Commission, and the Tredyffrin Township Police Department in Chester County*, it read. Tredyffrin Township. How ironic, he thought, snickering. My mother grew up in Tredyffrin Township. Nice little affluent suburb on the Main Line.

"Some day, mother," he cackled over wailing guitars, popping open the fifth can. "Some day."

He went back to his desk, pushing his writers' magazine aside and picking up the letter from his ex–lover. Caroline would not approve of his thoughts. She was so rational, so understanding. "But you loved Canada more than me," he scoffed, angrily ripping the letter to shreds. "I'm sorry, baby, really, I am."

* * *

"Can I borrow your *Night Crew* tape?" Kyle Lawry asked.

"Yeah, sure." Brian Haney disappeared into his house, returning a few seconds later. He tossed the cassette into Kyle's hands. "Have you seen your precious ex lately?"

"No," Kyle said, slipping the tape into his back pocket.

Brian lit a cigarette. "So you're really lettin' go?"

"Drop the subject. I don't want to talk about her, okay?"

Brian stepped off the porch. "She stopped by the shop three times last week to see her pretty boy." He took a long drag from his cigarette and blew the smoke in his buddy's face. He laughed. "He ain't gettin' none."

Kyle's eyes locked on his. "How do you know this?"

Brian sauntered back to his school bus parked in the driveway. "I can see the frustration on his face. It ain't so pretty anymore."

"I hear it wasn't Dale Ryzik," Kyle said, walking toward the bus.

Brian froze, cigarette in mouth, waiting for more. When Kyle said nothing further he quickly spoke up. "Yeah, heard that, too."

Kyle watched as Brian rummaged through his toolbox for a wrench. He was still working on the bus. Nothing better to do than drink, smoke, and fiddle with that damn bus. If the school district knew the real Brian Haney, that busing contract of his would be history.

"If I were you I'd be gettin' real scared," Brian cackled. "*You're* the one who watched her screw around with Ehrich and kept puttin' notes in her mailbox. Maybe she told the police about all that. You'd better go find yourself an alibi."

Lisa found Renee on the back porch.

"What the hell happened to you?" she asked, looking down at her sister sprawled out on the swing, pale and disheveled.

Renee moaned, rubbing her eyes. The sun had gone down. She must've fallen asleep. "What time is it?"

"A quarter to ten. You look like death warmed over."

"I feel like death warmed over." She labored into a sitting position, dropping her head back against the cushion.

Lisa surveyed the three empty beer bottles and the untouched sandwich on the plant stand. "That bad a day?" She motioned toward the bottles.

"Worse," Renee mumbled, covering her face with her hands. "Where've you been?"

"Out with Jimmy."

"Dad and Tony home?"

"No, not yet." Lisa rested against the railing. "Where's Rick? I thought you'd be together."

Renee's stomach turned, nausea resurging. "I wouldn't have been much company. I came home right after the train got back."

"I've got to talk to you about Rick," Lisa said tentatively.

Renee dropped her hands in her lap and exhaled loudly. "About what? Can't it wait? I feel like I'm gonna barf."

Lisa inwardly mocked her sister's beer binge. "If you want me to wait I'll stop by your office tomorrow."

"No. Tell me now. What'd he do now?"

"Alex went through our reports yesterday. It's routine and means nothing, but—"

"But what?"

"She had to highlight all of our hostile incidents."

"What you're trying to tell me is he's under suspicion, right?"

"No, there's no probable cause. She just had to point out his raunchiness. Like I said it probably means nothing. But it had to be done."

Probable cause. Does a letter hinting at rash behavior constitute probable cause? Renee sighed, staring down at the porch–floor planks. "How's Alex doing?" she asked, deliberately avoiding a response to Lisa's statements.

"It's hard for her to stay focused."

Renee threw her head back against the cushion. "This is killing me."

"What is?" Lisa's eyes narrowed suspiciously.

"What happened to her. It's so...detestable."

"And the longer the creep stays on the streets, the harder it gets for her to deal with it."

"What has to be done with Rick has to be done. I understand."

Lisa stared at her sister, shocked. Renee's acceptance of these grave circumstances was nothing short of admirable. She wondered if Renee knew more than she was willing to reveal.

"I'm going upstairs to read. You staying out here for a while?"

"Yeah," Renee said.

Lisa straightened and reached for the handle on the screen door. "I'll let you know how my interview goes tomorrow."

"Yeah, okay."

Lisa studied her sister for a moment. Something was definitely bothering her. She bit her lip and entered the kitchen.

"Lise."

Lisa stuck her head back outside. "Yeah?"

Renee looked up from the swing. "The three of us should go out sometime. You, Al, and me. A girls' night out. We haven't done that in a while."

Lisa forced a smile. "Yeah. Sounds like fun. I'll mention it to Alex."

"Yeah. Do that. I really like her, you know."

CHAPTER 20

Probing Under Wraps

Lisa and Alex both arrived at the station at seven fifty–five.

Alex dilly–dallied outside.

"Are you going inside?" Lisa asked. "It's almost eight."

"I suppose."

"He doesn't know yet. Relax."

Alex glared at her partner. "That's easy for you to say. I'm terrified to death. I may have made the biggest mistake of my life."

"What if you didn't?"

"That's supposed to make me feel better?"

They entered the police station, Alex's eyes nervously darting around for signs of the chief. They signed in and were headed for the coffeemaker when Ted Peterson's demanding voice emanated from his office.

"In my office. Both of you."

"Oh, God," Alex whispered, her pulse pounding in her throat.

"He doesn't know yet," Lisa repeated, detouring past the coffeemaker to his office. Alex unwillingly followed.

"Close the door," Peterson ordered.

Alex did as instructed. They sat before his desk—the Monday–morning ritual of late.

"The Heritage Days Committee has requested we provide two officers for the festival this weekend. I'm assigning the two of you to Friday night, four to midnight."

"What about our regular duty that night?" Lisa asked.

"I couldn't work any reserves into the festival so Mike and Carl have agreed to work your shift."

"Why do *we* have to work the festival? Mike and Carl should be working it, not *our* regular tour."

Peterson raised his eyebrows. "Seniority. Do you have a problem with that, Officer Maselli?"

Yes, I do, but it's not going to amount to a hill of beans. "No problem," she answered.

"Is that okay with you, Griffin?" Peterson looked over at her, his voice less than accommodating.

"Yeah, sure, fine," she blurted, staring down at her sweaty hands fidgeting on her lap.

"Good, it's settled. A couple more things before you head out. One, good luck to both of you at Billy Ryzik's hearing this morning. Are you going to be able to handle it, Alex?"

Her eyes shot upward. "Why wouldn't I? Dale Ryzik wasn't the man who attacked me. He was set up. By someone who knew what went on at the school that night and who knew what the Ryziks were like."

She held his stare as if to say, *Someone like you.*

He lowered his eyes to a pile of papers scattered across his desk. "I was referring to the awkwardness."

"I'll get over it."

"What's the latest in the investigation?"

Alex immediately tensed. "I'm not at liberty to discuss it."

He shrugged, giving up. "If you don't think it's patronizing, Officer Griffin, I'd like to commend you on your baton–throwing ability Friday night. You did some quick thinking."

"I'll attest to that," Lisa said.

Peterson's attention instantly turned to her. "Yeah, Maselli, that's twice now she's gotten you out of a jam."

Let it slide, a voice inside her warned. Insults come with the territory. You're working in a man's profession in a small town divided along political lines. As long as your father is a county commissioner, Ted Peterson is never going to be fond of you.

Tolerance was the name of the game, but her patience was wearing thin. Her desire to attend law school resurfaced. She needed to get out of the department, and soon. A trip to the library to research jurist–doctoral programs loomed on the horizon.

"No one could have handled that situation alone," Alex told Peterson.

"You're full of piss and vinegar this morning. Aren't you, Griffin?"

"Are we through here?"

Peterson reclined in his seat. "Yeah, I've had about as much of you two as I can take for one day."

Lisa and Alex headed for the door. Alex glanced back at him for an instant. Please let there be an end to this nightmare soon, she prayed.

Before it goes too far.

Before I turn into the villain.

Greg Van Dien drove from the state–police barracks to the Mountain View Borough Building. Heading up Main Street he made a mental list of the individuals he planned on interviewing this week. Tomorrow he intended to speak with officials from Lumber Township on an arson investigation. Two weeks ago someone had torched the township's garage, destroying the building and two maintenance vehicles parked inside. Wednesday he had to travel down to Elk

Grove to look into a burglary. Thursday he contemplated making a stop at the auto repair shop to have a talk with Matthew Ehrich, Alex Griffin's latest love interest. If warranted, Friday he'd hunt down Kyle Lawry, the ex–boyfriend who was having a hard time accepting the "ex" part.

Today, right now, he would confront Ted Peterson. Greg was extremely uncomfortable about having to do this. If the public got whiff of Alex's allegations it would spell trouble for the regional police. Reputations would be destroyed. The department's second–rate image would suffer another severe blow. Greg was prepared to bend over backward to keep this inquiry under wraps until it became unconstitutional to do so. He honestly hoped this avenue of the investigation would dead end. Peterson would have an alibi. Something. The one thing he hated more than criminals was a bad cop, especially one in a high–ranking position.

Greg pulled into the borough parking lot and silenced the engine of the unmarked cruiser. Inside the station he flashed his badge at the desk clerk and reached into his pocket for an envelope. He asked that it be tacked on the message board under Lisa Maselli's name. He then requested to see the chief. Without hesitation the clerk showed him to Peterson's office.

"Ted, good morning."

Ted Peterson looked up from the paperwork on his desk. He rose to his feet. "Detective Van Dien. What can I do for you?"

Greg closed the door. "I need to speak with you. Official business."

"Sure. Have a seat." They settled on either side of the desk.

"I need to be straightforward, Ted. It's about Alex Griffin's sexual assault."

Peterson leaned forward, folding his hands on the desk. "What about it? I asked her this morning what was going on. She wouldn't tell me."

"Ted, Alex told me on Saturday that you harassed and assaulted her in this office exactly two weeks ago."

"What?"

"She informed me that if she slept with you, you'd squelch Ryzik's excessive–force charge. She also informed me that she refused, but you tried to change her mind by forcing a kiss on her. She said she pulled your hair to get your mouth off hers and you became angry and grabbed her by the collar and threw her against the wall."

Peterson shot out of his seat. "This is insane! Where does she get off saying those things?"

"She told the same story to Lisa Maselli in the ladies' room minutes after you threw her out of here."

"I can't believe this!" He began pacing nervously.

Greg watched his reaction, his every move. "We need to talk, Ted. You may want to get your lawyer on the phone."

"She thinks *I* attacked her?"

"That's not what I said, and before you say anything else, please, call your attorney. Have him meet us at the barracks in an hour."

"She's lying. I'm telling you she's lying."

"Please, Ted, call your attorney."

❧ ❧ ❧

An hour later Ted Peterson sat in an interrogation room at the state–police barracks with Greg Van Dien and Charles O'Shea, his lawyer and long–time friend. A tape recorder was placed near the center of the long table.

"What is the meaning of this nonsense?" O'Shea demanded.

"This is not nonsense, Mr. O'Shea," Greg said, spreading the case file before him on the conference table. He removed a pen from his shirt pocket and jotted some notes on a legal pad. He then briefed the attorney on Alex Griffin's statement. "A repulsive crime has been committed on this young lady, and I need to investigate every possibility. No one is being charged. I merely need to ask some questions and obtain some information."

"Do you realize the repercussions that could result from this if word gets around?"

"Yes, I do. Alex was extremely hesitant to even tell me because of what could result from it. She is not out to cause trouble. She only wants to see justice served. She does not want to bring sexual harassment charges against you, Ted. She simply told me what happened. *I'm* the one handling the investigation and, rest assured, I will be keeping everything under wraps."

"I cannot believe that this woman...concocted such a story!" O'Shea roared.

"Do you really think she *concocted* it?" Greg cast a firm glance at Peterson. He reached across the table and pushed the record button on the tape machine. He recited the case number, the names of the two men present before him, and a parade of constitutional rights. The interrogation lasted over an hour.

Ted Peterson denied everything vehemently. He denied a sexual interest in Alex. He denied the harassment allegation. Denied conspiring retaliation. Denied setting up Dale Ryzik. Denied ownership of any *Night Crew* tapes. Denied. Denied. Denied.

He had no alibi. No one to collaborate his whereabouts—he stated he was at home, alone, that entire evening. He explained he was divorced for two years now and wasn't into the bar scene. He preferred spending his weekends at home. He brought up the fact Officer Chris Wingate had phoned him that night to obtain permission for Lisa to witness the medical–legal and that he had gone to Alex's house to assist in the search for evidence. Greg had rebutted the statement by reminding the chief the phone call had been placed at two–thirty and the attack had occurred two hours earlier.

"What do you think of women cops in general, Ted?" Greg continued the inquiry.

"What kind of question is that?" O'Shea charged.

"I have nothing against them," Peterson replied.

"Why are Lisa Maselli and Alex Griffin assigned as partners?"

"They work well together."

"I see. It wouldn't have anything to do with the fact the dinosaurs on your squad refused to work with them."

"No, it has nothing to do with that."

"Then what *do* the guys on the force think of Lisa and Alex?"

"How should I know?"

"You're the chief. You should know everything about your men—and women. Have any of the guys ever bad mouthed Alex?"

"Not that I know of."

"What about you, Ted?"

"No. Never."

"Have any of them expressed a sexual interest in her?"

"Uh..." Peterson sputtered, visibly perspiring. "You've got to expect that sort of thing when women get involved."

"Involved?" Greg raised an eyebrow. "Involved in what?"

"Involved in a man's job," the chief snapped, instantly eating his words. "We never had women on the force until Maselli was hired two years ago. It's something to get used to."

Greg eyed the chief suspiciously. "Tell me what kind of remarks the guys have made about Alex."

"Jeez, Van Dien, it runs the gamut. I got young guys like Romanovich and Wingate who are gaga over her and Maselli. I got a few old–timers who won't acknowledge their presence, and I got some macho types making crude insinuations about using handcuffs on them."

"I want the names of all the guys who've made belligerent remarks."

"Ah, they're only shooting their mouths off. They don't mean anything by them."

"Are you going to cooperate with this investigation, or do I need to see the DA?"

"Would you like their first born, too?" Peterson retorted angrily.

Greg was not amused by the theatrical sarcasm. “Names will do. And I’m asking you at this time if you’d be willing to submit a blood sample.”

“Not without a search warrant!” O’Shea blasted.

“If you want a warrant I’ll get one,” Greg calmly told the lawyer. “Your client’s fingerprints were matched by AFIS on the cash register receipt found at the scene of the crime. Because of Alex’s statement that’s now probable cause for a warrant, and I need the blood sample, I’m hoping, to *eliminate* him from a suspect list. If everything he told me is true then he has nothing to worry about. The way I look at it, Ted, you’ve got two options. One, we can drive over to Lycoming County General Hospital and have the blood drawn so no one in town will know, or two, I get the warrant, escort you to Highlands Memorial for the sample, and hope nasty rumors don’t fly around town.”

Peterson sighed with resignation. “I’ll go to Lycoming.”

“Good choice.” Greg flipped the case folder shut. “And one more thing. You’re not to make contact with Alex Griffin, either in person or by phone, until further notice. If you need to speak with her on police business, do it through the assistant chief.”

O’Shea exploded. “This is ludicrous! We’re going to sue your ass, Van Dien.”

“Go right ahead, Mr. O’Shea. It’d make for great gossip at the corner barbershop. And what the hey, the state’s got some prestigious liability attorneys on its payroll. Maybe it’s high time they earn those big paychecks.”

* * *

“How’d the Ryzik hearing go today?” the desk clerk asked when Lisa and Alex returned to the station at four o’clock.

“He waved his right to the hearing,” Lisa said. “His lawyer convinced him to plead guilty and hope for leniency from the judge.” She smirked. “He’d have a better chance of hitting the lottery.”

Alex ignored the conversation and signed out. The sooner she got out of the building the better. She checked the message board and found an envelope tacked under her name. It was from the court administrator. She noticed the same envelope, plus another, was tacked to the board under Lisa's name. She removed all three, handing Lisa hers.

"A hearing must be coming up." Alex opened the envelope. "Yep, Friday morning, nine A.M." She scanned over the details of the hearing.

Commonwealth of Pennsylvania
Vs.
Richard A. Stanton

Charge: Driving Under the Influence

Arrested: 23 May

Location: Mountain Gap Road, Westfall Township

Arresting Officer: Ptlw. Alexandra Griffin

"Oh, no." Disgusted she released a huff of air. "Why did I have to sign that report?"

"What?" Lisa looked at her, baffled.

"Outside." Alex blew past the desk clerk and through the exit with Lisa on her heels.

In the parking lot Lisa asked, "What report? What are you talking about?"

"Stanton's DUI." Alex waved the notice in Lisa's face. "Friday's his hearing, and I'm the arresting officer."

"And?"

"And somehow I feel like I'm making enemies with the world. Peterson, and now Stanton. How I am supposed to face the magistrate with impartiality toward him?"

"You only called attention to his behavior. He's not a suspect. He may never be a suspect."

"I don't like this. It's making me crazy."

"Just stick to the facts."

"I still don't like it."

"Speaking of Stanton," Lisa said. "I've got an interview to go to."

Lisa left her car in the borough lot and walked the three blocks to the *Highlands Journal* on Centre Street. Along the way she opened the second envelope that had been tacked to the message board. It was a memo from Greg Van Dien, requesting to see her at five–thirty that afternoon in his office at the barracks. So much for an early dinner. She'd have to call Jim from Stanton's office to delay their date until seven. She folded up the memo and shoved it inside her shirt pocket with the hearing notice.

"I'm here to see Rick Stanton," Lisa told the receptionist upon entering the newspaper building.

The blonde once again gawked at her weapon then ushered her down the hallway to the editor's office.

"Officer Maselli, come in, please," Rick spoke from behind his desk with a rehearsed coolness. "Have a seat."

"Could I trouble you for a phone first? I need to make a call."

"Sure." He swung around his desk and showed her to a telephone in the layout room adjacent to his office. He returned to his office but not to his desk. He stood inside the doorway, eavesdropping on her conversation.

"Hi, it's me. Change in plans. Greg Van Dien wants to see me at five–thirty at the state–police barracks… No. I have no idea. I suppose it has to do with the investigation… Can you pick me up at seven instead? Okay. Yeah… How 'bout Chinese? Yeah, the Great Wall of China… See ya later… Bye."

Rick rushed back to his desk and nonchalantly waited for her to reappear in the office.

Lisa settled in the chair before him. "How'd you like playing conductor this weekend?"

He shrugged. "It was an easy sixty bucks for the twelve hours I stood around looking utterly ridiculous."

"Hey, you got to spend all that time with my sister. For some strange reason she's smitten with you."

"Is that so?" After her icy reception and behavior yesterday, Rick had to wonder about that statement.

"I hear you've got an interest in high–school girls' basketball," Lisa said. "Somehow that strikes me as odd, being the male chauvinist pig you are. I would have expected a piece on the Highlands Wolves football program. Six–time conference champs, sixty–three wins and nine losses over the past eight years. Quite an impressive program. I'm a big fan myself."

"Yeah, but I still think a state championship is more impressive than six conference titles. Even if it was the *girls'* team."

Lisa laughed. "Spoken like a devout sexist."

"Believe it or not I've been intrigued by your team's accomplishment from the day I got here."

"Don't you mean from the day we met on Mountain Gap Road?" She thought briefly about the hearing notice tucked inside her shirt pocket and assumed *his* notice was at home, lying in the mailbox. "C'mon now, you probably didn't even know this county had a high school, let alone an undefeated hoop team, until you went snooping through your files for dirt on me."

He chuckled, reclining in his seat and whisking his bangs away from his eyes. A crooked smile reeked of arrogance. "In case you haven't figured it out yet…" He shifted in his chair, leaning over the desk to emphasize the slam. "The world doesn't revolve around you. This may be quite a shock, but mark my word on it."

Lisa folded her arms across her chest. "Look, Stanton, do you want to talk about basketball or do you want to lob insults at each other? I can do both."

He rummaged for his notebook and a pencil. "Yes, you can. Let's talk basketball."

"Good idea."

"Okay, here's what I want to do with this piece." He verbally outlined what he intended to feature in the article: facts and highlights on the championship season, a short biography on the five starters, a sentence or two on their roles in the team's success, concluding with a note on their post–high–school accomplishments and current endeavors.

Lisa was neither impressed nor flattered. But she'd go along and make it sound fascinating. She'd lure him in. She was more than curious to know the real reason for his interest in the "team." She got the impression he hadn't made any attempt at contacting the other three starters or even detailing his ideas with Renee.

"Fire away," she said.

He started with a few basic questions. Her position on the team? Uniform number? Career points? Best game? Worst game?

The Q and A then became personal. How did it feel to be glorified by fellow classmates, by the townspeople? How'd she manage the transition from high school to college ball? Which level of competition was more fulfilling? What influenced her decision to pursue a career in law enforcement? Other interests? Hobbies? What are her ultimate goals in life?

Lisa had answered each question honestly but selectively. She had allowed him limited entry into her private life, and his pencil had flown across the pad's blue lines with lightening speed, recording every word, every feeling. He had clung to each and every reply, and Lisa took note of the engrossment, the spark in his dark eyes.

Now it was her turn.

She glanced down at her wristwatch. A quarter of five. Plenty of time to conduct her own interrogation.

"What about you, Rick? Did you play any kind of ball in high school?"

His pencil screeched to a halt, and he abruptly looked up. Those long, eccentric bangs dropped before his eyes, but he didn't bother to push them away. "No." Mother wouldn't allow him to participate in athletics. Only academics. Study. Study. Study. And still it wasn't good enough. *He* wasn't good enough. He had longed to play basketball or football. He envied every jock at Roxborough High who made a name for himself. He won the all–city English award. Look where it got him. Some hick town north of nowhere. Devon Carter won the all–city athlete award. Where'd it get him? Chicago, via the University of Virginia. Backup quarterback for the Bears. A measly million a year compared to his thirty grand. Yes, mother, academics *really* paid off.

"What kind of interests or hobbies do you have?" Lisa asked.

"I like sports, reading, music."

"What kind of music? I like soft rock, some country."

"Country? You've got to be kidding."

"No."

"Figures."

"Who do you like?"

"Definitely not country. I prefer classic rock."

"How about *Night Crew*?"

His eyes abruptly locked on hers. "What about them?"

"Do you like them?"

"I thought *I* was doing the interviewing."

Clever way around the *Night Crew* question. Missing any cassette tapes, Ricky? "I thought we were done. What else do you want to know about me? If I vote Democrat or Republican?"

"Real funny." He began playing with his pencil, twirling it through his fingers, sporadically tapping the eraser on the notebook.

The jitters are back, Lisa observed. He was fine until she turned the tables and tossed personal questions at him. Undeterred she continued the query. "Did you go to a private or public high school?"

"Public."

"Did it have a name?"

"Roxborough. I *doubt* you've heard of it."

"You're right. Was it a big school?"

"Pretty big." He habitually pushed the bangs away and huffed. "Anything else you want to know? I vote Republican in case you were wondering."

The anxiety was mushrooming into annoyance. Lisa slouched forward in her chair, resting an elbow on the edge of the desk. It was time to up the ante, pitch him an insult or two and see where it led. "What'd you and your friends, assuming you had any, do for fun in the big, bad city? Snort coke?"

He sneered. "Cheap shot, Officer, and one hundred percent stereotypical of a country bumpkin like yourself."

"Think so? You know what I think? I think this country bumpkin could match your Xs with Os and then some."

"I bet. What'd *you* do for fun, huh? Screw the *guys'* basketball team?"

Alas! Straight to the gutter, where she somehow knew it would end up.

"Or all those fag boys in the band?" he persisted.

"Cheaper shot, Stanton, and one not appreciated."

"Hey, I was matching your O."

"Don't push it."

Push? No way. I'll shove. "Jimmy boy was one of those fags, wasn't he?"

"How'd you know that?" she demanded.

"That he was a fag? Lucky guess."

"He's far from being a fag."

"I bet you showed him a thing or two about blowing a horn, huh?"

Lisa was on her feet. "It always comes back to that, doesn't it, Stanton? Is this how you act around all women? It's funny I never once heard my sister mention anything about your raunchy mouth."

Pencil still in hand he stood up to challenge her on a level playing field, a haughty grin spread across his face. "Fess up, Officer Maselli, you're dying for a taste of the city boy here."

"Get real. *You're* the one who's dying to get into *my* pants, but there's one little problem. There's a gun in the way. Isn't that right, Ricky? You got this ego thing about women and control. That's why you're schmoozing my sister. She's me without a badge."

He stood motionless, speechless, his face burning crimson. Perspiration surfaced behind those unkempt bangs as his eyes roamed over her body then bore down on the pistol, snug to her waist, menacingly resting in its holster.

Agent provocateur, that's what she was. And he wanted her bad. He wanted to hurdle the desk and show her a thing or two about the boy from the city.

"Take it off," he muttered, incited with lust. His eyes dipped to her pistol then raised up to lock on hers like a missile on a target. "Take your gun off. Take your uniform off. I'll do things to you that you couldn't even fantasize about."

Lisa met his fired eyes with a stone–faced stare. "*You* have a problem."

"*I* have a problem? How do you think Jimmy boy would feel about the way you tongued me last week? Or about those thoughts of me getting in your pants. Huh, Officer? You want me bad, don't you? *Tricking* me. How do you think your sister would feel about that little deception?"

"How would *you* feel about a rape charge?"

The pencil plummeted to the floor. He glared at her, shell–shocked. "What the hell are you talking about?"

"You tell me, Stanton."

"I'll tell you something. You're insane."

"Am I? It was awfully convenient of you to get sick and take my sister home early a couple Fridays ago. And you can learn a lot by reading those police reports you get every week, can't you, Ricky? Like what Billy Ryzik did at the school that night. Like all the times Dale Ryzik's been in trouble with the law. Is that why you went easy on Alex in the paper after the school vandalism? You were saving the knockout punch for your little visit to her house, weren't you? After all *she's* the one who busted you. She signed the paperwork."

The color drained from his face.

"You're insane," he repeated.

Her index finger found his face. "If I were you I'd be real careful." She reached inside her shirt pocket for the hearing notice. "Friday's the big day. Your day in court for the DUI, Stanton. Nine A.M." She held the paper before his eyes. "Start saying your prayers, Ricky, 'cause I might give Her Honor an earful. Defying authority, mouthing off, implying threats. That ought to double your DUI fine, maybe even get you a few days in the pokey. Wouldn't that look sporty on your record? It might even put a damper on your career ambitions. Jail time doesn't look good on a résumé."

She stuffed the notice back into her pocket and leaned over the desk to emphasize her forewarning. "And don't think the state police don't know about your belligerent behavior that night. 'Cause they do. Mark my word on this one." She played up her scare tactic with a wink and showed herself out.

Rick went ballistic. The boundary had been crossed. This was war. "You're going to mess up somewhere. And I'm going to be there to get you."

He went into the layout room and removed a digital camera and zoom lens from a storage cabinet. He packed it up with his laptop and headed home for a quick bite.

Next stop: the parking lot of the Great Wall of China.

"Talk to me, Lisa," Greg Van Dien said from behind his desk at the state–police barracks. He dropped two aspirins into his mouth and gulped half a glass of water. His dark hair was disheveled, his necktie discarded on the floor. His pale–yellow shirt was opened at the neck, stained under the arms, and his desk was haphazardly covered with papers, file folders, napkins, and a half–eaten cheeseburger.

"About what?" she asked from the chair before him.

He reclined in his seat, massaging his temples. "I don't know. Anything. Do you think communism will ever collapse in North Korea?" Abruptly he hunched over the desk and laid into her. "What do you think, for crying out loud? I've investigated dozens of sex crimes before, but this one takes the cake. Right out of a paperback novel. What the hell kinds of lives are you and your partner living any way?"

"I beg your pardon."

He fished for his notes. "Let's see here. You've got a boss who dislikes women cops, who allegedly tried to put the screws to your partner. *She's* got a psychotic ex–boyfriend, and one of the guys she named from the reports is now dating *your* sister. Enlighten me, please."

"What about Peterson? What happened with him today?"

"He denied it all as expected. But he had no alibi. I *was* able to convince him to submit a blood sample without a warrant. I'm sending it to the crime lab for analysis. Peterson's attorney has already threatened to sue, but it was a chance I had to take. I have to believe everything Alex is telling me. I know her. She's too damn honest to make up something like that."

"You've got that right."

"I'm not so sure he was the one. After Ryzik I'm not sure about anything. It was an open and shut case."

"It was a well thought–out setup."

"I know. I know. What are your thoughts on these brothers?" He handed her a sheet of paper with the names of the officers Peterson had supplied him. "Your boss claims they've been hinting of sadistic acts against you and Al."

Lisa studied the list. "Arrogant SOBs. Every one of them. Like their fearless leader."

Greg wrote himself a note to call the officers in for interviews on Thursday, his next full day devoted to this case. "Lisa, you know Alex better than anyone. Tell me more about Kyle Lawry, the ex, and Matthew Ehrich, the current."

"Lawry's a snake," Lisa said. "But Al's insisting it wasn't him. The intruder didn't have a mole below the belt, so to speak."

"Yeah, but I can't get over the fact he was harassing her."

"So was Peterson."

He nodded, running his hand through his messed hair. He longed for a long, hot shower and his soft, cool bed. "What about this Ehrich guy? He runs the auto–repair garage on Main Street. What kind of guy is he?"

"Nothing but a gentleman. Al is head over heels for this guy."

"How's he handling what happened to her?"

"He's being very supportive. Why does this interest you?"

"Alex is extremely attractive. A lot of the guys here at the barracks are drooling over her. Two or three of them have asked her out, but she's turned them down. I thought maybe this Ehrich guy had a jealous friend, a buddy who might've wanted Alex all to himself or was rejected by her."

Lisa thought long and hard about that possibility. "No one comes to mind. The only other person I've seen him associate with is the other mechanic who works for him."

"What's his name?"

"Brian Haney. He's really shy and quiet. Doesn't say much. In fact he's buddies with Kyle Lawry, not Matt."

He jotted the name on his notes. "Now there's an interesting piece of information: A common denominator between the ex and the current. What's this Haney guy think of Alex?"

"I couldn't tell you. All I know is he's quiet."

"You've got to watch those quiet ones," he remarked half–jokingly. "I'd bet a bundle this guy is feeding the ex tidbits on the current. I definitely have to discuss this with Alex."

"Anything else?" Lisa asked.

"Yeah, a couple things." Greg relaxed in the chair and eyed her with a genuine interest. "Tell me about this newspaper guy, Richard Stanton, the DUI who showered you with indecent proposals. Explain to me why he's now dating your twin sister."

Lisa drew in a deep breath and exhaled loudly. "Honestly I don't know how to take this guy. But he's doing one helluva job schmoozing my sister."

"Did your sister happen onto him, or did he happen onto her?"

"He conveniently happened onto her after he found out from old newspaper stories that she and I were sort of local celebrities."

"The basketball team?"

Lisa nodded.

"Think something's rotten in Denmark?"

"Possibly."

"Do you think he had it out for Alex because of the DUI charge?"

"I don't know."

"Do you think he has it out for you because of the DUI charge?"

"Again I don't know. But all I get is bad vibes from him."

"Where's he from?" Greg asked.

"Philadelphia. Moved here about two and a half months ago."

"What else do you know about him?"

"Not much. My sister told me his parents are divorced. His mother's some kind of high–ranking bank executive. Father's an architect. He says he went to Roxborough High School and Temple and used to work for a newspaper called the *Delaware Valley Tribune*. It's owned by the same company that owns the *Journal*."

"Want me to check up on him? I know some cops down in Philly."

"I'd love for you to dig up some dirt on this jerk. There's something very odd about him."

"Consider it done. I'll contact my colleagues from the Philly PD right away."

"It will be gratefully appreciated. What else did you want to discuss?"

"Uh, yeah." He hesitated, again shifting in his chair. "It's been working on my mind since Friday. You...you said something to Alex at her house about...fighting. About not being the coward you were. I'm sorry but I have to ask. What did you mean by that?"

Her stomach clenched. She felt sick. "W...what are you talking about?"

Greg studied her reaction. She was holding back on something. He had not earned his detective position because of looks. "C'mon, Lisa, as soon as you said it you tried to eat your words. You deliberately looked away from me."

"I...I..." She fumbled for an answer. Finally she closed her eyes and lowered her head, mortified.

"Lisa," he said softly, as sincerely as possible, "were you...sexually abused or assaulted?"

She could not look at him. How dare you ask such a despicable question! No. No way. Not the commissioner's daughter. Not the basketball star. Not the cop. She covered her eyes with her hand, holding her other arm across her abdomen, nauseated. She wanted to flee. But there was no way out of this. Admit it, her conscience pressed, stop being so gutless. You survived. You picked up the pieces and got on with your life. It wasn't your fault. You shouldn't be ashamed. Admit it, dammit.

She cleared her throat and lifted her head to face him. Slowly she nodded.

Greg swallowed hard, wiping perspiration from his forehead. "Recently?"

"No. In college. I was nineteen, and I was drunk. I never reported it. Alex is the only person who knows."

Suddenly things became awkward, a mix of guilt and embarrassment preventing him from meeting her eyes. "I'm...sorry. Was it someone you knew?"

"Sort of" was all she said. She rose from the chair to leave.

He glanced upward to see her eyes brimming with tears. "Lisa..."

"I've got to go now. Are we finished?"

"Yes."

After she'd gone, Greg dropped his head in his hands, cursing to himself.

❧ ❧ ❧

At their usual spot at Becker's Pond, Lisa and Jim lay on a blanket entangled in each other's arms. It was a quarter past eight, and the sun hung low in the sky above the lush green of the western mountains.

Jim lifted up on his elbows and rolled on top of her. "You feeling okay?" he asked, gently stroking her hair. "You hardly touched your dinner, and I don't think you said two words the entire time. I thought you wanted Chinese?"

Lisa gazed up into his blue eyes. "I did. I'm just exhausted. I've been going since six this morning." And a zillion things are on my mind, she added subconsciously. Things I'd rather not discuss. Like work. The investigation. Ted Peterson. Rick Stanton. Greg Van Dien. Calvin Anderson. What he did to me. What I never told you about. What I could *never* tell you about.

"How tired are you?" The mischievous grin on his face hinted of his desire for sex.

"I may need some persuasion."

"My pleasure." He undressed her slowly. Aching for his touch she watched him disrobe then return to her, his hands and lips caressing, awakening every inch of her body.

Jim went down on her, demanding she hold nothing back, pushing her to a pinnacle of wild abandon. She reciprocated the gratification by driving her body against his, forcing him down on his heels then on his back. She straddled his hips and took him into her, navigating the ride to seventh heaven. Beneath her, Jim moaned and panted indecencies until both surrendered to the unfurling waves of intense orgasm, Lisa collapsing on his sweaty chest.

They jumped into the water to cool off. On the way back to the blanket, Jim pulled her down in the grass near the pond and eased himself inside her for yet another strife at shameless physical pleasure.

In the bushes fifty yards away the camera whirled. Rick Stanton knelt on the ground, reeling off picture after picture through the zoom lens.

Psychotically aroused, he tossed his hair back triumphantly. He drew in several deep breaths, looking down at the camera. She'd handed him the perfect scandal on a silver platter. What were his chances of hitting pay dirt the first time around? On the camera were several frames of wild, devious—and damaging—sex. Photos that could be downloaded onto his computer and manipulated to replace this secluded location with a more public place. The commissioner's daughter—a public employee—and her schoolteacher boyfriend getting it on behind the tennis courts at the borough park. What a scream that would be: A blatant violation of the county's public nudity ordinance.

He suppressed the powerful urge to laugh at the top of his lungs as he tried to decide which board of hobnobs would enjoy the altered photos the most: the Regional Police Board, the Board of County Commissioners, or his personal favorite, the Board of Education.

Auf Wiedersehen, Jimmy.

CHAPTER 21

Masters of Manipulation

At seven–fifteen the next morning Alex met Greg at Seneca Cliff. He was seated at a weathered picnic bench when she arrived dressed for work. A bag of food from a local restaurant sat on the table. Ominous clouds were rolling in from the west, and soon the brilliant rays of sunshine bursting over the eastern ridges would be snuffed out. Forecasters were calling for an overcast day with a chance of showers.

"Morning," he said, digging into the bag as she settled across the table. "Thought you might like some coffee and a croissant. Sorry I got you up an hour earlier, but we need to talk and I have to be in Lumber Township at nine. Another case I'm working on."

Alex was touched by his thoughtfulness. This meeting was strictly business, and the breakfast offer by no means came out of the state's budget. "You shouldn't have gone through the trouble. It was no big deal to meet you now."

"No trouble at all. It's the least I could do after what I put you through this weekend."

"You're only doing your job. I know how it goes. You know what they say about doctors being the worst patients; I guess the same is true of cops. We're the worst victims."

He shook his head as they started on the coffee and croissants. "Al, there's no pleasant way to say it, but you knew exactly what to do. You kept your cool and provided us with everything possible to get this creep. I just hope it's enough."

She wrapped her hands around the warm plastic–foam cup. "Peterson denied the incident in his office, didn't he?"

Greg nodded. "No big surprise. We both knew he would."

"Yeah."

"He denied everything. I took him over to Lycoming General for a blood sample. It's already in Harrisburg. You won't have to worry about facing him until Friday. He's not allowed to make contact with you. He has to communicate through the assistant chief."

"Yippee." The sarcasm in her voice was unmistakable. "I'm screwed if the DNA doesn't match."

"His attorney's already threatened to sue. But I think he's bluffing. It'll be a lot of bad publicity."

"He's going to make my job a living hell. I'm going to be ostracized."

Greg tried to lighten the mood. "You'll always have the state police on your side."

Alex nodded, unconvinced. "I want this nightmare to end, Greg. I want my life back. But you know what? I'm never going to get it back." That recurring wave of anger sought to overwhelm her again, threatened to fill her eyes with tears. She immediately warded it off.

"Al, I have a couple more questions for you." His hand slipped around to retrieve his small notebook from his pants pocket.

She sipped her coffee anxiously. "Why am I not surprised?"

"Tell me about the guy who works for your new beau."

"Brian Haney?"

"That's the guy. Is it true he's one of your ex's buddies?"

"Yeah. Why?"

"Just covering all the bases. He's a common denominator between your ex and your current."

"He's a bum," Alex said. "Spends most of his free time at bars."

Greg jotted a few words in his notebook. "What do you think his feelings are toward you?"

"I don't know. He never talks to me."

"What about when you were dating Lawry?"

"He avoided me like the plague. Now that I stop by the garage a couple times a week, I see him more often."

"And he still doesn't talk to you?"

"No." An eerie, unexplainable feeling of vulnerability chilled her body, despite the warmth from the waning sunshine.

"I have to start considering a few more angles. One is the characters from the reports, the second is your coworkers, and the third, whether you like it or not, revolves around your past and current love interests."

"I told you it wasn't Kyle."

"But he, or Haney, may be involved somehow. Let me ask you this: Hasn't it crossed your mind, just once, that maybe this Haney guy was passing along information on your relationship with Matt Ehrich to Lawry? Perhaps on Lawry's request. Or maybe to stir up some trouble, fuel Lawry's jealousy. Ever think of that, Al?"

Alex pursed her lips in frustration. She couldn't lie. "Yes, I have." She swallowed the last mouthful of coffee and glanced down at her wristwatch. Seven–forty. "I've got to get going."

"I'll be back in town about five," Greg said. "Stop by my office at five–thirty. I want to know everything, and I mean *every*thing, about your relationship with Kyle Lawry."

Alex swung her legs around the bench and stood up slowly. She was sick and tired of his prying into her personal life. She sighed. "I hate this."

He looked her square in the eyes and said, "I hate doing this. But I have to do it."

"I know." The minute the 9–1–1 call had been placed, her right to privacy had been compromised. It was the price she was paying for justice, for closure. And she needed closure desperately. She needed to know whom. She needed to know why.

"Food's on me this time," she added, smiling appreciatively. "How 'bout a chef's salad?"

"I'd love one."

She was half way to her car when he came up behind her.

"Alex," he called.

She turned around. He couldn't help staring into her eyes. They were so blue, so enticing. So full of pain.

"I'm going to find this guy. I promise."

Those blue eyes stung with tears. "Didn't anyone ever tell you not to make promises you might not be able to keep?"

* * *

"Soon," Rick Stanton whispered menacingly. "I'm going to have you soon."

He couldn't peel his eyes away from the explicit photographs of Lisa Maselli and Jim Ostler. Lascivious electricity surged through his veins, flushing his face. His bangs hung over his eyes as he sat, hunched forward, inconspicuously flipping through the prints temporarily stashed in the top center drawer of his desk. The floppy disk containing the altered images was safely hidden away in his apartment.

He had downloaded the pictures from the digital camera onto his laptop about ten last night, after photographing an area of the borough park he could insert as a background. He lauded himself for mastering those undergraduate computer–graphics classes at Temple. He knew they'd come in handy some day. With his hearing for the DUI coming up on Friday, he decided he'd pay Lisa Maselli a visit Thursday morning about ten, ten–thirty. She'd be off–duty, her father and sister would be out of the house, and her brother—if he were like every other teenager on summer vacation—would still be asleep.

The plan was simple: Appease me or the photos end up in the laps and e–mail files of the county's big wigs.

First, she would "conveniently" forget about the hearing. And so would Blue Eyes, the official arresting officer. A no–show by both of them would mean an automatic dismissal of the charges filed against him.

Then—he grinned knavishly—the sexual favors. He shut his eyes and released an intense groan, insanely aroused by the thought of her giving him head.

An unexpected voice suddenly invaded his dream world. His eyes shot upward, and he practically leaped out of his seat, seeing her at the doorway. He shoved the pictures under some papers and banged the drawer shut.

"Sorry I startled you," she said, approaching his desk with a folded sheet of paper in her hand.

Renee. It had to be Renee. *She* was working. *She'd* be in her police blues. The civilian before him was Renee, not *her*.

Like a schoolboy caught peeking at a dirty magazine, he fabricated a gawky grin. "Uh, no, that's okay. I was proofing a piece for next week's edition."

"You were zoned out." Renee walked around to his side, propping herself up on the edge of the desk before him. She planted one foot on the floor and let the other dangle. She wore a denim miniskirt without panty hose and willfully afforded him a view of her black lace underwear. Raindrops from the passing shower outside spotted the white blouse she wore with one too many buttons undone.

For sure she had him. His eyes were lost in her crotch. She rubbed her calf against his thigh, enhancing the show between her legs.

He tried to stay focused, keep his raging hormones in check. He swallowed dryly and pried his eyes away from her panties. His gaze traveled upward to her breasts, lingering, then finally reached her eyes. "What brings you here?"

She dropped the folded sheet of paper into his lap. "Upcoming bureau events for next week's Community Calendar. You'll see they're printed, won't you?"

The egotistical smirk broadened, and he raised his eyebrows, dubious of her visit. "I'll see what I can do. Anything else you want?"

"Actually…there is." She let her eyes wander down the length of his tie to his crotch. "I want to apologize for Sunday. It must have been one of those twenty–four–hour bugs. Can you forgive me?"

Rick studied her face. His intuition told him she was lying. Now was the time to push her buttons. Who said you couldn't have your cake and eat it, too?

"I don't know." His hand found her knee and began working its way up her thigh. "I was really bummed."

She caught his pathetic expression. "Awh, I'm sorry. Let me make it up to you."

"And how would you do that?"

"Dinner tonight, my treat, then dessert at your place. I'll pick you up about six–thirty. How's that sound?"

"Sounds tempting. But what about now?"

"What about it?"

His hand slipped under her skirt, his thumb lightly brushing over the lace between her legs. "How 'bout brunch in the file room? *My* treat."

She outwardly grinned, inwardly cringed. "As much as I'd love to, I can't. Got a meeting with the big cheese in ten minutes." She hopped off the desk and leaned over him, the tip of her tongue grazing his ear lobe as she whispered seductively, "Tonight."

He moaned. "Act two. I can hardly wait."

She smiled guilefully.

The show hasn't even begun, Richard A. Stanton.

Jim was speaking on the telephone with a customer when Paula Sedlak walked through the door of Ostler Hardware. He acknowledged her with a slight smile but continued the phone conversation without interruption.

Paula waited, browsing the aisles of tools and saws and wires and other handyman gadgets with boredom.

Ten minutes passed before Jim hung up the phone.

"What brings you out on such a gloomy day?" he asked flatly, flipping through a mound of paperwork on the counter.

"I had some errands to run for my parents. They're gone on a cruise to Bermuda. Thought I'd stop in and see you about Thursday. Are you busy?"

"A little bit."

"I won't keep you," she said, disappointment in her voice. She leaned over, resting her folded arms on the counter. Her V–neck tee fell away from her chest, revealing more than he cared to see. "Do you want to drive to the seminar or should I?"

Jim stepped away from the counter, away from the show of cleavage. "I'll drive. I'll pick you up about seven–thirty."

Paula swung around to follow his moves. "Fine. I know a great place where we can stop afterward for a bite to—" Her eyes darted toward the street. "Isn't that Lisa?" She hurried for the door.

Outside, Lisa stood behind Paula's car, writing down the license–plate number on her citation pad.

Paula rushed across the sidewalk. "What are you doing?"

"You're parked alongside the fire hydrant." Lisa looked up and shot a condescending look in her direction. "Didn't I tell you about this last week?"

"I forgot, okay?"

"No, it's not okay. They teach you in driver's ed about parking fifteen feet from fire hydrants. It's not that difficult to remember." Lisa's attention went back to the citation but, before she resumed writing, her lips curled upward in a wily grin. She glanced up at Paula one more time. "You do know enough to stop when the red lights are flashing on a school bus? Or did you miss class that day, too?"

Paula's eyes blazed murderously. "Real funny. Look, I was only running in to see Jim for five minutes. Cut me a break."

Lisa stepped onto the sidewalk, dwarfing the blonde's petite body. "Sorry." She tore the citation from her pad and presented it to her. "You can pay the fine at the borough building or appeal it at the magistrate's."

Jim stuck his head out the door as Paula snatched the ticket from Lisa's hand.

"C'mon, Lise, let it go," he said.

Lisa did not appreciate his interference. She glared at him furiously. "Back off, Jimmy."

Jim looked at Paula and shrugged. "Can't argue with the law, I guess."

"Fine. You win." Paula stuffed the paper into her purse and extracted her car keys. Before she marched around to the driver's side to leave, her eyes locked on Lisa's. She smirked vindictively then tipped her head to Jim. "See you Thursday."

As she drove away Lisa turned to him.

"Don't get excited," he said, seeing her face flush.

"How could you tell me to let it go? For your information, James Ostler, every citation has to be accounted for at the end of the month. I can't let *anything* go."

"You're so threatened by her you jumped at the chance to nail her. What'd you think? We're driving to Scranton to get a motel room? Get a grip, Lisa. You're jumping to conclusions." He burst into laughter and went back inside the store.

Lisa followed on his heels. "Okay, maybe I was a little harsh. But, c'mon, she *was* parked alongside the hydrant, and I *did* tell her about it last week."

He returned to the paperwork on the counter. "Yeah, yeah, yeah. For sure she's going to make a play for me, now that you've *totally* pissed her off."

"Excuse me?"

"That's what you think, right? That she's scheming to get me into bed. Well, now she's going to pull out all the stops." He chuckled. "Hm. This may be worth my while."

"*Excuse me*?"

His chuckling snowballed into full–blown laughter as he walked into the stockroom to inspect a box of unpacked staple guns.

"I don't particularly care for your brand of humor." She was trying to sound threatening, but his uncontrollable cackling diluted her anger. She gave up and laughed along with him.

"Come here," he called to her.

"What?" She joined him in the stockroom. He abandoned the box of merchandise and wrapped his arms around her waist, backing her against the wall, nuzzling as close as the police paraphernalia affixed to her belt would allow. He kissed her, the silliness ceasing. "I'm sorry for interfering with your job," he said with sincerity. "She should have known better. Besides, you got rid of her a lot faster than I could." His right hand came around to fiddle with her badge. "And I got this thing for lady cops."

"All lady cops?" She arched her head back, exposing her neck to his hungry mouth. He lingered there, caressing and licking her soft skin, wandering as low as her uniform neckline would permit. Finally he raised his head and met her eyes.

He faked a shiver. "Hell, no, especially not those big, ugly mamas you see on TV."

Lisa burst into laughter.

"We're real lucky here in the sticks. We got ourselves two hot babes with badges."

"Two, huh?"

"Yeah, two. I can't lie and say I don't think Alex is hot, 'cause she's definitely a looker."

"Oh?" Lisa feigned surprise. She couldn't deny her partner's attributes. And the fact Jim found Alex attractive didn't bother her one bit. Alex was her best friend. Paula Sedlak was a different story. "How do you find your new colleague? The one who had—has—the hots for you."

"You don't know that for sure," he was quick to remind her, downplaying his own assumption that there was truth to that statement. "So she had a thing for me in high school. She's not my type, never was. I had this thing for these really tall twins. Actually I never stopped having a thing for the one I asked out. She's so incredibly sexy." He buckled his knees and rubbed his crotch on her thigh. "Feel that? That's what you do to me."

Lisa closed her eyes, her body aching from the feel of his hard–on against her pant leg. "Stop it. I have to get back to work."

"Later," he whispered.

Renee knocked Rick off his feet with dinner at the Mountain View Inn. They nestled at a corner table, sipping wine and making small talk, awaiting their meals.

He beamed with blissful arrogance.

She disguised her repulsion with a self–assured grin. "Am I forgiven for shunning you on Sunday?"

"Pretty much so."

Pretty much so? You wait. You haven't seen anything yet. "I'll see what I can do for you later."

His hand reached under the table, touching her knee. "I can hardly wait."

Her grin blossomed into a crafty smile. "Neither can I."

An awkward silence fell over them for several moments. His eyes were traveling over her body and for the first time since making his acquaintance, she honestly felt uncomfortable in his presence.

"Lisa said the interview went well yesterday," she blurted, attempting to resume the conversation, any conversation.

"She did?" Rick set his wine glass on the table, a little too quickly. His face flooded with color. Either Lisa had lied to her, or Renee was lying to him. Regardless he needed to lay fault with Lisa. "I'm sorry, but I thought your sister's attitude yesterday was nothing short of patronizing. She's made up her mind about me. I'm permanently on the shit list."

"Oh? That's not how she portrayed it. She said you're quite the talker, full of surprises." Renee assumed there was some truth to both versions of what had actually gone on yesterday. However, she was not taking either rendition as gospel. She mistrusted both of them.

But tonight she was playing *his* game, a game he was destined to lose.

"Your sister is an instigator. She'd better watch herself. She could get hurt real bad in her line of work."

His words stung like a hornet, sent a terrifying chill down her spine.

Hurt. How? Hurt like Alex? The one with the blue eyes. "What'd you mean by that?"

"I mean she might say the wrong thing to the wrong person one of these days."

Renee swallowed the lump in her throat and commanded herself to smile. "Don't worry about my sister. She can take care of herself."

It was nearly dusk when they arrived at his apartment. He uncorked a bottle of Chardonnay, and they nestled on the couch in the tiny living room, sipping the wine from stemmed glasses and listening to soft music on an FM station.

It didn't take long for Rick to make a move. The idle chatter had lasted all but ten minutes when he gathered up the glasses and set them on the end table.

"You are totally forgiven for your behavior on Sunday," he said, stroking her hair.

Renee took note the writers' magazine was missing from his desk. She began to speculate on the whereabouts of the letter from Caroline as his lips and hands roamed over her body.

She played up the passion, encouraged him to hold nothing back. As his hand went for the button on her pants, she suggested a move to the bedroom but intentionally dampened the mood by announcing a need to use the bathroom. With all the wine they had consumed, she was counting on him to do the same.

He did.

He stepped into the bathroom seconds after she had reappeared in the living room. Renee wasted no time. She went into his bedroom and into his dresser drawer, digging out the small revolver from under his shorts. She was thankful her sister had shown her a few months back how to load, unload, clean, and dissemble guns. She released the tumbler and removed all six bullets from the cylinders, slipping them into the front pocket of her pants. Her plan was risky to begin with; she couldn't chance having a loaded gun within easy reach. Hearing the toilet flush she quickly closed the dresser drawer and snapped the tumbler back into place. She sat on the bed and waited—the empty revolver clutched in her right hand, resting on her lap.

He sauntered into the bedroom with his shirt undone, expecting to complete what he started on the couch. The sight before him hit like a ton of bricks. "What are you doing?"

Renee drew in a deep breath, compelling herself to remain calm, in control.

"You did it, didn't you? You raped my sister's partner."

His piercing eyes fixed on the revolver then on her. He studied her face. This couldn't be Lisa before him. He was fairly sure it was Renee. "What the hell are you trying to prove?"

"I want answers, Rick."

"Answers? What kind of answers? Your sister already threatened me with this accusation! Now you! What are the two of you trying to prove? You played me up at work! *Now* you're sitting on my bed, holding my gun, and accusing me of attacking someone!"

"I fooled you pretty good, didn't I? I made you believe I felt bad, that I wanted you. It's easy to be taken. But you should know that. You're a pro at manipulating people." Renee rose to her feet, gripping the gun at her side. "Let me explain something, Richard Stanton. A police officer in this town, one who happens to be my friend, was hurt real bad. You were arrested by this cop for DUI after you made some rather lewd remarks. No big deal, right? That's what Alex thinks. She pointed out your disrespectful behavior to the state police only to cooperate with the investigation, reluctantly I might add, because she thought it was no big deal and you were harmless. And actually, it *is* no big deal. No establishment of probable cause because you mouthed off. My sister's always been suspicious of you for God knows what reasons, and to tell you the truth, I have no idea what went on between you and her yesterday. But you know what, Rick? I could make you or break you."

He glared at her, speechless, incoherent thoughts spinning through his mind.

"I found this letter Saturday night on your desk," Renee continued, her voice cracking, her heart pounding. "And you'd better start explaining what was meant by not doing anything rash and by likening the one with the blue eyes to your mother, who, I learned, beat you. 'Cause Alex Griffin has blue eyes, and you…you took me home early that night, and…" She paused to catch a breath, calm her nerves. "That letter, my so–called friend, is probable cause."

Rick swept his bangs away from his eyes and retreated to the living room, Renee tracking behind. He sat on the couch, dropping his head back and covering his face with his hands. "You found the letter?"

"Start talking, Rick, or I'm going to tell the police about it."

He grunted, reluctant to speak.

Renee was not going to tolerate stall–tactics. Holding this gun, albeit unloaded, terrified her out of her wits. She was paranoid he'd wrench it from her grasp and find it was empty, non–threatening. He was undoubtedly stronger and could easily overpower her. And she had no way of knowing what he'd do if he got the upper hand.

"Where is it? Where's the letter?" Keeping her eyes on him she went to the desk.

"It's not in there. I ripped it to shreds Sunday night. You've got *no* probable cause."

"Liar." She began tearing through the desk drawers with her free hand. She pulled a large manila envelope from the middle drawer and fumbled to open it.

He watched from the couch, helplessly. She was about to discover the newspaper articles and pictures of her and her sister and Alex Griffin—unquestionable probable cause in her eyes. He was thankful the computer disk with the images of Lisa and Jim was well hidden in a box in his bedroom closet.

Her eyes widened into saucers as she clumsily flipped through the clippings and pictures. "Oh, my God," she whispered, fighting to remain composed. She looked over at him, horrified.

"It's not what you think."

"What else could it be? You're obsessed with them. You loathed what they did to you, and you're hell–bent on getting even. And somehow your whole sick plan involves me…"

"No," he insisted. "You've got it all wrong. It may look that way, but it's not—"

"*Then what is it?*"

"Okay. The truth." He drew in a deep breath and began explaining. "The letter was from my former girlfriend. We met at grad school. She's Canadian and went back to Ontario after graduation. She's the only woman I ever trusted, and I still confide in her about everything. As you read in the letter my mother beat me and abused me when I was growing up. I hated her. In her eyes I never did anything right. Never. B's should have been A's. A's should have been A–pluses. One award should have been two. I...I have a serious problem with women—because of what my mother did to me. I distrust them. But I've never, *ever*, retaliated against them, at least not physically. I'm passive aggressive. I especially have a problem with women with power 'cause my mother was a hotshot at the largest bank in Philly. And, yes, I dislike women with blue eyes. My mother had icy blue eyes. They'd stare down at me with absolutely no love or affection. They were so...cold."

Renee let the gun fall to her side as she listened, her stomach knotted with nausea. She could see tears in his eyes.

"Caroline taught me to trust her and to try to trust other women. She looks a lot like you: dark complexion, dark hair and eyes. I...after your sister and her partner busted me, my resentment was out of control. I called Caroline for help. I was fighting to keep my emotions in check. I won't deny I had passive–aggressive thoughts about hurting your sister and her partner, especially her partner, because of her eyes. I was looking for dirt, something I could use against them, maybe print in the paper. But I never did. I found out about you, and I didn't want to blow my chance...All my aggression took place in my mind. Caroline made me accept responsibility for my actions. That's why she sent me the letter, to reaffirm what she had told me over the phone. Renee, I didn't do that stuff to Alex Griffin, I swear. You've got to believe me."

As much as she wanted to believe him, she could not accept the explanation. Far too many questions remained unanswered. "What about me? What about Lisa?"

"I've already told you. I thought Lisa was gorgeous, but I hated what she represented. That's why I said those things to her. I wanted her, and I wanted to hurt her. When I found out about you, I thought I could befriend that person less the badge, less the resentment. I wanted our relationship to mean something. I wanted someone I could trust."

Renee covered her mouth with her trembling hand. She felt for his pain, his mental suffering. But she had no faith in his words. "I…wanted our relationship to mean something, too," she muttered, choking back tears. "You are a master of charm and romance…" She began shaking her head helplessly. "And deceit. Alex Griffin is too good a friend. I couldn't live with myself if I kept all this from the police. Rick, I'm sorry…I can't buy it."

"Renee, in the top left–hand drawer of the desk, there's a statement from the phone company. It came in the maii today. Get it out and look at it, please."

She gripped the gun tighter, apprehensive, and removed the bill as requested.

"On the third page there's a summary of calls billed to my account. On July 11, I made a call to Windsor, Ontario, after eleven P.M. I called Caroline. I was still feeling sick, but not sick enough to stay off the phone. We talked for almost two hours. According to the police report Alex Griffin was assaulted that night about twelve–thirty. Renee, I was here at that time on the phone. It's there in black and white."

She flipped to the third page. There it was, like he said: *11:10 PM, 11 July, 116 minutes, To Windsor, Ontario, 519–555–1381.* She wanted desperately to believe him, to believe what this phone bill was proving to her. But her instincts were still waving red flags.

"I've got to get out of here. I've got to think about all this." She threw the statement onto the desk and hurried for the door. She deposited the gun on the kitchen table and bolted from his apartment.

She drove to Lake Iroquois and wandered down to the shoreline. Seeing no one in sight, Renee extracted the six bullets from her pocket and flung them, one at a time, into the water.

CHAPTER 22

Conduct Unbecoming

Wiped out, Matt collapsed on the grass alongside the high–school track. He rolled onto his back, sweating and gulping for air. Alex came up beside him, her breath heavy but controlled. She bent over, clutching her knees. Her disheveled ponytail flopped over her right shoulder and hung before her face.

"You're pathetic," she teased between huffs. "Don't lay down. It's the worst thing you could do after running."

"That's easy for you to say," he panted, his arm sliding over his eyes to block the early–evening sun. "You're in such good shape it makes me sick."

"With a body like yours, you'd think *you'd* be in shape."

"What's that supposed to mean?"

She eyed his limbs with admiration. "You're solid. No flab on those arms and legs."

"Working on cars, my dear. Lots of lifting and elbow grease."

"Literally and figuratively. The elbow grease, that is."

He managed a meek laugh between gasps for air.

"Seriously," Alex said. "It's not good to lay down. C'mon, get up."

He lifted his arm, slightly, peeking at her with his right eye. She offered a hand. "Man, I am pathetic," he said, reluctantly accepting her assistance.

She helped him to his feet, and they walked off the tiresome effects of the mile jog along the way back to her place.

Passing by Kyle's house Alex took note he wasn't at home, his car missing from the driveway.

Late yesterday afternoon she and Greg Van Dien had discussed her involvement with Kyle in great detail. Greg had been especially interested in her reasons for ending the relationship, Kyle's reluctance to accept it, and his stalking behavior including the notes he had deposited in her mailbox. Brian Haney's "shy boy" demeanor and his constant avoidance of her also had disturbed Greg. He theorized Haney might have been jealous of her relationship with Kyle.

"I'm getting a bad feeling about these two," Greg had said to her from behind his desk at the barracks, papers and takeout food and napkins strewn before him. "I'm going to have to do some checking up on both of them, and I need to talk to your boyfriend about Haney."

Alex realized it was inevitable, perhaps even imperative. "May I at least forewarn him?"

"I don't see why not."

After the meeting at the barracks, despite the threat of rain, Alex had gone for her nightly jog. However, last night, while her sneakers had been rhythmically pounding the macadam track, she had racked her brain sorting over what Greg had suggested about Brian Haney. After running the four laps and walking a fifth to wind down, she had climbed the bleachers to the top row. She sat alone, with a false sense of security from her elevated location, and chewed a glucose tablet to replenish her blood sugar. With elbows on her knees, Alex had slouched forward, burying her head in her hands, and forced herself to relive the nightmare over and over again in her mind. She had fought futilely to control the sobs and tremors as she searched for something, anything, that would link the intruder to someone she knew. The muffled voice. The harrowing words. His clothing. His actions. Those dark, cruel eyes.

Nothing.

Nothing made sense. Nothing triggered in her mind. She had been psychologically terrorized into believing the man behind the black mask was Dale Ryzik, and from that point on, her ability to reason ceased. Depressed and feeling helpless she had cowered on the bleachers, sobbing into her hands while a fine misty rain had begun falling from the sky.

Inside her living room Matt plopped onto the couch, face down, while Alex went through the ritual of testing her blood sugar in the kitchen. She drank some juice then poured two tall glasses of water. Carrying the water into the living room, she quietly stood alongside the couch, gazing down at him, once again admiring his masculine form. Her body craved for his touch, for release, but the thought of intimacy knotted her stomach. She set the glasses down on the end table and inwardly cursed her absurd fears.

She nestled on the edge of the cushion and leaned over him, slipping her hands under his tee shirt and around his waist.

He moaned pleasurably. "Officer Griffin, are you trying to pat me down?"

She laughed, allowing her fingers to roam under the band of his shorts, slightly. She wanted desperately to feel him, disassociate him from the horror of that night. She reminded herself she was in control of this moment; she could stop at any time. "Why do you ask? Are you concealing a dangerous weapon?"

Matt sighed. "Wow, was that a loaded question." He twisted his head around and looked up at her. "No weapon in there. Just six inches of purely adult entertainment. You may see for yourself."

Alex exhaled heavily. She couldn't make the separation. "I can't." She quickly withdrew her hands.

Matt sat up and took her into his arms. "It's okay, no problem. The choice is yours. But whenever you're ready," he said softly, "I promise you'll be in the driver's seat. You understand that, lady? I love you. I'd never hurt you."

"I know."

"I'd wait an eternity if I had to."

"Matt, Greg Van Dien wants to talk to you, tomorrow sometime."

"The detective? Why?"

"He's looking for information…on Brian Haney."

Matt pulled away, staring at her. "He doesn't think Brian's—"

"He doesn't know *what* to think anymore. I've managed to piss enough people off *I* don't know what to think anymore, either."

"But why Brian?" His voice sounded alarmed.

"Because of his association with Kyle and you."

"That's it?" Matt reached for the water on the end table and downed the glassful in one long swallow. Gut-wrenching thoughts of Brian Haney torturing her raced through his mind, inciting an explosion of rage. "I…I'll…I'll *kill* him!"

Alex bit her lip, suppressing the need to vent her displeasure with this whole guessing game she was being forced to play. "Matt, there isn't one inkling of evidence or probable cause. So calm down, okay? Just be honest with Greg and keep an open mind. Don't jump to any conclusions. As far as Greg's concerned—"

"As far as Greg's concerned? What about you, Alex?"

"Matt, if there's no positive fingerprint or DNA match, this guy's free for the rest of his life. I can't identify anyone. I only saw eyes. And nothing's triggering in my mind. Without a physical match there's no case. You know what frightens me the most?"

Matt slowly shook his head.

"The fact I have no idea who it was," she muttered, her eyes brimming with tears, "and that so many people had it out for me."

He held her protectively. "I hate this as much as you do. The thought of this guy being out there frustrates me to death. I feel so helpless."

Alex buried her face in his shoulder. "If they don't find him, I don't know what I'll do. Every guy I look at with dark eyes, I'll be thinking: Was it him? I can't…deal with that."

Matt gently stroked her ponytail. "They'll find him. You've got to be positive." He lifted her chin, dried her watery eyes, and kissed her softly. "Let's not dwell on that. What do you say we shower and change and go down to the lake? We can watch the sun set from the overlook."

Alex's face brightened. "Sounds great."

Lisa found Renee in the garage cleaning out the interior of her car.

"I'm going to the plaza with Jimmy in a little while," she said. "Need anything?"

"No, thanks," Renee said coldly. She was crouched under the steering wheel, her legs protruding out from under the opened door as she swept dirt and pebbles from the car floor. She did not bother to look up at her sister.

"Is something wrong?" Lisa asked.

"No."

Lisa pursed her lips, skeptically. Renee hadn't been too talkative the last few days, and Lisa was becoming a bit more than curious to know the reason. She pulled a stool out from underneath her father's workbench and sat down, resting her feet on the lowest rung. "You're lying. Talk to me."

Renee dropped the whiskbroom and straightened to face her sister. "What's your problem? You said you were going shopping. So go. Get out of my hair."

"Jimmy won't be here until eight. That gives us plenty of time to chat."

"I'm busy." Renee resumed her cleaning.

"C'mon. What's bothering you?"

Renee exhaled angrily. "Look, Lisa, I'm fine. Okay? Work's been tough, that's all."

"Uh–huh."

Hidden by the car door Renee clenched her teeth. She drew in a deep breath to settle her irritation, contain her feelings of guilt. "Really. I'm okay."

Lisa slapped her hands on her thighs and shrugged. "If you say so." She stepped off the stool and walked out of the garage.

"Lisa, wait," Renee called, standing up. Her sister reappeared. "How's Alex?"

"She's…okay."

"What's happening with the investigation?"

Lisa eyed her sibling suspiciously. "I can't say. I'll know more on Friday. Why are you asking?"

"I'm concerned, that's all."

"Why?"

"Because Alex is a friend," Renee snapped. "Can't I be concerned?"

Lisa settled on the stool for a second time. "Renee, do you know something you're keeping to yourself?"

"No."

"Something about Stanton?"

"No! What is it between you and him? He said you were an instigator. I'm beginning to believe him."

"He said *I* was an instigator?" Lisa's face flared with anger. "I'm sorry, but *he's* got a problem."

"Why don't you leave him alone?"

"Do you want to know what he really said to me Monday afternoon?"

"No, I don't! I want you to leave him alone, and I want you to stay out of my life! I'm sick and tired of you, Lisa. I'm sick and tired of your attitude. Of your self–righteousness, your suspicions." The floodgates opened, envious words spilling out. "You always got everything! I never got anything! You got the scholarship. You got all the attention. You even got assigned that stupid study hall in eleventh grade! Maybe if I did, maybe I'd be with Jim Ostler right now instead of you. Maybe I'd be...happy."

Lisa stared at her sister, devastated, words failing her. Tears stung her eyes. "Is that what you think? You hate me?" She looked away, fixing on an old saw hanging on the wall. "I never tried to one–up you. I never saw any of it that way. We were always a team, you and I..." She stopped, overwhelmed by emotion. "I...I...don't know what...to say."

Renee lowered her head. "I don't hate you, Lisa. I envy your life. You've got it all. Everything always went your way."

"Everything always went my way? If everything went my way, Mom would still be alive."

"I'm not talking about Mom. I'm not talking about our family. I'm talking about *you*. You do everything right. You're so...perfect."

"Have you got it all wrong," Lisa muttered, shaking her head. Perhaps now was the time to own up to the mistake that had destroyed her self–respect, her ability to trust. Perhaps Renee needed to know how "perfect" she was.

Lisa's eyes made their way back to her sister. She cleared her throat. "Ever go to a party in college and get shit–faced?"

Renee looked at her, bewildered and annoyed. "What?"

"Answer me, Renee. I know you have."

"Yeah, so? Like you *haven't*?"

"Yes, I have. I also know you've picked up quite a few guys at those parties."

"What's it to you? Some of us didn't have the boy–toy you had at your beck and call."

Lisa let out a short, cynical laugh. "I picked up a guy, once, when my boy–toy, as you so put it, was in Europe. Your so–called perfect sister got hammered at a frat party one weekend during her sophomore year and started flirting with a black football player. One thing led to another, and he ended up walking me back to my room." She paused, momentarily, to glance up at the deadpan expression on Renee's face. "And I invited him in—"

"You slept with a *black* guy behind Jimmy's back?" Renee's voice was tinged with amusement and spite.

"It didn't go like I thought. He wanted to hurt me." She paused again to assess Renee's reaction. There was none. Her sister simply stared down at her, arms folded across her chest. "You don't get it, do you? He raped me."

Renee's arms fell away. "What?" she whispered, horrified. "W…what the hell are you talking about?"

"I'm talking about something I've kept to myself for five years." Lisa inhaled deeply to calm the uneasiness that threatened her composure before she described what had happened in her dorm room. "All I kept thinking the entire time was how could I have been so stupid, how could I have fallen into a trap. I hated myself for being so naive. I should have known better."

Renee was numb. She stared down at her sister, frozen with disbelief. "Oh, God," she whispered, ashamed of her malicious, petty behavior. She squeezed her eyes shut, a stream of tears gushing out from under her lids. "The knife at the school… Lise, I'm so sorry."

Lisa finally allowed her own tears to materialize. "I couldn't report it. I didn't think I could prove it, and I was…scared. Scared of Jimmy's reaction. Scared of what would happen to Mom and Dad if they found out, especially Mom. It doesn't always happen to strangers. Look at Alex. Do you understand now why I'm leery of people? I'm sorry for acting suspiciously, but I can't help the way I've become. That night changed the way I see people. It put me on the defense all the time, and I have a hard time trusting people. I hope you can understand that."

Renee shook her head and cried. Her mind raced wildly with thoughts of all the times she had acted recklessly, immorally. With guys at college, with a few guys in town. With Rick Stanton. She knew little about him. Only what he *chose* to tell her. How selfish, how depraved could she be to keep what she had discovered about him to herself?

"I...I don't know what to say about your feelings toward me," Lisa muttered, dejected by Renee's revelation of envy. "I never, ever, meant to hurt you, but if I did, I'm sorry...you mean the world to me. I don't know what to say about Jimmy, either. Sometimes I wonder myself if he would have been better off with you...especially after...after what I did...was going to do. I guess...I paid for it."

Consumed with self–anger, Renee forced herself to meet her sister's eyes. "Lisa, I've acted like such a fool. I need to talk to you about Rick, about some things I found in his apartment."

She perched herself up on the hood of the car and revealed what she had discovered: the gun, the letter, the newspaper pictures. She explained the contents of the letter and everything she had done to coerce him into telling the truth, including the visit to his office. She also brought forth the phone bill with the call to Canada documented during the time of the assault.

"I believed he was telling the truth," Renee admitted. "That's why I kept quiet. And because I wanted you to be wrong. I'm sorry. I feel so bad for Alex."

Lisa slowly digested the information. "His mother beat him? It's no wonder he hates women. He's a classic example of a textbook rapist, and you put yourself in a dangerous situation," she blasted.

"He didn't hurt me. He didn't even try. He sat there and explained everything. He didn't try to stop me when I left, either, which also led me to believe he was telling the truth."

"You're *sure* the phone bill was authentic?"

"It looked like the bill we get every month."

"And he said the gun is registered?"

"He told me I could check it out."

"That means nothing. The gun that was used has been recovered. He could have had a registered gun *and* an unregistered one."

"What are you going to do now?" Renee asked.

"He destroyed the letter?"

"He said he ripped it to shreds."

"Greg may be able to bring him in for questioning and get a search warrant for his apartment based on what you told me, but you're going to have to retell everything to him. He's looking into a few other possibilities."

"What other possibilities?"

"I'm sorry, I can't say. You'll find out in due time. But I can tell you Greg is having some cops down in Philly check on Rick. I…asked him to. Because of my suspicion."

"I understand," Renee said, then added with hope, "If he's clean we can put all this behind us. Maybe I can help him, like his old girlfriend. But only if he's clean."

"I have to admit I've been antagonizing him. Maybe I wasn't thinking objectively."

"You know, Lisa," Renee interrupted, remembering something else that had been working on her mind. "Do you think Rick would know where Dale Ryzik lived? Since whoever did this planted the evidence in his car."

Lisa raised her eyebrows in a quandary. "He could have gotten the address easily through the newspaper files. The Ryziks have been arrested a number of times."

"But it's a rural–route address with a box number. Do you think he could find it without a road name? I mean, c'mon, Dale Ryzik lives in a dumpy trailer at the end of an unnamed dirt road no one uses but him. The mail carrier doesn't even travel on it."

Lisa pressed her lips together and nodded. "That logic may be the answer we need. But Greg still needs to know about everything."

"I should have had faith in you right from the beginning."

Lisa sighed. "Your sister is no saint. I've done some pretty stupid things in my life."

"About what happened at North Penn," Renee said timidly. "Y...you never told *anyone*?"

"Not until last week. I told Alex. She needed to know she wasn't alone. And Greg got it out of me Monday afternoon. I accidentally said something to Alex that made him figure it out."

"What about Jimmy?"

"I can't tell him. You have to promise me this stays between us. I don't want Dad or Tony finding out about it, either. They'd never be able to accept the fact I wanted to sleep with a black guy behind Jim's back, for obvious reasons, and for the sad fact most people in this county are prejudice."

Renee slid off the car and Lisa stood up, glancing down at her wristwatch. It was seven forty–five. "Jimmy should be here soon," Lisa said.

Simultaneously they walked out of the garage, and simultaneously they froze at the sight before them. Jim and Tony stood perfectly still alongside the overhead–door opening, their faces aghast.

"J...Jimmy," Lisa sputtered. "How long have you been standing there?"

The look on his face provided the answer. His eyes glistened with disbelief, with anger, with betrayal.

"Jimmy?"

"Long enough." He grabbed her by the arm and jerked her toward the house.

Jim slammed the bedroom door shut and pushed her against the wall. "What did I just hear? About you sleeping with a black guy behind my back! Did I hear right? Did I?"

"N…no. You d…don't under…stand," Lisa stammered, on the verge of panic, staring into his flaring blue eyes. She had never wanted to be in this situation!

"What's there to understand? I heard you say you slept with a black guy!"

She shook her head, frantically. "No, you heard wrong."

"You're lying!"

"No!"

"Then what *did* you do?" He dropped onto the bed, burying his face in his hands. "How could you do this to me? I can't believe what I heard you say!"

"I didn't sleep with him."

Jim shot her a fierce glare. "How could you stand there and *lie* to me. I *heard* you say it."

"You heard the tail end of it. You took it out of context."

"Then tell me the whole story," he said, bitterly. "I'm real curious to hear it."

"No." She shook her head in desperation. "I…I can't. Don't make me do it…please."

An eerie silence fell between them as he glared into her eyes. "Why don't you want to tell me? Lisa, you're my life. How could you do this to me?" The shock, the breech in their unyielding faith was more than he could handle. The tears came involuntarily.

Lisa couldn't deal with his tears. "Jimmy, I'm so sorry." She sank to the floor and sobbed guiltily. She had to tell him. There was no way out. Stammering word after word she painstakingly confessed her harrowing secret. "I'm so sorry. I'm so sorry. I…I…I never meant to hurt you."

Jim sat, staring at the carpet, shell–shocked. "Y…you were… After all this with Alex you're telling me now that you were…too?"

"Yes," she muttered, barely above a whisper.

"Whoa, wait a minute. Let me get this straight. You whooped it up and came on to a football player." The anger in his voice intensified as he ground out each word. "And you had every *intention* of sleeping with him, but he roughed you up so you changed your mind. And then he got mad, so he put a knife to your throat and *forced* you." He snickered. "You know what?" He raised his eyes to burn hers with malice. "You deserved it."

His words hit with such force Lisa did nothing but shut her eyes and cry. Heartbroken she accepted her fate. "I'm so sorry I hurt you. I never meant to hurt you. You have to believe me."

"Why didn't you report it to the police?"

"I didn't know what to do. I was scared."

"You, scared? The criminal justice major. Don't give me that shit."

"Jimmy, how could you say these things? You don't understand. I didn't think I could...prove it. And my mother was dying at the time. How could I put her through that? How could I tell my mom I was raped?"

Jim scoffed, rising to his feet. "You couldn't tell her because you asked for it." Shock and bitterness overwhelmed his ability to think, to console, and thoughtless, taunting words flew from his mouth. "Was he bigger than me? Isn't that what they say about black guys? Was it *worth* it?"

He threw open the door and flew down the stairs and out of the house.

Alex and Matt relaxed on a bench at the Lake Iroquois overlook, casually watching motorboats cruise the lake. The brightest stars appeared in the gray–blue sky as the sun dipped behind the distant mountains, its fading rays glimmering across the water. Several couples strolled along the scenic path, and a group of teenagers lounged on the grassy hill descending to the shoreline.

"It's such a beautiful night," Alex said as a warm breeze swirled off the water. "I needed this distraction."

He intertwined his fingers with hers. “I’m glad you’ve cheered up.” Softly he touched her chin. “I love to see that smile of yours.”

That smile appeared, self–consciously. “You’re such a charmer.”

“I’ll take that as a compliment.”

“It was meant to be a compliment.” Alex’s eyes wandered around. There was nothing like a clear, summer night in the country.

“What’re you looking at?”

“Everything. I love the outdoors. But you knew that already.”

“We have so much in common. We were meant to be together.”

Alex met his gaze, squeezing his hand. Her feelings for him were genuine, and she needed badly to put her sexual apprehensions behind her. She *had* to make the separation from her assailant. For self–esteem. For a sense of normalcy. If destroying her sexual freedom had been one of that bastard’s goals, she’d be damned if she’d let him achieve it.

“Let’s take a walk down to the rocks,” she said, the expression on her face hinting of urgency. “I want to talk out of earshot.”

They nonchalantly made their way down the wooded trail to the large boulders hugging the shoreline. Leaning with her back against the same rock they had made love on two weeks earlier, Alex lifted herself up onto the flat surface and invited him to embrace her. He stood before her, nuzzling his upper body against hers as she loosely wrapped her legs around his thighs. Her arms maneuvered around his neck, and she kissed him.

When she finally pulled away Matt smiled exuberantly. “I have a fond recollection of this spot.”

She returned the smile. “So do I. That’s why I wanted to come down here.” She slid her hands over his shoulders, down his arms, pressing her palms against his rough, dry hands and interlocking her fingers with his. “You are the most sensual, caring man I’ve ever met,” she said, gazing into his pale green eyes. “I know how I feel about you, but for you to stick by me after what I’ve been through—even go out and get a book to help me—that tells me so much more than words could ever say. That…book you got from the library was both…frightening and enlightening. It put a lot into perspective for me, things I needed to understand and deal with. Matt, about our being intimate—"

He stopped her with a shake of his head. "Al, please, don't try to explain. I told you it's okay."

"No, listen to me. I need to make the separation. What happened in my bedroom wasn't sex, and I don't want to go on being afraid, because there's no reason I should." She freed her fingers and slowly ran her hands across the soft cotton material of his golf shirt, massaging his chest. "I want to be with you, tonight. I want to take it real slow."

"Are you sure?"

"Yes."

Matt held her chin gently between his thumb and index finger as his lips delicately found hers. "The pleasure is all mine. My place?"

"No, my place. It's got to be my place. My…bedroom."

Alex opened the window and lowered the shade to a few inches above the sill. It provided privacy, yet allowed the warm summer breeze to infiltrate her bedroom.

She turned to Matt, standing alongside the bed. Without saying a word, she went to him, and he drew her into his arms.

He kissed her softly, his hands trailing down the back of her shirt, slipping underneath. "Stop me if I go too fast, please."

She looked into his eyes. "It's okay."

He undressed her slowly, carefully, dropping onto his knees before her. His eyes gazed with adoration as he pressed close, caressing her abdomen with his lips.

Alex closed her eyes and allowed her fingers to rake his hair. Her body ached with a long–overdue desire for release.

"You're so beautiful," he breathed, rising to his feet, unable to concentrate on anything but the sensuality of her body craving to be loved, healed of emotional wounds. He pulled his shirt over his head, letting it fall to the floor behind him, and unfastened his shorts.

"Let me," she said, bringing herself closer, hesitantly burrowing her hands under the waistband. Her fingers lingered for a few seconds, and he could see the apprehension in her eyes.

"Al, you don't have to."

She held his gaze. "I want to." Slowly, timidly exploring, she permitted herself to touch him.

He groaned with burgeoning desire.

She let his shorts and underwear drop around his ankles, her hands gliding up to splay his chest hairs. He stepped out of his clothes and scooped her into his arms, laying her across the bed. "I love you so much."

He pushed a few strands of her long, wild hair away from her face and kissed her deeply. Then, his mouth began a slow, searing, downward journey, his lips and tongue caressing, licking. He felt her body trembling and looked up. "Are you all right? I'll stop."

She whispered, "Please, don't."

He exhaled heavily, his mouth returning to her breasts, her abdomen, and then venturing lower. He took it especially slow there, loving the way she moaned in rhythm with his moves. He was deliberate, unyielding. It was his innermost display of the passion he felt for her, of the commitment he vowed to preserve. And it was his way of assuring her he expected no reciprocation, he understood her trepidation to please him in the same manner.

Tears of physical pleasure and mental pain rolled onto the sheets from her eyes as he finally brought her to that euphoric crest.

He rose to his knees and readied himself. She welcomed his weight, his warmth, as he returned to her, slowly easing himself inside. She arched against him, and he moved with her body, at her pace. His eyes blazed with a passionate fire as he watched her, felt her lead him to a powerful climax.

Afterward he held her in his arms. She pressed her face against his chest and sobbed. She had cleared the most emotional hurdle of the healing process.

He gently stroked her hair as he kissed the top of her head and whispered, "I love you."

Rick sat at the desk in the living room of his apartment operating his laptop computer. He was engrossed in the desktop–publishing program he had recently purchased from a catalog warehouse. The design and graphic capabilities of this particular software system were endless. It would undoubtedly enhance the layout of the *Journal*, and sharpen the appearance of office forms and invoice slips. He had already experimented with some documents of his own. He had scanned their images onto the system at work, copied them to a floppy disk, and manipulated the formats and numbers at home on his laptop. The program was worth every penny of its five–hundred–dollar price tag.

He took a swig from the bottle of beer close at hand and wailed out a few lines of the classic–rock song blaring through the stereo speakers. He wrapped his fingers on the edge of the desk to the beat of the music and lit up a cigarette. He only smoked when stressed out, and the encounter with Renee Maselli last night had taxed his nerves—and his lungs—to a detrimental two–pack binge. He needed to engross himself in computer work to keep his mind off her—and her accusations.

He was so absorbed in the computer and music he jumped out of his chair when a forceful knock came at the door. He fumbled for the ashtray to deposit the cigarette and quickly silenced the stereo. Who the hell was at the door? He immediately froze, a panicky thought entering his mind: It was the police. She didn't believe him. She had gone to the police with the information she had learned. He glanced around for a means of escape. What was he trying to run from? He had an alibi. He walked into the kitchen and glanced at the wall clock. A quarter to ten. Cautiously he peaked through the blind to see who it was. Ill–at–ease he tossed his bangs back and opened the door.

"Renee," he muttered, his eyes scanning the figure before him. She wore a Pittsburgh Steelers tee shirt and black shorts. Her hair was a mess, her eyes red and swollen, her face streaked from tears. In her right hand she gripped an empty pint bottle of whiskey, her breath reeking of its missing contents.

"Maybe, maybe not," she mumbled, staggering past him into the kitchen.

"What's that supposed to mean?" His eyes widened at the mind–blowing possibility it was *Lisa* Maselli barging into his apartment. As he closed the door he studied her features intently but could not make a determination.

She tossed the empty liquor bottle into the garbage basket. "Who do *you* think it is?"

He stared at her, shaking his head. "I…I don't know."

She stepped close to him, pinching his cheek. "Do you think Lisa Maselli would get wasted and drive over here drunk off her ass? Do you? Hey, she's lucky she didn't get picked up for DUI. Ain't that right, Ricky? Wouldn't that be so ironic? Huh? Me getting arrested for DUI? With your hearing coming up Friday."

Me! She said me! Rick's heart pounded. It *was* Lisa, and she was intoxicated well beyond the legal limit. What the hell was she doing here? Why had she been drinking? And crying? It was obvious she had been crying for quite some time.

"Lisa?" he mumbled, barely audible.

"Yeah, it's me. Came for a little visit, that's all." She went into the living room and swaggered around, snooping. He followed on her heels, nervous and confused.

"Nice computer." She leaned over the desk, clutching the top of the chair to steady herself. She squinted in an attempt to focus on the screen. It was some kind of billing statement. She moved her index finger to the "delete" key. "What would happen if I hit this?"

He rushed over and ushered her away before she could touch the keyboard. Her next stop was the stereo. She began rummaging through his CDs and cassette tapes, nonchalantly reviewing the titles. "No *Night Crew* tapes, huh?"

"What's with you and *Night Crew*?"

She burst into a peevish laughter. "If you don't know then don't worry about it."

He dropped into a chair, whisking his hair from his eyes, leaning back with his legs spread. "What are you doing here? You're totally wasted, and frankly, I don't trust you as far as I can throw you."

The silliness continued. She plopped down on the floor and crossed her legs. "You couldn't throw me."

He shook his head in amusement, disbelief. "Where have you been?"

Lisa giggled. "D…drowning my sorrows."

"With whom?" His voice was stern.

"By myself at the cliff. And I've been d…driving under the infl…fluence. Ain't that a fine how–da–ya–do?"

The sight of her before him, stewed to the gills, was rather entertaining. If he played along, she'd spill her guts. Knowledge was power. "What happened? Why are you here?"

Lisa began shaking her head, slowly. Her eyes brimmed with tears. "It doesn't matter, not anymore."

He repeated in a level voice, "Why are you here?"

She raised her eyes up and said with a frightening seriousness, "Because I'm a whore and who better to punish me than the man who hates women."

Rick sat paralyzed. He held her stare with narrowing eyes as an array of emotions surged through his veins. It went without saying

Renee had disclosed the undignified details of his childhood. Was this visit a setup? A trick devised by the two of them? But how could it be? She was genuinely drunk.

"Renee told me everything. The letter, the gun, all about your mother, your girlfriend, all those clippings from the p...paper, your feelings toward me."

He continued to glare at her in stone silence.

"I don't know wh...what to make of you. A lot of strange things started happening since you moved here. Coincidence...or not?"

Rick raised an eyebrow. "What do *you* think, Officer?"

She threw her hands up in the air. "What the hell do I know? I'm so messed up. It was only a matter of time before it all caught up to me."

He couldn't remove his eyes from hers. They were locked together in some kind of disturbing, arousing manner. He held his ground. "You're not making any sense."

Lisa lifted up on her knees. "What's there to make sense of? You got a thing for me, Stanton, and...Friday, we're gonna clash. Cuz I gotta do my job. But now, I ain't wearing my badge..." She maneuvered herself between his lanky legs and unfastened the snap on his jeans. "You be the judge. Tell me if I give good head. You've been dying to know."

Stop her! a voice inside screamed. Stop her! It's a setup. It's a trick. She's going to burn you, good.

Her fingers lowered his zipper—and he did nothing. Nothing but respond to her unmistakable intention, his heart pounding through his chest, his breath heaving with lust, his blood surging. He dropped his head back on the chair, gripped the armrests—and did absolutely nothing.

"Oh...Christ," he rushed the words as her mouth found his erection. He moaned and gasped and muttered incoherently as she consumed him.

It was over in seconds.

Staring at the ceiling, wallowing in his victory, he breathed heavily. "Oh...God," he gasped, running a hand through his hair. He lifted his head to meet her eyes. "I had you pegged the minute I saw you."

Lisa fell back on her heels, her head spinning from the alcohol, from her wanton behavior. You're right, Jimmy, she mocked inwardly, I deserve everything I get. I'm a whore, and I don't deserve respect, from anyone. Not even from this woman–hater. Hell, I got burned once, what's another time? Let him beat me if he wants. Let him kill me. *I don't care.*

Not anymore.

She met Stanton's eyes with a forbidding, salacious glare. "It's your turn, City Boy. C'mon, do those things to me I couldn't fantasize about. I'm not wearing a uniform. I ain't got a gun."

Rick was on his knees, his mouth devouring hers with a forceful kiss. But a vision of Caroline suddenly flashed before him, and his heart opened up. He pulled Lisa into his arms and simply held her.

"I don't know what happened," he said, cradling her head in his hand as she broke down. "But I can't do this to you, not now. You're going to be sober when I nail you, Officer Maselli."

CHAPTER 23

Techno–Savvy Mind Games

Matt arrived for work at seven–fifteen, forty–five minutes earlier than usual. He unlocked the office and tossed his keys on the desk then immediately marched across the garage to Haney's locker. He carefully rummaged through the junk stored in the old, beat–up compartment, finding a comb, two packs of cigarettes, a pack of gum, a few quarters and dimes, a candy bar, and three cassette tapes—none *Night Crew*.

Matt closed his eyes, sorting over his troublesome thoughts. What had he expected to find in the locker? Something that would link Haney to the assault? The mere speculation Brian had been behind that mask worked on his mind all through the night. Brian's shy behavior, his tendency to be a loner, now bothered Matt. Before it meant nothing. It would have never occurred to him Brian could have been capable of committing such a crime, but now...

Now he didn't know what to think.

Matt went back into the office and brewed a pot of coffee. While he waited for the water to heat and filter through the machine, he sat in an old wooden chair, hunched forward, and called to mind the instances when he had mentioned his interest in Alex to Brian.

"Man, that new cop in town is drop dead gorgeous," Matt remembered telling Brian a few weeks after Alex had started on the downtown patrol. "Those blue eyes of hers are enough to get my motor running."

Brian had responded to the statement with a smirk and shake of the head. Not once had Brian let on Alex was dating Lawry—his friend. Extremely peculiar, Matt now thought. He recalled Alex telling him Brian never came around during that ill–fated relationship with Lawry. Why was that? Was Brian jealous? Did he dislike her?

Questions with no answers.

Matt reached for his mug and filled it with the steaming–fresh coffee. Sipping the hot beverage, its potent aroma penetrating his nostrils, he began pacing back and forth in the office, considering what the police knew about the assailant.

Brown eyes.

Brian.

Dark brown hair.

Brian.

A dropped *Night Crew* tape.

Brian had played *Night Crew* constantly on that boom box of his on the wall shelf. But he hadn't heard the tape recently. Not in the last two weeks. Did Brian lose interest?

Or did Brian lose the tape?

Matt snarled in frustration, clenching a fist and slamming it down on the desktop. "I swear, Haney, if you did this to her…"

Tears stung Jim's eyes as he drove to Paula Sedlak's place. The morning sun, low on the horizon, blazed blinding rays of light and heat at the driver's side of the car. He cursed loudly.

This educational seminar in Scranton could not have come at a worse time. He was simply going through the motions, operating the car like a programmed robot. His head pounded, and he nursed coffee from a plastic–foam cup to settle the nausea in his stomach.

After storming out of the Maselli's house last night, he had driven to the hardware store, closed for the evening, and let himself in through the back–alley door. Raging depths of deception and betrayal had engulfed his mind as he threw cartons of merchandise around the stockroom. His love for Lisa was steadfast. *She* had made a mockery of his devotion. Not once in the past eight years had he breached their monogamy, albeit with some temptations at North Penn and despite audacious offers in France and Germany. Especially in France. French college girls had some unexplainable *idee fixe* with American guys, and he had been tempted on a few occasions to satisfy their curiosity—and his own—rationalizing with his scruples Lisa would never know. But he had resisted. The guilt would have wreaked havoc on his conscience.

The thought of her with another man was more than he could handle. The ungovernable anger that burned within him masked what actually had occurred in her dorm room that snowy night.

"How could you do this to me?" he had shouted, succumbing to his knees. Physically drained he doubled over, selfish despair consuming his thoughts. He had not seen the whole picture. He only had seen betrayal. And it had hit like the A–bomb. Out of nowhere. With total devastation.

Not until he sat back against the stockroom wall—and got a hold of himself—did he realize what Lisa had acknowledged. Not her reckless action, not the deception, but the cold hard fact she had been raped.

Numbness washed over him as her agonizing words finally had registered. Then, out of the blue, he had remembered Lisa coming to his house, two Sundays ago, after Alex had been attacked. They had been talking about Alex's relationship with Matt Ehrich… *If he's any kind of decent guy and really does have feelings for her, then he'd better damn well be understanding and supportive.* Those had been his exact words.

Jim arched his head against the wall. Lisa had then asked if he'd feel the same way if it had been her... She had been seeking his support, his understanding. And what had he done? What had he said to her?

You deserved it. You asked for it. Was it worth it?

He had slain her with a double–edged sword.

He had wanted to go back, tell her he reacted irrationally, that he was sorry and didn't mean what he had said. He had wanted to talk, work it out. But he couldn't go back. He had delivered the knockout punch. Lisa would never forgive him. And he couldn't blame her. No one deserved to be terrorized and degraded.

"What have I done?" He had destroyed eight years of love and trust and openness in the seconds it took to thoughtlessly spew those inhumane words at her.

He had sat on the stockroom floor, despondent, as the night waned away. Tears had rolled down his cheeks as he realized the mental anguish she must have endured, alone, all these years. She had not wanted anyone to suffer as a result of her mistake. Including him. And look what he had done. He had thrown it back in her face.

About ten o'clock he pressed himself to straighten up the boxes of stock he had ransacked then drove to Vic's and purchased a couple six packs of beer. He took them to Becker's Pond and drank in misery along the edge of the water. Lying in the tall grass, in the still and darkness of the muggy night, he had stared up into the starry sky, praying she'd forgive him. He couldn't bear to be without her. He couldn't *live* without her. Sometime after midnight he had drifted asleep only to be awakened four hours later by an earsplitting rumble of thunder from an approaching storm.

He pulled into Paula's driveway and honked the horn. She sauntered out of the house dressed in a snug silk–knit blouse and rayon pants and slid in on the passenger side. Jim barely acknowledged her presence, throwing the car into reverse, then into drive, and accelerating down the road.

She tipped her head and looked at him apprehensively. She hesitated a moment before muttering, "Good morning."

"It's anything but that," he hissed, locking his eyes on the road ahead. He surmised what she had planned for the day in Scranton—and he wanted *no* part of it.

Renee sat at the kitchen table, staring down at the front page of yesterday's *Journal*. The heading of the article in the lower right corner read: *Ryzik Cleared of Sexual Assault. Search for Assailant Continues.*

She skimmed through the piece, authored by Richard A. Stanton himself, Editor–In–Chief. But it was hard for her to concentrate on the newspaper or think about the investigation, the uncertainty with Rick. Her mind was preoccupied with the staggering events of the night before.

Renee's heart had sunk at the sight of Jim and Tony standing outside the garage, and she had been overcome with a sense of helplessness as Jim grabbed Lisa's arm and took her into the house. Renee had stood in the driveway, frozen by fear. How much had Jim heard? She exchanged a worried, inquisitive glance with her younger brother. Tony had responded by blabbing in exasperation, "Correct me if I'm wrong. But did I hear Lisa say she did the nasty with a nigger?"

The back of her hand came across his face with such force the blow knocked him off balance.

"What the hell?" Tony cursed, babying his injured cheek.

"Don't you *ever* use that word again!" Renee seized his shirt and jerked him forward. "And you heard *wrong*!"

Tony's face flushed with embarrassment. He had not appreciated his sister manhandling him. "Then what'd I hear?"

"Nothing. You heard nothing."

"C'mon. Jimmy heard it, too."

"You didn't hear the whole conversation. And the rest is none of your business."

"Why not?"

"Because..." She had paused, anxiously glancing at the house. "Because it was supposed to be between Lisa and me. And don't you dare breathe a word of this to Dad. I'm dead serious about this, Tony. Do you understand me?"

"No, I don't!"

Renee had exhaled to calm herself, releasing his shirt. "Look, Lisa didn't sleep with anybody behind Jim's back. Trust me on this, okay? I know it sounded that way, but it's *not* what happened."

"So what's going to happen between her and Jim now? He heard what I heard."

"I...don't know."

When she and Tony walked into the kitchen minutes later, the sound of the confrontation upstairs had been disheartening. She had wanted to keep Tony away, but she didn't know how. She couldn't leave. She needed to be there for Lisa. Horrified, Tony had stood in the foyer at the bottom of the staircase, listening to his sister's pleading voice and Jim's rage emanating from the bedroom above. Their words had been as plain as day. Stunned he looked over at his sister standing in the doorway to the kitchen. His voice cracked when he finally spoke, and his eyes quickly filled with tears.

"Lisa was..."

Renee's own tears had rolled untouched down her cheeks. Slowly she nodded, sadly whispering, "Yeah."

Numbly Tony shook his head. "By that—"

"Don't say it." Renee muttered through sobs.

"By that *nigger*?"

Renee squeezed her eyes shut, torn between her strong disapproval of racial slurs and her vile hatred for this individual who had violated her sister. "I warned you about that language."

Tony stared at her, ignoring the admonishment. "W...why didn't she do something about it?" he had asked with the innocence and ignorance only a seventeen–year–old could possess. "Why'd she let him get away with it?"

"Only Lisa can tell you that," Renee had said. "It wouldn't be fair if I told you."

Before she could say anything further, he hurried out of the foyer to the rec–room in the basement. Down there he could hide from the painful reality of what was transpiring two stories above.

Not long after, Jim bolted from the house like a bat out of hell. Renee had tried to console Lisa, but in a rebellious fury, Lisa grabbed her car keys and fled.

The night had dragged on endlessly, Renee worrying terribly about her sister's whereabouts and volatile state of mind. She couldn't even have begun to fathom what Lisa was going through and as darkness fell her anxiety had mushroomed into a real fear. When her father walked into the house at ten P.M. after a lengthy commissioners' meeting, Renee had faked a cheery greeting.

"Where's the other two?" Robert Maselli had asked.

"Tony's downstairs. Lisa's out," had been her reply. Nothing unusual about that. Her father had showered, enjoyed a beer on the back porch, and retired to his room upstairs, unaware of the earlier commotion.

A few minutes past eleven–thirty Renee rousted her brother from his safe haven in the basement to accompany her on a search for Lisa. They drove up to the cliff, past Jim's house, by Alex's place. They had been heading north on Main Street, en route to Becker's Pond, when Tony spotted Lisa turning onto Main from Centre Street. They followed close behind as Lisa drove home at a snail's pace.

"Where have you been?" Renee insisted after jumping from her car and running up to Lisa's door.

"Here, there, and everywhere," Lisa had scoffed, stumbling out of the car and trudging across the front lawn.

Renee and Tony exchanged concerned glances. Lisa's face was flushed, her hair disheveled, her favorite Pittsburgh Steelers shirt torn at the side seam. And it went without saying she had been drinking heavily.

"Lisa, c'mon," Renee had pleaded. "Don't shut me out. I want to help you."

Stopping abruptly at the porch steps Lisa turned around and stared at them, stupefied. "Help me with what? He said I deserved it. He was right."

Renee slept fitfully, and her concern for Lisa's well being had prompted her to use a sick day. The annoyance in her boss's voice had been evident. It was the height of the tourist season, and she had only been on the job six weeks. But Renee couldn't care less whether he believed her lame stomach–virus story or not. Today the only thing of importance was her sister.

It was a quarter past ten, and Lisa and Tony were both still in bed. Renee folded up the newspaper then shuffled around the kitchen, rinsing her coffee mug and wiping up the toast crumbs from the table. She frowned at the noticeable coffee stain she had gotten on the tee shirt she wore—it was Lisa's from North Penn—and decided to change.

As she headed through the foyer a car door shut in the driveway. She detoured to the front door to see who was calling.

The sight before her was an eye opener. Rick Stanton stepped onto the porch, a large manila envelope in his hand and an equally large cocksure smirk on his face.

"Morning, Officer Maselli," he greeted, his voice nothing short of patronizing. "You look much better than I anticipated, considering all that booze you washed down last night."

Puzzled, Renee stared at him through the screen door. Officer Maselli? The shirt, of course. He was associating North Penn with Lisa. And he must have assumed she'd be working. The next thought hit like a ton of bricks. *How did he know Lisa had been drinking last night?* Had she been with *him*? Impossible. They loathed one another. Had her sister been angered—and intoxicated—enough to do something that rash? Renee did not have to think twice about accommodating this visit—Officer Maselli she would be.

"C'mon out here." He gestured with his free hand, and Renee walked onto the porch. "Have a seat." Again he made a motion, toward the swing, and again Renee did as requested, all the while speechless, her eyes questioning.

He sat alongside her and forced a hard, lewd kiss on her lips, driving his tongue deep inside her mouth.

Renee's eyes flew open. She furiously pushed him away. *What the hell was going on*? *What the hell had gone on between him and Lisa*?

Rick snickered, grinning, his fingers making slow, suggestive circles over her kneecaps. "Don't you remember what you did to me last night?"

"What are you talking about?" Renee gasped, struggling to control the emotional upheaval that mounted within her. Her head spun with outrageous thoughts.

"You don't remember? You know, Officer, you shouldn't be acting recklessly. You're supposed to be a pillar of the community, and we're supposed to be able to respect our law enforcement officers." He savored the expression of perplexity on her flushed face as he set the manila envelope on her lap. "Go 'head. Open it. See what I mean."

Renee's stomach knotted from seething anger as trembling fingers fumbled to pull open the metal clasp. She lifted the flap and removed the contents. Her eyes bulged in horror as the images in the top photograph came into view.

It seemed like an eternity as she sat, shell–shocked, her eyes burning holes in the pornographic blowups of Lisa and Jim. "You…you…*took* these pictures?"

"Yep. You and Jimmy boy are quite entertaining, of the adult form that is." Rick nonchalantly leaned back in the swing, an arm coming around her shoulder. "So how do you think the school board would react to those pictures? Doesn't this county have an ordinance banning public nudity?"

She shoved the pictures into his chest and jumped from the swing. "I don't know what you're trying to prove, but you're *sick*! You'd better get help. How could you do this…" To her. She almost said her. She almost blew the guise. He was engaged in a vendetta to avenge his arrest at all costs. Had Alex already paid the price? Was it Lisa's turn? Or had he already gotten that revenge last night? While her sister had been vulnerable. Had he lied to *her* the other night? Falsified the phone bill? Nauseated, Renee covered her mouth, her hand reaching for the porch railing to steady herself.

He left the photos on the swing and rose to his feet, stepping close to her. One arm slid around her waist, trapping her against the railing. His other hand pushed her hair away from her shoulder.

She flinched. "Get away from me."

His hot breath was on her neck, his tongue running over her ear. "*You're* the one who came to *me* last night."

Renee twisted her head away from him and stared into his dark eyes, terrified. What had happened between them?

"You make me sick," she spit out the words, propelling him backward, and darted for the door.

"Whoa." His hand flew out, seizing her arm. "Hold on a minute. Here's the deal with those rather compromising pictures. You're going to conveniently forget about my hearing tomorrow. And so is your partner. I want this little DUI problem of mine dismissed unconditionally."

Renee jerked her arm free. "Fuck you."

Rick Stanton laughed demonically. "You got that backward, honey."

Renee reeled back into the screen door.

"I gotcha now, Officer. Tomorrow, say elevenish, at my office. For an encore performance of last night's head show. And you'd better be there. 'Cause I got those *photos* on a computer disk. You wouldn't want fag boy or, God forbid, your *father* to suffer as a result of your scandalous conduct? Would you now?"

His Nissan had barely vanished from sight when Renee scooped up the pictures from the swing, stuffing them back in the mailer. She tore open the screen door and flew up the steps two at a time. She flung Lisa's bedroom door open, barging inside.

"Get the hell out of bed. Now!" Renee yanked the crumpled sheet off her sister's lifeless body.

Lisa winced.

"Get up! Now!"

Slowly Lisa's eyes parted, the daylight assaulting her throbbing head. She moaned in agony and quickly squeezed her eyes shut. "Leave me alone." Her hand came up to shield the light. A dull, ruthless ache penetrated every inch of her body.

"You got some explaining to do." Renee tossed the envelope onto the dresser and folded her arms across her chest. She stared down at the pathetic sight of her sister, sprawled out facedown, and clad in the same grungy clothing from the night before.

One eye peeked between two fingers. "Go away." With great effort Lisa rolled onto her back. A sudden, unstoppable wave of nausea swelled in her stomach. She cupped her hand over her mouth and leaped from the bed, darting down the hallway to the bathroom. Dropping before the toilet, she vomited, again and again.

When it was over she slumped back against the vanity. Her life as she knew it was no longer, blown to bits in a matter of hours. And she had no one to blame but herself. She thought about the different types of pills stored in the medicine cabinet directly above her. A bottle of painkillers ought to end it all. Or maybe she should crawl back to her bedroom, reach for her pistol hanging in its holster in the closet, shove it into her mouth, and—bang!

"I want to die. Let me die," she cried, burying her head in her hands. A vague recollection of her salacious behavior with Rick Stanton grew clearer as Jim's haunting words echoed in her mind. She drew her knees up close to her chest, wrapping her arms around her legs, and rocked back and forth.

"You deserve everything you get!" She sprang from the floor, her hands swooping around the room in an all–out assault. Candles, soap dishes, the tumbler and toothbrush holder, everything on the vanity and toilet went crashing into the tile wall around the tub.

Renee was in the bathroom in seconds, wresting a hand mirror from her sister's grip. "Get a hold of yourself!"

Roused from bed by the loud clamor, Tony appeared in the doorway dressed only in his briefs, his dark, curly hair tousled. The heart–wrenching pain he felt showed in his dark eyes as he stood, unnoticed, watching Renee's struggle to subdue Lisa. "Is she okay?"

Renee waved him off. "Leave us alone."

Reluctantly Tony returned to the solitude of his bedroom.

Drained, Lisa collapsed onto her knees. "I'm worthless. I want you to hate me."

"Stop it! You're not worthless. You made a mistake. We all make mistakes."

"You don't understand," she sobbed guiltily. "I went to Rick's last night. I wanted to be…punished."

"Punished?" And he undoubtedly obliged. That bastard! His mysterious visit now made sense. He had taken those photographs days earlier and planned to use them to his advantage, regardless of what had happened last night.

She could not hate her sister. She could only hate Rick, for everything he had done, planned to do…to her, to Lisa, to…Alex. What if it *had* been him behind that mask? What had Lisa done to herself?

Stanton needed to be exposed. She had to be the one to do it.

"Did he hurt you?" Renee asked, her voice indicative of nothing but genuine concern. "Tell me. I need to know."

Lisa fell back on her heels, staring at the floor and crying. Slowly she shook her head. "No."

"Why is your shirt ripped?"

Lisa pressed her memory for the truth. She saw a nail protruding from the wooden banister, heard something tear on her way down the steps from his apartment. "I got it caught on a nail."

"Where?"

"On the banister at his place."

Renee eyed her dubiously. "Are you sure?"

"Yes."

She had to believe that explanation. To preserve her peace of mind. Renee held a hand out to her sister. "C'mon, let's get you cleaned up and get something in your stomach."

The pictures would have to wait awhile longer.

❧ ❧ ❧

Renee watched from across the kitchen table as Lisa sat with her face buried in her hands, Stanton's photographs lying before her. "What exactly does he plan to accomplish with these?" Lisa asked, rather calmly, finally lifting her head to face her sister.

"First, he wants you to forget about the DUI hearing tomorrow. You *and* Alex."

"And then…what?"

"Then he wants an encore performance of, and I quote, last night's head show. Tomorrow morning in his office."

"And if I don't go along he's sending copies to the school board?"

Renee nodded. "And I'm assuming since he mentioned something about Dad suffering to the county commissioners as well."

Lisa closed her eyes for a long moment, weighing her options. "He certainly works wonders on that computer of his."

Renee stared at her in silence, flabbergasted by her lackadaisical reaction to Stanton's illicit ultimatums. "Aren't you the least bit appalled by the fact he *watched* you and Jim to get these pictures? And then cut and pasted your images onto a picture of the park?"

Lisa exhaled harshly. "After last night…I'm in no position to be appalled by anything."

"How could you say that?"

"After what I did last night, Renee, I shouldn't be *allowed* in the courtroom for his hearing. How do you think the magistrate would feel about *me* driving under the influence? Or about me going down on the defendant? She'd have my badge in the blink of an eye."

"You're going to let him get away with this?"

Lisa shook her head helplessly. "I have no idea what I'm going to do. But I won't allow him to hurt Jimmy or Dad. I've already hurt Jimmy as it is. His job would be in jeopardy. I can't let that happen."

Anger flared in Renee's eyes. "Jimmy hurt *himself*. He hurt *you*. He had no right saying what he said to you. Stop feeling sorry for yourself! None of it was your fault!" She stood up quickly. "I want to go to the state police. I want to come clean about Rick. His vendetta against you and Alex has to be stopped. Now!"

"He has an alibi. He showed you the phone bill…" Her voice trailed off as something she had seen in his apartment last night suddenly registered in her mind. She jumped to her feet. "There may be something. C'mon."

As Lisa grabbed her car keys from the desk in the foyer, she reached out for Renee's arm, pulling her up close. "Not a word to Greg about the pictures."

By coincidence Greg Van Dien was returning to the barracks from lunch as Lisa and Renee were arriving.

"You're just the person I've been meaning to talk to," Greg said, holding the door open for them to enter the building. "At least one of you." He studied each twin but could not determine who was Lisa. "It's much easier to pick the cop out when she's in uniform."

Lisa came forth, formally introducing him to her sister. He escorted them to his office, and they settled around his desk.

"About this Stanton guy," Greg began, leaning back in his chair, intertwining his hands behind his head. "I got a call from my friends down in Philly this morning. He's as clean as a whistle. Never even had a parking ticket. Comes from a well–to–do family from the upper–middle class neighborhood of Roxborough in the northwest section of the city. Anyhow, his parents are divorced. Father's an architect; mother's some hotshot bank vice–president. The kid was a good student right through college and grad school. Had a falling out with his boss at Penn Publishing, and the next thing he knew, they shipped him up here."

"Yeah, well," Lisa interrupted. "He has a gun stashed in his dresser drawer, and that hotshot mother of his beat him senseless when he was a kid. And it gets better. Mamma has steel–blue eyes, like Alex. That clean–as–a–whistle, stereotypical student hates assertive women, especially blue–eyed ones."

The expression on Greg's face turned dead serious. He shifted in his seat, hovering over the desk like an eagle on its prey. "How do you know this?"

"My sister's been seeing him, and she found out some interesting information. Go ahead, Renee, spill your guts."

Greg listened intently as Renee described everything she knew about Rick, what she had discovered in his apartment, his explanation of it all, and the phone bill with a documented call to Canada at the time of the assault.

Greg's mind whirled from this latest barrage of facts. Scratching his head he drew in a deep breath. Yet another wrench had been thrown into this already bizarre investigation. Exactly how many people had it out for Alex Griffin? He shook his head and huffed in frustration.

"You should *not* have confronted him with what you learned," he berated the civilian twin. "Because now you've tipped him off, and, truthfully, I don't like the sound of anything you told me. Especially the fact he was harboring pictures of Alex and of you two." He rubbed his hands over his face, mentally sorting over the numerous speculations surrounding this mind–boggling case. "This may blow the other theories right out the window. But this phone bill is cramping my style."

"It may not have been an authentic bill," Lisa said. "With the computer technology out there, it's a possibility he may have created his *own* version of the bill." It was more than a possibility. She had *seen* a statement from the phone company on his computer last night. He was a pro at computer graphics. Those photos of her and Jim were beyond proof. "He could have scanned in the real bill and easily inserted the call to Canada, or increased its duration."

"Does he have access to a computer system that elaborate?" Greg asked.

Renee nodded. "Absolutely. The newspaper has computers and scanners and printers, and he's got a laptop he takes back and forth to work."

Greg reached for a notepad. "There's only one way to find out if the bill was fudged. What's his phone number?"

Renee called out the seven numbers, and Greg buzzed another extension in the barracks. "I need two things done right away," he spoke into the phone. "I want you to get in touch with Keystone Central Telephone and confirm a call from this number…" He recited the number, "…was placed to Windsor, Ontario, Canada, on July 11 between eleven and eleven–thirty P.M. and also get a confirmation on the duration of the call, five minutes, ten minutes, whatever. Okay? Second thing: If the call *is* confirmed, I want you on the horn with the Windsor PD to find out the name of the person or persons and the address assigned that number. I also want a confirmation from the boys north of the border someone in that household indeed spoke with a Richard Stanton from Mountain View, Pennsylvania, on the night in question during that time frame. Got all that? Yeah, ASAP, this afternoon. If they give you a hard time get a hold of the Ontario Provincial Police…No, I'm not kidding. Let me know if you have any problems. Right."

He set the phone down forcefully. "The wheels are turning. All we can do now is wait a couple hours. If none of this checks out, the search warrants for his apartment, his vehicle, and his office will be processed before I leave here tonight at five–thirty. If he's legit then it's back to my other game plans: Interviewing your sadistic brethren and having a one–on–one with Alex's beau about the ex's friend, both of which I'm hoping to accomplish later today."

Greg stood to show them out. "I'll call as soon as I hear something."

Lisa asked Renee to meet her in the car. As her sister disappeared around a corner, she looked back at Greg. "She just shared this information with me last night."

"Why'd you wait this long to tell me? You could've called me at home the minute she told you."

Lisa shifted her eyes from his gaze. The lingering headache pounding at her temples instantly reminded her of the reason. "Something personal came up."

His eyes were questioning, but he let it go. He paused briefly, awkwardly, before speaking again. "Lisa, about what I pried out of you Monday afternoon…I'm sorry if I brought back bad memories, I didn't mean to—"

Her hand came up to silence him. She bit back tears. "Just stop it. It's coming back to haunt me in ways you can't even imagine."

She was gone before he could respond to her statement.

"It's legitimate," Greg told Lisa over the phone. "The phone company verified the call. The Windsor Police visited the residence, an apartment rented by a twenty–eight–year–old woman named Caroline Farr. She confirmed she talked with Stanton that night. Her story matched his to the letter. Your sister's friend may have contemplated evil intentions, but he didn't act on them."

Greg ended the brief conversation and drove to Ehrich's garage on Main Street. As he walked into the service area, a thirtysomething dark–haired man in greasy coveralls greeted him.

"What can I do for you?"

Greg studied the mechanic's features as he spoke. "I'm looking for the owner, Matthew Ehrich."

"I'm Matt Ehrich." The voice came from under the hood of a Ford Explorer, and Greg turned in that direction. A blonde mechanic stepped around the vehicle.

"Mr. Ehrich, Detective Gregory Van Dien of the Pennsylvania State Police." Greg reached into his pocket and flashed his badge. "I need to speak with you in private."

Matt grabbed a rag and wiped off his greasy hands. He motioned the detective into the office, inconspicuously casting a glance in Brian's direction. But Haney had already returned to the engine of the Oldsmobile in the bay next to the Explorer. He appeared uninterested.

"I'm assuming Alex has filled you in about this," Van Dien said after Matt closed the office door for privacy.

"Yes, she has."

"Good. I'd like to meet with you tonight at your residence, say about six, six–fifteen. Is that convenient for you?"

"Yeah, that's fine. I'll have Brian close up. Why then and not now?"

"It'll be more comfortable at your place, and I don't want any ears listening in. I came by to check him out, make him wonder what's going on. If he's hiding something, he might start acting anxious. Keep an eye on him. Let me know if his behavior changes."

Matt agreed to be observant, but Greg warned him not to breathe a word about the investigation. "If he asks why I was here, tell him you're not at liberty to discuss it. Make him sweat some more, if he's got something to sweat over."

Greg was gone in a matter of minutes, Matt returning to work on the Explorer.

Under the hood of the Olds, Brian Haney nervously fiddled with the electrical system.

"I know it's short notice but see what you can do. Yeah, thanks." Renee hung up the phone, grabbed a can of soda from the refrigerator, and headed for the back door. Quietly standing at the screen door, she glanced out at her sister. Lisa was sitting on a porch chair, her long legs bent upward with her feet resting on the edge of the seat. She was staring off into the mid–afternoon sky, but Renee surmised the beauty of the clear, summer day went unnoticed in her sister's eyes.

Renee popped open the can and stepped onto the porch. Lisa looked up at her, a deadpan expression on her face. "Who were you on the phone with?"

"The office. I'm trying to get another conductor for the remainder of the excursions."

"Oh."

They were silent for a few moments. Renee leaned against the railing, sipping her drink.

Lisa finally ended the awkwardness. "You didn't have to stay home on my account."

"I wanted to be here for you. Feel like talking?"

"I don't think there's anything you could say that would make me feel better."

"Maybe not. But I could listen."

"You want to hear about how despicable I acted last night?"

"If you need to talk about it, then yeah, I want to hear it. What you did…I don't hate you for acting out your anger."

Lisa looked away, ashamed, her eyes brimming with tears. "It was wrong. It was *stupid*. But I was so…I…hated myself…It had nothing to do with you…or Rick. It was all aimed at myself…" Her voice broke. "And Jimmy. His words… They cut me down to size, made me truly believe what I've been trying to deny since that…night. That I really did ask for it."

"If that's what Jimmy thinks," Renee fired back. "He's got a serious problem."

"But I was going to betray him."

"Maybe he has a right to be angry about that, but he had no right, none whatsoever, to say you deserved what actually happened. He has to realize that, and I think he will. Question is: Will you be able to forgive him for what he said?"

The tears came faster. "Renee, I love him so much. I can't imagine my life without him. But I hurt him. He hurt *me* so bad."

"You've got to talk it through with him. Don't throw it all away. You've got to be totally honest with one another."

"I don't know if he'll ever be able to trust me again." As she thought about the seminar he was attending that very moment with Paula Sedlak, she wondered if he'd feel compelled to even the score. An eye for an eye. Tit for tat. She'd have no right to condemn a rash reaction to her shocking revelation.

"You've been trusting one another for eight years," Renee said matter–of–factly. "You made a mistake. You didn't mean to hurt him."

Lisa averted her eyes from her sister's stare. "I don't mean to do a lot of things." Her voice was tinged with sarcasm; the sigh that followed resigned. "Or do I?"

Renee's forehead furrowed. She set the soda down on the railing, regarding her sibling with bewilderment.

"I've been thinking about Rick," Lisa said. "I egged him on so much, even accused him of attacking Alex. Renee, I got what was coming to me, the pictures and all. He was hell–bent on getting back at me, not because of the DUI, but because of the way I was treating him. Like a royal bitch. Like his mother."

"Are you crazy? He's a master of manipulation. He has nothing but sex and malice and control on his mind. I wish I had seen it earlier, before he made a fool of me. Before I fell for his act."

Lisa disagreed adamantly. "After what you told me about his mother, and after Greg confirmed that phone call, I realized something about him. We're in the same boat. Someone hurt him, like I was hurt, and he needs to be treated with kid gloves. He needs affection. He needs someone to…love him."

Renee could not believe what she was hearing. "He took pictures of you while you were with Jimmy. He *watched* you. He manipulated the images, and now he's trying to blackmail you!"

"He took those pictures on Monday night. That's when Jimmy and I were at the pond. It was a little while after we went at it in his office, after I accused him of attacking Alex. He was right, I started it. I lobbed the first insult at him. I was trying to trap him. I was trying to get him to do something that would prove my suspicions of him. But now I could see clearer. I think he was telling you the truth on Tuesday night."

"How do you know that?"

"I don't know it for sure," Lisa admitted. "It's a gut feeling. Renee, I gave him the perfect opportunity last night for an ultimate retaliation. If he truly hated me, he could have hurt me. He could have picked up the telephone and turned me in for DUI. I set myself up for disaster. But he didn't do anything like that. He held me in his arms. He let me cry my heart out."

"Hello there, Officer Maselli!" Renee threw her arms out in exasperation. "Richard A. Stanton is a master manipulator, and he's going to use those pictures to *control* you."

Lisa got up from the chair and went to the kitchen door. "Stanton needs someone he could trust. Like his friend in Canada. He's doing all this because he's full of anger and resentment and distrust. There's a monster in him that needs to be tamed before he actually *does* hurt someone. But there's also a part of him capable of love and trust. He's already shown you some of it. He's preparing himself for a battle with me over these pictures. I wonder what a little reverse psychology will do to his game plan. Maybe it's time Rick Stanton met the real Lisa Maselli."

"You must have gotten an A in photography class."

Rick's chair shot backward from the computer terminal, slamming into the drawers of his desk. His face aghast he turned toward the voice in the doorway, watching as she stepped into his office, closing the door behind her.

"Scared you, huh?" She walked over to his desk and tossed the manila envelope into his lap, the fright and confusion evident in his staring, saucer–wide eyes. "You weren't expecting me today?"

No reply. He sat motionless, his mouth agape.

"Maybe I should clear things up. My sister forgot to identify herself this morning. So you're going to have to give *me* an encore performance of that shakedown you laid on her."

He leaned back in his chair and snickered. "You're going to have to do better than that."

"Renee called off sick from work today. She was wearing my tee shirt when you saw her. You put the squeeze on *her* this morning, not me. And frankly, I'm a little disheartened by the fact you still can't tell us apart."

Venom coursed through his veins. His face flushed. What was she trying to prove? He set the envelope on his desk and slowly rose to his feet, slithering around her. She stood perfectly still as his hand pushed her hair away, exposing her ear and neck. His tongue was running over her ear, probing lewdly, but when his other hand came over her breast, Lisa struck back.

She spun around and seized him by the throat, driving him back against the wall. She forced her leg between his, her knee inches from his groin. "Don't make me hurt you."

His eyes burned with contempt as they met her uncompromising glare. "You're in no position to strong–arm me, Officer," he said, undaunted by her surprising physical strength. "I could ruin your reputation for the cost of a first–class stamp or by a simple send–mail click on my computer."

"You don't want to hurt me, Rick," she said with conviction. "You're really not that kind of guy, are you?" She released her hold on his neck and boosted herself up on his desk, her feet dangling close to the floor.

He fought to control his raging hormones. She was playing with his mind. "You're a dick tease."

Lisa took the insult with a grain of salt. "Look, Rick, I'm sorry for the way I've been treating you: putting you down, instigating confrontations, accusing you of things I had no right to say without solid proof. It was bad judgment on my part, totally unprofessional. And I'm sorry for…last night."

Laughing, Rick returned to his seat. "You're real clever. Trying to con your way free of my chokehold. I gotcha, don't I? And actually…" He reclined in the chair, intertwining his hands behind his head, a haughty smirk plastered across his face. "I didn't think you'd be so averse to going down on me at my beck and call since you so willingly proved to me last night what I've known all along. They don't get *any* better than you."

His attack bounced right off her. She had to let it go. She was trying desperately to heal the wounds she had irreverently afflicted. "Let me ask you something: When I came to your apartment last night, drunk off my ass, why didn't you pick up the phone and turn me in for DUI after I left? It would have been a most–appropriate retribution."

"Who are you kidding? You would've gotten away with it. What cop in this town would have busted you? They would have covered your ass big time. I know all about small–town politics."

"So you're using that knowledge of small–town politics to *create* these pictures. Real clever, Rick. A sure–fire way to get Jimmy and I fired from our jobs." She angrily scooped up the envelope and flung it at his chest. "I hate you for this, Rick. Did you get off while you were watching us?"

"Does that turn you on? The fact I watched you."

"Get help, Rick," Lisa said flatly. "Deep down you're a decent guy. I honestly believe that. Your mother messed up your mind. You don't want to hurt people like this. That's what you needed Caroline for, to talk you through your problems, get you through your bad days. My sister wanted to do that for you. She wanted to help you. But after she saw these pictures…she doesn't believe in you anymore. But I do."

Those last three words threw him off guard. He could not conjure up a response—any type of response. He simply stared at her, his body fixed in the chair like a department–store mannequin.

"I'm sorry I made you mistrust me," Lisa continued. "It's just that *I* have a hard time trusting people myself. Look, after what I did last night, you have every right in the world to have those charges against you thrown out. It was against the law for me to drink and drive, and totally unethical for me to…you know. But Alex is the arresting officer. Technically I'm only a witness. I'm going to try my best to convince her to not show up, but I can't make promises. It's an automatic reprimand for intentional no–shows. As for your other so–called request…" She drew in a breath, held it, and then exhaled. "Please don't hurt me like that. You could have hurt me last night. But you didn't. You respected me…respected my body, despite our less–than–civil confrontations." She met his eyes and held them courageously. "Let's not hurt each other anymore. Okay?"

He countered her openness with aloofness, turning toward the window, pretending to stare out. "Why did you go out and get drunk last night? What made you act so recklessly?"

An explanation was inevitable, and Lisa met the challenge head–on. Her decision had been made: Total honesty from this point forward. "I had a fight with Jim, over something that happened to me in college. Something he never knew about."

His eyes found hers once again. This time they were questioning—sincerely.

Lisa looked away, but only momentarily. "I acted reckless back then and someone hurt me, bad."

"What are you saying?"

"I'm saying I was…raped by someone I thought I could trust."

His bangs dropped over his face. Automatically he whisked them back. It all made sense now: her accusations, her misgivings, her defensive disposition. They were destined to clash.

"Now you know about the real Lisa Maselli," she said, sliding off the desk to leave. "I'm sorry for everything I've done to you."

She left the envelope with the damaging photographs behind. And for a long, hard moment, he stared down at it, remembering with disdain all the times his mother had cut him down to size, humbled and degraded him. With a wrath as violent as his mother's stinging backhand, he flung the manila folder at the wall, vehemently cursing that heartless bitch.

He hated the monster his mother had created.

* * *

Matt had stepped out of the shower and was pulling a clean shirt over his head when a knock came at the door. Right on time, he thought. Six o'clock on the nose. He quickly answered it, showing the state–police detective into the kitchen.

"Can I get you something to drink, Detective…?"

"Van Dien. No, thank you. I'm anxious to get started."

"Fine."

They sat at the table. Van Dien's manner was methodical. He pulled out a small notebook from his shirt pocket and positioned it before him. A pen appeared next. Matt stiffened, intimidated by the detective's businesslike approach.

"Okay, Mr. Ehrich," Greg began. "I'm under the impression Alex has been clueing you in on the investigation."

"Yes, she has. And please, call me Matt."

"Okay, Matt. Let's get right to it. How long have you and Alex been seeing each other?"

Matt hesitated. Didn't he already know that? "Three weeks to the day."

"But you knew her long before that?"

"I've known *of* her for several months. We'd make small talk a lot when she'd pass by on the foot patrol."

"But you never knew she had dated Kyle Lawry?"

"No. Like I said it was small talk. Nothing personal."

Greg made some notes on his pad. "How long has Brian Haney been working for you?"

"About two years."

"Did you know him before that?"

"Yeah, I went to high school with Haney, and Lawry. We're all the same age."

Van Dien's pen rolled across the paper. "And not once during those several months did Mr. Haney mention his best bud was seeing that foot–patrol cop that walked by your garage?"

Matt shook his head. "Not once. Not even after I made it known to him I thought she was…attractive, you know."

An agreeable grin appeared on Greg's impassive face. "Yes, I understand where you're coming from."

With the mood lightened Matt opened up a bit more. "Brian's backward and, to tell you the truth, I don't know if he's ever dated anyone since he's been working for me. He doesn't talk much."

Greg slouched back in the chair. "Matt, I want you to tell me everything you can remember about Haney and Lawry, from high school, or anything personal you know about them, anything you may have overheard Haney say at work. Whatever. Tell me it all. I'm not from around here. I was transferred here about four years ago from Blair County. I'm interested in learning a lot about these two guys. Even though Alex has been adamant about the attacker not being Lawry, I'm still not convinced he had *nothing* to do with it. Which leads me to believe, his buddy, Haney, may have done his dirty work."

Matt brought to light a considerable amount of information on both Haney and Lawry. He informed Greg that Kyle's parents moved to Florida awhile back and that Brian's parents were both dead. He explained what they were like in high school: into cars—he mentioned Brian now drove a bus for the school district—and drinking and smoking. They were not very popular with their female classmates, especially not Haney.

"Do you remember either of them slapping any girls around?" Greg asked.

"No, nothing like that. And I had no idea how possessive Kyle was, until Alex told me about his behavior."

"Did Alex tell you about the notes Lawry left in her mailbox?"

Matt huffed angrily. "Oh, yeah. But she begged me not to do anything about it, because of what happened and the investigation and all."

"Did Alex ever suggest to you that Lawry may have slapped her around?"

Alarmed, Matt immediately straightened up. "No."

Greg nodded, flipping the notebook paper over for a clean sheet. It was the fourth time he had turned a page. "Don't get the wrong idea. I was fishing for information. She denied any kind of physical abuse from Lawry to me as well. I believe she's telling the truth."

Matt exhaled in relief.

"What about their music interests? Specifically their interest, or disinterest, in *Night Crew*?"

"Brian loves *Night Crew*. He used to play their tapes constantly."

"*Used to*?" Greg's eyes shot up from the paper.

"I haven't heard *Night Crew* playing on his portable stereo in the shop in the last two weeks."

Greg grimaced. "How'd Haney behave after I left the shop this afternoon?"

"To be honest he acted like usual: Quiet. Barely said two words to me."

Greg returned the notebook and pen to his pocket and stood up from the table. "Matt, you've been a great help. Thank you for your time."

Back in his car Greg assessed what had come to light. The road leading toward suspicions of the regional cops who had bad–mouthed Alex had dead–ended earlier that afternoon. Each of the officers interviewed at the barracks had alibis. If Peterson's DNA analysis came back from the crime lab unmatched tomorrow, he'd have to pay a visit to Mr. Lawry. Those notes Lawry dropped in Alex's mailbox were reason enough for questioning. Haney, on the other hand, left nothing for him to go on. The fact he hadn't played *Night Crew* in two weeks wasn't grounds for shit. It may have been purely coincidental. But Greg's gut feeling was it was more than a coincidence.

He had to start with Lawry. He couldn't touch Haney unless Lawry gave him probable cause.

Lisa picked her way through the tall grass leading to Becker's Pond. She sought the solitude of the rustic surroundings to cope with the repercussions of the events of the past twenty–four hours.

When she opened up to Stanton earlier, she had made up her mind to come forth with her secret, to deal with it openly. Shortly after dinner she had called her father into the den and confessed with careful detail the nightmare she had endured in her dorm room at North Penn University that February night.

As she sat down in the grass near the edge of the water, her father's reaction to her revelation persisted to haunt her. It would be forever etched in her mind, the shock and horror of his voice contradicting the disillusionment she had seen in his eyes. He had expressed his strong disapproval of her racy behavior—the drinking and flirting and sexual forwardness—but compassionately unburdened her self–guilt with words only a father could say to a daughter. Afterward she had wept in his protective arms. The one thing in life she had always striven for was her father's approval.

Had she ultimately let him down?

Gazing up into the mid–evening sky, Lisa reflected on her mother's death. "I hope you're able to understand why I kept it a secret," she muttered tearfully. "You were suffering enough as it was. I…couldn't do that to you. Please forgive me, Mom."

She drew her legs up close to her chest and rested her head on her knees, sobbing quietly.

Stanton now held the key to her future. If he made good on his threat to forward the photographs to the school board, Jimmy's employment as a teacher would be in jeopardy. In a matter of two days she single–handedly would destroy both his personal and professional lives. The love and trust they had shared for eight wonderful years would be reduced to hatred and despair. And revelation of her devious behavior would deal a serious blow to her father's flawless record. For her a contented life in Highlands County would no longer be an option. Perhaps she'd move out West. Wyoming or Colorado. She'd always visualized the beauty and peace of the Rockies whenever Alex spoke of her college days at Colorado State.

"Lisa, can we talk? Please."

She gasped, startled, her head whirling around in search of the low, timid voice.

"Jimmy." He stood in the grass a few yards away, dressed in a shirt and tie, his hands fidgeting in and out of his pants pockets. "How'd you know I was here?"

"Renee told me. I drove straight to your house the minute I got back in town from the seminar." Hesitantly he stepped toward her. "Can we talk? Please."

She looked away, making a feeble attempt at drying her eyes. She didn't want to face him, not tonight. Not after what she had done with Stanton. Not until she knew the fate of her future, their future, if any hope of one existed.

"Lisa, please listen to me," he begged, kneeling in the grass alongside her, the tears coming involuntarily. "I'm so sorry for what I said to you last night. Please, please, you've got to believe me. I don't know why I said those things. I was…overwhelmed. Please, baby, please, believe me."

Lisa couldn't bring herself to face him, her tearful eyes fixing on a huge weeping willow tree across the pond.

Jim wanted desperately to embrace her in his arms, feel her warmth and forgiveness. She would not allow it. There would be no forgiveness. "Lisa, I'm so, so sorry about what happened. You don't know how sorry. I was totally out of line by saying you deserved it. You've got to believe me. I love you so much. Please, Lisa…" His voice trailed off into uncontrollable sobbing. "I'm so sorry. Please forgive me…please."

She couldn't bear to see the pain and suffering in those baby blue eyes of his. Those same eyes that would turn her to putty every time they'd beg for affection or hint of devilish desire.

"I can't forgive myself," she cried. "Please, leave me alone. I need to be alone."

"Lisa, please—"

"Jimmy, please. Go. I want to be alone."

Heartbroken he acquiesced to her request.

He drove around aimlessly. An hour later he couldn't deal with the loneliness any longer. As if powered by an evil being from the nether world, his car led him to Paula Sedlak's house.

She answered the door in a skimpy black bikini, the inviting smile on her face unmistakable.

"Does that offer for a burger and a swim still stand?" he asked.

Paula stepped aside, allowing him in. "Absolutely."

CHAPTER 24

To Hell And Back

The public defender impatiently glanced at the clock on the courtroom wall.

"Your Honor," the young man said, rising to his feet. "It's twenty–five minutes after nine. I believe we've given Officers Griffin and Maselli ample time to be here. I move the charges against my client be dismissed."

Behind the elevated bench the magistrate removed her glasses and set them before her. She rubbed her eyes and sighed angrily. "Very well," she spoke curtly. "Mr. Stanton, I have no choice but to dismiss the charges filed against you for Driving Under the Influence because of the failure of the arresting officer to appear here today. Count your lucky stars, young man. I don't want to see you before me again. Understood?"

Rick sprang to his feet. "I understand, Your Honor. Thank you."

Shaking her head, obviously irritated, the magistrate scooped up his file. "Don't thank me. Thank those two irresponsible police–officers who just wasted a half hour of my life." She left the courtroom in a huff.

"She's pissed," the public defender said, sliding the paperwork into his briefcase. "Guaranteed she's going straight for the phone to report them." He extended his hand to Rick. "I don't know what you did, or who you prayed to, but congratulations. This doesn't happen much around here. Not since the police board cracked down on the cops. Stay sober." The young man patted him on the back and departed to meet another court–appointed client.

Loosening his tie Rick sat in the quiet and solitude of the courtroom for a few moments, lost in thought. He was free and clear of the charges. He had gotten everything he wanted—in more ways than one.

He should have been exuberant.

He felt like shit.

"I owe you another one," Lisa told Alex while they sat at the table inside Alex's kitchen, conversing over coffee.

Alex shrugged. "I signed the complaint. Take the credit, take the blame."

"I should be taking the blame. You don't deserve a reprimand because of my stupidity."

"I'll survive. What would I be gaining by refusing to help you?"

"You'd be keeping your self–respect."

"How's that?"

"Because right now I don't have any, and I brought you down to my level."

"Don't be ridiculous. But you've got to do something about Stanton. He needs help, professionally. Blowing off the hearing was one thing, but you're going to have to draw the line."

Lisa stared at the tablecloth, her fingers fiddling with her coffee mug. "I had to give in on the DUI. It was only fair. And right now my concerns are for Jimmy and my father. I don't want them to suffer because of me."

"You're going to have *another* reprimand put on your record in less than a month's time because of the no–show," Alex warned.

"You'd better start being concerned about *yourself* because you might be jeopardizing your law career."

"My future hinges on today—"

Lisa was interrupted by the jingle of the telephone.

Alex immediately looked at the digital clock on the microwave, her heartbeat accelerating. Nine forty–five. She knew who was calling. Greg Van Dien with Peterson's DNA results. Right on schedule, like the crime lab had promised.

She got up from the table to answer the phone. Hesitantly she raised the receiver to her ear. "Hello."

"Al, it's Greg."

"Somehow I knew that already."

"Sit down, Al, we got a lot to discuss."

She pulled up a chair, heeding his suggestion. "I'm sitting."

"No match," Greg said. "It wasn't Peterson."

Emotionally exhausted from fourteen days of nothing but dead ends, Alex simply shut her eyes and exhaled harshly. Across the table Lisa knew by the resigned expression on her face the DNA had come back unmatched.

"Now what?" Alex asked.

"I've got a bad feeling about Brian Haney, but I need to grill Lawry first. He's got to give me probable cause."

Alex shivered as thoughts of Brian Haney beating her surfaced. Her faint snicker hinted of irony. "The wimp," she muttered, barely audible.

"Pardon me?"

"It's so ironic," Alex mumbled, her voice full of resignation. "I called him a wimp. Maybe he was trying to prove a point."

"Keep those blue eyes of yours dry. 'Cause the last laugh's going to be on him. Rest assured."

"What about Peterson? What's going to happen?"

"I'm making that phone call next. Alex, he can't touch you legally. Just watch your back. It's my ass that's going to get fried."

"Greg, I'm sorry."

"For what? You told the truth. If he's got a conscience maybe he'll keep quiet."

"Yeah, right."

"I'll be in touch," Greg assured her. "Keep that chin up, Officer. They don't get any better than you."

Rick stared at the computer screen, his hands idle on the keyboard. He had been writing and rewriting the same introductory paragraph for a piece on the centennial celebration of the local fire department for over an hour. He couldn't stay focused on the article, his eyes kept drifting up to the time bar in the upper–right corner of the screen. It was now two minutes past eleven. He anxiously wondered if she'd show.

The words she had uttered to him yesterday afternoon had been playing over and over in his mind. *I believe in you. You respected me. Let's not hurt each other anymore.* Was she being sincere? No one other than Caroline had believed in him. He rarely got a second chance.

But Lisa Maselli had given him a second chance with the law. And she somehow had convinced her partner to do the same. They had afforded him the opportunity to prove his integrity and would consequently be rebuked by their superiors for their irresponsible action.

Lisa had lived up to her promise, but the uncertainty of her intentions had been eating at him since he had returned to the office from the hearing. Could he trust her? Open up to her? Or was she manipulating him to free herself from the chokehold? After all, a reprimand for failing to show at a hearing was far less detrimental than her boyfriend losing his job for public lewdness. He wanted badly to believe her since he couldn't deny the strong physical attraction he had to her. For someone he detested professionally he realized they were unarguably alike in many ways.

He was attempting to compose the lead paragraph for the fifth or sixth time when a light rap came at his office door.

He turned from the computer and watched in silence as she stepped inside, closing the door behind her. She was dressed casually in a pair of white shorts and a peach tee shirt. Rick assumed it was Lisa and, for the first time since making the twins' acquaintance, he wished he could find a way to tell them apart.

"Lisa?"

"You didn't think it'd be Renee, did you?" She neared him, leaning against the side of the desk, and folded her hands across her chest.

"No. I guess not," he said in a low, sheepish voice.

"Congratulations on beating the DUI charge."

Guilt made him look away.

"Was the magistrate angry?"

Rick nodded slightly, his eyes wandering around the room. "Yeah, she was pissed."

"We figured that."

"How'd you get your partner to go along?"

"I told her the truth, Rick. She didn't want to see me get hurt. But she also told me to wise up. That's what I admire the most about Alex. She's brutally honest."

"What'd she say about me?"

"She thinks you have some problems to work out."

"She does?" He nervously tapped his fingers on the edge of desk then abruptly sprang from his chair. He went over to a metal file–cabinet and stared at the poster of the Philadelphia skyline hanging on the wall above.

Lisa sensed the emotional turmoil within him as he peered at the poster, his hands fidgeting with the handle of the top drawer. It was as if he wanted to say something but couldn't bring himself to doing so. "Go ahead. Say what's on your mind."

Rick shook his head angrily, torn between the hostility his mother had spawned and the compassion Caroline had nurtured within him. *She's being sincere. She believes in you*, his conscience insisted. *Don't let her off*, his evil being retorted. *She deserves what she's getting.*

Test her, another silent voice ordered.

He spun around to face her, his bangs falling before his eyes. "I believe you still owe me something."

Lisa's heart sank. How could she have been so wrong about him?

"Rick, c'mon. I kept my promise on the hearing. I don't want to do this."

"Then don't do it. Just tell me one thing."

"What?"

"When's the next school–board meeting? So I can be there when they fire Jimmy boy."

Lisa sadly realized she had no choice but to appease him this one time. But never again. She would not allow this sick game to continue. Tomorrow she would go to her father and explain the situation. Perhaps he could make some calls, soften the blow before it hit. Then she'd fess up to Jimmy, tell him how sorry she was for the pain she caused. He'd never want to see her again. In a few months she'd move away. Wyoming, she decided. Cheyenne. Maybe the local sheriff's office would hire her.

Lisa straightened from the desk and moved before him. She raised her right hand to his face, clearing those scraggly bangs from his vision, and met his icy glare with one of resolution. "I guess I was wrong about you." She continued to hold his stare as her left hand dutifully found the zipper on his pants. "I hope you enjoy this, Stanton, because you're hurting me real bad."

Self–hatred permeated the lust that coursed through his veins and in a rush of desperation he intercepted her wrist. His hands came around her neck, entangling her hair in his fingers, pulling her face to his. "Don't fight this. Let it happen." His lips locked on hers in a long, fiery embrace.

Her reaction was to pull away, but the passion in his kiss was so strong, so undeniable, she quickly melted against his body, her own hands vigorously splaying his tousled hair.

When it was over he released her, neither saying a word as they struggled for a breath.

"I couldn't help myself," he finally spoke, wiping away the sweat that cooled his burning brow. "You…drive me crazy." He hurried over to the desk and removed an envelope from the top middle drawer. "Here, take this, please. It's the disk. Get rid of it. Burn it. Get it away from me. I don't want to hurt you anymore."

Her lips curled up in a heartwarming smile as she reached for the envelope. "I wasn't wrong after all."

His whisked his bangs back with both hands, his eyes acknowledging her statement. "No one except Caroline has ever said they believed in me. It was those words that made me realize how wrong I was about you."

Lisa was drawn to him. Her hand came up to gently caress the smoothness of his cheek. "I want you to trust me. We can honestly relate to the bad things that have happened in our lives. I want to be your friend, Rick, but only your friend. I love Jimmy. I want to be with him for the rest of my life."

He stroked her hair. "I know."

Lisa's hand swept under his chin, guiding his lips to hers. It was a parting kiss, one last taste of the forbidden passion they felt for each other.

"I've got to go," she muttered, pulling away from his embrace. "I need to get my life back in order." She reached for his hand. "Friends?"

His smile was genuine. "Friends."

She turned to leave, but he called her back.

"You were right," he said. "You and your sister *are* a lot alike."

The inference was unmistakable. She nodded. "Talk to her. Apologize. She may find it in her heart to forgive you."

A customer was browsing the aisles and Jim was on the phone with another when Lisa walked into the hardware store. He turned from the counter, freezing at the sight of her.

Quietly she headed for the stockroom, tipping her head in that direction and mouthing, “We need to talk.”

He cut the phone inquiry short but as he hung up, the elderly man who had been mulling over a cordless screwdriver for the past twenty minutes approached the counter.

“May I return this if I’m not happy with it?” the man asked.

“Of course. Save your receipt.” Jim rang up the sale. He gave the customer his change and slipped the purchase into a bag. “Have a nice day.”

The man dilly–dallied on his way out the door, stopping to examine a display of power tools. It seemed like an eternity, but he finally moseyed out of the store. Jim anxiously hurried into the stockroom.

“Hi,” Lisa said warmly.

“H…hi.” He eyed her with apprehension.

“I…we need to talk. You…have to hear me out. I need to be honest with you.”

“Okay.” His fidgeting hands clearly indicated the awkwardness of the moment as he searched for something more to say.

“Not now. There’d be too many interruptions. Later, tonight, after I get off duty from the festival. We could go to the pond.”

“Lisa, I’m so sorry, please, you’ve got to believe me—”

She stepped before him, silencing his words with the tip of her finger against his lips. “Not as sorry as I am.”

“I love you so much. I can’t bear to lose you. Let me hold you, please. I can’t wait until tonight. Please.”

The desperation in his eyes was pitiful. She nodded passively, and his arms engulfed her in a frantic embrace. The floodgates opened and the tears poured out. Time stood still as they crushed their bodies together. Lisa trembled in his arms, overwhelmed by the intensity of his reception. She needed to feel that warmth, to know the revelation of her deceitful intentions hadn't lessened his love for her.

"You feel so good," she muttered, her voice cracking with emotion. "I'm so sorry I hurt you."

"No, baby." His hands cradled her head. "I reacted like a jerk. I should have picked up on the messages you were sending me all along. Oh, Lise, I'm the one who's sorry. You can't imagine how much—"

She shook her head, signaling him to stop. "Not now. Later. We'll have all night to talk this through."

"Okay, later." Their eyes locked together in a solemn truce, each begging for forgiveness. Slowly their lips were drawn together but at the same time, the bell over the front door jingled, signifying someone had entered the store.

Drying his eyes Jim cringed at the interruption. "Not now. Go away." He didn't want the moment to end. He wanted to hold her in his arms forever.

"You'd better get back to work," Lisa said reluctantly. "I'll see you tonight."

They walked out to the retail floor. Another elderly gentleman was perusing the aisles. Jim escorted her to the door. "I'll see you later. Be careful tonight."

Turning his attention back to the customer, Jim agonized over whether or not he should tell her about his visit to Paula Sedlak's last night.

Honesty.

She wanted to be honest with him.

He needed to be honest with her.

"Peterson's clean," Lisa informed her father over the telephone. She sat at the kitchen table, snacking on a piece of chicken left over from last night's dinner. "But I'm terrified about what he might do to Alex now. I can't see him letting it go. He's going to make her job a living hell… Yeah… I'd hate to see it come to that… Yeah, I know… Okay, Dad, see you in the morning… No, I'm working the festival tonight, then Jimmy and I are going to get together. Yeah… Thanks."

Rising from the table to hang up the phone, she ran headlong into her brother.

"Gosh, Tony, sorry. I didn't hear you come into the room."

He quickly backed away. "No problem," he mumbled coolly, deliberately avoiding eye contact with her as he opened the refrigerator for a drink.

Lisa frowned at his standoffishness. "Tony, what's bothering you?"

He shot her an alarmed look, hurrying for the back door. "Nothing."

She stepped in front of him, blocking his escape. "I have a good idea why you've been sidestepping me. Want to talk about it?"

"No."

He tried to get around her, but she seized his arm.

"It's not going to go away. I know you overheard the fight Jimmy and I had."

"Yeah, so? What'd you want me to do?"

"I don't want you to *do* anything," Lisa snapped. "I thought you might want to talk about it. I realize it must have been a shock for you."

"A shock?" He snickered. "No, not at all. The fact my sister was—" He stopped in mid–sentence and angrily looked away.

"Was what?"

He jerked his arm free and slammed the soda can down on the counter. "What is it with black guys, anyhow? What the hell made you want to…screw a nigger?"

"Where do you get off using that kind of narrow–minded word? That's disgusting."

The feelings of resentment and disappointment Tony had been harboring the last two days blazed out of control, and he showed no mercy. "You know what's *really* disgusting? You. You let a *black* guy touch you and—"

"And what, little brother?" Lisa glared at him, appalled by his guttural language and racial convictions. "I can't believe what I'm hearing. Do you know what I went through?"

"You let him get away with it! I can't believe what you did, Lisa. I never imagined my sister being a…*slut*."

Her eyes filled with tears. "Wow," she exhaled, devastated, walking away. "That one hurt." She stood at the sink with her back toward him and quietly began to cry.

His mind whirled with wrenching emotions. "You wanted to know. I told you. What'd you want from me anyhow?" Frustrated he grabbed his drink and bolted out the back door.

Alex picked up Lisa at three–thirty, and they headed for the borough building to sign in before the start of their shift at the festival grounds.

"You're wearing your glasses!" Lisa exclaimed as soon as she climbed into the Tracker.

Alex smirked. "Thanks for calling that to my attention. I tore a lens this afternoon."

"You look fine in your glasses."

"What happened after you left my place? Is it good news or bad?"

"It's good news." Lisa briefly recounted the morning's events. "But my brother dealt me an unexpected blow below the belt," she then said, dejected, repeating his hurtful words to Alex.

"Does he plan on going to college?" she asked.

"He's got his heart set on Penn State."

"Perhaps the rude awakening he's in for will paint a clearer picture for him. He's only seventeen, Lise, he doesn't understand yet. Don't dwell on it, okay?"

Lisa accepted Alex's advice halfheartedly. As they pulled into the borough lot and parked the Tracker, nausea churned in Alex's stomach.

"I hope he's gone for the day. I have no idea what *I'm* in for."

"I'll be right beside you."

They entered the police station and made small talk with the desk clerk as they signed in for duty.

"We're working the festival tonight," Alex told him. "We're heading up there now."

"Like hell you are!" The irate voice emanated from the chief's office. "I want you both in here. Now!"

Alex said a quick prayer to herself. Lisa touched her arm lightly, assuring her of support, and together they walked into Ted Peterson's office.

"The door." He sat on the edge of his desk, arms folded across his chest. The look on his face was one of anger and authority.

Lisa had barely shut the door when he flew off the desk and bore down on Alex. "Officer Griffin, you'd better have a damn good reason you didn't show at that DUI hearing this morning!"

Alex immediately diverted her eyes from his. "I forgot about it."

"You *forgot*? Well, *I* haven't *forgotten* to take disciplinary action against you," he shouted, inches from her face. "There will be an official written reprimand in your file first thing Monday morning."

"I understand completely. I take full responsibility for my failure to show at the hearing."

"You're damn right you will." He then glared at Lisa. "You can expect the same, Maselli."

She nodded passively. "I understand."

"That's two, Maselli! One more and you're out of here until the board evaluates your performance."

"Yes, sir. I understand."

"Get lost. I want to speak with Officer Griffin in private."

Alex's eyes flew open, her heart racing.

"With all due respect, Chief," Lisa said. "You could speak to her in front of me."

Peterson's nostrils flared. "You want that third reprimand right now, Maselli?"

She refused to go back on her word. Lisa swallowed the lump in her throat and started to speak, but Alex interjected.

"I'll be fine."

Hesitantly Lisa turned to exit the office. "I'll be waiting out at the desk."

As the door closed behind her, Ted Peterson's eyes shot daggers at his new enemy. "How *dare* you accuse me," he ground out the words with utter resentment. "How *dare* you think I was capable of such a thing!"

Alex drew in a breath to settle the fear he was instilling in her. "I didn't *accuse* you of anything. I told the state police the truth about you."

He let out a short, vindictive laugh. "The state police. When I get through with Van Dien's ass, he'll be back in a cruiser on the interstate. If he's lucky."

Alex did not respond to his statement. Instead she stood perfectly still as Peterson began walking circles around her, his eyes meticulously inspecting her uniform.

"You have a smudge on your left shoe," he informed her, vengeance in his voice. "Get it off, now."

Alex's face flushed with anger and humility as she fished for a handkerchief in her pocket and bent over to buff her shoe. When she straightened, his index finger came up to trace the opening of her shirt at the neckline.

"A little deep here. I don't think it's proper for a police officer. Button up."

A vivid remembrance of her attacker's unwanted touch chilled her bones as she fastened the second button on her uniform. "Are you through finding fault with me?"

Ted Peterson leaned in to her ear, his breath hot on her neck. "I'm going to be finding fault with you for the remainder of your employment with this department. Now get the hell out of my sight."

Renee left work at four–thirty. As she approached her car in the dirt lot behind Main Street, she found Rick Stanton leaning on the front fender.

"What the hell do you want?" It had been a long, busy day, and the last thing she wanted was a confrontation.

"I want to talk," he said, straightening up. "I'd like for you to hear me out."

"Get away from my car. I don't want to hear anything you have to say, and you could forget about the conductor's job. I want your outfit back in the bureau office by eleven tomorrow morning."

"Renee, I'm sorry for everything I've done to you and your sister."

Unmoved she inserted her key in the door lock. "Save your sermon. You're going to need it at the gates of hell."

"I gave your sister the disk with the altered images."

"Before or after she sucked your cock?"

Rick looked away, but her verbal bashing continued. "How does it feel to blackmail your way out of a criminal record?"

"Like shit." He stepped away from the car. "Renee, I'm sorry. I was hoping for a second chance. You're so much like Caroline."

She exhaled in exasperation, opening the car door and tossing her briefcase onto the back seat. What was it about this guy?

He was poison. She had to get away before she gave in.

She quickly slipped behind the wheel. "It's too late, Rick."

"Let me finish out the summer with the excursions. I promised to help, and I want to keep that promise. You haven't replaced me, have you?"

"No, I haven't," she reluctantly admitted.

"Then I'll be there tomorrow at noon for the excursion. Please, let me do this."

Infuriated with his persistence she heaved her door shut. "No. Stay away from me."

She started the engine and drove away, leaving him behind in a cloud of dust.

Kyle Lawry parked the delivery truck in the loading zone behind Zeller's Furniture Store at precisely five P.M.

Quitting time. Friday. Pay day. He was heading over to the bank to cash his check and then it was straight to Vic's for Happy Hour.

As he left the dock and walked to his car in the rear lot, a man in a suit quickly approached him.

"Kyle Lawry?" the man called out.

Kyle stopped dead in his tracks and turned cautiously. "Who wants to know?"

A badge flashed before his eyes. "Detective Gregory Van Dien of the Pennsylvania State Police."

Kyle's mouth dropped. He stood, frozen, gaping at him. He remembered being questioned by this same man two weeks ago. He'd been asking if he had seen anyone suspicious–looking in the neighborhood.

"I'd like to talk to you, Mr. Lawry," Greg said. "At the state–police barracks."

"What for?"

"I'm investigating a sexual assault, and I've been informed by an extremely reliable source that you knew the victim quite well."

Kyle's heart pounded against his chest as he sputtered for a reply. "I'm not sure I know what you're talking about, Detective."

Greg cut right to the chase. "I know all about those little notes you dropped in Alex Griffin's mailbox. Need I say more?"

Panic instantly washed over Kyle. "I had nothing to do with it. I swear."

Greg motioned him to an unmarked cruiser. "Let's talk."

Inside the interrogation room, Greg wasted no time grilling Lawry.

"Is it true Alex Griffin broke it off with you about two months ago?"

"Yes."

"And you had a hard time accepting that?"

"I suppose. I was…in love with Alex."

Greg's eyes narrowed. "Oh, really?"

"C'mon." Kyle fidgeted in his seat like an anxious five–year–old. "I was head–over–heels for her. I couldn't bear the thought of her dating other guys."

"And then she started dating Matthew Ehrich. Divorced, lonely, Mr. Ex–Class Flirt."

"Yeah."

"So you told her about it."

"Yeah."

"And what'd she tell you?"

"She told me to leave her alone."

"But you didn't. Instead you started watching her and leaving notes in her mailbox. You watched her have sex with Matthew Ehrich two nights before she was attacked, didn't you?"

Kyle hesitated to answer.

"Need I remind you loitering and prowling at night is a third–degree misdemeanor? You help me out I may conveniently overlook that fact."

"Okay, okay. Yeah, I watched her and Ehrich get it on. It made me sick."

"Sick enough to seek revenge?"

Kyle's fist came down hard on the table. "No! I'd never dream of hurting Alex that way. Never. Not in my life."

"Why were you leaving her those notes? What'd you plan on accomplishing with them?"

"I…I wanted her to know I was…keeping tab. I didn't want her to be happy. 'Cuz I wasn't…happy. I was…jealous, extremely jealous."

"But you'd never dream of *physically* hurting Alex?"

"N…no."

"What about your friends?"

"What?"

"Maybe you put one of your buddies up to it."

"*No! I didn't, man! I didn't do this to her. You gotta believe me.*"

Greg calmly doodled on his notepad, smiling on the inside. He was scaring the living daylights out of Lawry, as planned. "Tell me about your buddy, Brian Haney."

Kyle wiped a stream of sweat from his forehead with trembling hands. Slowly his head raised up to face the detective. "What about him?"

"What's he think of Alex?"

Kyle's thoughts instantly shot back to the exchange of words he and Brian had had the Wednesday after the assault, when news of it had first appeared in the *Journal*. It was Brian who had hinted Alex was the victim, telling him in a supposedly joking manner to find an alibi. And Brian's opinion of the assault had been nonchalant. Had his best friend done this to her? Acute nausea swelled within him. He had to come clean with Brian's hateful feelings toward Alex.

"Brian never liked her. He's shy, and her forwardness intimidated him."

"Does Haney have other friends?"

"No. None."

"What kind of social life did he have while you were dating Alex?"

"Stayed home a lot or drank by himself. But I spent some time with him. I didn't ditch him totally."

Greg slouched forward and rubbed his temples, digesting the alarming information Lawry was readily disclosing. "What was Haney's reaction to Alex and Ehrich dating?"

"Brian told me to forget about her, no woman was worth a shit. He said she used me then dumped me for the pretty boy."

Greg's eyes shot upward, but he downplayed his alarm. "Pretty Boy? Is that what he calls Ehrich?"

Kyle nodded. "Let's just say they have different personalities."

"Does Haney have any *Night Crew* cassette tapes?"

"Yeah, three or four. What's that gotta do with any of this?"

Greg ignored the question. "How 'bout *Full Moon*?"

"Yeah, as a matter of fact I borrowed it from him last week. Why?"

"I'm asking the questions, Lawry. You still got this tape?"

"Yeah, it's in my car."

"What was Haney's reaction to Alex being attacked?"

Kyle hesitated.

"I don't have all day, dammit it!"

"In a nut shell he was really cool about it, like he couldn't care less. He even joked that maybe I needed an alibi. We got into a fight over that remark. I'm talking I yanked him off the ladder he was standing on and threw him to the ground. He said she wasn't gonna wanna…get it on with Pretty Boy anymore, and if she couldn't defend herself without her gun then maybe she deserved it."

Greg was on his feet at once. No one had known Alex was not wearing her duty belt at the time of the assault.

No one but the police—and the assailant.

"I want to see that tape. I'll drive you back to your car."

* * *

"How long has Haney owned this tape?" Greg demanded after carefully inspecting the cassette and its plastic case.

"Couple years, I think," Kyle said.

"A couple years? No way. This tape is brand new. Look at it, Lawry." Greg held the case up to his eyes. "Not a scratch or mark on it. Haney just bought this tape. Let me ask you this," Greg said anxiously. "Does Haney know about the Ryziks' reputation with the law?"

"Who doesn't?"

"Where's Haney now?"

"At the Heritage Days Festival. He had to bus the kids from the school band up there for some kind of show or something."

"Thank you for your time." Greg hurried to the cruiser. Now he could bring Haney in for questioning. But he also needed a search warrant for his house.

Greg rushed back to the barracks and put in a call to Judge Conroy. It was Friday afternoon, and the probable cause for the warrant was borderline, at best.

"I hope the good judge is in a good mood," he mumbled, impatiently awaiting the return call.

* * *

Kyle Lawry immediately drove to Brian Haney's house.

No way were the police getting to the prick before him. He was going to kill the bastard himself.

But he needed to be absolutely sure. Before that detective got a search warrant.

Kyle stepped onto the back porch, nonchalantly surveying the surroundings. Confident none of the neighbors was within eyeshot, he cautiously opened the screen door and slid his credit card between the door and the jamb, tripping the lock. Brian had never been concerned about intruders and had flimsy locks on the doors. Let them take what they want, he often joked. There ain't nothing in this house worth a damn.

"We'll see about that," Kyle whispered, heading straight for Haney's bedroom upstairs. Kyle figured if Brian were hiding something, it'd be in his bedroom.

He tore the room apart, rummaging through the dresser drawers and closet. He fished around under the bed. There he discovered a pair of black sneakers, a spiral–bound tablet, a shoebox full of junk, a few back issues of a porn magazine, and two clippings from the most recent editions of the *Highlands Journal.*

He examined the clippings. The first one, from the July 9 paper, pertained to the vandalism at the high school involving Billy Ryzik. The second, from the July 16 edition, was the report on Alex's assault.

Kyle's heart raced as he opened the tablet. A yellowed newspaper photograph cut from an April edition of the *Journal* was tucked between two pages. In the picture were four teachers, the principal of West Highlands Elementary School—and Alex, taken at the school during Safety Week. On the tablet's pages were written records of Alex's daily routine, with a highlighted note that she habitually removed her duty belt as soon as she entered her home after work; information on police defense and disarmament tactics referenced to Internet sites; planned details of the assault, including the scheme to frame Dale Ryzik; and a hand–sketched layout of Alex's house.

The rage that boiled within Kyle was mind consuming. He bolted down the stairs and out the back door.

"*God help me! I'm gonna kill you!*"

He peeled out of the driveway and sped toward the festival grounds.

The Highlands High School Band warmed up on the grandstand stage for a six–thirty show as a light crowd filtered through the grounds of the Highlands Heritage Days festival three miles north of town.

Near the center of the activities, Lisa and Alex chatted with the festival organizers then casually strolled around the various food, games, and entertainment concessions.

"Let's split up for a while," Lisa suggested. "I'll meet you back here in fifteen minutes. We could grab something to eat."

Alex agreed, and they each went in a different direction. Lisa headed for the game trailers. Alex stepped inside the ladies restroom and pulled a syringe, insulin pen, and rubbing–alcohol packet from her shirt pocket. A packet of glucose gel and an extra insulin pen remained tucked away. She discreetly administered her nightly slow–release and quick–acting mealtime insulin, each by separate injection. She then wandered toward the grandstand.

The bleachers were quickly filling as it neared six–thirty. The kids from the band were tuning their instruments, and Alex stopped near the entrance gate to listen awhile. An elderly man with a walking cane came up to her and winked. She acknowledged his innocent gesture with a broad grin.

"Honey, you want to pat me down? You got such pretty eyes and a beautiful smile."

Alex laughed, self–consciously aware of her eyeglasses. "C'mon, sir, behave yourself. You're making me blush."

He cackled and continued through the gate.

The old man's candid compliment lingered in her mind. Smiling she nonchalantly turned to walk around the stage. But as her eyes locked on the figure across the way, her merriment instantly vanished.

Brian Haney stood alongside a school bus, presumably his, wolfing down a chilidog. His mouth full of food he suddenly looked up, his eyes meeting hers for a split second. Anxiously he turned away.

A frightening chill shot down Alex's spine, and she immediately reversed directions, heading back into the grounds to look for Lisa.

She found her near the last game trailer.

"What's up?" Lisa asked.

"Haney's here."

"Where?"

"Over by the grandstand," Alex said. "He's scarfing down a hot dog by his bus. He must've driven the kids from the band up here."

Lisa strained her eyesight for a glimpse of the school bus. "The band will be done in an hour, and he'll be out of here. Hungry?"

"I was till I saw him. But I've got to eat something soon; I just shot up with both kinds of insulin."

Lisa glared at her. "Let's go. I don't even want to *think* about you having one of those insulin episodes in front of me."

"Eh, the ambulance crew's right behind us."

"Real funny. What do you feel like eating?"

Alex pondered the question for a few seconds. "Pizza."

Lisa grimaced. "I'll pass. I'm going for a cheese steak. I'll meet you at the picnic tables under the pavilion."

His fury raged out of control.

Kyle Lawry raced across the parking lot toward the grandstand, oblivious to the stares and looks of perplexity he attracted from festival patrons.

He spotted Brian heading for the men's restroom in the small cinderblock building several yards from the grandstand entrance. He charged past the school bus and came up behind him, his arm whipping around Haney's neck.

"What the—" Brian hollered as he was jerked backward and thrown to the ground.

In a flash Kyle was on top of him, his fists pummeling Haney's face. "You did it to her, didn't you?" He seized Brian's shirt by the neck, wrenching his head off the dirt. "I found your little tablet under the bed, ol' buddy! I'm gonna kill you!"

In panicked desperation, Brian grabbed Kyle by the throat and flipped him around.

An all–out war had begun.

Screams from the horrified onlookers echoed through the grounds. Someone ran to summon a police officer.

Lisa was closest, and she quickly radioed Alex for help. She had no idea who was involved in the altercation as she detached and expanded her baton to full length.

Reaching down to interject, she shouted, "Hey! Hey! Guys! Break it up! Now!"

Haney's arm flew up to dislodge the weapon from her grasp. It shot upward and caught her right eye.

Dazed and blinded, Lisa staggered backward, losing her balance. She went down on a knee and raised her hand to her eye, wiping blood from the gash above her brow.

In a wild frenzy, Haney broke free from Kyle and sprang to his feet, grabbing the baton from the ground. He swung it like a bat at Lisa's head. She collapsed onto her side. Fading into blackness she didn't feel him roll her onto her back and snatch the pistol from her holster. He fled into the chaotic crowd.

Terror and panic consumed the eyewitnesses. They were diving for cover as Alex came upon the scene, aghast.

Kyle pulled himself up from the ground. "Stay away from him, Al! He'll kill you!"

"Stay out of this, Kyle!" She drew her weapon and frantically relayed a "Help Me Quick" message on her portable. "Get the paramedics," she shouted indiscriminately, running after Haney.

Brian bulled his way around horrified people. He had to get to his bus. He had to get away.

"Get down! Get out of the way!" Alex directed the crowd as she closed in behind him.

Do something! a voice from within ordered. *She's going to have a clear shot at you when you get to the bus! Do something! Now!*

He lunged out and grabbed a little boy trying to flee the chaos.

The boy screamed in horror as Brian seized him by the neck, jabbing Lisa's pistol into his temple.

"Oh, Christ." Alex stopped dead in her tracks and tightly gripped her weapon with both hands, leveling it directly at him.

"Take another step, and I swear I'll blow his brains out!"

Battered and bleeding above her brow, Lisa lay lifelessly on the dirt. The ambulance crew rushed to treat her.

A paramedic knelt alongside her and reached inside his first–aid kit for antiseptic to clean her laceration. He examined her head for signs of traumatic injury and checked the responsiveness of her pupils to the sunlight. He found no indication of severe cranial damage.

He bandaged the cut then jolted her awake with an ammonia inhalant.

"Take it easy," he said, restraining her from lifting up with her elbows. "Lay still. You got whacked pretty good."

"What happened?" she moaned.

"Some crazy guy clubbed you in the head with your baton."

Her head throbbing and her vision fading in and out of focus, she struggled to assess the surroundings. A crowd of onlookers encircled them. Her baton lay on the dirt a few yards away. She twisted in pain. The equipment attached to the back of her duty belt was pressing against her, making her extremely uncomfortable.

"My belt's hurting me," she muttered in distress, tilting her head up to watch the paramedic remove it.

She gasped in horror. "My gun! Where's my gun?"

* * *

"Take it easy, Brian," Alex said. "Please, don't hurt the kid."

Haney's eyes darted around wildly, perspiration streamed from his brow. "Stay away from me, or I'll kill him!"

Terrified, Alex met his crazed eyes straight on. "Oh, God," she whispered.

She had seen that same psychotic look before.

Through the black ski mask.

"Let the boy go," she pleaded, struggling to hold her composure intact. "You're not making matters any better by hurting him."

"Save it, bitch. Drop your gun! Now!"

Her eyes dropped to the horrified ones of the little boy, tears streaking his cheeks. He couldn't have been more than eight years old, and the terror in his eyes begged her for help.

"I said drop it! I'll kill him!"

From somewhere in the benumbed crowd Alex heard the hysterical plea of the boy's mother. Giving up her pistol was against procedure. It would leave her virtually powerless—against the man who had beaten and violated her. She knew it beyond a doubt. She had seen that same hatred in those eyes two Fridays ago.

She held her ground. "You'd better think long and hard about that. You kill him; I'm going to kill you the second after. This is between you and me, Haney. Let the kid go."

"No way." He began dragging the boy toward the bus. "He's my ticket outta here."

A bone–chilling scream from the boy's mother pierced the air.

"Brian, please—"

"Shut up! I should have killed you when I had the chance!"

Unconsciously Alex took a step toward them.

"Get back!"

She quickly retracted her movement. But she couldn't deal with the thought of that innocent boy going through hell. She had to do something. Swallowing hard, she made a split–second decision to go completely against hostage–negotiation procedures. "Look, Haney, if you want a hostage, take me. Just, please, let the kid go."

"No, Al!" a horrified voice emanated from behind her. It was Kyle. "Don't do this to yourself. There's backup on the way. They'll be here any minute."

"I told you to stay out of this, Kyle! Don't make it any worse."

Brian went ballistic with the revelation more cops were en route. As he pulled the boy onto the bus, Alex's negotiation grew desperate, a matter of life or death. "Please, Brian. Let him go. How much of his crying are you going to be able to handle? C'mon, don't do this. I'm willing to trade places with him. You've got a problem with me, not with him. Don't make him suffer for it."

Brian's eyes darted around in paranoia, his breathing wildly irregular. He had to act now before reinforcements converged on the scene.

"Come toward me!" he ordered from the top of the steps, shielding himself with the boy. "One stupid move, and I swear I'll kill him."

"Alex, don't!" Kyle shouted.

"Stay out of this! Before the kid gets hurt." Her pistol remained leveled at Haney as she commanded her legs to move forward, slowly, stopping at the base of the bus's steps.

"It's okay, sweetheart," she said to the trembling boy. "Everything's going to be okay. Trust me. I won't let him hurt you." She raised her eyes to meet Haney's. "Let him go. I'm not going to do anything to jeopardize his life."

"Unhook your cuffs with your left hand."

Gripping the pistol with her right hand, she moved her left hand around to the back of her belt and unhooked her handcuffs.

"Cuff your right wrist."

She did as told.

"Unbuckle your belt and let it drop to the ground! Hurry up!"

Her left hand hastily fumbled to unfasten her belt. It fell to the ground with a forceful thug; with it went her radio, baton, pepper spray, keys, and a clip of extra bullets.

"Let him go," Alex said.

"Drop the gun!"

"Not until you let him go."

"*I'm* running the show here. It's my way, or he's dead. Now drop the gun!"

"*Not* until you let him go. I want assurance he doesn't get hurt."

"You're testing my patience!"

"Okay, look." She drew in a breath to ease her fear. "I'm going to lower the gun to my side, but I'm not giving it up until he's off the bus."

Haney trained Lisa's pistol on Alex's head as she brought her weapon to her side. "You fuck this up; you're dead!" He abruptly released the boy, sent him tumbling down the steps onto the dirt.

"Go on. Get away from here," she instructed the kid with urgency, her eyes never deviating from Haney's. "Okay, Brian, it's you and me."

"Drop the gun! Now!"

She swallowed dryly and let her pistol fall to the ground beside her.

"Get your hands up and get on the bus!"

As she climbed aboard he swiftly grabbed the free handcuff and jerked her around, cuffing her wrists together behind her back. He seized her by the collar and thrust the pistol under her chest.

"You too, Lawry. Get on this fuckin' bus, or I'll finish her off right this minute."

"Brian, please," Kyle begged, moving toward the bus. "Think about what you're doing, man."

"Get on the bus and drive!"

❧ ❧ ❧

"You're not going anywhere!" the paramedic sternly informed Lisa. "You need stitches."

She grew hostile, jerking her arm free of his grip and laboring onto her feet. "You don't understand! I've got to find my gun. Where's my partner? What happened to the guy who hit me?"

"He took your gun after he knocked you out and ran toward the parking lot," a visibly shaken man from the crowd explained. "That other woman cop and the guy he was fighting with went after him."

Lisa staggered in that direction. The paramedic followed on her heels, insisting she be taken to the hospital.

At the edge of the parking lot she found chaos: horrified eyewitnesses, a hysterical young woman clutching a screaming little boy, Alex's weapon and duty belt lying on the dirt.

She approached the woman with the crying child. "What happened, ma'am? Tell me what happened?"

The traumatized mother sputtered erratically through heavy sobbing. "Grabbed…my…little…boy. Gonna…kill…him. On…bus…with—"

"What bus? Who's on the bus?" Lisa struggled to control a panicky outburst.

A second woman appeared from the crowd and explained what had taken place.

"Which way did they go?" Lisa urged desperately. Greg's theory about Brian had to be true. And now Haney had Alex as a hostage.

"North."

Lisa felt around for the keys to the cruiser, but her belt had been removed from her waist.

"This can't be happening." She scooped up Alex's pistol and unhooked the other set of car keys from Alex's belt. She rushed to the cruiser.

Her heart racing, her mind whirling, she was oblivious of the blood seeping from her bandaged brow and the throbbing pain in her head. She jumped into the car and sped onto the highway, a cloud of dust billowing behind.

The activity at the grounds of the Highlands Heritage Days Festival was nothing short of bedlam. State and regional police–cars swarmed the parking lot near the grandstand.

Greg Van Dien had just returned to his car after obtaining the search warrant from Judge Conroy when the radio went berserk. He'd listened in horror to the urgent transmissions between the Comm Center dispatcher and police units as he raced to the festival. An officer had been injured in an altercation, and now he was hearing reports of another—along with a male civilian—being taken hostage on a school bus by the gunman.

Greg knew who was working the festival. He also knew who owned the school bus. As he pulled up alongside a state–police cruiser, he feared the worst.

He hurried to the mass of police officers besieging the area near the restrooms. Witnesses were being questioned.

He immediately spotted Ted Peterson talking with a trooper.

"What the hell happened?"

Peterson whirled around. "Get out of my face, Van Dien. This doesn't concern you."

Greg's hand flew up for Peterson's collar. "The hell it doesn't! I have a gut feeling whatever the hell happened here is directly related to Alex's case. I want answers, Peterson, and I want them now!"

Peterson glared at him. "I'm going to have your ass."

Greg was in his face. "I'm going to have *yours*, for obstruction of justice. Now give me answers." He abruptly released the chief's collar.

Peterson exhaled in exasperation. "Apparently it all started when Maselli tried to break up a fight between two guys. One of them went ballistic on her, knocked her baton out of her hand and whacked her unconscious with it. Witnesses said he took her gun and ran off with it. Took a little boy hostage but—"

"Who's he got on the bus?"

"Griffin, and an unidentified male."

"Damn it," he muttered under his breath, visibly shaken, then spoke up, "Tell me it's not Brian Haney."

Peterson's eyes narrowed in awe. "Yes, it is. How did you know that? She traded herself for the kid, a fuckin' stupid move…"

Greg began pacing back and forth, swearing loudly. "He's the one for Chrissake! He's the guy who attacked her! Where's Lisa?"

"She went after the bus in the cruiser. The paramedics said she refused medical treatment, and they're not sure what kind of condition she's in. She got whacked pretty good, bleeding and everything."

"Which way did they go?"

"North. Your boys got two cruisers trying to locate the bus—"

"Nobody knows where they're at? How fast can a school bus go? We've got to find them! Before he kills her!"

Greg sprinted back to his car.

In a matter of seconds he was racing north on the highway.

Kyle Lawry steered the bus off the highway and onto a secondary road, heading northeast as instructed. He raised one eye to peer in the overhead mirror above the driver's seat, keeping the other on the road.

"C'mon, Brian," he pleaded, watching Haney positioned next to Alex in the seat directly behind him. Haney's eyes darted out the windows, wildly, from the front of the bus to the back, looking out for cop cars. "Think about this. You can't get away with it, whatever you're thinking. Give up. It'll be better in the long run."

"You caused all this, ol' buddy, ol' pal," Brian retorted with a bone–chilling madness. "Dumpin' me like a pile of trash when you met this bitch. Then she dumped you, but you wouldn't let go. No, you still wanted her. Kept hounding her, pumpin' me for dirt on her. She's a piece of trash, got everything she deserved…" He directed his fury at Alex. "No, not everything. I ain't through with her yet."

Alex turned away, staring out the window at the passing trees and fields, consumed with thoughts of what lie ahead for her. He was going to kill her, she was sure of it. He was going to pick up where he left off that night in her bedroom, when he had been frightened into flight by the police–car sirens, and make damn sure nothing got in his way this time around. She was going to pay the ultimate price once and for all. Alex propped her head against the glass and silently prayed for her life.

"You're out of your mind," Kyle insisted. "The cops are gonna be on your ass in a matter of minutes. There's no way out. Think about it, man."

"Shut up!" Haney's hand flew over the driver's seat, whipping Kyle in the shoulder with the butt of the pistol.

Kyle pitched forward, bellowing in pain. The bus veered off the pavement, and he struggled to regain control. "What're you trying to get us killed?"

"Just drive!" Haney motioned with the gun to a cut in the trees. "Up there to the right. Turn off there. Follow that dirt road till I tell you to stop."

His free hand brutally seized Alex's ponytail, jerking her head back against the top of the seat and pulling her hair taut until he saw tears in her eyes.

He savored the fear he was instilling in her. "Like I said, I ain't through with her yet."

No one noticed the police cruiser approaching from a distance.

"You're mine, Haney."

Lisa clenched her teeth as she caught sight of the bus ahead. She was sweating heavily and shivering. Blood dripped from her brow. She floored the gas petal and gripped the steering wheel tighter, driven by an all–consuming vengeance.

"You're mine. So help me, God."

Alex tried to stay calm. The rutted road was a dead end leading into state–forest land, and it could only mean one thing: The end of the line. *The end of her life.*

A half–mile into the woods Brian ordered Kyle to stop, spotting a run–down hunting cabin.

"C'mon, Brian," Kyle again pleaded. "Don't be foolish. Give yourself up. Don't do this."

In one violent blow to the head, Brian knocked him unconscious with the butt of the gun.

Alex flinched, gasping, as Kyle slumped against the side window, blood oozing from above his right ear.

"Please, Brian, please." Her arms and legs were numbing with panic. "Think about what you're doing."

He snickered, shoving the pistol under her chin. "I'm thinking about what I'm *gonna* do." He reached under the driver's seat for a metal box and pulled out a piece of rope, tying Kyle's wrists together and fastening them to the steering wheel.

Alex watched in horror, her pulse pounding in her throat. The scene before her slowly blurred then quickly refocused. Lightheaded, she drew in a deep breath and slouched back in the seat, making a futile attempt to remain calm. She hadn't had time to eat her pizza, leaving it at the concession stand and rushing across the grounds to help Lisa. Her blood sugar was dangerously low, and her quick–acting insulin was at maximum release. As her heart raced with terror, a severe, perhaps deadly, hypoglycemic reaction loomed inevitably.

Haney's crazed eyes turned on her, and he motioned with the pistol. "Let's go. Ain't nothin' gonna interrupt us this time."

Her head spun. She needed glucose, and the packet of gel she carried with her would not be enough to raise her blood sugar to a prolonged safe level. But she didn't want to die from irreversible hypoglycemia. She had to try to delay it, at least. *He* was going to have to kill her.

"B...Brian, I haven't had anything to eat since lunch. I need something with sugar. There's a pack of glucose gel in my shirt pocket. Please, I need it, or I'm going to pass out."

Her plea provoked wicked laughter. "Ah, yes. Officer Griffin, the diabetic." Menacingly his free hand reached under her collar for the chain that held her medical tag, twisting it repeatedly around his hand. "Remember this?" He thrust his fist under her chin.

Tears welled in her eyes. She refused to answer.

"You still haven't learned! Answer me!"

"Yeah...I remember."

More evil laughter. He abruptly released the chain and fished through her pocket, pulling out the small packet containing the gel and also a pen–like instrument.

He eyed the pen demonically. "Insulin, huh? I could kill you with this." The ominous cackling grew louder, deeper, as he held it before her eyes. "Or this." The gun was thrust under her chin. "No sirens out here, Officer. You *ain't* gettin' lucky this time." He slipped the pen into his back pocket and ripped open the glucose packet, squeezing the substance into her mouth.

He waited until she swallowed before pulling her to her feet. He dragged her off the bus and over to the abandoned hunting cabin.

Alex went without resistance. What good would it have done her to fight? If she somehow managed to get away, how far would she get running through the woods with her hands cuffed behind her back? Her legs were weak from fear and low blood sugar. He'd be on her in seconds.

Haney shot off the rusted padlock from the wooden door and violently pushed her inside.

❧ ❧ ❧

Greg Van Dien's car skidded to a halt behind the regional–police cruiser blocking the dirt lane at the highway entrance.

He radioed for backup and rescue units and leaped from his car. Lisa was nowhere in sight. He cursed her under his breath. She should not have taken matters into her own hands. With a head injury and no backup, she was foolishly putting her life on the line. And she was too emotionally involved to remain levelheaded.

Greg armed himself with a high–powered rifle from the trunk of his cruiser and headed into the woods.

He had to find Alex—and stop Lisa—before it was too late.

❧ ❧ ❧

The one–room hunting–cabin was filthy and devoid of any furniture. Ashes lay in an old fireplace and shards of glass from a shot–out window were strewn over the warped floor.

The damp, musty smell of the abandoned shack filled Alex's nostrils as Brian Haney backed her against a wall, raising the pistol to her throat and violently seizing her chin. "It's just you and me, Officer—again. And they say lightening never strikes twice." He grinned demonically. "Where did we leave off? Oh, yeah, I remember." He released his grip and slapped her hard across the face. The force of the blow sent her eyeglasses across the room and knocked her off balance. Unable to use her hands to cushion the fall, her left knee came down hard on a razor–edged fragment of broken glass.

She cried out and grit her teeth as a fiery hell shot through her body. Gasping in pain she sank back against the wall. Everything was a blur, and her head spun dizzily. He cursed at the sight of her bloody knee.

"Why are you doing this to me?" she cried, trying to no avail to focus on the towering nemesis before her. "What did I do to you?"

"What did you do to *me*?" he mocked, crunching over the glass to retrieve her eyeglasses. They were bent but unbroken. He knelt alongside her and slid them back on her face. Grabbing her chin he compelled her to look at him. "You stole my life! You took my buddy for all he was worth, used him then tossed him aside."

Horrified, Alex stared into his crazed eyes. "You got it all wrong. You don't understand—"

"Shut up!" He thrust the gun under her chin. "*You* don't understand! He wouldn't let go. You *used* him, yet he wouldn't let go! You screwed up his mind!" He abruptly seized her collar, jerking her forward, his hot, vile breath less than an inch from her face. "Do you know how much I *hate* you? You're nothing but a whore so high and mighty wearing that piece of tin." He ripped her badge from her shirt. "Never saw this side of the *wimp* before, huh? But I put it to you real good. Didn't I, bitch? Had ya *all* fooled. I was plannin' it out for some time now, then those Ryzik fuckers helped me along. I was pretty damn clever comin' up with that setup. Yeah, the newspaper spelled everything out for me." More evil laughter. "But who'd've thought the one I was doing it for would be the one who betrayed me in the end?" He raised the pistol to her ear, lewdly running his left hand across her throat then down over her heaving chest.

His touch made her flinch. He had total control of her body but not of her mind. She would not allow herself to die begging and whimpering. She would fight with the only weapon she had: Her mouth.

Alex lifted her eyes to meet his with a brave, defiant glare. "You proved to me how *much* of a wimp you are, Haney. You didn't have the guts to show your face. Yeah, you're a real *he*–man."

She held his stare, despite the terrifying madness she saw there, mentally preparing herself for a swift, brutal retaliation.

Instead a bone–chilling silence fell over the cabin as he began shaking his head, slowly, thoughtfully, his face flushing with intense anger. "You whores never learn, do you?" Then, in an explosive rage, he straddled her hips, his hand reaching around and jerking her ponytail. He forced her down flat onto her back and pressed his upper body against hers. Underneath, shards of glass picked and cut and pierced her. She gasped and grit her teeth, feeling a sharp edge slice deep into the palm of her left hand. A large, triangular piece of glass lay precariously close to the side of her head, and as his tongue slid into her ear, licking her lewdly, tormenting, she dared not jerk her head for fear of being cut.

"You wanna see my face. Here it is." His tongue came across her cheek, sending shivers down her spine. He drove it between her lips, deep into her mouth. "I'm gonna kill you, Officer Griffin. But I haven't decided how yet." He thrust the pistol between her legs. "Maybe I'll fuck you with this then, *bang*, pull the trigger."

Alex trembled violently, the tears coming automatically. She refused to acknowledge his gruesome portrayal of what lie ahead. Instead she fixed her eyes on a spider web spun in a ceiling nook, blocking out his words with silent prayers.

He dug out the insulin pen from his back pocket, removing the plastic cover and poking her neck with the fine needle. "Or I could jab you with this and press the plunger. No mess that way." A roar of psychotic laughter pierced the air as he returned the device to his pocket.

Her tremors intensified and the room began spinning out of control. Alex waited for the end, accepting her fate—however it came. She prayed for her parents, and for her brother and sister, that they'd somehow find the courage and strength to deal with her death.

"Or I could slice you to death," he proclaimed matter–of–factly, lifting the triangular piece of glass, slowly running it along her skin beneath her ear. A hairline of blood seeped from the cut.

Alex's mind whirled with incoherent thoughts as she strove for an ounce of control.

She had none.

She felt Haney rip open her uniform, heard buttons ricocheting off the floor. The nausea in her stomach became overpowering, her vision was failing her, the room slipping into darkness…

Behind a thicket of forest brush near the parked school bus, Lisa surveyed the surroundings.

There seemed to be no activity on the bus, the driver lifelessly slumped against the side window.

I'm too late, she instinctively thought. Alex is dead. They're all dead.

Then she heard a raging male voice emanate from the cabin beyond the bus. She gripped Alex's pistol in her right hand and cautiously crept around the bus, coming up alongside the cabin.

She pressed her back against the outside wall next to the window and glimpsed inside. They were on the floor, Haney on top of Alex. Pulling back against the cabin, Lisa trembled violently as blood ran down her face from the saturated bandage. She squeezed her eyes shut, a vision of Calvin Anderson mixed in her mind.

She slid toward the door. Drawing in a breath to steady her tremors, she raised the pistol with both hands. On a silent count of three she swung toward the door and swiftly kicked it open.

"Freeze! Police!"

Haney whirled around. Two shots rang out.

Brian flew backward, crashing onto the shards of glass, the pistol tumbling from his grip. A hole in his chest, he lay dead on the cabin floor.

Lisa pitched forward, her weapon falling to the floor. She collapsed onto all fours, her right hand coming up to clutch herself below the left shoulder.

She coughed up vomit, blood running between her fingers and down her arm and rapidly spreading across her shirt. She fell onto her right shoulder and rolled onto her back, sucking air into resistant lungs.

Minutes later, when Greg Van Dien rushed into the cabin, three bodies lay on the floor before him. He dropped the rifle and quickly radioed for medical assistance. Haney was dead. Alex was unconscious and bleeding from several cuts.

He knelt alongside Lisa and hastily removed his shirt, rolling it up into a ball and stuffing it inside her uniform against her wound.

She struggled to form words. "Al…okay?"

"She's alive. Hang on, kid. Help's on the way."

"M…my b…back. W…wet. C…can't m…move m…my arm."

Greg saw blood on the floor above her shoulder. The bullet had shot right through her.

His hand reached for hers, squeezing it tightly. "You'll be okay. Lay still." But he wasn't too sure of that statement. His hands and arms were covered with her blood. It was everywhere.

"H…Ha…ney?"

"He's dead."

"W…won't h…hurt any…b…body again. C…Cal…vin An'er…s…son, n…no more."

Greg suspected she was hallucinating, her thoughts jumbled between Brian Haney and the creep who had assaulted her. He pressed his lips together, forced an empathetic smile. This was Lisa's revenge—justice served. "That's right, kid. He won't hurt anyone again."

Lisa managed a slight nod as a crushing pressure and bone-numbing cold gripped her. "D…don't let…m…me d…die," she begged weakly, shivering convulsively. Her blood pressure was in free fall.

He gripped her bloody hand with perseverance, fighting to keep his emotions in check. "I won't. I promise."

CHAPTER 25

Justice Served—And Long Overdue

"Lisa, can you hear me?"

She struggled to part her eyelids, heavy from sedation, as a painful light permeated the peaceful darkness. Her head throbbed; a figure hovered over her, fading in and out of focus. With great effort she forced the word "where" through parched lips, her face contorting in agony from a raw, irritated throat.

The surgeon motioned for the nurse. "Get some ice and wet her lips."

As the woman went for ice chips, he glanced at his wristwatch. It was a quarter of seven. The surgery had gone without complication nearly eight hours earlier.

"Talking is going to be painful for a while, Lisa," the surgeon said. She had been intubated from the time the ambulance crew had rushed her into the emergency room until less than an hour ago. "You're in the IC Unit at Highlands Memorial. Do you remember what happened last night?"

Her eyes roamed around the room, assessing the surroundings. A struggle flashed before her. Through a clouded memory she felt something strike her eye and reflexively her right hand jerked upward.

The surgeon quickly pushed it down. "Whoa, no drastic movements. You're hooked to an IV and chest tubes."

Lisa drifted in and out of cognizance for a brief moment, a hazy vision of a hunting cabin in her mind. Brian Haney. A loud bang and then wetness, no air. She couldn't breathe. Above her, a face. A familiar face. Greg Van Dien.

She looked up at the strange man before her and mumbled weakly, "Sh…shot?"

"Yes, but you're going to be fine, thanks to your brother's and sister's generosity."

Her eyes narrowed with bewilderment.

"You owe them each a unit of blood. You needed six, and we only had four of your blood type on hand."

Lisa stared at him blankly. "B…blood type?" she mumbled then struggled to swallow.

The nurse returned with ice in a plastic–foam cup. She held it against Lisa's mouth, just long enough to allow her to wet her lips and ease the soreness in her throat.

"Easy does it," the nurse said. "You've been through some serious trauma."

The surgeon checked Lisa's blood pressure while discussing a few signs of progression in her condition with the nurse. Gently he took her left hand. "Can you squeeze my hand? Give it a good try."

Laboriously she bent her fingers and feebly pressed them against his.

"That a girl. This is going to be painful, but try to lift your arm up as far as you can and bend your elbow. Take your time."

Her arm started up, slowly, shakily. Her teeth clamped together and her face twisted in agony as a stabbing pain shot out from her left shoulder. She let it fall back to her side. "I c…can't. Hurts…bad."

The surgeon was extremely pleased with the slight movement he saw. It was still too early to make a diagnosis, but he felt confident she'd regain full use of the arm after several weeks of physical therapy.

He turned to the nurse. "I'm going to call her family. Have the day–shift nurse make arrangements to move her to a private room as soon as possible."

Brian Haney's onslaught lived on in a haunting nightmare. Alex shot upright in bed, gasping and drenched in sweat.

Jolted awake, Matt sprang to her aid, enveloping her with his strong arms. "It was only a dream. It's all over."

She buried her head against his bare chest, the horror subsiding.

Matt cradled her protectively. She had come close to dying from severe hypoglycemia, but the paramedics had gotten to her in the nick of time, injecting her with a maximum dose of glucagons. A silent rage burned within him as his eyes skimmed over the cuts on her arms and legs. Her left hand and knee had been stitched and bandaged in the hospital emergency room, the minor lacerations cleaned and treated with antiseptic.

Alex abruptly pulled away. "What time is it? You've got to get to work."

She turned to hop out of bed, but Matt reached for her arm. He gently pushed her down across the sheet, his lips smothering hers with an unhurried, passionate kiss.

Giggling she tried to squirm out from underneath his embrace. "Cut it out. You've got to get going."

"Did I tell you lately how much I love you?" Matt said, lifting his face to gaze into her eyes, masking the emotional upheaval that churned deep inside him.

Alex laughed. "About a zillion times."

* * *

"I'm not being a good hostess, am I?" Lisa muttered, weak and groggy, tipping her head to the side to see her sister and brother seated across the room. "I keep zoning out on you guys."

"Considering what you've been through," Renee said, "the fact you're lying there mumbling to us is the best thing we could ask for."

"Where'd Dad and Jimmy go?"

"Dad is talking to the doctor. Jimmy said he'd be back in a little while."

"The doc says I owe you guys some blood."

Tony swallowed the lump that stuck in his throat, his eyes stinging with tears. "I'll…be right back." He sprang from the chair and vanished into the hospital corridor.

"Was it something I said?" Lisa asked.

Renee got up and moved alongside the bed. "Actually I think it's something *he* said."

Lisa looked up at her, confused.

"He's upset about what he said to you yesterday."

"You guys came through for me. I love you two, you know that, don't you?"

"Lise, you saved Alex's life. You're a hero in our hearts. And besides," she teased. "What's a little blood? No big deal."

Lisa wanted to laugh. She was too weak. Instead she pursed her lips. "Always a joker."

"Always a fool, actually."

Lisa turned her head to see the digital clock on the bed stand. It was nine–fifteen. "What time does the train leave?"

"I'm not going."

"Why not?"

"I'm not leaving you, no way. Not after I almost lost you…" Renee's voice cracked with emotion. She looked away.

"Hey, don't get soft on me. I'm going to be okay. At least that's what they're telling me."

Renee dried her eyes. "You're going to be back to normal in no time."

"So go on the excursion. Do me a favor. Talk to Rick. Give him the chance to be your friend, if nothing else."

"I...don't know."

"Go."

"Only if you promise me one thing."

"What's that?"

"Don't ever get shot again."

Lisa's involuntary laugh was short–lived. She gasped in agony.

"Take it easy. I didn't mean to make you laugh."

"It's okay," Lisa whispered.

A soft footstep and a presence behind her made Renee look around. Her brother stood inside the doorway.

"Can I talk to Lisa, alone?"

"Sure." She looked back at Lisa and lightly touched her arm. "I'm going to get some coffee. I'll be back."

Tony Maselli approached his sister, timidly, hesitantly. "Lise, about yesterday—"

"Forget it," she muttered.

"No, I want to apologize. I love you, and I hurt you, and I thought I wasn't going to get the chance to tell you that."

She tipped her head to the side. "I love you, too, and nothing you could say would ever lessen that love. You said what you felt. I respect you for that."

"We all love you. Dad and Renee and me. You really gave us a scare."

A single tear ran out from the corner of her eye and rolled toward her ear. His hand reached over and wiped it away.

"Don't worry, kiddo," she whispered. "We got a lot of years ahead of us."

Alex sat at the kitchen table, alone, nursing a cup of cold coffee, the same beverage she had been drinking when Matt left for work an hour and a half ago.

Her assailant was dead. His life had gone awry, been destined for destruction. For her the fallout from his attack had gone full circle. She now had closure, peace of mind.

At other people's expense.

She picked herself up from the table, rinsed out her cup, and called the hospital to check on Lisa's condition. She then phoned Greg Van Dien's home. His wife informed her he was at the barracks, tackling the mound of paperwork effected by last night's pandemonium.

Alex hung up the telephone and limped into the bedroom to change into a tee shirt and pair of jeans. As she rummaged through her purse for her car keys, a knock came at the door.

It was Kyle.

She let him in, and for a long, trying moment they stared at each other, viewing the physical reminders of what they had endured together.

Finally Alex broke the silence. "How's your head feeling?"

Reflexively his hand touched the bandage on his temple. "Hurts like hell. How 'bout your cuts?"

She glanced down at her wounded hand. "Six stitches here; eight on my knee."

He forced a small, caring smile. "I…I had no idea Brian was…sick like that. I should have been more of a friend to him."

"It wasn't your fault."

"Al, I'm sorry for the way I was treating you, for the inexcusable things I did."

She nodded once. "I appreciate your sincerity, but…I can't quite forgive you…yet."

"I don't blame you. I just needed to apologize. I promise I'll let go."

Their eyes came together in a solemn truce.

"Thank you," Alex said.

❧ ❧ ❧

Greg Van Dien looked up from the mess on his desk, hearing a light wrap on the door. His eyes instantly lit up.

"Alex!" He sprang to his feet, taking her into his arms. "I'm so glad to see you."

It was out of character for her to break down so quickly, but nothing could stop the rush of tears. "Thank you for all you've done," she cried, wrapping her arms around his back, holding him tightly.

He cradled the back of her head, allowing a few of his own tears to escape his eyes. "You and your partner are one class act."

She slowly pulled away, sniffling, drying her eyes.

"What you guys did last night," Greg said. "Word's out to the governor."

Her mouth fell open. She looked away, angered. "My partner is lying in a hospital bed. The last thing I care about is what the governor thinks."

"That you're both heroes, that's what he thinks. You risked your life for that little boy...and Lisa...she should have gone to the hospital and had that head of hers examined...but she went after you..."

Alex fought off another emotional outburst.

"Peterson called earlier. You're on administrative leave until you're mentally and physically capable of returning to work."

"I bet he's thrilled about that. I'll be out of his hair for a while."

"I wouldn't worry too much about him. Commissioner Maselli laid into him at the hospital last night. He threatened to bring him down, and I quote, faster than a bomb on a 747 if he so much as looks at you funny. Why don't you take a vacation? Get away."

She was resigned over the suggestion. "I need something from you."

"Sure. Anything."

"I need the name and address of that little boy. I want him to see I'm okay, and I want to be there for him, help him through any emotional problems."

Greg searched through the paperwork on top of his desk for the report. He jotted the information on a note sheet and passed it to her.

"Al, I've got to ask you something," he said as she turned to leave.

She looked back.

"Did you know Haney was the one when you got on that bus?"

She nodded slowly. "Yeah, I did. But I couldn't let that kid go through hell. I'd been there already."

Alex hobbled down the hospital corridor, carrying a dozen red roses in a white ceramic vase. When she reached the room she hesitated, peering inside before entering.

Lisa was alone, resting with her eyes closed.

Quietly Alex stepped into the room, setting the flowers next to a few other arrangements on the small dresser near the bed.

Lisa opened her eyes, hearing the faint clunk. Her face immediately brightened.

"Hey, partner. I'm so glad to see you."

"Me, too. How're you feeling? I hear you're going to be up and around in no time."

"Couple days maybe. I've got five stitches on my forehead and a concussion. My lung was collapsed, and I have some nerve damage in my left arm. But other than that," Lisa managed a hearty smile, "I'm doing fine."

"When they told me what you did," Alex blurted with emotion, "I was numb. Lisa…I…I'm…" She burst into tears.

Lisa's right hand came up slightly, restrained by the IV connection. "I owed you a big one."

"No way," Alex muttered. "We're a team."

"Yeah." Lisa paused then whispered, "Al, I don't think I'm cut out for this job anymore."

"What? You're not abandoning me, are you?"

"I'm going to be off for three months, plenty of time to do some soul searching."

"Or some law–school searching," Alex added, disheartened. "When we split up to eat last night I didn't think we'd be splitting up for good."

Lisa's eyes stung with tears. She struggled to swallow the lump in her throat. "I have to make something out of my life, and law enforcement is not it. I guess now's as good a time as any to get out."

"If that's what you want then I'm behind you a hundred percent."

"How's Matt handling everything?"

"He hasn't said much. I think he's in shock. And he can't handle the shop by himself."

"He'll find another mechanic."

"Yeah."

The room fell silent until Lisa spoke up. "I'm going to have a lot of free time on my hands the next three months. Keep in touch, okay?"

"Keep in touch?" Alex burst into laughter. "You're not getting rid of me that easy. Just because you don't want to be my partner anymore doesn't mean you're losing my friendship. Ours is a keeper, Officer Maselli. I can still call you that, right? You're not a civilian yet. You haven't turned in your badge, have you?"

Lisa shook her head, smiling. "No, Officer Griffin, I haven't. And, yeah, ours is a keeper."

❧ ❧ ❧

Renee was testing the PA system on the first coach when Rick Stanton climbed aboard, draping his conductor's outfit over the last seat.

"Here it is," he said with resignation. "Eleven A.M. as you requested." He started to leave but hesitated. "How's Lisa? The…scanners were going crazy last night."

Renee set the microphone down, her eyes meeting his with an unspoken gratefulness. "She's…okay. Actually she's better than okay. Everything's looking good."

Rick nodded. "That's great news. I won't keep you." He lingered for a second, his eyes absorbing her for one last time.

"The flowers you sent to the hospital were beautiful."

"It was the least I could do." The havoc he had wreaked on the twins made him lower his eyes with shame and remorse. "Renee, I'm sorry for what I've done."

She nodded sympathetically, gesturing toward the conductor's suit. "You'd better get dressed. The train leaves in less than an hour. We'll talk at Elk Grove."

He raised his eyes and whisked those long, scraggly bangs away, smiling. "Yes, ma'am."

❧ ❧ ❧

Alex rushed into the garage as quickly as her injured leg would allow, hearing metal crash against metal. She found Matt hurling tools at Brian's beat–up locker, his anger so intense she saw blood vessels bulging under his crimson skin.

"What are you doing?"

"I hate him!" Matt walked away from her in a fury. "I *hate* him! I hate what he did. I hate who he was. He conned me. He lied to me…" His voice trailed off as his emotions got the best of him. He turned to face her, the turmoil in his eyes unmistakable, and whispered, "He hurt you so bad. And I never saw it in him. Not once. Alex, how could I have been so oblivious? I hope he rots in hell."

Alex limped over to him, her hand coming up to caress his face. "No one knew." She glanced around the garage. "How many cars do you have right now?"

His eyes were questioning. "Five."

"How long till they're fixed?"

"A few days. Why?"

"Ever been to West Virginia?"

A grin sprouted from his troubled face. "No."

"We need to get away. A visit to my sister's, some camping in the New River Gorge." She mischievously snuggled against his greasy coveralls. "You and I lying by a crystal–clear mountain stream under a starlit country sky. Am I tickling your fancy?"

He lifted her chin with his thumb and index finger. And just before his lips covered hers, he whispered, "Lady, you've been tickling my fancy since the day you set foot in this county."

Jim leaned over, softly kissing her on the cheek.

Lisa's eyes flew open. She smiled. "Where've you been?"

"Where's your family?" He deliberately evaded her question.

"My father and brother went home for lunch, and I made Renee go to work."

Jim laughed. "You *made* Renee go to work?"

"She was only going to sit here and stare at me. So where've you been?"

He nestled on the edge of the bed with one foot on the floor, cautious of the barrage of tubes protruding from her arm and under the sheets.

"Be real careful of those." She pointed to the tubes running out from under the sheet near her waist to a ventilation machine on the floor alongside the bed. "They're keeping my lung inflated."

"I'm not moving a muscle. I won't disturb them."

"So are you going to tell me where you've been? I'm getting this feeling you're intentionally avoiding an answer."

Jim carefully took her right hand in his. "We never got a chance to talk last night."

"You *are* avoiding an answer."

He giggled. "Would you hear me out, okay?"

He clutched her hand tighter. An appeal for forgiveness dampened his eyes as he spoke. "Lisa, you mean the world to me. I hope you can find it in your heart to believe that, after all those horrible things I said to you. I'm so sorry for reacting like I did, but I was devastated and felt cheated..."

Her lips parted to speak, but his index finger crossed his mouth.

"Sh. Let me finish. The reality of what happened to you didn't sink in until hours later, and I realized how vicious I had reacted. I thought I had lost you forever, and I couldn't bear to think of my life without you." One by one, tears rolled down his cheeks. "Then on Thursday at the pond you shunned me. I...it hurt me so much. I...I went to Paula's...and—"

"Don't," she immediately stopped him. "Don't...say anymore. I don't want to know. Whatever happened...happened. I want us to start over. I want to put these last three days behind us and...go on from here."

His tears came faster. "I was going to...but...I didn't."

He cleared his throat and made a feeble attempt at drying his eyes. "Lisa, I love you so much." His hand slipped into his shirt pocket, and he pulled out a diamond engagement ring.

She gasped, her face frozen with surprise.

He reached across her waist and gently lifted her left hand. "I know this arm hurts, but I have to do this the right way." Slowly, with some effort, he slid the ring onto her third finger. "Lisa Maselli, will you marry me?"

Painful laughter intermingled with her tears. "Yes," she whispered.

He leaned over and softly brushed his lips across her cheek. "I couldn't wait any longer. After last night, after I almost lost you for the second time in two days, I had to get it."

"It's beautiful," she cried, gazing at the stone, fluorescent light dancing off its facets. Swallowing the lump in her throat she looked up at him.

"So this is where you've been."

About the Author

M. L. Donato was born in the anthracite coal region of northeastern Pennsylvania and has been involved with the promotion of the area through local government and regional planning for the past fifteen years. A graduate of East Stroudsburg University, she lives near Scranton with her husband and son.

0-595-21195-X